Anonymous

Life and Light for Heathen Women

Anonymous

Life and Light for Heathen Women

ISBN/EAN: 9783743418240

Manufactured in Europe, USA, Canada, Australia, Japa

Cover: Foto ©Andreas Hilbeck / pixelio.de

Manufactured and distributed by brebook publishing software (www.brebook.com)

Anonymous

Life and Light for Heathen Women

LIFE AND LIGHT

FOR

Heathen Women.

VOL. I.　　　　MARCH, 1869.　　　　No. I.

A WORD TO OUR READERS.

WE offer you here the first number of a little publication, which, if the Lord will, we hope to send out quarterly to bear intelligence to the Christian women of America from our missionary sisters abroad, and from those for whom they are laboring.

We call it "Life and Light for Heathen Women." Does any sister object to this title as too high-sounding, or as implying more than the truth? Let her turn to the articles entitled "Triumph of Grace," "Earnestness in professing Christ," and to the story of Anna Maria White and her family, and then tell us if these heathen women did not indeed obtain life and light through the gospel.

We do not profess to be commencing a new work. Others have labored, and we are entering into their labors. And we love to look over the history of the American Board, and of other missionary societies, and gather up examples like those mentioned above, which prove beyond a doubt that Christ meant just what he said when he uttered those blessed words, "The Son of man is come to seek and to save that which was lost." For the Scripture saith, "Whosoever believeth on Him shall not be ashamed. For there is no difference between the Jew and the Greek." No difference, dear sisters, between ourselves and the lowest of heathen women in this respect; "for the same Lord over all is rich unto all that call upon him."

But just here come in those solemn queries, "How, then, shall they call on Him in whom they have not believed? and how shall they believe in Him of whom they have not heard? and how shall they hear without a preacher? and how shall they preach except they be sent?"

"Lift up your eyes and look on the fields, for they are white already to the harvest." We have indeed been praying the Lord of the harvest to send forth more laborers. Now let us heed his voice, saying to each one of us, "Go work to-day in my vineyard."

Christian sisters, to whom among you comes the command, — "Depart; for I will send thee far hence unto the Gentiles?" And to whom is the word put in another form, "Honor the Lord with thy substance, and with the first fruits of all thine increase?" Let us engage in the work of the Lord with faith, with earnestness, and with a humble spirit of prayer and consecration.

Our royal firman reads, "Go teach all nations," with the royal promise annexed, "Lo, I am with you alway, even unto the end of the world."

ANNUAL MEETING.

The first annual meeting of the Woman's Board of Missions was held at Mount-Vernon Church in Boston, Tuesday, Jan. 5.

Notwithstanding the inclemency of the weather, and the very bad state of the streets, over six hundred ladies were in attendance during the whole day; many coming in from the suburban towns, and some from distant places in this and the adjoining States.

In the devotional exercises conducted by Mrs. Bowker, the President of the Board, grateful acknowledgment was made of the good hand of the Lord upon this Society, which commenced its operations one year ago in great weakness, taking for its text of promise, "Fear not, thou worm Jacob, I will help thee, saith the Lord."

The congregation then united in singing an original hymn, composed by Mrs. Edwin Wright for the occasion.

The Recording Secretary, Mrs. J. A. Copp, presented a Report, which was accepted, and a copy requested for publication, and distribution among the friends of the Board.

A Report was then read by Mrs. Homer Bartlett, Treasurer, stating that the whole amount received during the past year exceeded five thousand dollars.

Mrs. George Gould, Corresponding Secretary, read interesting extracts from the correspondence of female missionaries and native Bible-readers, a portion of which will be given in another part of this publication.

The Board then proceeded to the election of officers for the ensuing year, when the old Board was re-elected with some additions.

ENLARGEMENT OF THE WORK.

Miss Myra A. Proctor, missionary teacher of the A. B. C. F. M. in Aintab, Turkey, gave a sketch of the enlargement of the work among women in that vicinity, and the consequent increased demand for laborers. Several mountain districts, that not more than five years ago were still in a state of rebellion against the Government, and were so filled with highway robbers that it was not safe to go among them, have recently been subjugated, and the inhabitants have been compelled to give up their former wild way of living.

In some of these places, little churches have been formed and schools opened. One bright mountain girl learned to read by looking over her brother's shoulder as he prepared his lessons, and is now studying in Aintab to fit herself to go back, and teach her sisters and neighbors in Hasan Beyli.

In the larger towns, that have been occupied for some time as mission-stations, there is a more ready access to Mohammedan women than formerly. They are not asking for teachers. The saddest fact of all is, that the heathen seldom do ask for the gospel. They do not know their need.

Public opinion in regard to female education has so changed, that there is a great opening for schools in the cities, where other means of grace have thus far failed to reach the women.

Sisters, will you heed these Macedonian cries? Then you must take greater responsibilities upon yourselves in sending out and sustaining more laborers. You will need to learn more of the *pleasures of self-denial.* The native Christian sisters in Central Turkey are accustomed to lay aside their jewelry when they begin to learn of Christ; believing that they are commanded to be adorned, "not with gold and pearls and costly array," but with "good works." If we deny ourselves only the *superfluities* of life, the treasury of this Society will never be empty.

Mothers, the enlargement of this work calls for your cherished daughters, for your most gifted, the sweetest and best. Is it too much to ask the best for Christ?

Thirty-three years he toiled and suffered on earth, "despised and rejected of men," suffered for us, leaving us an example that "we should follow in his steps."

O sisters, living in this favored land! O my missionary fellow-laborers, with all the love and the comforts that are showered upon us! O ye tender mothers who, for Christ's sake, have sent away with your blessings your noble sons and cherished daughters! what yet do we know of sacrifice?

Let us rather praise God that he graciously allows us to fill up that which is behind of the afflictions of Christ, and thus to become "heirs of God and joint heirs with Christ: if so be that we suffer with him, we may be also glorified together."

WHAT CAN WE DO?

Mrs. Dr. Anderson advocated earnestly the plan of enlisting every female church-member in New England and the Middle States to aid in this work.

Mrs. Bowker said, *We have pledged ourselves* to the support of seven missionaries and eleven Bible-readers; and we are asked to send more. Therefore our contributions must be largely increased. Let every woman connected with our churches have the opportunity to add her mite. A collector in one of the churches in this city called upon a poor widow supported by the charity of the church, and told her of the efforts of the Woman's Board, and of the progress of the work. The poor woman thanked her again and again for not passing her by, when she knew she could give but little; and, putting a ten-cent scrip into the hand of the collector, she said, " It's only a little; but I'll pray the Lord to make it worth more than ten dollars."

The Treasurer added, that the poor widow's mite was blessed by our Saviour, because it was all her living. The rich must give very largely in order to secure Christ's blessing.

OUR WEIGHT IN GOLD FOR CHRIST.

Mrs. Dr. Butler, formerly a missionary in India of the Methodist-Episcopal Church, related a custom of the last of the Mogul kings. On each birthday he caused himself to be carefully weighed, the other balance being filled with gold, and a few diamonds thrown in. When the balance was perfect, the gold and diamonds were distributed among the poor. Thus he was annually worth to his people his own weight in gold and diamonds.

Sisters, what were we worth last year to the cause of Christ? Did we find at its close the word *tekel* written against us? Our missionaries, who have given their lives to faithful labor for souls, are worth annually more than their weight in gold.

Stimulated by their example, shall we not aim this year to be of equal value to the cause of Christ ?

At twelve o'clock, at the cordial invitation of Mrs. Deacon Safford, the audience retired to the vestry, and partook of a bountiful collation, provided by ladies from the different churches of Boston.

AFTERNOON.

Dr. Kirk presided at the afternoon session. Rev. N. G. Clark, D.D., the Foreign Secretary, presented the salutations of the American Board, and of the two hundred female missionaries now in their service. He said that this great uprising of Christian women in behalf of their sex was one of the most cheering signs of the times. It was a revival of the missionary spirit of fifty years ago, when there were three hundred and twenty-seven auxiliary female societies in this country, which furnished one-eighth of all the contributions for the work. In 1837, there were laboring under the care of the Board, three hundred and sixty missionaries. Last year there were three hundred and twenty-two. In 1837, sixty men and women were sent out within three months, consecrated to the work, and trained for it by devoted Christian mothers. When it became known that new fields were opening for woman to work for her sex, scores of letters were received from those who were willing to go; and last year eighteen were sent out, making forty-five single women now laboring for the redemption of their own sex in heathen lands. There is *need* of this society as a support to the Board "I am glad I belong to you," said one of the seven missionaries, when first introduced to the President of the Woman's Board; and from each of these will come back frank, confiding letters, such as can only be written to mother and sisters.

Dr. Clark also gave interesting sketches of some of those who have recently gone out, as examples of the spirit which actuates them in this work. Just the noble-hearted and gifted women who cannot well be spared, are those needed to devise the best means for raising their degraded sisters. He concluded with an earnest " *God bless you!* "

Rev. George Washburn of Constantinople drew a very dark and gloomy picture of the condition of women throughout Turkey. They are not recognized in society, save as the servants and slaves of the men. A father, in numbering his children, never includes the girls, whose birth is regarded as a great calamity. They marry at a very early age, and then become subjects to their mothers-in-law, in whose presence they may not speak aloud for a year. Their manner of life forbids the growth of self-respect, or pride in well-doing. During a visit to a village, where he remained over night, Mr. Washburn was invited to the best house, to which he was conducted over two manure-heaps. The building was of stone, about six feet in height, with no windows, scarcely a door, no furniture save a few tattered coverlets, and something which answered for a cradle. In the only room lodged four men, three women, four or five children (one a young infant), five cows, two calves, two or three dogs, a dozen or fifteen chickens, some sheep, and a donkey. In Turkey they scarcely believe that it was possible for women to be educated. It was the gospel of Jesus Christ that raised woman up, and made her what she was in this country. In Turkey the influence of religion itself (Mohammedanism), was degrading. The Greeks and Armenians call themselves Christians, but their faith was little more than formality and superstition. The influence of Mohammedanism was still more degrading: it was purely sensual. There was no instruction given in connection with religion. These Turkish women had control of their children until ten years of age; and during that time they so carefully educated them in their own superstitions, that it was almost impossible afterwards to efface them. These women not only stood in the way of their children, but of their husbands. If they had any suspicion that their husbands were about to read the Bible, or to turn Protestants, they knew how to step in, and make the houses too hot to hold them.

Enough, however, has been accomplished among these women to prove that earnest labor was all that was needed to effect a reform. It was abundantly proved that they were capable of elevation and education, and that the influence of the gospel upon them was exactly the same as upon the women of America. The girls had to be gathered into the schools, of which many more were needed. In Constantinople, with a population of over five hundred thousand, there were no Protestant schools for girls. It was also necessary to train up these girls for teachers, and to make them instrumental in gathering others into the kingdom of Christ. There must be schools in all the great cities of Turkey to accomplish this work. They must have a system of visitation from house to house, — visitation by women who know how to care for the sick and suffering. All that work must be done by Christian women. It was, however, essential that the women who were sent out should be trained as missionaries for the work.

Rev. Dr. Webb, pastor of the Shawmut Church, who has just returned from extended travels in Egypt and in the East, confirmed the remarks of the previous speaker. The impression that was forcibly made upon him everywhere was, that the people had no homes, and that there was no pivot upon which to fix the lever by which to elevate them. They would find the work undertaken by the mission to be slow and heavy; and but for the omnipotence of God, and the fact that Christ had died, he would tell them that they would fail. If, however, they earnestly strove to imitate the spirit of the Master, they would not fail. He concluded by urging the opening of schools in Turkey by American women.

Dr. Kirk made a brief address, in which he enforced the absolute necessity of good home-influence on Turkish women.

One of the evil consequences of slavery was the utter absence of home-influence, and this was one of the great difficulties encountered in elevating the freedmen. This was the great evil crying for remedy in Turkey. There was, in the church, a vast amount of unemployed female talent, both of head and heart, that was pining for a worthy field upon which to bestow its beneficent labors. A large number of these women were unmarried, and many must remain so; and these long for work. This mission offered such a field. Dr. Kirk concluded with a powerful exhortation.

FIRST FRUITS OF THE ANNUAL MEETING.

The day following the annual meeting, a woman over sixty years of age, in plain but respectable attire, came more than two miles to call upon the president. She said that she earned her living by sewing in different families, but that she gave up the previous day to the Lord to attend the missionary meeting; " and what a wonderful meeting it was ! " she exclaimed. " I have been in the habit of attending such meetings in Boston for thirty years, but I never before enjoyed one as I did this. I felt I must give up to-day also to the Lord, and come and bring my thank-offering; for," said she, " you know that we were reminded yesterday, that whatsoever our hands find to do, we must do quickly."

This allusion was made in reference to an incident related by the treasurer during the meeting; stating, that, after she entered the church, an envelope was placed in her hands containing twenty-five dollars, found in the drawer of Mrs. Dr. Keep, recently deceased, with which she intended to make herself a life-member of the Woman's Board of Missions.

The treasurer spoke of this as a voice from the spirit-world ; and it seems that at least one heart was stirred by it to " work while it is day : " for this unknown friend from whom the collector possibly would have hesitated to ask one dollar (the annual membership), presented her "thank-offering " in two bills, — a five and a twenty, — saying, she should like much to make herself a life-member of the society ; but her friends, if they should see her name, would say she was beside herself, that she ought rather to have bought her a new dress. She was greatly pleased with the suggestion that she could make one of the missionary ladies a life-member ; and as Mrs. Wheeler, for eleven years a devoted missionary in Turkey, had manifested a deep interest in the work of the Society from its commencement, and had labored much in connection with its members during her recent visit to America, it was decided that the donation should be acknowledged as " from Persis," to constitute Mrs. Susan A. Wheeler of Harpoot a life-member of the Woman's Board of Missions.

Where is there another Persis to go and do likewise ? Be assured, such a token of loving remembrance is one your missionary sisters will prize ; and such a spirit of love and self-denial will not fail to win the approving smile of the Master.

BIBLE WOMEN IN INDIA.

BY MRS. FAIRBANK.

Two women have lately, i.e., within the past month, been appointed to go among the women in the villages around us, to read the Bible and to tell of Christ. One is Diûpatābāē, a young woman who was my first scholar after we entered upon our village-work, which was the second year (1858) after we arrived in India. Her father, on becoming a Christian, gave his children to the Lord in baptism except this one. She was ten years old, and had been married several years before, in her infancy to a heathen husband, and so her father felt he could not give her in baptism ; because she was not his. She felt very badly when she saw her brothers and sisters being baptized ; and told her father, " I will believe in Christ, and then they will baptize me on my own faith. I do not care what my husband or his friends say to me." She learned to read, write, and sew, and, above all, to love Christ, and was baptized, and joined the church. Her heathen husband told her she must do penance if she came to live with him. She said, " Then I will not go with you." He left her ; and afterwards she married a Christian young man, who died two years after. She was again married to a Christian, whose work it is to take care of the premises of the mission at Wadālē. We are just now out in another part of our work ; but the other day, when I went home, she came in to tell me her new experience in going to the women. She said she went to Kharawandi, quite a large village ; and a large number of women came, and some men too. The men said, " We don't want you to tell us any thing. What are your books ? nothing but ink smudged on paper." She said to them, " Just let me read to you a little, and you won't say so." So she read, and they listened. They would try to say things between : but she kept on reading ; and at last there was a large company gathered together, and they listened quietly.

The other woman I have employed is Yarmônābāi. Her husband is a farmer, and they live at Barhānpûr, two and half miles south of us.

She has seen a good deal of sorrow, and is an older woman than the first. She takes a deep interest in the work. I have not seen her since she commenced going out ; but I know she will sow the word faithfully. The first woman will have $1.50, and the second $3.00 in gold monthly. This is only a temporary arrange ment. We ought to build them a house near us, where I can superintend them carefully. They ought also to go to villages farther away; and for this they need an allowance, so that they can have a conveyance. They also ought to buy their own books.

We are now at Khokar. This is a sad place to visit in some respects. There were once many Christians here, i.e., members of the church; but some of them have turned back after their idols, and their heathen marriage-ceremonies, and much of this through the influence of one woman, whose husband was a pillar of the church, but died several years ago. Then his wife turned aside, and led away others. Last hot season, cholera came into her family, and took away her best beloved son, Then she felt as if the Lord had spoken to her to turn from her backsliding; and she sought again the prayer-meetings and the people of God, and the church has received her again to its fellowship. In my daily prayer-meetings with the women, she weeps, always weeps. Pray that she may be the means of bringing back many to Christ. She is very feeble now, and this sorrow has told heavily upon her. Poor miserable people! My heart pities them more and more.

EFFECTUAL PRAYER.

BY MRS. WHEELER.

One day I received a letter from Miss West, saying, "Somebody is praying for me, I am sure; for I have never had such success in teaching before."

I entered the house of God in Bangor, and, after the services, was introduced to a lady as from Harpoot. She at once asked, "Do you know Miss West? I have been drawn out to make special prayer for her." I found this lady an intelligent reader of the "Herald." She said she marked certain places to be remembered in the closet, and to be re-read. She searched with two pairs of spectacles on at once for the places on the map.

Did she stop here? Let her answer. "I have been to Hoveli to the woman's prayer-meeting to-day; and we had a precious season." She carried the "Herald" to her neighbors; and, her position being high in social life, she had influence; and many read the "Herald" who before had cast it into the waste-basket. I have no doubt the Master said, "Well done, good and faithful servant" to this sister.

Will not all our sisters do all they can to spread missionary intelligence; and, when they pray, do it with the understanding as well as the heart, and thus please God.

AFTER MANY DAYS.

A party of friends in Christ, and lovers of missions, met one evening in last February to bid farewell to two young men just departing to preach the Saviour in China. Being asked the reason of their determination to seek a foreign field, the elder of the two told this story. Twenty-seven years ago, Dr. Anderson wrote to a lady, then teaching in Western New York, asking her to consider seriously whether it was not her duty go on a mission to Siam. She could not go, and returned by her own hand neither consent nor denial. "But." said the young minister, "my brother and myself are her living answer. That lady, now in heaven, was our mother; and we, her sons, go to China to do her missionary work for her."

Besides this, she was long a teacher of young ladies, and had the happiness of seeing twelve of her pupils become missionaries.

Are there not mothers who read this, whose hearts have burned within them to go and tell the heathen about Christ? You may never go yourselves; but is there not in your home a little boy, the light of your eyes, the delight of your heart? Give him to Christ; train him as wisely as you can; tell the

Master, that, if he will accept the offering, that child is his-
Jesus will own your sacrifice. "After many days" you may
speak to the heathen through your son. Be faithful. "He is
faithful that promised."

LETTER FROM KOHAR.

The following extract is taken from a letter dated Harpoot,
Oct. 23, 1868, written by Kohar, assistant teacher in the
Girls' Boarding School, and addressed to a member of this
Board who had sent her valuable gifts. After expressing her
gratitude for the kindness, she says, "Perhaps you desire to
hear about our school. This year all the pupils were fifty-three ;
of which four were Arabic-speaking, the others Armenians.
Now it is vacation ; that is to say, the yearly course of the
school is finished, and the pupils will be scattered in the cities
and villages until spring.

I also, if the Lord wills, shall go to my father's house. My
brother has brought a horse, that I may go. But I do not wish
to remain there all the time. I wish and desire much to go to
work for the Lord in different places. But I have a request
to make to you, dear sisters ; although your presents rejoiced my
heart, a hundred times as much you will rejoice and encourage
me when you pray for me, that, as much as I feel I ought to
work or set a good example, I may not neglect any thing. I
also do not forget you, and will pray that the Lord bless you all
your life, also your labors. There is no such work in the world
that is so sweet and precious to me as the work of the Lord ;
although I feel that I cannot, as I should, fulfil my duties. I
wished also to relate more to you about other things, but my
time is very short. Excuse me.

Good night. With loving salutations to all of you,

I remain your sister,

KOHAR.

TRIUMPH OF GRACE.

[Extract from a letter written by Rev. Mr. Howland of India.]

One of the candidates for admission to the church is an old woman, who, after a long life spent in idolatry, seems to be taking hold of Jesus with firm faith. She is very regular in attending meeting, and says she understands what is said while she is hearing it, but cannot keep it " so as to tell it." Some months since she said, "Till lately I said, " O Vyravar ! " and " O Jesus ! " but now I only say, " O Jesus ! " She remarked recently, that, when she goes by a heathen temple, sometimes the name of the god, as Vyravar, or Prolliar, will come into her mind ; but she immediately says " Jesus," and they go away. Within a few days a Pandaram (or religious mendicant) came to the house where she lives with her heathen sister-in-law, and offered them some sacred ashes, as their custom is. Her sister took and marked them upon her forehead ; but she refused, when her sister said, " She worships Jesus now: she does not want this." Her manner of prayer is, " O Jesus ! since the teacher (referring to Mr. Anketell) told me about thee, I trust in thee." When about to take food, she says, " Jesus, now give me food ; " and, after she has taken it, " Jesus, thou gavest me this food." One day when alone in the house, a neighbor sent in food for her. She said to Mr. A., who called in the afternoon, " Christ sent me food to-day." Although very poor, she seems averse to receiving any aid from us, and was troubled when Mrs. H. gave her two or three pence to buy some oil for her sprained wrist. She said, " You must not give me this. I have nothing with which I can repay you. My sister gives me food, but I never had money." One day she received a little money from some source, and brought part of it, and put it in with others when our usual sabbath contribution for the support of the gospel was taken up. I have spoken of this woman thus in detail, because her simple faith has much interested us, and because the Lord has seemed to be showing us how he can lead an uneducated woman, who has spent her life in the darkness of heathenism, to himself, and by his Spirit teach so easily what all our efforts fail to do without the divine power.

VALUE OF EARLY CHRISTIAN INSTRUCTION.

BY REV. MR. HOWLAND.

The case of another woman may, on the other hand, be taken as showing the influence of Christian instruction. She is a woman, now a widow, who was formerly educated in the boarding-school of the English Church Mission ; and, while in connection with the school, received baptism, though she was not received to the communion.

She was taken from the school by her relations, and married to a heathen. Though the wife of a heathen for some years, she did not engage voluntarily in heathen rites, or attend heathen temples. She says, that, when she heard the church-bell ring on the sabbath, she used to long for the privilege of going to meeting again. She began to attend a few weeks before we came here ; and she improves the privilege as though she prized it. Scarcely any of the female church-members are so regular and constant as she is at all our meetings. She wanted a whole Bible ; and Mrs. H. promised to give her some sewing to do, that she might pay for one.

Great was the joy which lighted up her face, as she took the precious volume, to carry to her home a whole Bible, all her own. Her case also encouraged us. There may not be another one among the many females at this station who have studied in the mission-village schools, who hears the church-bell with a longing to come to its call. But we are shown that the Spirit may be leading souls heavenward where we are not aware of it. I trust the Lord has yet many in these villages whom he has chosen for his own, and whom he will bring unto the light in his own good way and time.

EARNESTNESS IN PROFESSING CHRIST.

BY MRS. GULICK.

The third day after our arrival at Yujo, while I was talking to a room full of women, an old woman came up to me, and, warmly taking my hand, said, " I am of the same religion as you are : I believe in Jesus.   Last New Year's Day I burned my idols : I wanted to begin the year right.   Now I pray only to the true God.   When can I be baptized ? " — " We will consult about it." — " But when ?   I am an old woman.   I have no husband or son.   I want to be baptized ; and then I shall have nothing to do but to die, and go to heaven."

You can imagine what a gleam of sunshine it was to my heart to see one come forward thus.   When she came, I was showing the women some pictures.   Amongst them was one of our Saviour on the cross.   This attracted her attention, and she staid a long time telling them of his love.   This old woman is a poor widow of the name of Feng.   She was, as we afterwards found out, the one who was the means of leading Mr. Gulick to pay his first visit to Singo nearly two years ago.   Before Tsai Ching was baptized, he went home for a holiday, and took with him the Gospel of John and a small catechism.   He was zealous in telling his family and friends about the truths he had been learning.   Widow Feng heard and believed.   She got some one to copy for her the whole of the Gospel of John and part of the other books : not that she could read herself ; but she wished to have them in her house, so that she might sometimes hear them read.

2*

On Friday, Mr. Gulick asked those who believed in Christ, and wished to be baptized, to meet together in our room early in the morning before breakfast, so as to avoid the crowd. This meeting was one I can never forget : we could feel that God was present with us. Three or four, who came from curiosity, were much moved. One old woman said, " I believe in Jesus. I want to be baptized." — " Wait," said Mrs. Tsai, " till you know more : if you worship Jesus, you must destroy your idols." " Wait ! I have no time to wait. I am nearly eighty years old. I ought to decide at once to worship one or the other ! " Two or three of the women offered up simple but earnest prayers : four expressed a wish to be baptized.

Let me entreat your prayers for this little feeble band of Christians, left without an earthly teacher, that God may teach them, guide them, and make their light to shine so brightly that many through them may be led to the Saviour.

THE SOUL-LOVING SOCIETY.

The following extract is taken from a letter written by Miss West from Yozgat to her pupils in Harpoot, giving some account of her labors among the women in the various towns visited by her during her homeward journey.

" The first sabbath I went to church in the city of Cesarea. They have a good-sized stone house of worship, with a high gallery. After the service I held a meeting with the women. I told them of you all, and gave them your greetings, which much pleased them. The sisters all agreed to become members of a ' Soul-loving Society,' and spend part of one day every week in visiting from house to house. There were over thirty present. One good woman said, ' When I earn ten piastres, after this, *one* shall be the Lord's ! ' It may please you to learn that pastor Heropi has given a tenth ever since his visit to Harpoot.

While there, I had several conversations witth his dear brother (whom I knew before), and with two or three of the oldest helpers in the field. All listened with deep interest to my story of the churches who support their own pastor, and are giving for the support of Koordish students in the seminary. All confessed it was the true way; and, when I spoke of the love and gratitude showed us by those for whom we have labored in the Lord, I saw their eyes glisten; and I think they felt almost proud of their own people, who had begun to do so nobly! Dear friends, I beg you will be careful to go on, that I'll not be "ashamed in this same confident boasting," as Paul says (2 Cor. ix. 4), but rather let the experiment of this ministration glorify God (2 Cor. ix. 13).

I must tell you of a sabbath spent in the village of Moon-jasoon, a few miles from Cesarea. There I found a little band of brothers and sisters who speak Armenian. Their chapel is a little gem. It is built of stone, the courtyard laid in mosaic (by one of the brethren), and nearly all the work and expense met by them when they were but few in number; and this their first love. Moonjasoon has but two hundred houses, — a very clean, pleasant, airy place. In the afternoon, I told the sisters of Christ's work in the places around us, of our schools at Harpoot, and what we hoped would be done through the giving of truths. The brethren wanted to hear; and a number of them came and sat near the chapel-door. In the evening, a number met to converse with Mr. Farnsworth and myself. They had been thinking of what they had heard. One old man, whom they feared would oppose it, said to his son that evening, "If we can't come up to this giving of a tenth, we may as well give up our religion!" They have no preacher or teacher. One of their number conducts worship on the sabbath; but all hearts and all eyes were turned to one who was, under God, the means of building up the work in their village soon to finish his course of study in Marsovan. It was delightful to hear them speak of their beloved teacher Krikore. He had evidently been a faithful worker for Christ; and the women especially seemed remarkably intelligent and earnest in their piety. I loved them at once. They hope Krikore will become their pastor. " Are you able and willing to support him?" I asked. " We thought we were not able till you talked to us; but now we think we can do it," said one of the leading men. His salary is fixed at $9.00 per month. The four or five sisters who are church-members, besides others, pledged themselves to become members of the "Soul-loving Society." One of them conducts family worship in the absence of her husband, and four women from without come every day to attend. Those who can read go often to teach others, and talk to them of Christ.

Monday morning they came to see us off. I was talking to them of doing more for the poor souls around them, when one of those dear good women exclaimed, " Last night I lay awake thinking how we could bring all the sisters to be more faithful and earnest. I resolved that we must make it a rule, that every one who does not attend onr weekly prayer-meeting for women must pay a piastre every time." — " Will it do," I asked, " to compel them?" — " Yes," they all said : " they will pay it if they don't come." Fifteen women now gather for prayer every week. They will let me know how their plan works in future. Pray for Moonjasoon, dear sisters. It is a little garden of the Lord, but they greatly need an under-gardener. I promised to see their dear Krikore in Marsovan, and also the others in both schools from that place.

MRS. ANNA MARIA WHITE.

Miss Agnew, teacher of the Oodooville Seminary, has kindly furnished us with a manuscript of forty pages, giving an account of some of her old pupils, which shows us most clearly what the heathen may become under Christian instruction, and the leading of the Holy Spirit.

We can give but a meagre sketch of the one whom we have chosen as the subject of this article; but we will not mar the simple beauty of the narrative by changing the person. She shall speak for herself.

"I was born of heathen parents in Tillepally, in 1823. At the age of seven years, I went to school. Mrs. Spaulding, the missionary's wife, used to give us good advice at the close of school. She frequently spoke the word 'Jesus, Jesus.' I used to pronounce that word in my house, but did not know who it was that bore the name of Jesus, nor any thing about what he had done for us. Although Mrs. Spaulding treated me very patiently and kindly, I was afraid to ask what these things meant.

"Soon after, Mrs. Spaulding told my parents to take me to the Oodooville school. Here I attended the meetings held by the missionaries, and heard many confessing their sins and praying with tears. I began to be anxious, and said, 'Am I not a sinner?' I then began to pray; but the thought came to me, I will repent after all the older girls have repented. If I repent now, everybody will laugh at me; yet day after day my anxiety of mind continued. Mr. Spaulding called me, and asked me if I thought myself a sinner. To which I replied, with much sorrow and crying, 'Yes, though I am a child, I am a great sinner: when I think what shall I do to be saved, I am in great trouble.' Mr. Spaulding said, 'Believe on the Lord Jesus Christ, and love him: you will then be saved. Confess and forsake your sins, and pray to him.'

"The next day was the sabbath: I went to the church. The missionary providentially preached about the Prodigal Son, and showed how he returned to the father, and how the father received him. I listened to the sermon with astonishment, and felt much comforted.

"In September, 1835, I was received to the church. My mother united with the church about six months before I did.

"In 1843, I was married to Mr. John White, one of the students of the Batticotta Seminary.

"My beloved pastor, who had guarded me from childhood, said, 'Put on godliness as a jewel, and live among the heathen as a bright light, and as an epistle which they can read. May the blessing of God be on all the vessels of the house where you dwell!' My kind teacher, Miss Agnew, said, 'May the Lord bless you! trust him, and strive to serve him.'

"With these blessings I left the school, and went with my husband. After teaching a girls' school for two months in Molai, my husband's native village, we were requested to go to Ramnad to teach the young Hindoo princess of that district. When we arrived at the Palace, the princess, her mother, and their relatives, urged us to rub ashes. As we would not consent, they declared we were "low-caste religionists," and should not be allowed to enter the palace or teach the princess. They also commanded us not to teach the children unless we had ashes on our foreheads. Then I said to them, 'I did not come here to deny my religion : I came here to teach the princess and others, and to make known the Christian religion."

"After two or three months, the inmates of the palace treated me very kindly. I then began to teach the Bible little by little, as I saw they were disposed to listen. At first, I told them how Jesus Christ came to this world, and that when he was born the heavenly angels sang praises. When I told them these things, they were glad, and heard attentively, and said, 'Let us hear you sing one of the songs of the angels.' I then sang, —

"'I am an angel sent from Heaven.'

(A Tamil hymn founded on 'Behold, I bring you good tidings,' &c.) They listened, and said, 'Very well : we never heard that before.' Afterwards, daily, they begged me to tell more about the Bible.

"In the course of a year, we returned to Jaffna. After the birth of my daughter Emily, we preferred to remain there. We collected twenty girls, and established a school, which I taught. I often held meetings with them, and spoke to them about loving the Saviour. Of the twenty children, two became anxious about their souls, and were in the habit of praying. They are now following Christ.

" While we were residing in Jaffna, two of our children took a severe fever, and died suddenly. One was six, and the other four years old. They died happily as Christian children.*

" We afterwards removed from Jaffna for a time to a place where I had a school of thirty girls, six of whom became Christians. During the three years we lived in this place, our two daughters, Emily and Eliza, were pupils in the female boarding-school at Oodooville. We then returned to Jaffna, and took charge of the girls' boarding-school in that place. It contained at that time thirty-five children. I selected fifteen of them, with whom I daily talked and prayed at six in the afternoon. Several of these girls united with the church. I was afterwards called to Molai, on account of the severe illness of my eldest daughter, Emily, who was married and residing there. God gave me this precious jewel, — a precious talent which I did not bury in the ground. On account of my being a wanderer, I committed her, at the age of ten years, to the care of Mr. and Mrs. Spaulding, who had watched over and taught me. She was taken suddenly from me, and left her little girl in my care. On this account I did not return to the boarding-school.

" In all these ways God has been with me. I am now forty-five years old ; yet whenever I hear the name of Jesus, which was taught me when eight years old, the promises of the gospel all come to my remembrance, with the times and the places where Mrs. Spaulding heard my lessons. There is no sound in the

---

* For an account of these two little girls, see " Mary and Harriet" in the *Children's Corner.*

world, as the sound of the name of Jesus. All his promises are precious, and no persons are so dear to me as those who taught them to me. I pray God to bless them and me.

(signed) ANNA MARIA WHITE."

Miss Agnew adds, "A few months ago, Anna Maria White heard a voice from heaven, saying, "Come up hither." ' She set her house in order, and triumphantly ascended to meet her Saviour."

A PRIVILEGE.

The silver and the gold are the Lord's: why should we give for the missionary cause? Because it is a privilege so to do, and God condescends to accept our offerings, and to give a rich reward. Will the women of our churches avail themselves of this great privilege the present year? A dollar a year from every female member of our churches would make the treasury overflow. There are comparatively, few, who, if they should bear the subject on their hearts, could not by special effort do this; but there are enough who could easily give a larger sum, and make up the deficiency. Shall not a vigorous effort be made this year to bring up those who have given nothing for this cause? and will not those who have heretofore given smaller sums increase their subscriptions? Let this be a year of retrenchment for the sake of saving the souls of our sisters in heathen lands. We have heard of their ignorance and degradation. We can individually do something for them. The way is open, the means at hand.

Let no woman who loves the Saviour delay to do something to save those for whom he died. Let officers of societies be in earnest; let collectors be faithful, and bring the call to the hearts of all those who should give; and may every Christian woman avail herself of the privilege of doing something for this blessed cause!

Children's Corner.

"LIGHT ON THE DARK RIVER."

A STORY OF TWO LITTLE TAMIL GIRLS.

BY THEIR MOTHER.

Mary was six years and three months, and Harriet was four years and three months, in this world. "I love them that love me, and those that seek me shall find me." According to this proverb did these two children live, and then slept in Jesus. While here in this world, they were two choice jewels, beloved by all. They were very fond of study. Their father, seeing their desire to learn, taught them in the evenings, and also heard their prayers. I early taught them the hymn, "Gentle Jesus, meek and mild." They not only learned it by heart, but sung it with me. These two little children were regular in their conduct, ardent in spirit, and very obedient. A few days before they were taken sick, a little girl six years old in a Christian family suddenly died. When she was to be buried, these two children went with me, and saw the corpse in the coffin. Mary asked, "Mother was this little child like us." I replied, "Yes: this child was a little child just your age. Yesterday she went to heaven. Thus you also must die; and will both of you go to heaven?" They said, "Yes : we too will go to heaven." — "But whom will you see in heaven?" Both cheerfully replied, "We shall see gentle Jesus there."

After a few days, Harriet was very sick of fever. When I held her in my lap, Mary came and looked at her for some time, and said, "Mother, our beloved little sister is now very

3

sick. Does the heavenly Father know it?" — "Yes: he knows it very well." — "Then," said the child, " if he knows, has he no compassion?" — "Yes: he is very good. He is very merciful. He sent this sickness for our good. My child, go and pray that God may give little sister health again." Mary went immediately to another room, knelt down, and prayed. When she came back, she said, " Mother, I have prayed to our heavenly Father with tears that little sister may get well."

Two days after this, Mary came to me, and said, " Mother, my head aches." I feared she was going to have fever, and was much distressed, exclaiming, " What shall we do?" I tried to say, " The will of the Lord be done." The child, seeing I was troubled, concealed her sufferings, took her book, and said, " I will not lie down: I will go and study. You need not be troubled about me." Though she spake thus, she became worse, and laid down. The father, seeing both children very sick, raising his hands, said "O Father, thy will be done!" The children, seeing this, prayed also. The next day Mary prayed many times. Seeing this, I said, " My child, does it not hurt you to pray so much? Better wait a little." She replied, " Mother this is not hard for me ; " and then repeated,

> " Gentle Jesus, meek and mild,
> Look upon a little child."

Just before her death, I asked her if I should pray. She made a sign, meaning " Yes." After prayer she spoke, and said, " Father, I am now going to sleep; come and lie down near me." She then raised her eyes, and, clasping her little hands, said, " O Lord! O Jesus!" and died.

Three days after this, Harriet said, " Come, mother, the bandy has come : let us go in it." She then repeated several times, " Gentle Jesus ; " and just before her death, she repeated the whole hymn. At the close, she said, " Mother, I am going." The Rev. J. Philip, who was present, prayed. She remained quiet; but, as soon as he had finished, she began to pray. Soon she turned towards me, and said, "Mother, I am going into the bandy," and immediately died. Mary was sick fourteen days, and Harriet thirty days. They are not dead. As Christ lives, they also live.

Does not this record prove that there is "light on the dark river," even for children?

OUR MISSIONARY BOYS.

Perhaps some of you, who read the story above of Mary and Harriet White, will think, as did another little girl, that you do not want to be good; for all good children die.

Now, I am acquainted with several remarkably good children, who lived to grow up, and are living still. It won't do to talk much about those who are living among us in America; for they might read this story, and not be pleased to find themselves in print. But I will tell you about two little Armenian boys. who live in Aintab, Syria.

In 1861, when the war broke out in America, and the people were obliged to pay heavy taxes to support the army, the native Christians at Aintab began to fear that the people in America would forget them, and thus their preachers and schools would not be supported. They wisely resolved to do more to help themselves and those about them than they had ever done before.

One day we saw quite a little party coming into our yard. It was Pastor Kukore and his wife and their eight children, dressed in their Sunday clothes; and one could see from their faces that they had something important to say.

After the greetings were over, and all were quietly seated, the father explained why they had come.

They had heard with sorrow of the war in America: they

could not expect that the American Board would send them as much help as they had formerly done. But they could not bear to have any of the schools and churches closed; so they had formed themselves into a family missionary society, and had contributed enough among themselves to support the preacher at Birijik (a town on the Euphrates) for three months. They all then brought forward their offerings. Even baby Rebecca held out a ten para piece (about a cent) to the missionary in her little fingers.

There were two nice little boys in the group, about ten and twelve years of age : and, when they brought their gifts to the missionary (Mr. Schneider), he took their hands, and asked them, " Arteen and Nazar, would you like to be missionaries yourselves ? "

They hung their heads bashfully at first, but said they would like to be missionaries when they grew up.

Mr. Schneider told them that their missionaries had come across the ocean to preach the gospel to their parents and people; but that Africa lay close by them, and in all that great continent there were yet but few who knew of Christ. Couldn't they go to Africa, and carry the Bible there? Their eyes brightened, and they said they would like to go.

Their father and mother also said, that if God should " open their hearts," and give them a desire to work for him, they would be very glad to let them go wherever they were needed.

Well, we often looked at these boys with interest after that : we noticed them at church because they looked so tidy (they had a good mother, you see) ; we noticed them at school-examinations, because they recited so promptly ; we noticed them at home, because they were so helpful to their father and mother, and so kind to their little brothers and sister. I used to go there often, and at all hours of the day ; and sometimes I found them at work, sometimes at play, and sometimes reading or studying : but, although there were so many children in the family, I never found these boys cross, or quarrelling with the others.

After a while, their father, although he was a minister, and wished nothing better for his sons than that they should be ministers too, took these boys out of school, and put then to learn a trade; because he said he thought every boy ought to learn how to work as well as how to study, and ought also to have a trade to fall back upon in case he should need it.

So Arteen commenced working with a dyer, and Nazar with a shoemaker. They did not forget their books, however, but spent many of their evenings in study.

They also talked sometimes with their father and mother about their own souls, and how they could become the true children of God. They both gave themselves to God, and united with the church, when they were quite young.

Not long after, they asked permission of their father to attend school again, and fit themselves to preach.

This he readily granted; but he told Arteen that he feared that he would not be able to keep up with his class, as he was rather hard to learn. At the end of the first half year, when the examination was past, Arteen wrote a most joyful letter to his father, saying that he had passed his examination well, and could go on.

When the long vacation came, they both went up into the villages in the mountains, and taught school. Their mother could hardly spare them, when they were away all the year beside; but she put up many little niceties for them, and prepared their clothing carefully, and sent them away with her blessing.

At the first village where Nazar stopped, the people sent him away. They told him they didn't want any Protestant teachers there. So he went to another place. There he gathered a school, and taught in his own little room by day, and slept there at night. It was very hard for him; for the children were very dirty, and covered with vermin.

Arteen had a better place; but you would say, if you could

3*

see it, that you would much rather live in your father's barn. When the vacation closed, they went back to school again.

These two boys, or *young men* we must now call them, have two years longer to remain in the Theological Seminary, and then they will be ready to commence preaching.

They were good boys; they are good young men; and I should not be one bit surprised if they should indeed go to Africa some day, and work for Christ there. No, boys: children do *not* all die young; and those who live are a great deal happier, and a great deal more useful all their lives, because they began early to live for Christ.

A HEAVY SUBSCRIPTION.

Some months since, a lady received a little blue box, containing between six and seven dollars in coin, neatly done up in twenty-five-cent packages. It was collected in an infant sabbath-school class, and sent as a donation to the Woman's Board of Missions. It weighed six pounds avoirdupois, and was probably the *heaviest* contribution ever received by the Society.

Weighed in the heavenly balances, what was its value?

He who sits over against the treasury may have noticed that some of those little ones gave more than those who gave larger sums of their abundance. But, more than this, the interest awakened in those little minds may be like a seed, which, in after years, will bring forth an hundred fold, and may perhaps lead to a life consecrated to the cause of missions.

THE LITTLE SOWERS.

In the same sabbath-school, two classes united, and sent five dollars to the Woman's Board of Missions, with a note requesting missionary intelligence, calling themselves the *little sowers*.

That note was brought before the Executive Committee as a fragrant flower.

Will not Christian parents and teachers encourage the little ones of our land to bring their offerings, till there arise a cloud of sweet incense, well pleasing to the Lord.

THE MOTHER'S JEWEL.

BY A NATIVE CHRISTIAN WOMAN.

Emily was a Tamil girl, the daughter of John and Anna Maria White. She was born April 20, 1844, and was received into the Oodooville Seminary when ten years of age.

She possessed a meek and amiable disposition; she was industrious in her habits, neat and tidy in her person, and was never known to have any disagreement with her schoolmates. She won their affections, and all esteemed her highly. In 1858 she united with the people of God. In August of the following year she was married to Robert Breckenridge, Principal of the English High School at Batticotta. She died April 25, 1863, age nineteen.

The love of Christ was a favorite topic with her. Whenever she perceived any of her family neglecting closet-duties, she would go and pray for them, and then exhort them to be faithful and prayerful. She was anxious about the salvation of the lads in her husband's school, and would frequently inquire if those boys with whom she was acquainted loved the Saviour. If she received a reply in the negative, she would ask her husband, " What are you doing there?" (i.e. in the school). Her heathen relatives were the subjects of frequent prayer. She was very anxious for the formation of a church in the village in which she resided, and for which she often poured out her heart to the throne of grace. The women of her neighborhood were invited by her to the bungalow where the regular ministrations of the Sabbath were held; and she was faithful in conversing with them on the duty of worshipping the only living and true God.

It was her custom to speak freely of death; and her mind dwelt on her departure to a better land, apparently overcoming the world through faith in God's dear Son. She said all earthly property and jewelry seemed as dross. Her husband and parents were often surprised at her remarks, owing to the comfortable health she enjoyed.

On the 7th of April, 1863, she was attacked with a severe headache and slow fever. Her friends tried to cheer her with the hope that she would soon be well; but she told them, "No: you must not think so." Her disease afterwards assumed the typhoid form.

During her sickness she frequently asked her aunt and sister to sing "Rock of ages" and other favorite hymns, and would join with them.

At one time, noticing that her sister read a letter from her husband several times during the day, she asked, "Sister, how many times have you read the *Bible* to-day? I feel very anxious about you. You do not love God as you love your husband."

To her mother she said, "Mother, when you get all your work done, please take the Bible and read to me." Her mother read the eleventh and twelfth verses of the third chapter of Proverbs. She listened, and said, "All that the Lord doeth is good." That night she prayed, "O Lord, have mercy upon me! forget me not."

As her disease progressed, it became evident to all that she must die. While her friends wept, Emily said, "Why do you hinder me? I am going to our home. My dear mother, let me go." Her mother asked, "Do you feel afraid?" She smiled, and said, "I have no fear."

On the morning of her death, her mother witnessed her sufferings with a heavy heart, and said, "Daughter, oh that I could relieve you! but Jesus will cure your pains. He will comfort you. Is it not so?" Emily signified that it was so. Some catechists present, who witnessed her sufferings, shed tears. Then the mother asked, "Daughter, does Jesus ease your pains?" She tried to speak, but could not. She motioned affirmatively, which the catechists observing, rejoiced. After a pause she looked upward, and, with a joyful countenance, uttered "*Yes!*" and breathed her last. Her husband, sitting beside her, took her right hand in his a moment before her death, and said, "Father, thus thou gavest her to me: in the same manner I give her back to thee. Praised be thy name!"

Those who witnessed these scenes felt deeply. The Christians, and even the heathen, said, "This is a call from God. Blessed are the dead who die in the Lord!"

DEPARTURE AND ARRIVAL OF MISSIONARIES SUPPORTED BY THIS SOCIETY.

Miss Mary E. Andrews, for Toung Chow, China, sailed March 22, and arrived June 13, 1868.

Miss Rebecca D. Tracy, for Sivas, Western Turkey, sailed July 11, and arrived Sept, 5, 1868.

Miss Olive L. Parmelee, for Mardin, Eastern Turkey, sailed Aug. 15, and arrived Sept. 17, 1868.

Mrs. Mary K. Edwards, for the Zulu Mission, South Africa, sailed Aug. 19, and arrived Nov. 16, 1868.

Miss Ursula C. Clark, for Broosa, Western Turkey, sailed Oct. 10, and arrived Nov. 18, 1858.

Miss Maggie Webster, for Ceylon, sailed Oct. 28, 1868, and has not yet been heard from.

Miss Adelia M. Payson, for Foochow, China, sailed Oct. 31, 1868, not heard from.

DONATIONS.

THE receipts of the WOMAN'S BOARD OF MISSIONS for the year ending Jan. 5, 1869, were $5031.13. At the Anniversary, and since, we have received,—

1869.

Jan. 5.—*Boston*—	From Mrs. David Coit Scudder, annual subscription .	$5.00
" "	Mrs. M. Fearing, O. S. Church, Life Membership	25.00
" "	Mrs. A. Ramsay, Essex-st. Church, Life Membership.	25.00
" "	Mrs. J. R. Stacey	5.00
" "	Miss Chadwick	5.00
" "	Mrs. Baldwin	2.00
" "	Mrs. Richmond, Mount-Vernon Church . . .	2.00
" "	Miss R. R., and Mrs. J. B. Simmons, $1 each . .	2.00
" "	Mrs. T. M. Noble, Mrs. Case, and Mrs. Hooker, $1 each	3.00
" "	Mrs. Munger, Boston Highlands	2.00
"	*Newton Corner*—Miss Ada L. Sears	20.00
"	" " Miss Snow and sister, $1 each . .	2.00
"	*Charlestown*—Mrs. A. W. Grant, Life Membership . .	25.00
"	*Lowell*—Mrs. Stevens	1.00
"	*Brighton*—Mrs. D. T. Packard	1.00
"	*Somerville*—Mrs. Oakman and Mrs. B. W. Eldridge, $1 each .	2.00
"	*Arlington*—Mrs. Henry Mott	1.00
"	*Jamaica Plain*—By Mrs. Perkins, additional . . .	2.00
"	*Andover*—Mrs. John Smith, Life Membership . . .	25.00
"	" Mrs. George W. Coburn, Life Membership .	25.00
"	*East Boston*—Maverick Church, Mrs. Stephen N. Stockwell .	50.00
"	*Lynn*—Mrs. James Flint	5.00
"	*Wells, Me.*—Miss Sarah Lindsay	1.00
"	*Colchester, Conn.*—Mrs. Martha T. Clarke, made Life Member by her mother, Mrs. Joshua Clarke .	25.00
"	" " Mrs. William S. Curtis	1.00
"	" " Mrs. J. B. Wheeler, Life Membership .	25.00
"	*Meriden, N.H.*—Miss Mary A. Bryant	2.00
"	*Dubuque, Iowa*—Mrs. George R. Ransom . . .	1.00
Jan. 7.—*Boston*—	Miss E. S. Tappan, Life Membership . . ⁊	25.00
"	By a Persis, to constitute Mrs. Charles H. Wheeler of Harpoot, Life Member	25.00

Jan. 8. — *Boston.* — Mrs. Greenwood of Shawmut-ave. Cong. Ch., L. M. . $25.00
"   *Detroit, Mich.* — Mrs. Charles Noble, Life Membership .   . 25.00
"   *Concord*, "   Presb. Ch. to make Mrs. C. F. Foucher L. M. , 25.00
"   *Norwichtown, Conn.* — Additional from Cong. Church   .   . 3.00
Jan. 9. — *Charlestown* — Mrs. Wm. Abbott, donation $5, and sub. $1   . 6.00
"   *Boston* — Mrs. A. W. Tufts, Life Membership and subscription 26.00
"   "   Mrs. E. A. R. Winslow, annual subscription   .   . 10.00
"   "   Miss S. Farrington 2.00
Jan. 10.   "   Mrs. Willson, O. S., and Miss Amy Foster, Cen. Ch. . 2.00
Jan. 11. — *Williamstown* — Mrs. Prof. Tatlock 4.00
"   *Chelsea* — By ladies of Chestnut-street Church, Mrs. Albert H.
               Plumb, Life Membership 25.00
"   "   By ladies of Chestnut-street Church, Mrs. I. P. Lang-
               worthy, Life Membership 25.00
"   *Pittsfield, Conn.* — Mrs. A. C. Morley. 10.00
"   *East Haddam, Conn.* — From A. H. 1.00
Jan. 12. — *Townsend* — From Ladies' Society, auxiliary   .   .   . 10.00
Jan. 15. — *Utica, N. Y.* — Mrs. A. W. Crittenden, Life Membership .   . 25.00
Jan. 16. — *Boston* — A Friend in Essex-street Church 100.00
"   "   Miss A. Newman, Essex-st. Ch., Life Membership . 25.00
Jan. 17. — *Boston* — O. S. Church, from J. C. for L. P. Gordon, L. M.   . 25.00
"   "   "   "   " Mrs. S. T. Armstrong, L. M.   . 25.00
"   "   "   "   " Mr. Cragiu, in memoriam   .   . 10.00
Jan. 18. — *Newton Corner* — Mrs. Alfred B. Ely, Life Membership .   . 25.00
"   *Boston* — Mrs. Freeman Allen, donation 100.00
Jan. 19. — *Wellesley* — Ladies' Missionary Society, constituting Mrs. Au-
               gustus Fuller Life Member 25.00
"   "   Auxiliary Society for sabbath school   .   .   . 40.00
"   *Ipswich* — Ladies of First Church : a New-Year offering .   . 10.00
"   *Bedford, N. H.* — From Presbyterian Church, a part constitut-
               ing Mrs. Stephen C. Damon L. M. .   .   . 31.75
"   *Hollis, N. H.* — From Mrs. J. B. Day, to make Mrs. Julia A.
               Grinnell Life Member 25.00
Jan. 22. — *Boston* — Mrs. Hale, subscription, $1; Mrs. C. M. Putnam, $5 . 6.00
"   "   Additional from Mrs. C.   30
"   *Bolton, Conn.* — Mrs. Talcot Carpenter, Mrs. Henry Alvord,
               Mrs. E. C. Ruggles, Mrs. William Loomis,
               Mrs. E. B. Morse, $1 each 5.00
Jan. 23. — *North Woodstock, Conn.* — Mrs. Peleg Child, Life Membership . 25.00
"   "   "   Mrs. T. H. Brown,   "   .   .   . 25.00
"   *Boston* — Old South Church, Homer Bartlett, to constitute Mrs.
               Almena B. Morgan Life Member   .   .   . 25.00
"   "   From Mrs. Homer Bartlett, Life Membership for Mrs.
               Susan H. Morgan, and Miss Myra Proctor of Tur-
               key; annual subscription 50.00
"   "   Old South Ch., Miss Mary Fowler, annual subscrip. . 5.00
Jan. 25. — *East Randolph* — Young ladies in church and sabbath school,
               constituting Mrs. Louisa S. Russell L. M. 30.05
Jan. 26. — *Littleton* — Ladies' Benevolent Society in Cong. Church .   . 10.00

Jan. 26. — *Belfree, O.* — Congregational Church $11.63
"   *Boston* — Central Church. From Mr. Wm. S. Houghton, L. M.   25.00
"   "   "   same, an annual subscription   20.00
Jan. 29. — *Stockbridge* — From Mrs. Anna J. Whitney, Life Membership .   25.00
"   *Westhampton* — From Mrs. Newman Clark, $10; Miss Hattie
         F. Clapp, $5; Mrs. Ansel Clapp, $2; Mrs
         Clark Bridgman, Mrs. Submit Bridgman,
         Mrs. Lucas Bridgman, and Mrs. Alfred
         Montague, $1 each 21.00
Jan. 30. — *Poughkeepsie, N.Y.* — Vassar College. Miss Hannah W. Ly-
         man, Life Membership . . 25.00
Feb. 1. — *Ipswich* — Seminary. Young ladies 9.50
"   *Boston* — Old South. Miss Lillie 2.00
"   "   Mt. Vernon Church. Mrs. J. C. Tyler, annual sub. .   5.00
"   "   Miss Esther S. and Miss Cutler, $1 each . .   2.00
"   "   Miss Rebecca Reed, Mt. Vernon Church . .   5.00
"   "   Shawmut-ave. Cong. Ch., Mrs. John Erskine, L. M. .   25.00
"   "   "   "   Subscriptions in part . .   80.00
"   *Chelsea* — Mrs. Joseph Sweetser, Life Membership . .   25.00
"   *New York* — Mrs. E. W. Chester, annual subscription .   5.00
Feb. 2. — *South Amherst* — Ladies' Benevolent Society, constituting Mrs.
         Clara B. Hutchings Life Member .   25.00
"   *New Haven, Conn.* — Ladies of North Church . . .   25.00
Feb. 5. — *West Amesbury* — Ladies' Social Circle, less express . .   37.75
"   *Northampton* — From C. E. L. 1.00
Feb. 6. — *Sand Lake, N.Y.* — Mrs. W. H. Scram, to constitute Mrs. Isa-
         bella Brooks Life Member . .   25.00
"   *Boston* — Old South Ch. Mrs. Bancroft and Mrs. Gray, L. M. .   50.00
"   "   "   "   Subscriptions in part 5.00
Feb. 8.   "   Essex-st. Ch. A Friend, $2; Mrs. E. Keep, L. M. .   27.00
"   *East Boston* — Maverick Church. Mrs. Albert Bowker, to con-
         stitute Miss Sarah F. Bowker and Miss Mary
         F. Bowker, Life Members . . .   50.00
"   "   Maverick Church. Mrs. Elizabeth Hammet, an-
         nual subscription 10.00
"   *Boston* — Salem-street Church. Collections in part . .   10.00
Feb. 9. — *Spencerport, N.Y.* — From Mrs. S. Weare, for China . .   10.00
"   *Columbia, Conn.* — Miss Emily C. Williams, subscription . .   1.00
Feb. 10. — *Oxford* — Mrs. B. F. Bardwell 5.00

          Total $1,754.98

LIFE AND LIGHT

FOR

Heathen Women.

| VOL. I. | JUNE, 1869. | No. 2. |

LEAVES FROM A MISSIONARY'S JOURNAL.

BEFORE it is crowded out of my more vivid recollection, I must try to tell you of a visit I have had to-day.

By way of explanation, I need to say, that one morning last week, while I was hearing my usual class from the English school, two Brahmins came, and begged me to go and see a young woman who was very ill. Her first infant was eight days old, and the young mother was in convulsions. I refused, saying that I had been often called too late, and I did not feel as if I could go and see another mother of a newly-born infant in a dying state. They begged me to go, if only to show my kindness of heart; to which I replied, "Yes, I will show you that;" and I went.

I was conducted to one of the largest and finest houses in the town. The street seemed thronged with people. The Mànsiff (County Judge) opened the Bandy door for me, and waited on me to the house. The Tahsildar was there, and it seemed to me every man I knew in the town. One Brahmin woman — who called to-day — came forward to recognize me; but not another woman was to be seen. Entering the house, I asked for the father of the young woman, and found that he was a man whom I had more than once received at our house; and he cordially recognized me. He led the way in, and guided me to the dark room, where his only daughter was dying. There were lamps burning, so that we could see her face. An aunt was there, a weird-looking woman, very old, and a sort of a hag, whom I have fancied was the midwife. The mother was away in another house. The little baby was in a sort of hammock. In that room were also as many as twenty Brahmins, all looking on as I had my first glimpse of the poor woman.

"She is dying," I said.

"Do give something to her," said the father.

I shook my head : " She is dying : let me turn to the living ! " I said; while, with such an audience as I never had before, I, surprised at my own boldness, gave them an earnest talk upon the terrible practices attending child-births among them, and referred them to cases which I had seen. They listened with the greatest attention, while others filled the doorway. There being no reason for remaining, I expressed my sympathy for the father, who, having offered me betel-leaf and the abeca-nut, upon a showy brass tray, as a token of hospitality, led the way out.

I soon after heard of the death ; and at evening the smoke of the funeral pile went up from the bank of the river.

Just as I was finishing my Wednesday religious lesson with the school, the old Brahmin woman mentioned came. She sat down, and heard me finish the story of Jonah, seeming greatly interested. She then heard us sing "Gentle Jesus." After dismissing the school, I said to her, "I am really very glad to see you. I was very glad to see you the other day too. It was pleasant to see an old face."

With great respect she replied, "You honor me too much. I have been very much taken up in the house which you visited, or I would have come before. I cannot tell you what a desolation there is. There was only this one daughter : she was so happy and so rich ! She had two boxes full of jewels, — very fine jewels ! a large gold plate for here (pointing to the top of her head) ; and another for here (pointing to the back of her head) ; and a string of pearls for here (from the tip of the ear to the back of the head) ; and bracelets and anklets and gold beads not to be counted ! " and, with a most expressive gesture, she added, " And now they are all lying useless ! "

"How is the baby?" I asked.

"It is well enough. They are giving it cow's milk. If it had only been a girl, there would be some joy in it."

" A boy ! " I exclaimed, " and not glad, and wishing it was a girl ! "

" If it was a girl there would be somebody to wear all those jewels ; but now they are of no use or pleasure to anybody."

I then made inquiries about the case, and received very full accounts of it, accompanied by expressions of satisfaction at my coming. There being a pause, I said, " And you are getting old : your turn to die is coming."

" What of it ! they will take me up, and carry me out, and lay me down by the river, and burn me up ; and that is the end of me."

" No, not the end of *you*," I said : " they cannot burn *you* up ! "

" Then what?" she asked, with rather a credulous, sarcastic air.

" You will drop your body as you lay off your clothes ; and that of you which is glad and sorry will live on."

" What am I going to do when I am only a handful of ashes?" she replied, with a poorly-concealed sneer.

Now, if other missionaries take the comfort, and a sort of pride, in saying " The Lord *my* God," that I do, they will enjoy David's loyalty as I do ; so I said, with a feeling of triumphant loyalty to the great Jehovah, —

" The Lord my God, who made all these trees, made you ; and,

when he pleases, you have got to die, and all the idols in
Mana Madura can't help it.   Arn't you afraid to die ? "

" No : why should I be afraid ? "

" But," I replied, " you will be afraid, as soon as you once
think that perhaps, very possibly, you may, after all, not *vanish*
while you are dying."

She began to look incredulous, and, having satisfied herself
that no one was listening, said, —

" How do you know what people are going to do after they
are burned to ashes ? "

" You are not so sure that you are going to turn to nothing
when you die : there is something about this ' after death ' which
troubles you and every heathen about us.   Is there not ? "

" Perhaps so," she said, evidently thinking soberly ; but,
wishing to make her own it, I said, —

" It is my God who sends the rain, who blesses us with har-
vests and fruits, and who created you and me, and who knows
how and when we are to die,"   She was forgetting herself
listening, while I continued, " If we bow down and worship
him, and obey him, he will take us to that beautiful city ; if
you bow down and worship that idol which my God abominates
and has foridden, you will have to be punished.   Do you think
you can bear this punishment ? "

" No : I couldn't, I am sure ; " and in an instant, seeing
how much she had committed herself, she rose to go.

" Stay," I said, " and hear about the city whose streets are
paved with gold, where you can go if only you will let me
tell you about it."   She did not need urging.   It is a beautiful description : even the names of the twelve precious stones
are fascinating to an Oriental ear ; and her eyes shone to think of
gates of one pearl.   Poor idolater ! she never will forget it, I am
sure.   She listened to me very attentively, without asking
questions of particular interest ; and I could only obey the command, " Sow thy seed beside all waters," hoping that the dear
Lord would bless this effort like so many others in this land.

TURKEY.

THE GLAD WELCOME.

Miss Olive L. Parmelee reached her destination, Mardin, Eastern Turkey, in September. She writes under date of Jan. 25, "Arriving at Harpoot, we were welcomed to the dear missionary homes there, as warmly as sisters could have anticipated or desired. For several hours before we reached the city, happy faces beamed on Mr. and Mrs. Wheeler, showing great joy at their return. One such welcome as that must be good pay for ten years of labor. I could not restrain my tears of sympathy. Wasn't it delightful for me, before I had scarcely begun to feel the cost, to be so far let into the secret of the great reward?"

A HAPPY HOME.

I can never tell what a happy home we have here with Mr. and Mrs. Williams, and the dear sunny Andrews. Did I give you the impression that it was a trial to come away from the work I had so long enjoyed at South Hadley? I do not repent the step. The ties that bind me to America are very strong, and I do not anticipate that they will weaken as the years go by. But I am so happy here in the Lord's work, and he has done such great things for me, that I have not the least inclination to look back with any thought of turning.

SARA OF MARDIN.

Should you attend service with us of a sabbath, you would notice that the men are far more intelligent-looking than the women, having had greater privileges. This is the rule, although there are exceptions. At your feet would be Sara, whom you would notice for two reasons: first, because she wears a white sheet. The married women in Mardin wear a

blue sheet ; and the girls a calico, light colored.   But Sara is
from Diarbehir, and still holds to the fashion there.   Her face is
very beautiful ; and she is one of the few favored women in this
land ; for her husband loves her, and is proud of her, and was so
before either of them became Protestants.   He was at first very
angry when he found she wanted to unite with the church, and
had a long, indignant talk with Mr. Wiliams, but was finally
convinced that he had no right to stand between her and what
she considered her duty.   He said if she offered herself, " of
course they would take her, because she was pretty."   She was
accepted ; and the next day, when the candidates rose to enter
into covenant with the church, greatly to every one's surprise,
he came out and took his place beside her.   Love and pride got
the better of his anger ; and he wanted to testify, that, even
if she could be so silly, he would stand by and protect her
just the same.   He is now a very firm Protestant, but not a
member of the church.

WEEK OF PRAYER.

I must tell you about our week of prayer, just closed, while
the memory of it is fresh in my mind.   Will you have quite
forgotten there was such a week, by the time this old Mesopo-
tamian letter reaches you ?   Then it may be good for you to be
reminded, that somebody's heart in this far-off land was very
warm, for at least a whole week, because of the assurance, that
it was specially prayed for in other places than in our own little
chapel in ˙Mardin.   Many times, as I sat devoutly listening
(apparently) to earnest Arabic prayers, I heard, instead,
familiar voices in the dear old lecture-room across the waters,
uttering well-remembered petitions ; and my prayer was all a
thanksgiving for the " communion of the saints even here on
earth."   The meetings were held at half-past three, P. M.,
each day, and from eighty to a hundred persons — about the
usual sabbath congregation — attended.   I was able to go regu-

larly, and enjoyed it more than I can tell you, though I could understand only an occasional word or phrase. But I loved to hear them sing our familiar tunes, — to see their earnest, attentive faces, their readiness in prayer, so that we often had six prayers in succession with not a moment's pause. My heart could interpret their earnest pleadings; and I came home with more intense longing for the souls of this dear people.

LETTER FROM BROOSA.

An interesting letter, dated Jan. 29, has been received from Miss Ursula C. Clark, who reached her field of labor, Broosa, Western Turkey, in November. Omitting the details of her delightful journey, we commence the narrative from her arrival. She writes, —

" Dr. Schneider came up from Broosa to meet me at Bebek; and Thanksgiving Day found me fairly established in my new home, very glad and thankful to be here, — thankful for all the way in which I had been led, and most thankful of all for the work opening before me.

" Mr. Wheeler, I know, claims Harpoot as the ' Beautiful for situation, the joy of the whole earth ; ' but, if you could only see Broosa as I have, through all the golden October days ! for we had October till the first of January. The city lies along one of the lower slopes of Mt. Olympus, which rises above the city in broken and irregular peaks to a height of some six thousand feet. All the lower slopes of the mountain are covered with mulberry gardens and vineyards ; above are pastures, from which wind down every night long lines of goats ; and up above all are bare rocks, covered with snow the year round. Below the city, there stretches away, miles in length, a broad fertile plain, green even in December, and in summer covered with

most luxuriant crops. Beyond this plain, there is a range of
hills in outline not unlike our own Holyoke. From among
these hills, and from the plain, all manner of fruits and vegetables are brought into the city. We have all the variety one
could wish, — all we know at home, and many more.

"Broosa itself is a gem worthy its setting. Of course, being
an Eastern city, it has some narrow and crooked streets, ruins of
mosques, and various indescribable Oriental sights and sounds :
but its streets, if narrow, are clean ; and in the Armenian quarter, where we live, they are wide and well paved. There are
innumerable mosques still in good repair ; and, as you know,
there is nothing in architecture more graceful than the minarets,
of which each mosque has at least one, and some two or three.
About all these mosques are tall, solemn-looking cypresses, which
contrast finely with the white minarets. But the charm and
health of Broosa are its fountains, which are at every street-
corner, as well as in all the houses of the better class, — great
streams coming down clear and cold from the mountains, and
flowing into marble basins : wherever one may go, one hears
the music of these waters. You will bear with me for dwelling
so long on the charms of Broosa, one's surroundings have so
much to do with one's happiness ; and mine are so delightful,
in every respect, that I sometimes fear so much happiness is not
mine by right. I do not deserve to have every thing just to my
mind. You told me, I remember, that Mrs. Schneider would
be a mother to me ; so I expected that, but you did not tell me
that I should find in her, besides, a sister, and a host of congenial
friends ; neither did you tell me that Dr. S. would be next to
my own dear father.

"In regard to the work itself, as yet there is nothing very
definite to be said. In fact, I'm only devoting my energies to
getting ready to take charge of the good ship when Dr. Schneider and Mr. Richardson shall have launched it.

"It is pleasant to find that interest in the proposed school is not confined to Protestants, but is felt also by Armenians, and even Turks. We could, no doubt, have as many pupils as we wished from this city alone ; but while such scholars are of course desirable, in order that the school may accomplish the greatest amount of good, we must have girls from the villages, — girls who, going back to their homes to teach, will spread the light they may have gained. Broosa girls seldom leave the city, except to go to Constantinople. We have already heard of several who are ready to come, and only waiting for permission from us : several of these would be supported by their fathers. There has been great difficulty in finding a suitable house for the school ; but an arrangement has at last been made for the summer, which may perhaps be permanent, and we are hoping that the first term may commence in May. It seems to me at times almost an impossibility that I shall *ever* be able to talk so easily with everybody and about every thing as dear Mrs. Schneider does. She is unwearied in her visits among the people, making calls here and there among Armenians and Protestants. I frequently go with her, and occasionally make visits by myself, learning faster in that way than from books. These people are so quick to understand what one wishes to say, and so kind in helping me out of lingual flounderings ; and they never laugh at my mistakes, though I often make very absurd ones. I enjoy, especially, talking with Favaria the new Bible-woman of the place. She is a lovely Christian, and is really, as she promised, a sister to me. Indeed, I've found a great many whom I know I shall love, not simply from interest in their souls, but, just as I love my American friends, because they are so loveable. But oh how I do *long* to get my lips open to these women who don't know or care for any of these things. The Armenian church is near us ; and there are such crowds of them going in and out of it : they have bright, pleasant faces, — persons whom I think it would be a pleasure to teach.''

PASSAGES FROM MRS. KNAPP'S MANUSCRIPT.

One woman, who has withstood all our endeavors to draw her towards us until just before we left for America, tells me now, that, after we were gone, there was not a day for a year that her tears did not flow freely in remembrance of us. Such was her opposition to the truth, that, hearing one day that her son had been to our meeting, she fainted, and remained unconscious for some time. Another woman, who had opposed her husband and children, and had been a great trial to us, as she threw her arms around me, said, "I have remembered all your words to me just before you left, and now I love you very much." We daily see evidence that Christianity has finally reached the hearts of the women; though in no city in this country that I have visited do the customs of the people furnish so many obstacles to the enlightenment of women as in Bitlis. They are kept very secluded, living year after year with their faces closely veiled, and never speaking above a whisper; thus being deprived of all opportunities to speak or hardly think for themselves, but believe just what their ignorant priests tell them. Superstitious ideas are so deeply rooted in their minds, that it is very difficult to make an impression that will mark progress. We hope that a few of the number, who constantly attend our meetings, are Christians; but the pastor and brethren are very slow to admit them to church-membership, knowing their ignorance. Seeing the women in this condition, we are constrained to feel the great necessity of bringing their daughters under our influence, and Christianizing them while quite young; being more and more convinced that Protestantism cannot flourish until the women are thoroughly renovated, and their old superstitious notions are rooted out. We cannot have much hope of those who are already mothers; but for the young we *do* hope, if we can reach and educate them.

THE SCHOOL AT BITLIS.

Our people are so scattered, that we could not, if we would, reach them all by a day-school. We must have a boarding-school for them if we would educate them ; and, by education, we do not mean placing before them the sciences, and telling them they must reach up and grasp : neither do we mean giving them a new style of dress, and thereby create in them a love for outward adorning. They need no more to change their style of dress than their language. Both are adapted to their country and circumstances. We wish to place Christ, and him crucified, before them, and teach them to be Christians.

We desire it to be a school for the poor as well as rich ; for those less favored as to mental capacities, as well as the favored ones. Such a school that the poor villagers will wish to patronize it, without fear that their daughters will come back to them proud and spoiled.

The people here had become somewhat interested and awakened to the subject of educating their daughters before we went away ; and we had collected a school of fifteen girls, eight of whom were from fourteen to twenty-five years of age, and the remainder younger. These eight girls were in the school two years, and their pastor believes that all are converted. Six of these, before we had arrived here, had married young men who hope to become preachers of the gospel. Since our return, we have been trying to interest the people, and make them feel that every girl in the community must come to this school. The 31st chapter of Proverbs has been explained to them, and held up as the model for their wives and daughters.

Teaching there is to be our work ; but the pupils must be brought to us, and provision made for all their temporal wants. This they agree to do, and have chosen four men to constitute a committee to calculate how much will be needed annually for each girl. The parents, if able, are to bring it with their daughters when they come to school. Those who need help apply to the committee; and they, knowing their circumstances better than we, can decide the amount, but having for a rule, that every one, however poor, must give something; for, if the daughter stayed at home, she must eat bread, and therefore her parents must supply a portion of her food at school. We expect five girls this year from the neighboring villages to come to our school, whom we hope in a year or two to send back to teach their friends. This plan of carrying on the school is new and untried with us, and we do not know as it will succeed ; but it promises well so far, and relieves us of a burden of cares. It is also better for the people to feel that the school is theirs, and to bear responsibilities and grow strong.

CONTRIBUTIONS OF THE WOMEN.

The women have a share in the good work of sustaining our school. At our last weekly prayer-meeting, four women were chosen, who should have the care of providing clothes for the poor girls who wish to come to school. The women have sold their ear-rings, and nose-rings, and other useless ornaments, and with the money bought cotton, spun, wove, and dyed it red ; and now they have given the proceeds to help poor girls get an education.

Yesterday they purchased about three hundred piastres worth of material; and to-day a woman has walked two miles through the snow, and in a pouring rain, to cut garments for four girls, and distribute them among those who have volunteered to sew them.

There are as many more who need help ; and next week they will decide what to do for them. Our women number about thirty ; and, besides this work, they expect to support a Bible-reader. One woman brought three small gold pieces (worth thirty piastres), which she had taken from her head, and said she wished it to be used to send a preacher to adjacent villages. Said she, "I want to give all I have to Christ." Another woman, who is not permitted to come to our meetings, stole away from her house long enough to go to a neighbor who was to attend, and gave her some money to bring for *her*. The women in Bitlis can earn but about two cents, or twelve piastres, in a day, when engaged in their most profitable employment, which is spinning cotton.

MARRYING A BLIND MAN.

One of the converted girls in our school went with the pastor, B. Simons, to Marash, expecting to be married to John Concordance, the blind man that we read about in the book entitled "Ten years on the Euphrates," and whose sermon on giving tithes has been printed in "The Missionary Herald."

She is a brave, noble girl, and showed much Christian fortitude in this affair. Her friends opposed her; and one brother went so far as to threaten to shoot her if she attempted to go. The night before she was to start, her opposers collected in great numbers, and made such a noise and confusion, that the pastor, at whose house she had sought refuge, sent for his Mussulman neighbors to still them. These men called the girl, and inquired if she desired to marry this blind man, or if she had been influenced by others. She distinctly answered that it was her choice. Then the pastor told them how, a year ago, she had prayed much, that, if God saw fit to give her a husband, "he might be a Christian man : though he be blind, let him be a Christian." And, when John wished her to become his wife, she could not refuse, because she felt sure that God had sent him in answer to her prayers. Then the Mussulmans said that no one could interfere with her marriage, and also that they would be witnesses for her. So, without the farewell blessing of her mother and brothers, fearing God more than man, she went away, and will live in Havadoric, a poor village near Moosh, and teach the people the way of salvation : while her husband, led by a little boy, goes from village to village during the week, selling Bibles and preaching; coming home on Saturday, that he may preach to the people in this village on the sabbath.

5

FOOCHOW, CHINA.

[EXTRACTS FROM A LETTER BY MISS PAYSON.]

A letter received April 26, from Miss Adelia M. Payson, one of our missionaries at Foochow, gives intelligence of her "safe arrival, and cordial reception by the missionaries." Her journey was very prosperous; and, among pleasant incidents, she gives the following: "We were detained in Panama Bay on account of freight, and did not reach California until the 26th of November. We were tired of sea-life, and were rejoiced to have the privilege of eating our 'roast turkey' on shore."

She reached Foochow on the 18th of January, and is at present domiciled in Mr. Peet's family. She says, "I am trying to master this barbarous tongue, with a native teacher, at the rate of four hours a day; repeating final syllables and their proportions until my throat is hoarse. Even after twenty years' study, I am told that I shall not be independent of teachers. The missionaries are surely sowing the seeds of what will one day be a plentiful harvest; and they are very impatient to obtain recruits. I hope the time is not far distant when these heathen temples, crowning so many hill-tops, shall give place to churches of the Christian's God. I am striving to learn this foreign tongue, so that I may do something towards helping on the good work."

AFRICA.

THE PIONEER TO THE ZULUS.

The following extracts from letters written thirty-five years ago by Mrs. Geo. Champion, cannot fail to interest our readers, as giving us the first impressions of that pioneer band, as they then commenced their labors for the poor Zulus.

"As we neared Capetown, the cry 'Land ho!' was heard in merry mood on deck. Our party were immediately mounted on the shrouds in order to gain a first view of the country on which our thoughts and prayers had so long centred. Then, with eyes turned towards the land of the ill-fated African, we sung, —

> ' O'er the gloomy hills of darkness,
> Look my soul, be still and gaze.'

And, safely moored after our long voyage, we could but exclaim, ' What shall we render to God for all his mercies ! ' We commenced our journey to Port Natal in bullock-wagons. Each had a wagon and twenty-four oxen, twelve or fourteen attached at a time, as the case might require. Thus equipped, we went on our way at the rate of two or three miles per hour. Our journey of five or six hundred miles was performed in nine weeks. We bade adieu to Port Natal after a residence of a few months, although I had fondly hoped that we might remain there. In obedience to what all felt to be the will of our heavenly Father, we commenced our journey inland to the Zulus. After journeying ten days, we pitched our tent in a vale, looking towards the north. There we commenced building some rude houses of stone, sticks, and mud, with a roof of grass. But, as the rain often detained us, it was not until three moons had waxed and waned, that we had a shelter from the pitiless storm. A few weeks after entering our dwelling, a son was born ; but, as his birth was premature, he soon yielded up his breath. This was a severe trial to me. O my M. ! I thought of you in that hour, with no mother, no sister, no female friend nigh. But think you I envied her, who, at home in such an event, would have had the support of a fond mother ! No : my tongue was filled with praise for the mercies which surrounded me. Yet I often think of the days we so delightfully passed together, and of my grief at parting, which was but the beginning of partings with me. To parents, brothers, sisters, all I have bidden adieu. As I parted with them forever, my heart was wrung with anguish, while at the same time it was filled with joy unspeakable and full of glory. It was a strange, sad hour ; and, as the recollection comes over me, tears fill my eyes : but think you I regret it, — that I would have left one thing of it undone ? Not unless I had forgotten Jesus, — him who died on Calvary, he who bore my sins in his own body on the tree. No : I regret it not. Again and again would I separate those ties if duty called, and say farewell to all I held dear, and go out not knowing whither I went.

MRS. EDWARDS AND THE ZULUS.

FIRST IMPRESSIONS.

Mrs. Mary K. Edwards, the first missionary of our adoption, safely reached her destination, Inanda, Nov. 18. "The Missionary Herald" of April gives the following extract of a letter written by her Dec. 4 : "If I say that I am filled with astonishment at the degree of cultivation, or rather Christianization, among the natives, others have written enthusiastically of first impressions, and then in sorrow acknowledged that they were mistaken. There are three native missionaries supported by the native Christians of this mission. This is done by a people extremely poor. Poor Christians at home know nothing of poverty : they live in luxury, compared with these people. There are four on this station who preach; and Mr. Lindley says the arrangement, appropriateness, and point of the sermons would compare favorably with many preached in America.

"The country is fine; the road from Durban to Inanda is delightful; the scenery is picturesque, sometimes bold and rugged. The seminary building stands on the east side, and fronting Mr. Lindley's house. It is built of brick, one story high, and covered with zinc. It contains ten rooms, — dining-room, kitchen, school-room, sitting-room, and six bedrooms. Three rooms have board floors : the others are made of earth. The grounds between the two houses are tastefully laid out, and ornamented with trees, shrubs, and flowers."

In another communication, just received, she says, "It is a source of joy that I did not choose my field of labor. As to the country, there cannot be a more beautiful one ; and, as to the people, Mr. Lindley says there is not a race of barbarians on the earth who are so honest, so faithful, and trustworthy as the Zulus. There has been the time when he would send money to Durban for the purchase of articles by any strange native who chanced to be passing. The errand would be done, and the change returned. My boxes were open for two weeks, and the doors and windows unlocked night and day. When I expressed some concern about it, Mr. Lindley said, 'Give yourself no uneasiness, for they are perfectly safe.' "

AN APPEAL FOR ZULU WOMEN.

"The women are the beasts of burden. They dig, plant, gather the corn, thresh it, and carry it to market. If Christian women could realize what the Bible has done for them, they would not, they could not, be happy without doing all in their power to send to those who have never received it. I am sure you have not forgotten your promise to pray for me. If you could see the degradation of the women, and the hopefulness of the work, every prayer offered would bear a petition to the throne, that the Father would pour out his Holy Spirit. Pray that this school, teacher and scholars, may be in a special manner in his keeping, that we may walk with him, that every girl who is taught may be a light to all around her.

" A poor old woman came to the chapel in a tattered garment. I gave her one of my dresses : she was so grateful, she went to the hut of Cingway, and, weeping, begged her to come and ask me to take her. She is a heathen, but said she wanted to learn the words of the Inkasi before she died. How I wished that some of the money so foolishly spent at home could be used here ! "

5 *

Light and Life.

BY MRS. EMILY C. PEARSON.

From our sisters comes the wail,
" Give us light : our idols fail !
Help us bury in the dust
Hoary fanes in which we trust !
" Give us light !" thus, ceaselessly,
Call they o'er the Bengal Sea ;
Cry they, too, from Turkey's strand,
And from Afric's darkened land.

They are groping in the night :
Shall we hide from them the light ?
Shall we harden each our heart, —
In Christ's giving have no part ?
Where the Pagan women roam,
Why was not our earthly home
Why of Jesus have we heard,
If 'tis not to spread his Word ?

Lo ! 'tis now the Lord's own time :
Open is each heathen clime.
Let us send of Life the light ;
Let us go in God's own might.
Have we not the promise heard ?
" Always with you " is his word.
Sowers, reapers, hasten on,
And the nations shall be won.

By the sufferings Christ hath borne,
By the Holy Father's frown
Cast on him for thy sins' sake,
Christian sister, offerings make ;
Speed the story of the cross ;
For Christ's sake, count all things loss ;
Be thou faithful, toil and pray,
Till earth's kingdoms own his sway.

A MORNING'S WORK.

BY ONE OF OUR LIFE-MEMBERS IN INDIA.

How busy I am ! Even my evenings are becoming engrossed with school exercises, which I cannot find time for in the day. My time is also much taken up by attending to the sick. I don't like to send any one away; and I make many friends where I am able to benefit. I am obliged to make a rule, that I can attend to no one after seven in the morning. Of course in case of accidents, or of persons from a distance, I make an exception. One morning I had eighteen cases to look after before seven ; then I had, in Mr. —— 's absence, to open the school, and have charge of it till nine, when I breakfasted. I have been very successful with children and infants. Older people are very apt to come when they have become discouraged under native treatment. I might mention many items of interest to you in this connection. I *must* tell you of a mother, who brought a daughter, a young woman grown, and laid her down upon our verandah steps. The poor thing was in the last stages of consumption ; and I *never, never,* can forget the way she stretched out her hands to me, and with an imploring look said, —

" I have heard of you ; and here I am."

The mother seemed strong and well, though quite advanced in years. Said she, —

" We have come two miles. This poor child would give me no rest ; and I took her up and brought her."

" Brought her yourself ! " I exclaimed," — " yourself all the way ! "

" I helped her a little," said a nice woman, who had been every day for a week, and whose young daughter was nearly cured of an obstinate fever; " but I thought many times we must give it up."

Those imploring eyes were fixed upon me, as I turned away to others who were waiting.

There was a mother with a little girl, who has had a fearful sore, but who was so nearly well that I dismissed her; a young woman with a disease in the scalp, and too proud to have her hair shaven, and to whom I have given the same advice so many times, that I declined doing any thing more.

Then there was a mother with a baby; and another; and another. Oh, dear! how my heart aches for the neglected babies of this country!

I often talk with these women, if I have not too much to do for them. There was a woman with a sore foot, whom I passed over to my young maid. She helps me nicely.

There were two more cases of eruptive disease, and a new case of fever, — one more sick baby, and they had gone.

The poor young woman had been lying on the verandah, watching wearily all that had been going on. I went down the steps to her, and said, as kindly as I could, that "she was very sick, and that no medicine would cure her now, — it would only make her sicker and more uncomfortable;" and I said many other things. She listened to me, and then burst into tears, and turned to her mother and said, —

"How can we ever get home?" The mother turned to me.

"We never can get home with no hope to help us. Show me a place, and we will stay here till she dies."

It was distressing beyond expression to me. I talked a while longer with her, and called the bandyman, and told him to put plenty of straw in the bandy, and take her home.

I went into the house, thankful that the bullocks were at home, so that these poor creatures should not be compelled to such a forlorn walk home.

SYRIA.

Miss Everett writes from Beirût, March 9. Among items of interest are her first impressions of the place. She says, "I had repressed all high anticipations, and was happily surprised.

The school building is so good, the grounds about it are so pleasant, and we have so many home comforts and so much choice society in our large missionary band, and Beirût affords so large a supply of temporal comforts, that it cannot involve hardship to come here as a missionary, and I cannot be thankful enough for what I enjoy. The dear companionship ceases when we go beyond our garden wall; but what is this, when compared with what earlier missionaries suffered, and multitudes are now suffering, and more than all, I blush to name it, when I think of the sacrifice of Calvary for these souls and for mine?"

THE SCHOOL.

" I find the pupils far more attractive in manner, and apt to learn than I expected. Many have awakened in me an intense interest, and some are really bewitching. I never was in a school, even a Sunday school, where they showed such familiarity with the Bible as our pupils do. Not simply Bible stories are they well versed in, but more difficult subjects, as Paul's missionary tours, the full description of Solomon's Temple and the Chronology of the Bible. They are all very ready to talk upon the subject of personal religion; but conscience seems dormant, and they have little idea of doing right for the sake of the right, with few exceptions.

" Our great want is the Holy Spirit's influence. I am heavily burdened in heart because of this dearth. Outwardly the school is prosperous; but I want to see souls converted: this must be the Spirit's work. We have to pray a great deal for patience while being tongue-tied.

" The girls listen very attentively to religious instruction in Arabic, and many are thoughtful. Several have pious parents, and seem not far from the kingdom of heaven. Most of them are under the age at which we really expect children at home to be converted. But do we not often limit God in that regard?"

NEED OF WOMAN'S WORK.

Dr. Jessup of Syria, in a letter dated Beirût, March 16, says, " I regard woman's work among the women as, at the present time, of pressing importance. Mission schools and missionary preaching have opened the door of access to thousands of families in foreign lands, where none but women can enter. In Shakir, a widow from the massacre of Hasbeiya is now laboring as a Bible woman and reader in Beirût. She has access now to some fifty Mohammedan families. Miss Taylor, a devoted Scotch lady, who co-operated cordially with us, has a school in Beirût of seventy-five Mohammedan girls. She has no regular support, trusting in the Lord for means to carry on her interesting work from month to month.

NESTORIA.

REPORT OF HÂNÉE AT TABREEZ.

Translated by Mrs. Labaree.

An interesting letter has been received from Hânée, the wife of the native helper at Tabreez. Five years since, she commenced her labors in that city, then enshrouded in deep moral darkness, — such darkness, as she expressed it, that she could do nothing till she had prayed a great deal. She continues : —

" There are now young men and young women who are much enlightened. In reading the Bible, and looking out references, they find that in the gospel alone is made known the way of salvation by the death of the Lord Jesus Christ, our beloved Saviour, and there is no way of salvation under the sun, except through him. There are large schools for boys and girls here, which are supported by the people themselves; and the parents are very much in earnest that their children should be taught. All, whether rich or poor, are equally desirous of having their children learn to read. If poor, they lighten their other expenses, that they may be able to afford teachers for them. At this time, there are only schools for boys. The girls' school has been discontinued, because there is no female teacher for it. Therefore, I undertook with much zeal to learn to read the Armenian language, that I might be able to read the Holy Scripture to the poor women and girls who are left without instruction. Although many of them read, they are very ignorant; for what they have learned has had no effect to enlighten them, because their teachers have only taught them reading and the forms of their religion. These teachers themselves have little knowledge of godliness and the light of life. Seeing this absence of light and understanding, I made an effort to explain to them what they have read and learned; and many understand and accept. But it is very difficult to meet with them as much as I wish, since it is not the custom to go to their houses, except by invitation."

QUARTERLY REPORT.

The quarterly meeting of the Woman's Board of Missions was held in Old South Chapel, Boston, Tuesday, April 6, at 3 P. M., notice of the meeting having been given, one week previous, in "The Congregationalist and Boston Recorder."

The fact that no quarterly meeting has as yet been so largely attended, as well as the increased contributions reported by the Treasurer, gives gratifying evidence of a steadily growing interest in the Society, and the cause it represents.

The act of incorporation recently granted by the legislature of Massachusetts rendering it necessary, the Society proceeded, after the usual devotional exercises, to re-organize the Woman's Board of Missions, and unanimously re-appointed the officers elected at the annual meeting.

Mrs. Homer Bartlett, Treasurer, reported receipts for the quarter as $5,549 $\frac{76}{100}$, besides subscriptions for more than five hundred copies of "Life and Light."

She especially noticed two letters containing large remittances, — one from Providence, R.I., the other from Colchester, Conn., — in which it was distinctly mentioned that the moneys forwarded had not been obtained until after the usual collections for the A. B. C. F. M., one of which was the largest ever taken.

Mrs. Bartlett also read a letter from the venerable Dr. Storrs, of Braintree, Mass., enclosing $75.00 for life-membership of the three female members of his family.

He said, "My infirmities are such that I cannot visit Boston personally; but my whole heart is with you in the great and good work in which you are engaged. The good Lord, the blessed Saviour, *is* with you, and *will* be with you 'always.' . . . The Lord of Hosts be with you, and prosper you in your noble effort; and, though few days remain to *me* on earth, may *your* days be many, and your angelic ministries to the forlorn daughters of idolatry and superstition carry joy up to the courts of God!"

The benediction of this beloved father in the ministry seemed like the voice of God through the lips of his servant, and made a profound impression upon all who heard it.

Mrs. George Gould, Corresponding Secretary, read extracts of letters from Miss Olive L. Parmelee, Miss Ursula C. Clarke, and others. Another was from Mrs. L. S. Parker, missionary of the M. E. Church in India, now in this country, regretting that she could not be present at the meeting, and expressing great sympathy in our work, and an earnest desire for our prosperity.

The meeting being cheered by the presence of several missionaries, one of them, Mrs. Walker, from Diarbekir, after prayer by Mrs. Safford, related, in a simple and touching manner, many incidents in her own missionary life, concluding by saying that she blessed God for all the way in which he had led her, and for the great privilege of being a missionary.

After singing an original hymn by Mrs. Emily C. Pearson, followed by the doxology, the audience dispersed, some of them mentally asking the question, "How much longer will the Old South Chapel be large enough to hold our quarterly meetings?"

Mrs. J. A. Copp, *Rec. Sec'y.*

HOW WE FORMED OUR AUXILIARY.

Having received a Circular of the Woman's Board of Missions, our active Miss L. hastened to the sewing-circle, and made known its message. "Now, ladies," said she, "we must do our part. We are responsible to God, and are bound by the most weighty considerations to do all the good in our power." The ladies, concurring in this thought, at once appointed Miss L. directress of the new society, and her friend Carrie secretary and treasurer.

A list of the female membership of the church was obtained, districts portioned, and the three collectors started on their rounds the ensuing week. At the next meeting of the circle, a favorable report was returned by the collectors ; and Carrie, who fills the twofold offices of secretary and treasurer, promptly wrote the Treasurer of the "Woman's Board of Missions" at Boston, enclosing the amount obtained. It was agreed that a half-hour should be spent by the circle, quarterly, in listening to the reading of missionary intelligence, selected from "Light and Life for Heathen Women," "The Missionary Herald," and other authentic sources. It was also voted, that, at the annual meeting of the circle, the above offices be filled for the year ; and thus our auxiliary society, in working order, was successfully launched.   C.

6

OUR WORK.

It is gratifying to note an increased interest in every department of our home-work, as is shown in our report. The uniform testimony of our foreign correspondents to the joy and happiness afforded them in their labors is also exceedingly cheering.

A missionary in Madura, who had been laid aside by temporary sickness, writes, "The wish to devote a long life to Christ, in India, becomes more intense every day. I never felt a stronger assurance that this joy would be mine; and I never had cause for deeper gratitude than at present. The evidence I have had, that God was planning for me and directing my steps, has been sufficient to cheer me: even when the prospect of future usefulness seemed most uncertain, I knew that the Lord's plans were the only safe ones, and that they would surely promote his glory. I thank him for disappointment; for it has brought the joy of more entire trust in God, and I hope, also, a better preparation for his service."

Of a similar character are all the testimonies of the missionaries reported in our columns, from Mrs Champion, the pioneer to the Zulus thirty-five years ago, to the young sisters recently sent out by our Board.

Is other stimulus needed to excite us to more vigorous activity? let us find it in the generous contribution of means and labors by the converted Armenian women for the girls' school in Bitlis. If self-denial for Christ yields such precious fruit in foreign lands, why should not we, by corresponding efforts, gain a like blessing?

It is "the day of small things" with us, compared with the immensity of the opening field; and, as we become more and more conscious of the magnitude of the work, we feel the inadequacy of our strength and resources to meet the demand. Yet "we can do all things through Christ strengthening us;" and we echo the notes of joy wafted us from our sisters afar, and bless God that he has called us to be co-workers with his dear Son in the world's redemption. Do we not well to cherish the inspiring thought, that, when the sheaves shall all be gathered into the heavenly granaries, not the reapers, but the sowers who dropped the seed of the Word amid darkness and discouragement, thus rooting a work for Christ, nurturing it by their tears and prayers, shall sing forever the loudest, sweetest songs of praise.

The issue of our Quarterly has introduced us to a large circle of Christian ladies, many of whom cheer us by words of hope and sympathy, while a few fear that we have not counted the cost. They bid us look at the time, means, and labor involved in carrying on our operations, at the apathy of large numbers of the women in our churches, of the depths to be reached, of the heights to be climbed, and of giant difficulties to be overcome, that will continually impede our progress. In reply we say, He who has appointed our work is able to carry it on ; and therefore we expect to bridge the chasms, scale the mountains, vanquish the giants, and, with grateful memory of what God has done for us, step by step removing obstacles and clearing the way, can we doubt that he will give us the victory in every conflict ? With the banner of the cross, and Jesus for our leader, " we are able " to go forth and enlist the heathen women for him, and carry " light and life " into the region and shadow of death.

Dear readers, speeding our work by your prayers, will you not come and bear with us the burdens, and share the glorious reward of those " who weary not in well doing ? "

SELF-DENIAL AND ITS REWARD.

" There is that scattereth and yet increaseth." So we thought the other day when a young servant of God brought a donation to constitute his wife a life-member of the W. B. M.

Knowing that his health had become so much impaired as to oblige him to relinquish his pastoral charge, and that several children of tender years were dependent upon his small income, we hardly felt justified in retaining the gift.

When the fear was afterwards expressed to him that he had carried self-denial too far, he replied, "I love the cause of missions; and I gave because I felt it a privilege, saying to my wife that I thought we could perhaps do without the money. And *we did not lose by it either;* for the next day a friend owning a woollen mill sent me a piece of cloth sufficient to clothe my family!"

Relating this incident to another, whose contribution to the same object had involved considerable self-denial, her instant rejoinder was, "Oh, yes! that is just like our heavenly Father; he always keeps his promises, and 'gives good measure, pressed down, and running over.' He returned my gift in a very few days, just tenfold; and I felt ashamed that I had not given more."

"THE WOMAN'S BOARD OF MISSIONS FOR THE INTERIOR."

CHICAGO.

This Society reports an auspicious commencement and prospects. Its receipts for the three months ending March 1 were $1,226.55. God speed the work!

"WOMAN'S MISSIONARY SOCIETY."

JACKSON, MICHIGAN.

This is an enterprising auxiliary of the Chicago W. B. M. I., and is engrafted upon the female prayer-meeting; which meets weekly in five neighborhood meetings, and monthly at the parsonage. At the monthly meetings the members bring the aggregate of the sums they have pledged each week, an example well worth imitation by all auxiliaries.

We are glad to learn of the enthusiastic welcome extended our missionary friends, Mrs. Lydia V. Snow and Miss Myra Proctor, on their tour West in the enterprise of awakening special interest among the churches in behalf of heathen women. They addressed audiences of ladies in various places. Miss Proctor met fifteen hundred mission children in Detroit, and made them a short, earnest address. At Kalamazoo, they were entertained at the Michigan Mt. Holyoke Seminary, and each addressed the young ladies. Now, more than ever, is the time for women to work for Christ, who so graciously opens the way.

A CALL FOR AUXILIARIES.

Dear Christian Sisters, — Thirty years ago, our mothers and grandmothers supported three hundred and twenty mission societies, auxiliary to the American Board. Shall we, their children, with our increased opportunities, do less? Then missions were in their infancy, considered by many an experiment : now they have been so owned and blessed of God, that the Christian public feel it a duty as well as a privilege to support them. If you have faithfully and gladly given a tenth already, can you not spare a little more to help the women whom heathenism has made drudges and slaves?

We wish to have an auxiliary society in every town. Any number of ladies contributing not less than ten dollars a year may form a society. It is not necessary to have a cumbrous organization. The sewing-circle may have within it a mission-circle. Intelligence can be obtained from the different fields, so that you may know how the work goes on. Who is there that has a heart for the work?

For Treasurer's Report, see " Missionary Herald," for March, April, and May, 1869.

6*

In Memoriam.

We were startled last week, for the first time as a society, by the messenger of death. To-day we are called to mournfully record the decease of one of our directors, — our beloved

MRS. GILES PEASE,

WHO WENT HOME ON APRIL 19.

Very early in life she became a Christian, and for nearly fifty years adorned her profession. Hers were rare domestic virtues : she was the oak to whom the home-tendrils lovingly clung, and as a wife and mother was most exemplary. But, while so faithful in these relations, she did not rest there, or limit her charities to her fireside circle ; but her sympathizing heart was moved, and her ready ear listened to every cause for the succor of the suffering that came within her reach. She was very efficient in helping forward "The Moral Reform" enterprise, which reaches down the hand of love to uplift fallen women. Who can say but that it may be she vacated the presiding chair of that society, to come to them again, "a ministering spirit" to guide, comfort, and strengthen the returning prodigal ? From the beginning, she identified herself as an earnest worker in the "Young Women's Christian Association" of this city, and never ceased active efforts in its behalf, so long as her health allowed. The first prayer-meeting was held in her parlor, which initiated that movement. She was also present at the meeting of the little band of Christian women in the Old South Chapel, which led to the inauguration of our society. The last public act of her life was to speak in our quarterly meeting, after having made self-denying efforts to be present. She expressed joy on her sick-bed, that she had been permitted to unite with us in our mission work, which seeks the world's redemption. Just before she went to the Saviour, whose cause had ever been dear to her, her thoughts were directed to those with whom she had been associated in active efforts to obey his last command ; and she sent a farewell remembrance to us, and bade her dear ones bear her love to the members of our board.

Children's Corner.

WHAT CAN CHILDREN DO?

Let me tell you, dear children, of a little girl scarce three years old, a tiny, bright-eyed body, of whom you would say in passing: "Isn't she cunning; isn't she pretty?" and yet so wisely trained and guarded, that she is not in the least spoiled.

A lady called to see her mother a short time since, to ask the annual collection of the Woman's Board of Missions, when little May, attracted by the earnest conversation, ran to her, saying, " I'se going to be a missionary! I 'ant to be a missionary!" The lady took her up, and told her some stories about the poor little heathen; and then, in response to the glistening eye and quick heart-throb, said, —

" You shall be a little missionary, if you ask papa to give you twenty-five dollars to make you a life-member of our society."

This satisfied the child, and soon after the lady left. When she called the second time, the little girl was summoned, and came running to the visitor, all alive with, " I'se a little missionary *now*," at the same time putting twenty-five dollars into her hand.

She had climbed into her papa's lap at her earliest opportunity, and lavished all the wealth of her love and pretty endearments upon him; and so pleadingly asked for the twenty-five dollars, that the father, deeply grateful to God for the gift of this precious child, could not deny her request.

But you ask, "How did twenty-five dollars make her a missionary ?"

Suppose you very much desire to make your father a present of a beautiful watch-case, but are too small to embroider it, and still know how to knit, crochet, pick berries, take care of babies, or do something else by which you could gain a little money : you would have no need to sigh and say, "I cannot give him the beautiful watch-case, because I do not know how to work it ;" for you could use many spare minutes, — and they would be real love minutes, — and earn here a few pennies, and there a few more, until, almost before you know it, you would have money enough to get the materials, and pay somebody else to make it for you, so that, when you presented it, you could say, " Father, this is all my own present : I bought it with my money ! "

Now, although May is too young to go to teach heathen children herself, the twenty-five dollars can be given to a good Bible-reader, who will visit the little mud-floored cottages, and, gathering the mothers and children around her, tell them the story of the Cross, and show how even the little ones may please and serve Jesus.

Thus little May is a real missionary, because she can provide a Christian teacher. Will she not grow into a deeper pity and love for the heathen as the years pass on ? And will not her dear mother be likely to train her for missionary service ?

But you say, " My father is not rich enough to give me twenty-five dollars." Now, please listen : just want to be a missionary, and want it *ever so much*, because you are so sorry for children who will never know how to be good unless somebody is sent to teach them, and then go and tell Jesus, asking him to direct you what to do for him, while you are young.

Every child cannot do what this little girl did ; but there is a work which God will give you, and which no one else can do quite as well.

Can you not talk with some of your mates, and persuade them

to join you in forming a little mission-band, a berry or sewing circle, to earn money for the Board of Missions. Jesus will own and prosper it; and will say to you, too, from the throne of his glory, " Well done ! "

THE LITTLE ARAB GIRL.

At the time of the massacres in Syria, in 1860, very many women and children fled to Beirût for safety. The mothers especially suffered much from hunger, as they gave what little food they could get to their children.

Among other Arab women who escaped from Hasbeiya was a native Christian, who not only loved Jesus herself, but taught her little girl, Miriam, the prayer our Saviour gave us. One night Miriam, who was only three years old, being very hungry, kneeled down beside her mother, and began to say " Our Father." She went on till she came to " Give us this day our daily bread." She stopped, then began again. " Give us this day our daily bread, and please do, dear Jesus, give us bread and olives, and *enough for mother and me too.*"

Was her prayer answered? Yes. God sent them food, and made her *sing for joy.* " Enough for mother and me too."

Little children, if you are in any trouble, go and tell Jesus. He has *promised,* " If ye shall ask any thing in my name *I* will do it."

MRS. S. A. CLOSSON,

A life-member of the Woman's Board in Cesarea, writes, Jan. 7th, from Yallas, " As I have never regretted that I came here, only regret that I have done so little for Christ. This week we are having prayer-meetings morning and evening : they are well attended, and a good spirit manifested. May this new year be one of blessing to all our missions ! Pray much for us, that we may be good soldiers of the Cross."

Onward.

BY MRS. EMILY C. PEARSON.

Will not our young readers call to mind the story of the spies, and their report of the land, as found in Num. xiii.

AIR, — " *Waiting by the river.*"

We are going, onward going,
  To possess the promised land,
Fearing not the hostile legions,
  Since we go at Christ's command.

CHORUS.

We are able, fully able,
  To possess the promised land ;
Though the hindrances are mighty,
  We'll go on at Christ's command.

II.

Heeding not the " high-walled cities,"
  We are marching fearless on,
Trusting in the faithful promise,
  That the kingdom shall be won.

Chorus. — We are able, fully able, &c.

III.

Glory be to Christ our Saviour,
  Who is Leader in the strife,
Who doth order well the battle,
  With his watchword " Endless Life."

Chorus. — We are able, &c.

IV.

Flee away, old superstition !
  Soul-debasing errors rife !
Haste away, ye powers of darkness :
  Christ alone is Light and Life !

Chorus. — We are able, &c.

v.

Endless Life for those who perish :
Let this cheer us on our way !
And oh let us never falter
Till the nations Christ obey !

Chorus. — We are able, &c.

Dear young friends, you have many times sung "Waiting by the River ; " but have you truly enlisted for Christ ? He is calling every one of you to his service. As you sing our hymn, will you not join our army, and be faithful soldiers of the cross, so that, when you have forded the "river," you may wear the victor's crown on the heavenly shore ?

ACT OF INCORPORATION.

COMMONWEALTH OF MASSACHUSETTS.

In the Year One Thousand Eight Hundred and Sixty-nine.

AN ACT

TO INCORPORATE THE WOMAN'S BOARD OF MISSIONS.

Be it enacted by the Senate and House of Representatives, in General Court assembled, and by the authority of the same, as follows : —

SECTION 1. — Sarah L. Bowker, Eliza H. Anderson, and Berinthia M. Child, their associates and successors, are hereby constituted a body corporate, to be located in the city of Boston, under the name of "The Woman's Board of Missions ; " with all the powers and privileges, and subject to all the duties, liabilities, and restrictions, set forth in the general laws which now are, or may hereafter be, in force relating to corporations, so far as the same may be applicable.

SECT. 2. — Said corporation may hold real and personal estate to an amount not exceeding two hundred thousand dollars, to be devoted exclusively to the purposes and objects herein set forth.

SECT. 3. — The object and purpose of this corporation shall be to collect, receive, and hold money given by voluntary contributions, donations, bequests, or otherwise, to be exclusively expended in sending out and supporting such unmarried females as the Prudential Committee of the American Board of Commissioners for Foreign Missions shall, under the recommendation of the board of directors of this corporation, designate and appoint as assistant missionaries and teachers for the Christianization of women in foreign lands; and for the support of such other female missionaries, or native female helpers in the missionary work, as may be selected by the board of directors with the approbation of the said Prudential Committee.

SECT. 5. — This act shall take effect upon its passage.

HOUSE OF REPRESENTATIVES, March 3, 1869.

Passed to be enacted.

HARVEY JEWELL, *Speaker.*

IN SENATE, March 4, 1869.

Passed to be enacted.

ROBERT C. PITMAN, *President.*

March 6, 1869.

Approved.

WILLIAM CLAFLIN.

SECRETARY'S DEPARTMENT, BOSTON, March 17, 1869.

A true copy.

Attest.

OLIVER WARNER,
Secretary of the Commonwealth.

LIFE AND LIGHT

FOR

𝔥eathen 𝔚omen.

| VOL. I. | SEPTEMBER, 1869. | No. 3. |

LEAVES FROM A MISSIONARY'S JOURNAL.

NUMBER TWO.

I WAS called up Sunday night at eleven o'clock : fortunately I had retired at an unusually early hour, and had some sleep. A Brahmin woman was supposed to be in danger, and would I only come ! The husband himself came, and I went. I remained till 5, A.M., and then left in great perplexity, and yet feeling that no one else could do better. I wanted some tea, and I wanted change of air, and I wanted to pray too.

Before 7 o'clock, although I promised to come back in two hours, there were no less than eight men, — brothers, husband, and uncles, one after the other, to hasten my return. I accompanied them ; and it was no small comfort to think that the poor woman was so much more quiet. Staying four hours, I came home at 11, as tired as could be, but with the hope that the mother might live, although the long-wished for, first-born son had perished. I have daily visited her since, and now the whole street is thrown open to me ; and ever ringing in my ears — beginning with that long, anxious night — are the words, "Woe is me, if I preach not the gospel ! "

It was touching to see the woman reach for my hand and say,
" It feels so good." Undoubtedly it was an immense relief to
have some one calm and collected in the midst of so much
absurd tumult.

Tuesday, while I was standing by her, she stretched out her
hand; and, when her aunt asked her what she wanted, she said,
" I want to take hold of that hand again : I could bless it."
And when I patted her cheek, and gave it to her, she stroked
it with true, affectionate gratitude.

She is not going to spurn me from her door, is she ?

Do you remember the Brahmin woman who was so faint for
food ? She is always at her door with a truly cordial greeting ;
and her husband I am just bringing out from an intermittent
fever.

Wednesday night I was very anxious about this woman, and
I still consider that there are unfavorable symptoms. I fervently hope that her life will be given to me for my encouragement, and for my better hope of usefulness in that
street.

At such a time, one comes into familiar acquaintance with
the women. They are anxious, and they listen with respect.

To-day they were all thrown into great perturbation by what
I suppose was a turn of nervous agitation. From eleven until
two, there was a succession of arrivals, each one with some
astonishing report, and every one half frightened out of his
wits. One came with bandy and bullocks to carry me ; and,
though I was startled, I remembered my head and the noonday
sun, and preferred to wait till a composing dose had been tried.
Little Laura said, " They keep coming and coming, one and
another, all bringers of bad news : it makes me think of the
time when one and then another came to tell that good man
(Job) of his trouble. They came just about as fast, and
Satan was making all the trouble."

It was not prudent to say to the child that I thought Satan

was keeping idlers busy now ; but I did say, " I hope I shall be as patient as Job was."

The customs of these people are vexatious sometimes. Their inner rooms are so dark, that to see at all I must have a light ; and one day, I not only needed some one to hold the light, but still another person to aid me.

The mother of the sick woman was standing a little distance off ; and I said, " Will you come and help me ? "

" I cannot come. I am the only one to cook, and I mustn't come."

" Will you hold the light ? " I asked.

" No : I mustn't go inside the door.

To this I replied, " You don't deserve the honor of my coming : go and call your husband's sister." I knew her well.

" She will not come," was the reply : " she has not eaten."

" Neither have I," I replied ; " but, if she is not here in five minutes, I will go straight home. I came here to help you, and you won't even hold a light for me ! " Never having seen me angry, as I confess I was, they began to be afraid I would go, and the husband's sister soon came.

" Oh ! " said she, " if I come, I've got to go to the river and bathe, and say all the mutherams over."

" I don't care how much you bathe," I replied : " as for the mutherams, just tell the ' Swamy ' you'll say them twice to-morrow." So she came ; and since then I insist upon her being in the room before I go into it, which has saved further annoyance.

" Behold the Lord hath proclaimed unto the end of the world, Say ye to the Daughter of Zion, Behold thy salvation cometh." — Isaiah, lxii. : 11.

CHINA.

WOMEN IN THEIR TEMPLES.

BY MRS. NEVIUS.

One of the most common sights in China is that of women going, either in groups or singly, to the temples. They usually carry a little basket, containing incense-sticks and candles. On reaching her destination, the worshipper at once lights both candles and incense, and places them either in front of some one particular image, or, as is more often the case, before several. This duty performed, she returns to her starting-place, and commences her prostrations. Folding her hands before her, she first makes a profound bow, then kneels upon a cushion placed for the purpose, and, bending slowly forward, strikes her forehead upon it, or upon the floor or ground. This act is usually repeated at least three times before each idol, and sometimes much oftener. After this, she goes to a priest, and buys a paper upon which is a picture of Buddha. Her name is also written upon it, together with the year, month, day, and hour of her birth. It contains, too, an assurance of happiness in a future state. This paper is, at first, of little importance ; but, after the name of Buddha has been chanted over it a great number of times, its value becomes inestimable. Having received it, she goes off by herself, and, either sitting or kneeling on a cushion, spends hours repeating as rapidly as her lips can form the words, " Na-mi-O-mi-to-Fuh ! Na-mi-O-mi-to-Fuh ! " one of the names of Veh, or Buddha, assisting her memory by means of a rosary, in the same way that the Romanists do. Sometimes, instead of remaining apart, the worshippers sit in rows ; and then they often vary their employment by interchanging bits of gossip, congratulations, or condolences. When they are chanting together, as they sometimes do, the sound is very peculiar : it always seemed to me like the mournful whistling of the wind.

INDIA.

A VISIT TO HINDOO WOMEN.

BY MRS. DEAN, MAHRATTA.

The villages in India are usually made up of a clump of mud houses, with narrow, winding, dirty lanes and alleys. As the missionary lady, accompanied by her husband, enters the village to visit the house of a wealthy and influential man, dogs get up from the doorways and bark; children emerge from every nook and corner, some boldly following, others peeping with curious eyes; women come to the doors, and look over each other's shoulders to see the strange white faces. The man of the house approaches to meet them, when the husband, seeing his wife safely received, continues his walk to the public place near by, and preaches to the crowd assembled. Meanwhile the lady is asked to walk across a court to the verandah which surrounds it, where she is politely invited to sit upon a mat. Not a woman in sight, and a dozen men looking in at the street-door. "I have come to see the women," she says: "will you not allow them to come out and sit by me?" — "They are afraid of such as you: they have never spoken to a white woman." "Oh, no! they are not afraid: if you will call them, and drive those men away from the door, they will be glad to appear." So the host calls his mother or brother's wife; for a Hindoo man never notices his own wife. The old mother makes her appearance, and stands silently by. The missionary lady says. "Will you sit beside me? I am here to talk with you: will you not allow your daughters-in-law to listen also?" At her call, the younger women come from their rooms, accompanied by a number of timid neighbors, who had preceded the visitor, and were awaiting her arrival. By this time, other women from the street enter, and sit or stand around. Then begins a torrent of remarks, all talking aloud and at the same time. "Do see! she

7 *

cannot sit like us on the mat!" "Why, she talks as we do!"
"Why does she not wear jewels?" "Wouldn't she look
handsome in a nose-ring?" "I hear she has several boys:
she must be a favorite of the gods." The lady tries to make
herself heard : "Friends, if you will keep still, I will not only
read to you and talk with you, but will answer your questions."
A moment's hush, and then for two minutes a perfect jargon.
"Keep still, can't you? One would think this was a market!" "Those screaming 'keep still' have been making
more noise than the rest of us." "Now, see here," says the
lady, "if each of you will be silent, without telling others to do
so, we shall soon have quiet." She then proceeds to tell them
that she has brought with her the word of God, and reads one
of the parables of our Lord, and explains the way of salvation.
In order to fix their attention, she says, "Suppose two of you
should be coming from the field, each with a heavy load on your
head, and one is tired and faint, would it be of any use for that
one to ask the other to help carry her load? If a strong, willing woman, who had no load, should come along, she could relieve the weary one. You all have a Guru (spiritual teacher),
to whom you pay something to answer for your sins. How will
you manage this, when his own sins will be as great a burden
as he can carry?" Trying to show them the foolishness of
some of their customs, she says, "You are in constant fear lest
you or your children be tortured by evil spirits; so a company
of you women go with a mother, and her babe twelve days old,
into the fields, there make offerings of fruit and flowers to the
goddess Satwaee, and implore her to be propitious. I have
never been to Satwaee with any of my children; and yet not
one of them has had his liver eaten out, nor has any spirit come
in the night to sit on their little chests." — "Why, how strange!
What *do* you do, unless you go to Satwaee?" — "Just what I
wish you would do, ask my heavenly Father, the one who made
you and me, every morning and night to take care of my little

ones." — "Of course that is the true way; but what do we poor creatures know? If we can bake bread and bring water, that is all we are expected to understand. If you could come often and read to us, we could remember; but we are so dull you will have to tell us over and over again."

So closes an hour's visit; and with her heart full of pity, and the joy of having had so good an opportunity of speaking of Jesus, the missionary's wife joins her husband, and they return to their tents, hoping to visit the place again as soon as possible. The number of women who are brought together in this way varies from a very few to even one hundred. It is a cheering fact, that, as the visits are repeated, the interest increases, more come to hear, and other houses in the village are opened for the reading of God's Word.

KURRAPAI, THE HINDOO CONVERT.

BY MRS. CAPRON, MADURA.

Sabbath afternoon, I sent Virginia and Jewel of Life to a village half a mile on the north-west; and I took Kurrapai and Martha to another village in the north-east. Virginia said that they "found most of the women picking greens; but that three women sat down with them, and listened to all they said." Kurrapai was embarrassed at first. She got up, and began to get some very tall cactus flowers; and I quietly said, "Two will do, Kurrapai." I did not want to hurt her feelings. She sat down again. After Martha had finished, while I was hesitating about Kurrapai, she began a strain of remark about worshipping mud and stone images, that, for irony and sarcasm, I could not surpass. Indeed, I never attack idol-worship: but she, a heathen redeemed, knows the depths better; and she set forth the mud that man makes to look worse than he himself does, — such eyes and ears as no man ever had, — and that cannot save himself from sinking into the slime of a tank, if he who worships it hurls him there. So she went on, and had the attention of us all, you may be sure. Then looking up at the grand heavens above us, she said, "He who spread out *that* is my Swamy" (my Lord). Her speech was done; and I could not but think that the Lord our God would receive Kurrapai's tribute of praise, amid the worship of the sabbath-keeping millions throughout the world.

TURKEY.

AINTAB SCHOOL.

A very interesting report has been received from Miss Hollister, associate principal of the female boarding-school, Aintab, dated April 15, from which our limits only permit brief extracts. The school is divided into three classes, and embraces a wide range of practical studies, which are thoroughly pursued by the pupils, as will be seen by the testimony of Mr. Schneider, who was present at the semi-annual examination.

The domestic department, which involves great care and responsibility, is still under the charge of Mrs. William Perry.

The pupils, besides the work required of them in the house, teach, in classes of six, a small school for Armenian girls, each one teaching an hour a day. The school has succeeded so well, that it is thought advisable to sustain it, provided it does not injure our pupils, and the Armenian children continue to attend.

The progress of the seminary girls is commendable; and it is pleasant indeed to report them as having been almost uniformly obedient. We have been obliged to insist upon prompt attendance; and repeated violations of this rule have resulted in suspending the offender from the privileges of the school, which we hope has cured the evil. While we regret that there are no cases of conversion to report, we still trust that the silent influences of the Holy Spirit have not been in vain."

SEMI-ANNUAL EXAMINATION.

The following cheering testimony from Mr. Schneider was written under date of April 15, 1869.

Among the pleasant occurrences during my visit to Aintab, was the semi-annual examination of the female boarding-school. It continued through two entire days, and was attended by a crowd, not only of Protestants, but also of Armenians and Mussulmans. It was thorough, embracing Turkish in the Arabic character, arithmetic, astronomy, history of the Armenian and Turkish nations, universal history, the art of teaching, physiology, and Bible-lessons. While the examination on all these branches was good, the pupils were entirely at home on the Bible-lessons. The missionaries present were surprised and highly gratified by their complete familiarity with all the subjects embraced in these exercises. It was evident that Miss Hollister had thoroughly drilled them in their studies; and it would have done the friends of the Board and this institution good to have been present, and witnessed these fruits of their benevolence.

The singing of the girls, trained by Mr. Perry, was most admirable, and left a delightful impression on the audience : hardly any thing could have been better in this respect.

At the close of the analysis of the Book of Revelation, a chant, in which Christ was particularly extolled, came in most appropriately, and touched all hearts. As a whole, the impression of the occasion was most happy. All were charmed, and with manifest reason, especially the Protestants. The interesting scenes here brought to view stand in such bold contrast to their former condition of ignorance and degradation, as deeply to impress upon them the changes wrought. They abounded in expressions of satisfaction. At the close of the exercises, the pastor elect of the first church delivered an interesting address on general improvement ; in which it was laid down as

a principle, that, for this progress, they must mainly depend on
their own efforts ; and it was so forcibly illustrated, as to carry
with him the convictions of his audience.

THE CHANGED SHOE.

Just before leaving Corfa, a month ago, one of the most
devoted women in the church there came to my room, and
communicated the following : —

A day or two previous, there had been an examination of a
girls' school, taught by a graduate of the Aintab Female Seminary. This woman, whom I will call Salome, on the morning
of that examination day, went to the women of three Armenian
families, and invited them to attend the exercises, in the hope,
that if they should once enter the church, and be interested in
the school, they might be induced to attend the Protestant service. All refused, and Salome returned home.

She had prayed for success in this thing ; and does not God
hear prayer? Again she called, only to get the same reply.
Then, pleading with still greater importunity that God would
bless her efforts, she called a third time, and gained their consent to be present. They did so, and evidently enjoyed the
exercises ; but, on leaving, one of them found that one of her
shoes had been changed (all Orientals take off their shoes at
the door), and was much troubled about it. Salome said,
" Do you see : God means you shall come here again? Now,
if you will come to church next sabbath, you will find your shoe.

" A year ago, an Armenian woman, coming from mere curiosity, had her shoes changed as yours has been. She returned
for it the next sabbath, and was so interested in what she heard,
that she has since been a constant hearer. Now, do you come
next sabbath, and find your shoe ; and I trust you, too, will be
glad to attend regularly."

I mention this little incident to show that there are "mothers in Israel" here, who *work for* God, and to show *how* they work. God bless all such, whether at home or abroad !

Rev. P. C. Powers, *Ain'ab, Turkey.*

------◄♦►------

LETTER FROM BITLIS.

SKETCH OF SARKIS.

The following, from Miss Mary A. C. Ely, gives the encouraging result of work in the villages : —

"It was the last of December, 1868, when, as we were enjoying a review, a native knock interrupted us. Our call, 'open,' was answered by the entrance of Pastor Simon, accompanied by a middle-aged man, of fine, erect figure, in peasant costume, who was presented to us as *Sarkis.* He had come on foot, four days' journey, from the village of Havordoric. I have never before seen such a manifestation of earnestness as he exhibited. His full, speaking eyes were beaming with fervor, while his face was radiant with intelligence. His singular language, — a mixture of Armenian and Koordish, — with expressive gesticulations of shrugging the shoulders, raising and lowering the eyebrows, and various motions of the hands and arms, manifested the intense earnestness of this ardent seeker after truth. Upon being asked what led him to come, he said that he had learned to read a little from *Ava-dis,* — one of the native helpers, — and had since read by himself twenty-one chapters in Matthew ; and when he came to the words, 'He that loveth father or mother more than me is not worthy of me,' &c., they 'shook' him ; and he resolved to try and get an education, and be a preacher for the villages. He had left home without the knowledge of his friends, knowing that they would, if possible, hinder his coming.

Said he, ' Doubtless my nephew is now weeping, as it were drops of blood, on account of my absence ; but I will send a letter and explain it.' Giving an account of his journey, he remarked, ' When I left Moosh, I was joined by two travellers, who were so profane that I rebuked them. Having reached a village, we entered a house, and sat down to converse. My companion asked where I was going. I said, " To Bitlis." " You are not going to Pastor Simon ? " — " Yes : I am going to learn to read." — " Then you are a Proto ? " — " Yes." " When you told us it was a sin to swear, we thought you were ; and, had we known it, we would have thrown you in the river ! " — " You could not." — " Why not ? we are two, you are one." — " You could not." — " Well, we will try when you leave this village." They further inquired, " You are poor ? " " No : I have two hundred sheep." Calling the priest of the village, they asked him, " Which is the first commandment ? " " To keep the fast-days." ' Sarkis wished them to get a Bible, and prove it. After further conversation, he rose to go, the two travellers accompanying him to carry out their threat. But Sarkis continued talking to them ; and, before they had gone far, God turned their hearts, and they became ' brothers.' In the exchange of friendly words they parted : Sarkis telling them, that, when he had learned how, he should come and preach to them in their village.

" Baron Simon read some from a Koordish primer, to which our earnest friend listened with deep attention. Being asked if he understood, he said with joyful emphasis, ' Ha ! every word ! ' — ' Do you love the Bible ? ' said one of the missionaries to him. ' Ha ! that brought me here.' — ' Do you love Ava-dis ? ' (the native helper formerly at Havordoric). ' Shall I strike your head with a beetle ? ' was the significant reply. He read aloud a few verses from Matthew, and, after further conversation, left. His intense desire to learn made him a zealous student ; and he was doing well, when, to the sorrow of our entire circle, his brother came, and obliged him to return with him to Havordoric. With many tears and entreaties that we would pray for him, he left.

" We hope yet to hear more of his progress."

NEED OF A NEW SCHOOLROOM.

We have no place adequate for our girls' school. As far as possible, we adopt Holyoke modes of teaching, yet laboring under discomfort, as the only available room, both as school-room and sleeping-room, is an apartment belonging to a house rented by Pastor Simon. The room is sixteen by thirteen feet, having one window, and is directly over a stable owned by a Turkish neighbor, and entirely beyond our control. Sister has visited the school daily since its commencement in December last. She soon discovered that the room was very close, and the air exceedingly impure. Mr. Knapp kindly arranged the best ventilator he could devise ; but this proves insufficient. In sister's daily visits, she has felt repeated attacks of nausea and headache, which is also the experience of others of our missionary circle. Yesterday she returned from school quite ill.

Mr. Knapp thinks with us, that a new schoolroom is indispensable to the welfare of the school. The only room possible to use for a school, besides the one now occupied, is the chapel, which is very damp ; and I will frankly add, that we feel, even if native constitutions could endure to occupy it, we could not. Our missionary circle, after careful consultation, have decided that the best thing to be done is to add a second story to the chapel. The situation of the building, in a high, airy locality, with no house adjoining, is most favorable. The expense would be about $500 gold. Deducting $100, which is, as I suppose, already allowed for first year's repairs and rent, also $100 additional, which sister and I desire jointly to contribute, — which sum we direct to be sent in gold to the treasurer, in July next,

8

— we apply for only $300. Material for building is at this
season of the year much cheaper than later; and our need is
so urgent and pressing, that we feel constrained to make some
preliminary preparations at once, in order that we may, if possible, have a suitable room for next winter. Begging your kind
and immediate attention to this subject, we hope for a speedy
and favorable reply.

I cannot close without saying, that we have manifest tokens
of the Holy Spirit's presence in our community. Eight persons
have already been accepted for admittance to the church at our
next communion season : others also entreat, " receive us."
May the blessed work of evangelization spread on every hand,
and the church at home feel and supply the increasing call for
aid !

MARDIN.

EXTRACTS FROM A LETTER BY MISS PARMALEE.

FIRST LABORS.

Miss Parmalee writes from Mardin, under date of May 4,
" You are expecting to hear, now that we are happily settled in
our new home, something of our labors. Well, stammerers as
we are, and able to express only a few ideas as we would like,
we are engaged in something this summer that is helping us
more than any teacher could, — a little opportunity to practise
what we do know, and come more in contact with the women,
whose dialect is very different from the Arabic of books.
Perhaps you know that the plan of opening the girls' boarding-
school this spring had to be given up, because it was impossible to secure suitable buildings. However, the men came
together as usual in the theological school ; and, as three of

them brought their wives, it seemed best, both for their sakes and our own, to organize a little class. This gives us something to do, and relieves us of the uneasy feeling that we are idlers in our Lord's vineyard.

As I sat before them this morning, I wished you could look in upon us for a few moments, and see these five pupils seated on the floor, with their queer silver head-dresses, and their embroidered or bright-colored veils thrown gracefully over their heads, sheltering their faces as they bend over their books. I have half a mind to introduce them to you, if you will permit me. First, there is *little* Miriam, as we call her, to distinguish her from another Miriam who sits beside her. She is from Sert, a village some two days distant from us. I cannot tell her age, though I presume she may not be more than fifteen ; but I find I cannot judge of ages in this country with any thing like accuracy. The women marry so very young, that they are deprived of all those pretty girlish years from twelve to twenty : one sees among them only little girls and women. Miriam is but just learning to read, and pursues her studies under some difficulties, as she is obliged to bring her tiny six-months-old baby to school with her. Next to her sits Miriam from Hullaat, a village an hour from here to the south-east. She is not so quiet and prepossessing in her looks and manners as some of the others ; but she is bright and quick, and very eager to learn. She reads quite well, as do all except the other Miriam ; and we hope she may prove a worthy helpmeet for her husband, who is studying with the hope of being a native helper, and live to do a good work among the women of some of these villages. Then there is Shimone, who graduated at Harpoot, and comes here to be with her husband, and improve in her Arabic, which she dropped entirely at Harpoot. With her quiet, gentle spirit, and her knowledge of school ways, she is a great comfort

to us, and helps us over a good many difficult places. The two
other scholars are from the city, not the wives of those who are
to be helpers, but women from the congregation, who desired to
attend, and whom the pastor thought might profit by coming.
Saidie is the eldest of the five ; perhaps in America we should
call her a woman : but Shimmy has a fair, girlish face, which is
rarely found here when persons have been married some time.
As I look at her delicate face, with its almost childish look, I am
reminded of dear little girls of thirteen or fourteen in America,
whom we should shelter very carefully in the home circle for
many years ; and yet our little Shimmy has, for some time, had
a home of her own, and many womanly cares ! The Protestant
community are beginning to see some of the evils of marrying
their girls so young, and are using all their influence against
the custom.

We teach our pupils only a few simple things, put in a very
simple way. The time is filled up with reading, writing, singing, Scripture catechism, and easy lessons in arithmetic, geography, and the old, old story of the gospel as told by Matthew.
During this last lesson, Pastor Jujers sometimes comes in and
supplements our imperfect teachings, giving the women some of
the practical lessons we long to give, but are not able. The
unpleasant feature of our work is, that we must feel our way
along so slowly, and have our mouths closed so many times, when
our hearts burn within us to utter some of these precious gospel
truths. Shimone is a member of the church : as for the others,
we only know that they have the truth in their hands, and can
hear it faithfully preached. But though we can do so little, we
work in patience ; trying not to teach error, and praying that
the Holy Spirit will use these words of truth which they can
read, and through them sanctify their souls.

I have tried to tell you something about our girls and our
daily life, that would make you feel that we are not quite
strangers, but that you know us well enough to sometimes pray
for us by name."

TALK ABOUT IT.

BY MRS. DR. ANDERSON.

Talk about what? Just that in which you wish your friends to be interested. If there is any plan you wish to carry into effect, or any object you wish to promote, you talk about it. Christians in all our churches are mourning over the want of interest in the missionary work. The truth is, a great many good people know very little respecting it. They do not read or think or feel much about it. Let those who are interested talk more about it. 'At the present day, there is a great amount of conversational talent in our churches wasted. Oh, what a sad record would that be, if all the useless chit-chat, the gossip, the scandal of only good people, were written from day to day! Cannot something better be substituted? Yes. There are profitable topics on all sides. No Christian, young or old, ought to make a call or visit without saying something worthy of being remembered, — something that will make a good impression. It need not be a religious conversation, but something that savors of a good influence, of a Christian spirit. Sometimes a kindly smile or a look of sympathy diffuses a heavenly fragrance. An allusion to a profitable book, or the repetition of an interesting fact, will often be remembered, and lead to good results. And one very interesting and useful topic of conversation is the world-wide range of foreign missions, and the many suggestive subjects connected with them. All the countries of the world are open before us : every week, new facts are being brought to light. Books are published, and even our daily papers are giving items of interest respecting missions. Why, then, should Christians be ignorant? There will, no doubt, be much regret in heaven, that so little of this treasure was laid up in the head and heart while here on earth. Let Christians read, and get their hearts warm; let them obtain facts from missionaries going or returning; let them attend missionary meetings, and find out what is being done, and then let them talk about it. Let those who wish to interest others in the missionary cause take pains to get stories for the children, spicy narratives for the young people, and practical doings for their older friends. It will suggest thought, lead to effort, and warm and sanctify the heart.

QUARTERLY REPORT.

THE QUARTERLY MEETING in June was held as usual in Old South Chapel, Mrs. Bowker presiding.

The passage of scripture read was from the thirty-seventh chapter of Ezekiel, and was selected because several of our missionaries had requested special prayer for the influences of the Holy Spirit to rest upon their labors. After prayer by Mrs. Anderson, the ladies joined in singing an original hymn by Mrs. Emily C. Pearson, entitled " Death and Life."

The report of the treasurer noticed, among other interesting items, donations from Mount Holyoke Seminary and Bradford Academy.

Extracts from missionary correspondence were read by Mrs. Tyler, also letters from Mrs. Butler and Mrs. Parker of the M. E. Church, regretting their inability to be present at the meeting.

Miss MYRA A. PROCTOR of Aintab gave an interesting account of her journey West, with Mrs. Snow of Micronesia, in behalf of woman's work in foreign lands. In many places, an interest in this cause had already been awakened, and they were everywhere cordially received. She met, in the cars, an old lady who had attended one of the meetings in Cleveland, O., and who was now on her way to Rochester to care for the orphan children of her daughter. Her heart was full of sympathy for missions, but her purse too scanty to afford an offering; yet by sitting up all night, instead of allowing herself the comfort of a sleeping-car, she saved fifty cents, which she begged might be expended in Testaments for girls in the seminary at Aintab.

A very precious gift, said Miss Proctor, because the fruit of self-denial, of which I hope ere long to render a good account.

Miss P., who is expecting soon to return to her field of labor, as a missionary of the W. B. M., concluded with some farewell words, expressing the gratitude and thanksgiving with which she goes, as to her home, and quoting, as her own last wish, the words of the apostle, "Pray for us."

Mrs. Gould, corresponding secretary, also a returned missionary, then addressed the meeting, giving a thrilling sketch of missionary experiences in Syria, amid the scenes of massacre by the Koords, and other facts of interest.

A letter was read from Epping, N.H., presenting a pair of stockings, the last work of a lady ninety-seven years of age, who bequeathed them to the Woman's Board of Missions.

They had been repeatedly sold, and ten dollars, the avails of their sale, presented with them. At the suggestion of Mrs. Dr. Anderson, to whom the letter was addressed, fifteen dollars were added to this sum by ladies present, to constitute a granddaughter of the donor, bearing her name, a life-member.

After further devotional exercises, the meeting adjourned till the first Tuesday in November.

A MODEL AUXILIARY.

Our auxiliary, recently formed in B., may truly be said to be a model. Embracing among its members nearly every female communicant of the church with which it is connected, it is the first to approximate the standard, we hope ultimately to reach through all our auxiliaries, when the entire female membership of our churches shall be so represented.

8*

But better even than this, is the fact that, when these warm-hearted sisters formed their society, they also agreed to meet once in every month, to pray for a blessing on the Woman's Board of Missions, and upon their own contributions in particular, that thus "their prayers and their alms might come up together before God."

BREAD CAST UPON THE WATERS.

We were deeply impressed by a sense of God's faithfulness to his promises, in reading the following letter from Concord, received after the issue of the March number of "Life and Light : "—

"I have looked over the contents of your Quarterly ; and you can imagine the peculiar interest felt, when I found that several of the most touching notices of benefits received by heathen women and children were of those in whom the ladies of our church have long felt a deep interest. I refer to the statements of Mrs. Anna Maria White, in regard to herself and three daughters : for her husband, John White, was educated in the Balticotta Seminary by contributions from the ' Mite Society of Concord ; ' and I have now letters in my possession, written by him and his wife, while these children were very young. His case was a very interesting one ; and the success which crowned this simple effort of the ladies here has been a stimulus to constantly increasing efforts.' "

God's word *is sure ;* and though we may wait long to see the fruit of our labors, or may never see it, the promise shall forever stand, ' For this thing the Lord thy God shall bless thee in all thy works, and in all that thou puttest thy hand unto.' "

Nearly thirty years ago, that Mite Society gave their contributions for children in Ceylon ; and now, when they are grown to mature years, they understand the meaning of that passage, — " Cast thy bread upon the waters, and thou shalt find it after many days."

𝔇eath and 𝔏ife.

Ezek. xxxvii. 9 & 10.

"Then said he unto me, Prophesy unto the wind, prophesy, son of man, and say to the wind, Thus saith the Lord God: Come from the four winds, O breath, and breathe upon these slain, that they may live.

So I prophesied as he commanded me; and the breath came unto them, and they lived, and stood upon their feet, an exceeding great army."

By MRS. EMILY C. PEARSON.

In the regions dim with death,
Nations wait celestial breath :
Dead in trespasses and sin,
None can life eternal win.
Shine upon them from above,
Holy Spirit, Heavenly Dove, —
Shine upon the nations slain,
Wake them that they live again.

Low they lie as in the grave,
But thou hast all power to save :
Shall they in the dust remain,
And the prince of darkness reign ?
Holy One, come in thy power !
Come, for 'tis salvation's hour.
Let thy living voice be heard,
And the vale of death be stirred.

In the regions dim with death,
Come, O soul-transforming breath !
Breathe, oh, breathe, upon the slain,
Till they rise and live again !
Till the army, great and small,
Hearing, Lord, thy gracious call,
Rise a ransomed, holy band,
At the word of thy command.

EXTENSION OF OUR WORK.

Since our last issue, our Board has appropriated three thousand dollars to found a home in Constantinople for three single ladies, who are to labor for the women of that city. It is designed that one shall be an educated physician, who will readily gain access to Turkish homes, and that a girls' school shall be connected with the establishment. The location offers strong inducements to start this enterprise; and, for importance and prospective usefulness, it is deemed second to none in the foreign field.

Those who have read the report of the female boarding-school in Aintab will be gratified to learn that Miss Myra A. Proctor, under our auspices, intends sailing in August to resume her charge. Our members who have been privileged in hearing her earnest words, knowing her worth, will be glad to claim her as their missionary.

It will be noted also with interest, by those who remember the "Passages from Mrs. Knapp's Manuscript," in the June number, that we have adopted the Misses Ely, teachers of the girls' school in Bitlis, and have donated four hundred and twenty-five dollars, additional to their contribution, towards a new schoolroom. They also bear one-half of their own expenses. Miss Ely's letter cannot fail to please our readers; and the devotion of those sisters to the cause should stimulate us to more self-denying efforts.

We have also assumed the support of Miss Sarah A. Closson, who has begun her work, with great promise, in Cesarea; of Miss Roselthea A. Norcross, of the female boarding-school; Eski Zagra, in the Bulgarian Mission, Western Turkey; and of Miss Rosa A. Smith, Madura, India. Miss Smith has the care of sixty Tamil girls; and the school under the charge of Miss Norcross has enjoyed much of God's converting power.

We learn, from our treasurer's report, that about ten thousand dollars has been received since the fifth of January, which has warranted our assuming the support of more missionaries, for which " we thank God, and take courage ; " yet we blush that our offerings are so meagre, compared with the large and rightful demands of our Saviour, in whom are garnered all our hopes for time and eternity.

NEED OF ADDITIONAL CONTRIBUTIONS.

Since the world has so wonderfully opened for the spread of the gospel, the American Board need a great increase of means to enable them to do the part assigned them in the providence of God. Hence it has been suggested to us, that we sustain, by our contributions, the girls' schools under their charge, and also to assume the support of all the single ladies now in their employ. Ought we not to do it? On whom does it so appropriately devolve as ourselves? Who shall comprehend woman's woes and degradation like woman? Christian mothers, ponder the view of maternity presented in " Leaves from a Missionary's Journal," in our last two numbers, and when surrounded by every comfort, cheered by loving sympathy, supported by special divine promise, you welcome infancy to your "ceiled houses," and rock the cradle of your dearest hopes, illumined by gospel sunlight, will you not yearn with compassion over those who bear like burdens, sorrows, and responsibilities without sympathy, without grace, a Saviour, or a God? Was there ever a time, since Christ said, " It is finished! " that the way was so fully prepared for Christian women to work? And with the " pillar of cloud " moving before us, must we not " go forward " ?

INDIVIDUAL RESPONSIBILITY.

There are more than one hundred thousand female members belonging to the churches in sympathy with the American

Board, assigned to our mission-call. If every sister would ask, "Lord, what wilt thou have *me* to do?" and then obey his providential direction, how greatly would our hands be strengthened and our hearts encouraged. If each member would send us one dollar, what an increase to our treasury! Should the stewards of wealth give according to their ability, the glorious day would hasten when heathen women would crown Jesus "Lord of all." A votary of fashion, in this vicinity, spent last year, ten thousand dollars for jewelry to adorn her person. Where is the Christian woman of large means who will give a like sum to win souls to Christ, and thus do her part in obeying his last command!

CONTRAST.

We attended the peace festival recently held in our city; and as we listened to the wonderful voice of Parepa as she warbled "The Star Spangled Banner," filling that vast Coliseum with delicious melody, we longed for some seraphic voice to sing of "The Star of Bethlehem," thrilling even to earth's remotest bounds, and awakening all dead hearts to life and love.

As we beheld the assembly, and were awed by the grand choruses voiced by thousands, our thoughts reverted to that first peace jubilee, held more than eighteen hundred years ago, when angelic hosts chanted over Judean plains, "Glory to God in the highest, on earth peace, and good will to men!" The watching shepherds hearkened with amazement, and all heaven was filled with ecstatic praise.

Our festival cost more than five hundred thousand dollars: that first jubilee, the incarnation of the Son of God, sealed by his precious blood.

Our festival was daily announced through the length and breadth of the land, and triumphantly borne with lightning speed to foreign shores: that first jubilee has never been heralded to one-half the habitable globe, although millions have perished for lack of knowledge. "Tell it not in Gath, publish it not in the streets of Askelon, lest the daughters·of the Philistines rejoice, and the daughters of the uncircumcised triumph ; " but earnestly, tearfully proclaim it to the sisters of the dear Redeemer. Shall our "Elder Brother" be longer shorn of his glory, and robbed of "his inheritance in the uttermost parts of the earth." Is it not still a humiliating fact, "that the children of this world are wiser in their generation than the children of light." Five hundred thousand dollars raised to secure a great musical entertainment, to minister to innocent recreation, and to commemorate a grand historic event; and it was greatly applauded. A large part of the audience was composed of women, who contributed their quota of the expense ; and their patriotism was highly commended. Shall we, as Christian women, do less to testify our loyalty to· the King of kings ? Shall we not "bring all the tithes into the storehouse," and seek to win to his service every woman whom he died to save ; thus securing to him a vast revenue of grateful, everlasting praise.

BRIDGET'S COMMENT.

A domestic in a family of one of the members of our Board, hearing it remarked that $9,000 had been received since January, for our missionary work, exclaimed with much surprise, "What ! *only* $9,000 by so many women, from so many places, for that great work ? Why, our poor little Catholic society has given, in the same time, $20,000 to clear the church-debt, and are starting another church besides. Give me the Catholics yet ! " She and her comrade girl had each given $10, and were ready to contribute a like sum towards the new enterprise. Will our 100,000 church-members give us *one* dollar each?

9

OUR MISSIONARY ROOM.

The Woman's Board of Missions has recently opened a room for the transaction of business at the Missionary House, 33 Pemberton Square. The demands of our enterprise called for this movement. A large correspondence is growing on our hands, "The Quarterly" is to be issued, subscribers' names to be recorded, and information to be given to friends who wish to learn of our progress.

May the blessed Spirit's presence ever abide there! and thence may there be issued many leaves for the healing of the nation!

OUR METHODIST SISTERS.

It is with emotions of peculiar pleasure that we welcome to our Christian fellowship, "The Woman's Foreign Missionary Society" of the Methodist-Episcopal Church, recently organized in Boston. This association has entered on its labors with much zeal, and promise of wide-spread usefulness. Acting with the Methodist Board, it is in spirit and organization kindred to our own. It issues a monthly paper, called "The Heathen Woman's Friend," a neat, attractive, spirited little quarto, which we hope will be taken by every woman in the Methodist denomination.

In one of the worst streets of Aintab, a poor, half-starved little girl followed Mrs. Schneider into one of the houses, and, giving her a simple strain of "I am a pilgrim," asked for the rest. She had heard a Protestant child sing it, and was attracted by its beauty; and very beautiful it is in the Turkish language.

TREASURER'S STATEMENT.

As the Treasurer reports in full, in " The Missionary Herald," all moneys received for the Woman's Board, it is not deemed necessary to recapitulate in our Quarterly. We would state here, however, that, from Jan. 5 to July 23, our receipts were $10,111.81, of which $655 were for the Quarterly. The reports will show the disciple of ninety-seven years exerting her last strength to increase our fund; the youth in our seminaries and Sunday schools banding together, and pledging, as we hope, a life-interest in our work; and even children sending us a part of their candy-money, in pity for the little ones who have not heard of a Saviour, who, when on earth, "blessed them." To interest our young readers, we will give an extract from a letter which we received from Eddie's father, who lives in Vermont. " Please find enclosed $1.85 for the ' Woman's Board of Missions.' It comes from Eddie, six years old, on hearing his mother read from ' Life and Light for Heathen Women,' and from Henry, two and a half years old, who wished to do as his brother did. The little boys brought their all to their father, of their own accord, and wished him to send it at once to the heathen, that they might learn about Jesus the Saviour. Here it is, and may God grant his blessing! "

One dear sister, recently deceased, bequeathed her jewelry to our cause, consisting of a gold bracelet, a chatelaine and pin, three breast-pins, and one diamond-ring. Her dying wish was, that the proceeds might be used to extend to others a knowledge of that dear Saviour who was her support while passing through the dark valley. Whoever is in want of any of these articles may have the satisfaction, in purchasing them, of carrying out the aspirations of a spirit winged for heaven.

Address *Secretary B. W. M.*, 33 Pemberton Sq., Boston.

L. F. BARTLETT.

The Last Command.

BY MRS. EMILY C. PEARSON.

AIR. — *Shining Shore.*

I.

"Go teach all nations!" parting word
Of Christ to heaven returning :
Let us obey our risen Lord,
With " lamps " all " trimmed and burning."

CHORUS.

Should we profess to love our King,
His mandate disobeying,
He'd not accept our offering,
And vain would be our praying.

II.

"Go preach my gospel!" said our Lord :
" *Lo, I am with you ever !* "
In making known his saving word,
He will forsake us never.

CHORUS.

Through flood and flame he'll bear us on,
His message to deliver,
Till all " the heathen " shall be won,
And earth is his forever.

III.

Thou dear Redeemer, loving Friend!
Oh, help us to be willing
To do thy bidding to the end,
Thy last command fulfilling !

CHORUS.

That " all the world " thy praise may sing,
And sound salvation's story,
While ransomed nations tribute bring,
And crown thee, Lord of Glory !

Children's Corner.

OUR SCHOOL GIRLS.

BY MISS MYRA A. PROCTOR.

Some dear children whom I know, and many whom I have never seen, are in the habit of sending their contributions, from year to year, to educate Armenian girls in our seminary at Aintab. No doubt, children, you often wish you knew some of these girls ; and perhaps you wonder if your money really does any good. I would like to tell you of some of them, not because I think them perfect, or worthy to be held up as models, but simply that you may become acquainted with them, and that you may have the pleasure of knowing that they do improve the school privileges with which your money furnishes them.

On the southern slope of Mt. Casius, about forty miles from Antioch, there is a little hamlet of only twelve houses ; and *such* houses ! Four rough stone walls laid up in mud, a flat earth roof, and a floor of earth, with no windows, lighted only by the open door and the broad chimney. There was only one room in a house ; and, in the cold season, the sheep and goats occupy one end of that. In the summer, the children, as well as the lambs and kids, live out of doors, and enjoy it, too, very much.

Here lived a little girl whose name was Mariam, or Mary. The family had once been considered wealthy, but had lost their property, so that one season, when the father was suffering from a long sickness, there was often nothing in the house to eat, except as the neighbors sent it in. Some men, working in the fields near by, would give their noon-lunch to the children, and go without themselves until night.

At Kessab, about three miles from this little hamlet, called Ekiz-Olook, there was a missionary and a Protestant church, with a sabbath school; and Mariam and her friends often went up there to attend the sabbath services. Kessab people also sent teachers down to Ekiz-Olook; so Mariam learned to read when a child. When she was about twelve years old, Mrs. Coffing went to Kessab, and opened there a school for large girls. Mariam wished very much to go, but her mother thought she was too small. She was so earnest about it, however, that her mother applied for her, and she was admitted. All the summer and all the rainy winter, she bravely climbed the mountain-side, never wearying of her long walk of nearly three miles, so much did she love her dear school. In harvest-time, when her father and mother went out to work, she would rise early in the morning, and get some one to milk her cow; then she would pull grass for the calf, and prepare breakfast for herself and the three younger brothers and sisters, and set off for school, returning at night to perform the same work again.

After a time, Mrs. Coffing proposed to send some of her best girls to the seminary at Aintab, to complete a three years' course of study. One soon decided to go; and Mariam's heart burned within her, so great was her desire to go also. Her teacher, and the missionary and his wife, tried in vain to induce her parents to give their consent. Her mother was not a Christian, and her father not even a Protestant: all her friends were opposed to her going. Aintab was a great way off, — almost a hundred and fifty miles distant; and who ever heard of a young girl's going away from her parents, to be gone three years! They could not think of it.

Children, what would you do in such a case? Mariam remembered one Friend, who can do all things; and she cried unto him to help her, and open some way for her to go to school. One night in particular, as she lay in her bed, this was the burden of her heart and of her prayer. And did God hear her? She, only a young girl in that poor little hut on the mountain-side, — did the great God of heaven notice her, and listen to her prayer? Yes ; and he *answered* her. · He put it into the heart of her aged grandfather to say, "I think it is well for Mariam to go to school at Aintab;" and so Mariam came, in answer to her prayer.

During her course, she was supported by a mission sabbath school in New-York City. She was a dear good girl in school, so timid she couldn't be persuaded to go into a dark room alone, and not remarkable as a scholar ; and yet very faithful in her lessons, faithful in her domestic work, and always kind and forbearing towards her schoolmates. She was very earnest as a Christian, and tried to lead others to Christ. She spent one vacation at home ; and how her face glowed with joy when she told me, on her return, that her mother had become a Christian ! With all the more faith and hope, she then prayed for her father.

A year ago last spring, as she was about to graduate and leave us, I said to her, "Mariam, do you dread going home again?" "Oh, no!" she replied : "I am *glad* to go." — "But you will have many things to try you," I said, thinking how distasteful such a life must be to a tidy girl who had spent three years in a clean house. "Yes," she answered ; "but I am sure I can have a school there, and I do long to teach those children."

She went back, as she expected, and opened a very successful school for the children, which numbers twenty pupils, and engaged also, with much zeal and perseverance in labors for the women. The missionary writes of her, "Mariam, on going home to Ekiz-Olook, went right to work, and in every way pleased me."

The following extract is from a letter addressed to one of our mission circles in St. Johnsbury, Vt., who support a girl in Mrs. Edwards's school : —

OUR YOUNG FRIENDS.

BY MRS. MARY K. EDWARDS.

" You are anxious to know something of the school for Zulu girls, for the support of which you have given your money. It commenced, on the 1st of March ; and, during the previous week, we were gratified by the prompt arrival of twenty-two pupils, six of whom were from Inanda, and the rest from the neighboring villages. Each brought her bundle of clothes in her hand. All but one could read their own language fluently. Nine have been through the simple rules in arithmetic : the others, excepting one, can read and write numbers. The youngest and most backward pupil is Talitha Hawes, a little cripple, whose parents were very anxious to have her admitted, and gave her to me. Laurana, the daughter of George Champion, a native preacher at this station, teaches her. She is one of our most advanced pupils, understanding and speaking English, and is a member of the church. We have a pleasant schoolroom, furnished with Ross's desks and chairs. Maps, a few mottoes, and pictures adorn the walls ; and two shelves are filled with minerals, fossils, and shells.

" The girls do all the work of the establishment, even to grinding the corn. We have a little iron hand-mill for the purpose. We have one of Stewart's magnificent stoves, which they soon learn to use. Their food is corn, either ground, stamped, or cooked whole ; sweet potatoes, perhaps once a week, and nine or ten pounds of beef twice a week : sometimes we have beans. I am sure you would be pleased to know who are the workers this, the seventh week. Ujeni Umgwebu is cook ; Usibedane Nembula and Umtaka Biddlecome are dishwashers ; Rebecca

Usijwana and Martha Hawes grind; Annie Unomvukela and Lynia Jakobe bring water; Emma Kalo and Unyoni Umlonyeni bring wood; Umkawaka Umdekazi and Umonasi Ubosibasi make stamp; Abbie Umkiswane fills the lamps; and Unozeh-lohlo Unyokana attends to the schoolroom. We have six American hoes. The girls have prepared the ground, and there is already quite a lot of beans up for our winter use. You must remember that the sun is travelling north, lengthening our shadows towards the south; and we are beginning to draw our shawls around us, and think of fires. I believe the girls are honest and truthful. I keep nothing under lock and key, not even the outside doors. If a dish is broken, the offender reports immediately. They perform their work better than I expected. Four of the number think they are Christians, and three are members of the church. I have every reason to believe that the progress of this school will be watched with prayerful interest by many in America. Do not cease to pray that the experiment now being tried may succeed, and this school may become the beginning of better things for the degraded women of this beautiful land. 'There is that scattereth, and yet increaseth.' May this be the experience of all who have so generously assisted in planting this school among the Zulus."

CHILDREN SINGING.

BY MRS. GEORGE GOULD.

Who, of all you blue-eyed Marys or Fannys, or roguish, Johnnys, do not love to sing, —

"I want to be an angel;" —

or those sweeter words still, —

" Jesus loves me, this I know!"

Of course, you all do; but how shall the dear little children that never heard of Jesus learn these songs? I will tell you. Save the pennies that are given you, or that you may earn, this summer, the coming fall and winter, and send them to our treasurer to support a teacher.

I know a girl on Mount Lebanon, who was educated in part by money sent by pupils at Ipswich Female Seminary. She became a teacher; and one sabbath night, when I was in the village where she taught, I heard, far off down the mountain, the sound of many children's voices. I supposed, of course, they were quarrelling; but, stopping to listen, I was thrilled in a way I can never describe, by hearing them sing, in Arabic, —

> "There is a happy land; "

and, —

> "Joyfully, joyfully, onward we move; "

which they had learned at school.

Why not send these children teachers; and then, when you reach the "shining shore," you may meet some of them there to join you in praising Him who said of them, as well as of you, "Suffer little children to come unto me, and forbid them not; for of such is the kingdom of heaven!"

CELIA'S SACRIFICE.

BY MRS. EDWIN WRIGHT.

Celia has a baby-sister that is her joy and delight. She often says, "Mother, was there ever a prettier baby than our little Maggie, with her rosy cheeks, her beautiful brown eyes, and golden curls?" Celia has brothers and sisters younger, —

Mary, Nettie, Tommy, and Johnny, — who also think baby very pretty and cunning, but do not begin to love her as does Celia; and I think I know the reason why. She never said so; but I believe it is because she is obliged to think so much about her, and sacrifice so much for her.

Celia is just thirteen years old, but no larger than most children of ten; yet slight as is her frame, and tiny as are her hands, she is her mother's sole dependence as housekeeper. No loving father ever fondly strokes her hair, and gladdens her heart with some pleasant word of encouragement, or pets and caresses her darling Maggie. She has no nice clothes, although she always manages to have a neat white bib-apron peeping out from under her little drab sacque. She has no luxuries on her table: indeed, she has not tasted butter for more than a year, and scarce ever has a bit of meat. Why? Because her dear mother has so many mouths to feed, as you will see if you count them up, and no way of earning, except as she washes, irons, and scrubs at other people's houses from morning until night.

Now, if there were no little Johnnie and Maggie, by dint of all rising very early, and helping together, the three little rooms might be put in order, and Celia go to school with the other children (and Miss Jenks used to call her her little "model scholar);" but, as it is, she must stay at home, where mother must be at the wash-tub with the rising sun, and there must be clean aprons and smooth-combed hair for the three, and Maggie washed, dressed, and carefully watched. For when her motherly little sister has tucked her into the cradle, and promised herself to do so much "clearing up" while she sleeps, she is just as likely as not to open her large brown eyes, and, if they do not instantly light upon Celia, pop up, and reach out after her dolly-baby on the floor, bump her own little curly pate, and have to be picked up, and kissed, petted, and soothed, until all the long-drawn sighs have died away in real slumber. Now, if it were

not for this same "prettiest baby in all the world," Celia could
once in a while have a slide or coast in winter with the other
children, or in summer indulge herself with a run in the fields,
or walk in the woods to gather wild flowers : but baby cannot
go, and Mary is too giddy to be trusted with her ; and so poor
Celia in winter contents herself with bouncing little Maggie up
and down before the window, crying, "Look at Tommy,. Maggie.
He says, 'One, two, three, and away I be.'   Oh! wasn't that a
good slide ? — almost as long as this house.   Oh, dear ! he's
slipped down : now he's up again, and didn't hurt himself a
bit.   Hear him laugh !   We'll laugh, too, — 'He, he, he !' "
and "He, he, he !" crows baby; and Celia is almost as happy
as Tommy and Mary.   She says not a word about play for herself ; but she did wish, the other night, — when all the children
were in bed, and she was sitting in the dark with her mother,
who was drying her feet over the old stove, that is so worn out
that it will never bake, only boil and fry, — she did wish she
had some kind of a baby-carriage, no matter if it was ever so
old, — so that she could take little Maggie out into the sweet
sunshine, and dress her up in butter-cups, and necklace and
bracelet of dandelion-stems; and I know where there is a baby-
carriage, rather old, to be sure, but whole and strong.   And I
think Celia will get her wish ; for I do love her for sacrificing
self so much for baby, and trying to be a comfort to her mother.

And, as sacrifice begets love, I believe that one reason why
Jesus loves us so much is because he has done and suffered so
much for us ; and I know he wants us to love all those for whom
he has died, who "sit in darkness" in heathen lands ; and I
think the best way to begin is to do and sacrifice something for
them, until, from thinking so much about them, we get to feel a
real love in our sacrifice, and Jesus says, "Inasmuch as ye have
done it unto one of the least of these, my brethren, ye have done
it unto me."

LIFE AND LIGHT

FOR

𝕳eathen 𝕎omen.

| VOL. I. | DECEMBER, 1869. | No. 4. |

LEAVES FROM A MISSIONARY'S JOURNAL.

NUMBER THREE.

On Monday, I had a pleasant tour to a village five miles from us. We told the teacher of the school, on Sunday, that the following day we would come to his village, and that it was my wish to speak to the women in one of their houses. He is a heathen, but exceedingly kind, and manifested great interest in my plan. There are no Christians in the village; but we have a good school there, and Mr. C. generally holds a meeting in the schoolhouse, where I went once, but no women were present. I took our bandyman's wife, who, though a heathen, always attends my meetings, and who also belonged, as well as her husband, to this same village to which we were now going. We left before the dawn, the moon bright, the deep-blue sky starry and clear. Mr. C. followed on horseback. As we reached the village, the sun was just up, and even then bright and hot. Men and boys greeted us. As I met the teacher, he cheerfully said, "Every thing is ready;" and I followed him down a narrow street, lined on either side with mud houses, about the doorways of which were clusters of dark, wondering faces. A turn around a corner,

and we entered a roomy court, with apartments on each side, and
a low doorway in front.

" Is not this a good large place ? " asked the teacher. It surely
was.   The broad, covered platforms before the rooms were three
feet above the court, from which I looked up at the sky. A mat
had been spread, and a box furnished me with a seat. I sent
the bandyman's wife for her relatives. The women flocked in,
the more intelligent sitting about me on the platform. Others
gathered in the court; and I found that I had the best possible
place for seeing the faces of all. Having asked the teacher —
who had been usefully employed at the door, in telling the men
and boys that they were not wanted — to invite all outsiders to
the schoolhouse, I said to the women, after obtaining silence,
" Now I am going to say a few words to you : do you think you
will understand me ? "

" No," replied a woman with a noisy baby : " we shall not
understand you."

" Yes, you will," rejoined our bandyman's little wife, " if you
do not talk yourselves."

So I began the story of the Indian woman in Martha's Vineyard. I have always had a good meeting with that narrative.

" Who knows what an island is? I am going to tell you about
a woman who lived on one."

" One of her kind of plates, I suppose," said a tall, good
natured woman, turning to my little helper, who was not quite
sure herself, but who instantly brightened up, saying, " It's one
kind of a village."

" Can you go in a bandy? " I asked, to which a woman replied, " If it isn't the rainy season." I soon made them understand what an island was ; whereupon my little woman, who had
been much interested in our Sabbath-lessons on Paul's ship-
wreck, began to talk about a ship. Having suggested the post-
ponement of this subject, I said, " There were four villages on this
island, and in one of them lived a black woman like you, my

elder sister," addressing a nice-looking woman, loaded with jewels.

" Tell, tell ! " exclaimed she.

Just here, a cross-looking man came to the door, and snappishly asked a bright young woman near me, " What she had left pounding paddy for ? " — " Let me alone," she replied : " I want to hear this !" But, in spite of my entreaties, he insisted upon her going to her work.

" Was she married ? " asked the jewelled woman.

" Yes," I replied ; " but she had one great sorrow."

" Tell, tell ! " cried a dozen voices ; for these people have no idea of the formality of a meeting.

" What was her sorrow ? " I asked.

" Perhaps he beat her," suggested one. " Hadn't she any children ? " asked another.

" She had had five children," I replied ; " and every one died before it was ten days old."

" *Iyo ! Iyo !* " they cried ; and here the heart-sorrows came forth, and short histories of their dead children were recited. This was something they understood, and I let them comment on the subject.

" At last," I continued, " the sixth baby was born : and was the mother happy ? "

" No, indeed," said one : " this baby will die. What happiness in that ? " " Were there no doctors there ? " asked another. " That was very heavy trouble, *ammal*," remarked the teacher's wife.

A woman now came in, who seemed to have the respect of all ; and the jewelled woman repeated every thing that I said, adding, " Come and listen ! "

" When this child was four days old, the mother carried it out in a field, and sat on a stone."

" In six days must it die ? " asked the teacher's wife.

" Sorrow indeed ! " ejaculated another.

"She looked at it with many tears. Medicine was of no use: she could only gaze at it till it died, and then lay it away with the other five. While thus sad, she saw a bush growing beautifully, and ready to blossom. 'Why don't the bush die?' she said; and then she thought, "Why did I not die when a baby?'"

Here, as I reviewed my story, and was glad to find it entirely understood, a woman came noisily in, not even making salaam to me. The children, who had been very still, now became uproarious, and for some five minutes there was an interruption. As the new-comer would not be quiet, I insisted on her leaving.

"This sorrowful mother said to herself, 'There must be somebody who kept this bush and myself from dying. He must be a Great One, and I wish I could find him!'"

"Wasn't he in another village?" inquired a woman. "Didn't they have any 'Swamy' there?"

"Can that stone Swamy keep your child from dying?" I replied. "If you had been with that mother, would you have said, 'The stone Swamy in my village will keep your baby alive'?"

An open expression of incredulity overspread her face. She put her hand to her mouth, as if to say, "You have caught me now!"

"Did the baby die?" asked one.

"The mother said, 'This Great One must be near, and I will ask him to keep my baby alive.' And so she spoke out loud, and asked the Great One to keep her baby from dying; and she went to her house with much peace. The tenth day came, and the baby lived!"

It was interesting to see these women exchange looks of gladness.

"Now," I continued, "would that woman forget the Great One who had done this thing?"

"No," answered one: "she must try to make some fine present."

"What present could she make to Him who called the world His own? She gave her child, and spoke out loud to Him every day. She knew He was there, if she could not see Him, because she felt so happy afterwards." I finished the story much in this way. They seemed interested; but it was more of a task to make them comprehend spiritual truth. They understood when I called the 'speaking out loud,' prayer; also the evidences which I mentioned of a good God, who continually cared for us. But when I tried to show how all were sinners, and how they had entirely forgotten this great Father, I felt that they did not perceive it. Even some of our simplest words for salvation and holiness they did not know at all. ·How could their hearts be touched by the love of Christ to them, if they did not see why such love was needed? Many times I have thought of the words, " He shall bring all things to your remembrance, whatsoever I have said unto you." I spoke of sin and our Saviour as I have done before, in the faith that in the great outpouring of the Spirit yet surely to come to India, my words will be revived in some heart.

It was a very pleasant occasion to me, and the women cordially invited me to come again.

CHINA.

LETTER FROM MISS ANDREWS.

TUNGCHOW, June 1.

Miss ANDREWS communicates the following information about her work : —

A SUCCESSFUL SCHOOL.

" In the fall, finding several women and young girls in our neighborhood anxious for instruction, we commenced a school. One woman, who wished herself and little girl to learn, allowed us the use of her room. We went every day, teaching all who wished it to read, and to sing our sweet Sabbath-school hymns. With the latter they were especially delighted ; and we could but hope that the truth presented in that attractive form would make a deep impression. As might be expected, our class was somewhat irregular. A few were much interested, but many came from curiosity, or some other motive. Occasionally our little room was thronged; at other times only four or five were present. We worked on through the winter, and a great many heard more or less of salvation through Jesus. Our labor was not in vain: from several houses idols have been cast out, and prayer rises daily to the living God. Last Sabbath we welcomed to our little church, which was established during the winter, four women, two of whom first heard and were interested in the truth at our school. For one or two others we have hope."

VILLAGE WORK.

"During the spring, Mrs. Chapin and myself have been attempting some village work. Mounted on our donkeys, with one of the boys as a companion, we take long rides in the surrounding villages, stopping whenever an opportunity offers for talking with the people. Sometimes we ride through a village, and no one will pay the least attention to us; at another place, particularly if it is our first visit, a crowd will gather to look at us; but if we stop, or turn towards them, they are frightened, and run away. In other places the people will throng around, and ask questions about our ages, relationship, clothing, &c.; and a few will listen with some interest to the truth. In this way the Saviour has been held up in many villages."

CONVERSION OF A TEACHER.

"The study of the language I enjoy much. During the year I have had the happiness of seeing my teacher yield to the Saviour. Long and hard was the struggle before he could renounce Confucianism, and accept Jesus; but the decision, once made, was final. He is now an earnest, warm-hearted Christian. His conversion was in answer to many prayers. I hope he may become a native helper."

LETTER FROM MISS PAYSON.

MISS PAYSON writes from Foochow, June 10 : —

A USEFUL GRADUATE.

"We have now twenty pupils, in addition to two married women who have come to stay a year or two and learn to read, while their husbands, in Mr. Noodin's 'Training-School' in the city, are preparing, by a short course, to become preachers. One of our graduates, about nineteen years of age, renders herself very useful as teacher of the younger pupils, presiding with much dignity, opening the morning exercises with prayer, leading the singing, &c. Her young sister, a member of the church, having been betrothed when an infant to a heathen, was married some time since, and has been very badly beaten and ill-treated by her husband and his relatives, because she refused to work on the Sabbath : she stands in great dread of him. We can only pray God to give her strength to endure the heavy cross."

AN AGED SCHOLAR.

"Few of the women know how to read, and it is quite difficult to interest them in learning. Many, especially the field-women, work hard to earn four or five cents a day, and say they would starve if they took time to learn. Mrs. Hartwell has lately adopted the practice of paying boys and girls, who have been to school, for teaching their mothers and aunts. A few cash, equal to a half-cent, paid for each chapter or hymn taught, is a mere trifle, and yet may be the means of doing much good. One woman over sixty, who chanced to learn to read in youth, has been thus employed, and for a few cents has taught another, a year or two her senior, not only to read the 'Sermon on the Mount,' published in tract form, but also a large number of hymns. I went with Mrs. H. to hear the woman read the former, on which she had been engaged two months. Her house was low and small; in one room, two men were embroidering a handsome scarlet garment for an idol; in the other, perhaps six feet square, we sat on rude benches, and listened to the gray-haired scholar, who, pointing with her finger, slowly named each character of the three chapters, almost without correction, a half-dozen of the neighboring women quietly listening. The woman naïvely remarked, that since she had commenced reading Jesus' words, she had not quarrelled with her neighbors as before. Of the passage, ' Love your enemies,' she said, ' No one can do that: it is impossible.' Mrs. H., of course, explained to her that we could not obey the command if unaided by Christ."

INDIA.

Miss R. A. Smith, Madura, writes encouragingly. Her school consists of fifty-two pupils, who manifest deep interest in their studies.

" we'll try ! "

She says, "At the close of last term, I reminded them that vacation afforded many opportunities for doing good ; and, if they really loved the Saviour, they would make earnest efforts to lead others to Him. Their eager reply was, ' We will try.' The reports they brought back showed that the promise was not forgotten. One endeavored to convince her neighbors of the sin of idol-worship, relating also the story of Christ's sufferings and death. They said, ' What you have told us may be true, but our relatives will punish us if we become Christians.' — ' You need not dread them,' she replied ; ' but you must fear God.' To similar objections, another answered, ' Whatever may come, you ought to love Jesus.' A third, to show that they must strive to be saved, quoted, ' Straight is the gate,' &c. Nearly all had related the story of the cross. A little girl from Madura was urging some children to come to church. 'We cannot : we have no clean clothes to wear.' She quickly replied, ' The Lord will not look at your clothes, if your heart is clean.' In some cases, their simple arguments seem to awaken a desire to know more of our religion ; but if such a wish was mentioned, in the same breath was added, ' We cannot join you, for our friends and caste would persecute us ! ' They were assured by their young teachers that the Lord would be kinder than their friends, and that he would never forsake them. Pray for them."

TURKEY.

Miss Charlotte E. Ely, Bitlis, writes, under date Aug. 2, —

" By a recent letter from Rev. N. G. Clark, I learned that our wants for a girls' school-building had been made known to the Woman's Board ·of Missions, and that you had promptly and liberally responded, by voting the four hundred and twenty-five dollars necessary. For this pledge of your interest in us and our work, we beg you to accept our heartfelt thanks ; also our warm gratitude for your decision to assume us as your missionaries. It gives us great encouragement to hope that we shall now have a more defined and special place in your sympathies and prayers. The Lord helping us, we shall endeavor so to labor, that your care on our account may bring back to you, through the enlightenment and salvation of souls in this dark land, a rich reward.

DESCRIPTION OF THE CITY.

" Bitlis, our missionary-home, being comparatively a new station, and so far interior that it is not often visited by other missionaries, you may perhaps be interested to hear something of its position and peculiarities. Disembarking at Trebizond on the Black Sea, and proceeding southward by the slow method of horseback travelling, a month's journey brings one to our strange, quaint city, — it being about three hundred miles from Trebizond, and twelve miles from Lake Vau. Exceedingly unlike the compactly built cities of Asiatic Turkey in general, it is emphatically ' a straggling city among the mountains.' It lies about five thousand feet above the level of the sea, on the steep banks of a branch of the Tigris, — the Bitlis River, — which is for sixty miles a rushing torrent, as it descends a declivity of nearly three thousand feet. The dwellings of its thirty thousand inhabitants are scattered on the slopes and artificial terraces of mountains whose summits rise far above, and so shut us in from the world, that it is fifty minutes after the sun rises, before it is visible. I often look at these mountain walls and reflect, ' So the Lord is round about his people,' till that sweet verse has come to be very precious. One pleasant feature of this Eastern city is the number of trees and gardens, which in summer give it a fresh and inviting look. Mountain springs supply the city with an abundance of excellent water, and in many places mineral springs are found, possessing a variety of medicinal properties. Bitlis is divided into quarters, something like the wards of American cities; but there is great irregularity in the position of every thing. As no wheeled vehicle is used here, there is no approach to a good road. The streets are sometimes quite wide, again mere paths, and always extremely uneven and crooked.

BUILDINGS.

" On the terraces and lower slopes of these mountains, till close beside the narrow, rushing river, rise the rude but good-sized dwellings, scarcely distinguishable from the rock on which they stand, and from which their stones are taken. They are built of hewn stone, with flat mud roofs, usually two-storied, and enclosing a small court. The windows are heavily grated, giving the

buildings a decidedly gloomy and prison-like appearance to a new-
comer. In summer the windows remain open; in winter they
are covered with oiled paper, glass being rare and expensive.
Mr. K. brought the first pane ever seen in Bitlis, less than a
dozen years ago, as well as the first mirror and stove. When the
natives saw glass, they could with difficulty satisfy themselves
that any thing which would admit light could keep out cold; and
to this day a mirror is a profound mystery to many of them.

THE BOARDING-SCHOOL.

" You have kindly accepted our judgment as to the necessity of
a school-building, and nobly aided us in providing the means.
Permit me to tell you, somewhat at length, why a building is requisite for a boarding-school, in distinction from a day-school.
From the very scattered condition of the houses, it would be difficult for scholars to attend a day-school, even though there were
no other objection. But, added to the distance — which, during
our long winters, with their deep snows, often more than twelve
feet, it would be impossible for them to walk — is the long established custom, that it is improper for a girl to go in the streets
alone. In the present rude and opposing state of society, it is not
only wholly contrary to Oriental etiquette for a girl to traverse
the public street unattended, but — at least in our city — un-
safe. Battling with the arguments, promises, and threats of op-
ponents has chilled many a heart warmed with a desire to know
more of the truth; personal insult and cruelty obliged many a
brave, strong man to wait with aching heart for the day of deliverance. And can we suppose that these poor brethren will
send their daughters defenceless through the streets, to be laughed
and scoffed at? We do not expect it, and cannot, till the gospel
leaven has worked more largely through this great mass of cor-
rupt and sinful humanity. In addition to this, a strong reason
for gathering girls together in a boarding-school is found in the
fact that Christian influence is much more likely thus to become

a saving power, than when, by a daily return to their homes, they hear the truth controverted and ridiculed.

ONLY A GIRL!

" A little incident which occurred at Havordoric, a mountain village about two days' journey from B., will show how many of the natives look upon the education of girls. Mr. K., while on a tour among the villages of Moosh-plain, spent a night with the chief man of H. The next morning, seeing this man's daughters toiling up the hill, with heavy loads of wood on their backs, Mr. K. said to the father, ' Why do you not send your daughters to school, that they may learn to read, be useful and happy ? To which he replied, ' They are girls : they cannot learn any thing ! ' After some conversation, he admitted that perhaps they could ; but, with a shrug of his shoulders, and a peculiar tone of voice, objected, ' Who would bring the wood and water then ? ' Ah ! that is it : who will be the slaves and drudges, when these poor women and girls are elevated and Christianized !

AFRICA.

LETTER FROM MRS. EDWARDS.

NEED OF SYMPATHY.

Accept my heartfelt thanks for your words of love and cheer, and the assurance that I have "an abiding-place in the sympathies and prayers " of the Christian ladies with whom you are associated. Situated as I am, these loving messages are doubly precious. There are hours when the darkness is so thick that I cannot see the pathway, but only cry, " Lord, take my right hand ! " My burden is heavy : I need the grace and strength to lay it upon Jesus.

SECOND SCHOOL-TERM.

Our first term closed on the 11th of May: the second commenced June 28. There are twenty-two girls, the youngest seven and a half years old, and the eldest fifteen. The school is in favor with the people and the girls themselves. God has turned their minds, and there seems to be a thirsting for knowledge. Mrs. Grout wrote me that two girls, one quite lame, were so anxious to come, that they were willing to walk all the way, a distance of about forty miles. They did walk twelve. To-day a girl begged to be received. Her father is poor, and has attacks of epilepsy ; her mother is asthmatic. Her reply, when I asked why she wished to come, was, " *Ugi ya tanda ukufunda* " (I wish to learn). She is a member of the church, and I ought to receive her ; but six girls in each sleeping-room are too many ; there are five in each now : one has six. The Zulu women are very degraded ; even those who are members of the church enjoy sitting in the dirt and taking snuff. The preachers' wives are much inferior to their husbands.

A HAPPY OLD WOMAN.

A woman came from a kraal to the school on the first of March. I clothed and fed her. She says she is too old to learn with her eyes, but not with her heart. She felt so badly, when I tried to send her away, that I relented. If she was lazy, I should not encourage her to stop ; but she is careful of every thing, and, if she knew how, would be neat. The heathen women can do little beyond digging, planting, carrying wood, and making huts. A few mornings since, I found an old woman in the kitchen, who had only a piece of a filthy blanket to cover her ; she was cold, and asked for something to keep her warm. I put on her my last colored skirt and a print dress. The poor creature's joy fully repaid me. She thanked me in Zulu, " *Ugi ya bonga ;* " but, not satisfied, she asked the girls what she should say in English ; and, when I went out again, exclaimed, " Thankee ! thankee ! *Ugi ya jabula kakulu.* I am very happy ! "

THE CONSECRATED GOLD DOLLARS.

The following extract from a letter by Mrs. CYRUS STONE, who, after many years of labor in India, was compelled, on account of ill health, to return to this country, cannot fail to interest our readers : —

"I have an intense longing to become a life-member of that blessed 'WOMAN'S BOARD OF MISSIONS.' Earnestly I have prayed for the means whereby I might become so. A few days since, I found a tidy and infant's bib of past work nearly completed. I said, 'Cannot these be sold, and the avails go towards the desired object? Is not this the way God will answer my prayers?' And, putting on my glasses, the work of finishing these articles was commenced and completed; the mean while praying that many more laborers may go forth to elevate our degraded sex in heathen lands.

"Should the question arise, why I am so anxious to become a life-member of the WOMAN'S BOARD, I reply, Before my marriage, in the bloom of youth and strength of my days, I gave myself to the work in India. I went out, not knowing one with whom I was to be associated, till a week before we sailed. Bidding farewell to a widowed mother, for seven years I saw none of my former acquaintances, or met any one who knew my relatives.

"So earnestly is my heart engaged in the zenana work in India, and the salvation of the women in the dark lands of heathenism, that my thoughts by day and dreams by night are with them. Scarcely have I given up the long-cherished hope that my grave might be made beneath the tall cocoanut-trees of that land of idols. My heart thrills with joy when I hear of one and another giving themselves to the Heaven-inspired cause! It is with difficulty I realize that I am not young and strong as in 1835, when I entered the glorious work, — so great is my desire to be again engaged in it.

"Enclosed please find a gold dollar, sent me a short time since by a former parishioner, to procure delicacies so needful to an invalid. But, dear friends, it is *too* precious to be used in that way; and the most satisfactory disposition of it, to my mind, is, that it be used to send the knowledge of a Saviour to our sex in benighted lands, and also so much towards the object named. A widow's mite, indeed; but Jesus, who sits over against the treasury, can multiply it a thousand fold: and so, this morning, bolstered with pillows on my bed, and about to write you, I again took it in my hand, and reconsecrated it to his holy cause. I asked him, as I could not speak to the poor Hindoo women myself, to use this gold piece for the salvation of some one of those idol worshippers, who might become a star in his crown of rejoicing, in the glorious day of his espousal."

The gold dollar was not enclosed; and a piece of paper, stating the fact, slipped out in opening the letter, so that it was supposed to be lost. Considerable anxiety was felt about it; and the next morning, on reading the letters to a lady, she exclaimed, "How strange that I should have called this morning! I have a gold dollar, that was consecrated to the Lord, under peculiar circumstances, twelve years ago; and for a long while it has been missing, until yesterday, when, in looking over some old papers, it was found. I will now reconsecrate it to the cause of missions, and give it in the place of the one that has been lost."

Subsequently the first one was remitted, and both have been deposited in the treasury. What if the prayers of these sisters should be answered, and each dollar should be instrumental in saving one soul, and that soul others, and so on, until "all the earth shall know the Lord"! Who can compute the value of the dividend which would be declared on that investment in the great day of final account?

Are there not other gold dollars that should also be consecrated to the salvation of heathen women?

Freely Give.

" For ye know the grace of the Lord Jesus Christ, that, though he was rich yet for your sakes he became poor; that ye through his poverty might be rich."—2 COR. viii. 9.
" Freely ye have received, freely give."— MATT. x. 8.

BY MRS. EMILY C. PEARSON.

Lo ! each breeze bears on its wing
Moanings of the perishing,
Who to unblessed graves go down,
With no hope of palm or crown.
Christian, canst thou happy wear
Costly raiment, jewels rare,
If from all thy store is given
Naught to aid the lost to heaven ?

Christian, slumbering, canst thou stay
From the ripening fields away,
While vast millions throng the road
Leading swift to death's abode ?
Gird thee, loiterer, for the strife !
Spread o'er earth the news of life !
Self and all be freely given :
Freely gave the Lord of heaven.

Dear Redeemer, shall it be,
That we hoard our gifts from thee,
Serving worldliness and dross,
Bearing not thy sacred cross ?
Oh for grace like thee to live !
Oh for love like thee to give !
Moved with pity, help us, Lord :
Bear to all the world thy Word !

QUARTERLY REPORT.

THE quarterly meeting in November, held in Old South Chapel, was very fully attended.

After the singing of "Jesus shall reign where'er the sun," &c., Mrs. Bowker read the 72d Psalm, dwelling upon the passage, " Prayer also shall be made for him continually; " and enforced the duty of praying for Christ by praying for the prosperity of his kingdom. When we pray for missionaries and the success of their labors, when we pray for the silver and the gold to carry on the work, we are fulfilling this prediction. Let us show the sincerity of our prayers by corresponding practice, and heed the command of the Master, who is with us to-day, and says, " Go work in my vineyard."

After prayer by Mrs. Edwin Wright, the Recording Secretary, Mrs. Copp, presented a brief sketch of the Society's work during the last quarter.

Mrs. Bartlett, Treasurer, reported the receipts of the last two months as $2,122.89, besides $132.89 for "Life and Light."

Mrs. Gould, Corresponding Secretary, read extracts from a letter of Miss Andrews in China, and also from Mrs. Edwards of the Zulu boarding-school for girls, South Africa, which was full of encouragement in regard to the progress of her work, and asking if some one would not like to give her a melodeon for her school.

Mrs. Dr. Anderson then introduced to the audience Mrs. Fairbank, from the Mahratta Mission, temporarily in this country on account of her husband's health. Mrs. Anderson alluded to her parentage (she is the daughter of Mr. and Mrs. Ballantine), and her birthplace upon heathen ground, and related the interesting fact, that, from her earliest years, she had been imbued with a missionary spirit, so that the recreations of childhood had been attempts at missionary labor.

Mrs. Fairbank gave an interesting account of the labors of herself and of several native Bible readers among the women of India, showing how prejudice is giving way, and some time-honored heathen practices invaded. The better class of men now desire to have their wives and daughters educated, and, contrary to long-established custom, a Christian widow has recently been married.

After singing, Mrs. Bowker read a letter from Mrs. Cyrus Stone, expressing a strong desire to become a life-member of the Society, accompanied by some articles made by herself, which she desired might be sold for that object.

Mrs. Bartlett reported the gift of a quilt from a blind woman, and desired that the donor might also be made a life-member.

An appeal from Mrs. Bowker was generously responded to by some of the ladies present; and a sufficient sum was contributed to make the two, life-members of the Woman's Board of Missions.

Grateful mention was made respecting the safe return of our Corresponding Secretary, Mrs. Miron Winslow, from her European tour, who is now ready to resume the duties of her office.

MRS. J. A. COPP, *Rec. Sec'y.*

ECHO FROM PITTSBURGH.

"Give us a graphic account of the Pittsburgh meeting," said one of our subscribers to us the other day; — "so distinctly photographed, that we in Boston can attend, and breathe its spirit," said another. We shall not attempt to comply with the latter request, as its inspiration and magnetic power cannot be reproduced in these columns; but, as several reports have already been published, we shall be pardoned if we only refer to the occasion in our own way.

AUSPICIOUS DAY.

On Thursday, A.M., Oct. 7, in the pleasant First Presbyterian Church, a large number of ladies convened. It was a
delightful day. The sun shone brightly; and, as his beams
played through the beautiful stained glass, we were cheered and
enlivened. All the surroundings were propitious. The voice
of prayer had scarcely ceased in the temple; the earnest petitions of our brethren, for a blessing to rest upon the meeting,
still lingered in the ear; while the cordial welcome given us on
the preceding day, as we gathered in the same place for our
mothers' meeting, by Rev. F. A. Noble, and Rev. S. S.
Scovel (the latter the pastor of the church), was revived, never
to be forgotten.

At the right of the lady presiding were a large number of
returned missionary ladies, and on the left were the officers of
the Woman's Board of Missions of the Interior, and Woman's
Board of Missions located in Boston; while the front pews were
reserved for delegates of auxiliary societies, and members of kindred associations.

DEVOTIONAL EXERCISES.

The hearts of the assembly seemed to flow together, as they
sang in unison, " Come, Holy Spirit." A few verses from the
29th chapter of 1st Chronicles, were then read. " Who am I, and
what is my people, that we should be able to offer so willingly
after this sort; for all things come of Thee, and of thine own have
we given thee," suggested, that deep humility and right appre-
hension of stewardship were indispensable requisites for the
highest success of the enterprise we were seeking to promote.

" We are strangers before Thee, and sojourners as were all
our fathers," &c., directed our thoughts above to the " great cloud
of witnesses," among whom we believed was the lamented Mrs.
Samuel Hubbard, who was with us on our first anniversary, and

who for many years had been present at the annual meeting of the American Board, but who had received the call, "Come up higher," and in her earnest, life-long devotion to missions, "being dead, yet speaketh to us."

The importunate prayer of David, "Give unto Solomon, my son, a perfect heart," &c., led to the consideration, that, like the Psalmist, we are but making "provision" for the rearing of the "gospel temple," that "our children and our children's chil dren" shall be honored "to build," until its dimensions shall fill the whole earth. As we perceived the earnest attention from the body of the house, and the lively sympathy indicated by the occupants of the galleries, in leaning forward to listen, we felt that there were mothers present who would unite in the spirit of the royal prayer, and consecrate their offspring to the work and glory of "Jesus Christ, the chief Corner-stone."

REPORTS.

After prayer by Mrs. Dr. Anderson, minutes of the last year's meeting at Norwich, Conn., were then read by Miss Evans, Sec. *pro tem.*, and also a report of the W. B., Boston, by Mrs. Miron Winslow. As these have been published, we forbear to give extracts. The audience then united in singing an original hymn.

BOARD OF THE INTERIOR.

Mrs. Professor Bartlett of Chicago, President of the W. B. M. I. was then introduced, and gave a very interesting account of the formation, work, and success of the society she represented. Although not yet one year old, it has received three thousand six hundred dollars, has formed fifty auxiliaries, and employed six ladies in missionary fields. In alluding to its origin, she referred to the Women's Board of Boston as the "elder sister; nay, more, the mother;" and in other remarks upon this point, in connection with the response which followed from the Boston

board, evidenced a very cordial and dear relation existing between these kindred associations. She also read extracts from two
letters of recent date, as specimens of many being constantly received from feeble churches, showing their earnest desire to
become auxiliaries in the work. One was from a pastor's wife
in Wisconsin, enclosing ten dollars, the fruit of self-denial in
dispensing with the use of tea. Her statements were very encouraging; and, at the conclusion of them, was sung one verse of
the hymn, —

"Blest be the tie that binds."

TWENTY YEARS AMONG THE ZULUS.

Mrs. Wilder, from the Zulus, South Africa, was then presented. She had labored twenty years in one station, north of
Natal. "Do you ask," she said, "if the Zulus need the
gospel? We, who have witnessed for long years their extreme
degradation, can answer yes, with earnestness. When we first
went to them, they were destitute of clothing, save a blue cloth
worn about the hips, or an antelope skin trimmed with beads.
Their huts looked like bee-hives, without chimneys or floors;
and their beds consisted of mats, with wooden stools for pillows.
Women are owned by the men, and are paid for at marriage in
cattle, and, though degraded by it, are proud to be sold for
much cattle; yet, notwithstanding their low condition, they can
be reached by the gospel, and it has had a *wonderfully* transform-
ing power. Some of them have been educated, so that they are
able to be interpreters for the missionaries. They love to listen
to the truth, but say, 'it goes in one ear and out the other.'
Pray, that, instead, it may sink into their hearts. As they
learn to love the Saviour, they want the civilizing influences of
clothing, and comforts for their houses. The missionaries' work
has been to try and lift them out of the mire of heathen habits.
Prayer meetings and mothers' meetings have been held among

the women. Mrs. Edwards, who has been sent out by the 'Woman's Board,' Boston, will be a very valuable assistant. The work there is not inviting in itself; but it is done for Christ, and is the same which He came to our world to do."

WORK AMONG THE ARMENIANS.

Mrs. Allen of Harpoot followed, in remarks about the Armenians. "They are not heathen, but nominal Christians. We do not have to clear away the rubbish as among the Zulus; but we have a no less arduous work, in clearing away their deeply-rooted superstitions, on which they rely for salvation, rather than on the cross of Christ." She illustrated the power of the gospel among them, by the change it has recently wrought in Palu. A few years ago, they were entirely ignorant of the way of salvation; but recently many conversions have occurred among the women, and eighteen or twenty connected with the female prayer-meeting visit weekly from house to house, to pray and read with the inmates. Five years ago, there was a wife who was violently opposed to the truth converted, and immediately inquired, 'What can I do?' She learned to read, started a girls' school, and, though partly blind, is very useful, and is much beloved by the Armenian women. The work done is glorious, but there is much more needed. Who will do it? How can it be done? This Board is answering the question. But are you willing to give your daughters? There are mothers who feel that it is too great a sacrifice. Christ gave his life? Is it too much for us to ask of you to give your loved ones? Remember the words of Jesus, "He that loveth son or daughter more than me is not worthy of me."

One stanza of the hymn, written for the occasion, "Freely give," was then sung, ending with the lines, —

> "Self and all be freely given,
> Freely gave the Lord of heaven."

FRUITS FROM THE PERSIAN GARDEN.

We were then permitted to listen to words of encouragement from Miss Rice, who for eleven years was the associate of Fidelia Fiske, that sainted woman, whose praise is in all the churches. She said, " ' For Christ's sake ' is the missionary teacher's motto. ' For Christ's sake ' we stand here to speak of the work in distant lands. Our beloved sister, Miss Fiske, was raised up to make a garden for the Lord in the Persian wilderness. I come to bring some of its fruits. Of the seventy-nine graduates from the girls' seminary, Ooroomiah, all but six left with hope in Christ. Nearly all give us constant joy. Many of them are efficient laborers in the Lord's vineyard, as Bible-readers, or wives of native preachers. Some of them have been called to suffer persecution for the truth, and have proved steadfast. While the gospel has led many of them to live consistently, it has also enabled them to die triumphantly. One who was connected with the seminary said, in view of death, ' I am not afraid : Christ will carry me over.' In delirium, she called for her golden harp, and in her lucid moments sweetly reposed on the bosom of Jesus. Our pupils love to work and pray. They hold little voluntary meetings among the women, and often have answers to prayer. They have a prayer-meeting on Saturday evening. Let all, who love the Ooroomiah school, remember it at that time. Pray for us this winter. Only one word more, dear sisters : it is blessed to labor for Christ."

THE ARMENIAN EAR-RINGS.

Mrs. Coffing of Marash next addressed the meeting. " You say, give us facts. I hold in my hand a pair of ear-rings, with which is connected a fact. In a certain place in Central Turkey, twenty years ago, several men gathered to read the Bible, and one woman was converted. She took off her jewels, and has recently sent her ear-rings to us, to be disposed of for the benefit of her heathen sisters." The speaker related a number of instances, exhibiting a similar spirit of consecration on the part of the natives.

SCHOOL FOR PASTORS' WIVES.

Mrs. Dodd of Marsovan referred to the school under Miss Fritchner's care, as the only one in Western Turkey where pastors' wives are being educated. It is doing a very important work. Pray for that school. She then related many touching incidents of her own missionary life, which deeply moved the audience.

SUGGESTIVE THOUGHTS.

Attention was invited to words of counsel from the "mother of missionaries," Mrs. Dr. Anderson of Boston, who suggested, that one great want of the women of the land is more knowledge on these important subjects. She said, " We feel that we can never forget the impressions of this occasion ; but they will fade away. What we need, when we leave this meeting, is to make the missionary work a study. One of our auxiliaries regularly takes up missions, one after another, becoming acquainted with its geography, history, &c. Few know how much the minds and hearts of our women may become enlarged, enlightened, and quickened in duty, by such a course."

PLEAS FOR PERSIA.

Mrs. Rhea was then introduced. She commenced, " Beloved, greeting," and read from 1 John i. 1–5 ; remarking, that " she always liked to begin and end with the Bible, for, without it, we are as mariners without a compass. Come with me to an ancient mountain, Ararat ; " and, taking her audience with her, described that distant country, Persia, and made a stirring appeal in its behalf.

After a three hours' session of unabated interest, we were compelled to interrupt the earnest and impressive address of Mrs. Rhea, to bring the exercises to a close.

POWER OF THE CROSS.

As we looked upon the sunny faces of our missionary sisters, and listened to their cheerful words, we could scarcely realize, that nearly all of them had returned to us, bearing a heavier cross than that which led them forth at first.

A mother, from Turkey, had brought her first-born son ; another, from Africa, a son and daughter : all to be left in this land, while they should go back to their distant fields of labor.

Moreover, there were several widows in that missionary group. There was one whose memory never fails to remind her of that weary, suffering journey, when she accompanied her sick husband to the village of Ali Shah. She cannot forget the long hours of that eventful night, when, after " watching, praying, and agonizing " that his precious life might be spared, she was paralyzed with grief, on reaching the " quiet resting-place," to find that the angel convoy had stealthily borne him away to his eternal home, without his having given a farewell " look or word or sign."

And a second, who, in recalling her former work in Turkey, bade her heart-throbs be still, that she might tell the power of Jesus to change the spirits of those wicked men " who murdered her dear husband."

And there was still a third, who often lives over those nightly vigils, when she, too, was written a widow. She had laid her darling babe in the grave, — had watched a long while the strange disease that had attacked her surviving daughter, and which baffled all the remedies at command ; and, after weeks of anxious waiting, at length welcomed the physician who had been sent for to her home. But he did not come alone, for the angel of death accompanied him ; and that first night he was called to minister to the husband, who died of cholera, after a few hours' sickness, leaving the mother alone, and the child fatherless.

Yet in neither case was there a regretful or repining word, but only thanksgiving for sustaining grace. True: they had been called to drink at "Marah's" stream; but the healing branch had been cast into the "waters," and they told us only of the "sweetness."

Precious sisters! we cannot let you bear the cross alone. We must rally to your side, and help you in the conflict. We shall never more meet you all in the earthly temple; but we hope to greet you yet again in our "Father's house," where, having "turned many to righteousness," in "the dark places of the earth, amid the habitations of cruelty," you "shall shine as the stars for ever and ever."

PARTING WORDS.

In a few words, the President remarked, that the reports which had been read had exhibited mainly the bright features of our work: but there was another side; and for a moment she lifted the vail, and disclosed heavy burdens and responsibilities borne, because the receipts of the treasury were not equal to the demands, and the laborers were still too few for the "ripening fields." An appeal was then made to the ladies to start an auxiliary in every church. Reference was also made to the quarterly "Life and Light," our organ of communication for missionary intelligence, respecting woman's work in heathen lands. It will be seen to be desirable that it should have a wide circulation; and, as we are a band of voluntary workers, if every one present would act as an agent in its behalf, its efficiency for good would be greatly increased.

Jesus is calling every Christian woman to his service. In the great work of leading heathen women to him, he hath need of each of us. Christian sister, "the Master has come, and is calling for you." He hath need of you, of your treasures, of your children. We bear the message : echo it from city to village, from hill to valley, and let its reverberations be heard from sea to sea, until the whole earth shall be won by his dying love.

The audience then united in singing the doxology.

INSPIRING PROMISES.

Just then, as we were dispersing, we received cheering words, donations, and subscriptions for " Life and Light." The warm grasp of the hand, and the promises, " I will canvass our parish for you ; " " I will start an auxiliary ; " " I will get subscribers," were inspiring, and we hopefully await their realization.

A WORD TO OUR SUBSCRIBERS.

As the year closes with this number, our friends will greatly aid our work by immediately remitting subscriptions for our next volume. It will be remembered that our terms are fifty cents a year, payable in advance.

We hope that all who love missions will realize the importance of spreading a knowledge of the work ; and we ask every lady who takes this little quarterly to find us one new subscriber, and send the name with her own to " Secretary W. B. M., 33 Pemberton Square, Boston."

For Treasurer's Report, see " Missionary Herald " for August, September, and October, 1869.

Obituary

OF

MRS. SAMUEL HUBBARD.

BY MRS. DR. ANDERSON.

At our meeting for business in July, Mrs. Hubbard was with us, earnest, cheerful, interested, as she always was, in that which pertained to the prosperity of Zion. On the last Sabbath of July she was called to her heavenly home; and, when we met in August, each one of our number felt personally afflicted.

The varied excellences of Mrs. Hubbard's character are too well known to need any public notice; and religion was so blended with all the doings of her life, that she will live in the hearts of her Christian friends, only to be more and more highly appreciated. And yet, as an Association, we are constrained to give some expression of the feelings which press upon our hearts when we think of the loss we have sustained.

We miss her in our meetings; for she was with us when we first came together, a little company, to consult as to the expediency of forming this Association; and we well remember her decided impulse to go forward. She has seldom been absent from a meeting since, and never seemed more animated and hopeful than at the last meeting which she attended.

But it is not alone in our missionary work that we remember her. With some of us, precious recollections cluster around meetings for prayer and maternal consultations, where impressions were deepened by her presence; and in how many ways of doing good have we felt her influence!

Let us be stimulated by her example; for we can never forget her promptness to meet duty, her zeal in overcoming difficulties, her large-hearted benevolence in planning, her discretion in giving counsel, and her earnest solemnity in seeking the divine blessing upon all our measures.

We know, that, in infinite wisdom and love, she has been taken from us; and doubt not she is now rejoicing in all she was permitted to do while here on earth to promote the good of others.

And may we be hastened in our work to be more faithful and diligent in all we design to do for the salvation of others, kowning that there is no work nor device in the grave, to which we are all hastening.

Children's Corner.

A BEAUTIFUL SUM IN ADDITION.

BY A MISSIONARY LADY.

EVERY Wednesday afternoon I have a prayer-meeting with the girls; and week before last, while reading to them that beautiful first chapter of 2d Peter, I recalled one lovely warm afternoon in F——, my childhood's home, when we were having a church-meeting in the dear old vestry. I love to think over the morning prayer, and afternoon church-meetings, and verily believe that many a saint now in glory remembers, too, that dear old vestry! I recollect a remark of my honored father, then the pastor, as he commented on the chapter. He said, "The apostle has given us a beautiful sum in addition." This was the key-note of an afternoon prayer-meeting, that should take place years afterwards, on India's burning plains.

The thought was just suited to our girls. Their minds greatly enjoy such. Imagine their forty dusky faces, and wondering looks, as I told them that they knew I had given them many "sums" in arithmetic, but that I now had a new one, a beautiful sum in addition, found in this chapter. This surprised them all; and, while some turned over the Testament leaves, others were suspicious that this would do no good, and awaited my explanation. So I said, —

"Look at the fifth verse, and you will find it. It is to be performed not only mentally, but with all your best efforts; and there is a reward to any one of you who does this, which is as

grand as you can wish." Even the youngest followed me
eagerly as I developed my meaning. I asked little H., who is
most expert in mental arithmetic, if she thought it would be too
hard for her. "It isn't like our common sums?" she asked.
"It says 'giving all diligence,'—that is right for a difficult
lesson, is it not?" I answered. A., who had been studying
over her Bible, glanced up with a knowing smile, and exclaimed,
" I know you mean something about the soul."—"We'll see,"
I replied : " let us add. Can you add as fast as I can speak?"—
"No, no!" said half a dozen voices at once. "It is a problem
for our souls," I continued, and every head was bent over a
Testament. "What must you possess in order to begin to add
this wonderful sum?"—"Faith," said they in a breath.
"Perhaps you may not be able to do all this at once, and you
will notice that you can have a special work for every day in the
week. What part may you add on Sunday?"—"Virtue," was
the full response. "Monday?"—"Knowledge."—"Tuesday?"—"Temperance." And so on, I, of course, finding many
pleasant thoughts by the way ; and all were greatly interested.
When we came to the reward to those who do the work faithfully,
it was one of those impressive moments when you know that the.
blessed truth of God's word is sinking into the heart. "Neither
barren nor unfruitful in the knowledge of our Lord Jesus
Christ ;" and then followed even more solemnity as I said,
"Only see,—you who are unfaithful learners in God's word,—
what is your condition? 'But he that lacketh these things is
blind, and cannot see afar off, and hath forgotten that he was
purged from his old sins.' And to all those who are faithful,
only hear: 'For so an inheritance shall be administered unto
you abundantly, into the everlasting kingdom of our Lord and
Saviour Jesus Christ.'" I could not help adding, "My care
and teaching of you will soon cease : there are only three weeks
more of our school connection ; 'wherefore I will not be
negligent to put you always in remembrance of these things,
though ye know them.'"

Severy Ammal, the school ayah, or matron, closed our meeting with one of her fervent prayers; and then the girls' followed me down the steps in that crowded quiet way that they have when their hearts are in any wise made tender.

" Are we all going to do this ' sum ' in addition ? " I said, turning to receive their salaams.

" By the grace of God helping us, we must try," responded that warm-hearted woman, whose Christian virtues are already added one upon another, so that we say, " We know that for her there is ' an abundant entrance ' ! "

JENNY'S MISSION-CIRCLE.

A TRUE NARRATIVE.

"May I go with you to the missionary meeting ? " asked Jenny, bounding into the room from the play-ground.

" Are your lessons ready?" inquired the mother. " Yes, ma'am, and I've nothing to do but roll hoop, dress my doll, or play croquet; and, if I do only these things, I feel like such a little girl : and I shall not know how to act when I am a woman. I want to see what the grown-up folks are about ! " Mrs. Worth was glad to take her daughter with her ; for, since the ladies had formed their Auxiliary Society, they had not had a dull meeting. A returned missionary was present; and, as Jenny heard her tell about the poor heathen mothers and children, the tears filled her bright eyes, and she longed to help them. But what could she do ? She resolved to save all the money given her for candy : it cost her a great struggle, but when it was past, how happy she felt ! " O mother ! " she exclaimed, on the way home, " what a live meeting ! How much better than bug-ology and murder-ology ! " (referring to catching insects for the Natural-History class.) "Jesus was a real missionary, as the lady said ; and he came to seek and to save, that which was lost : I'll tell you my secret, mother dear, and don't you tell, till I'm ready. I'm going to start a mission-circle, and call it 'The Seek-and-Save Society.'" — "But where are the five dollars coming from ?" — "I shall give all my candy money, — that is one dollar a year. If I am not very big, my dollar's just as big as anybody's, and I can belong to a society !" So the dollar was put into the green mission-box.

The next day, at school recess, Jenny found time to interest the girls in missions. She was such a wide-awake little budget, and had so much heart in what she said, that she was the leaven of the school ; and one and another resolved to save their pennies for missions, instead of spending them for trifles.

Jenny enjoyed play ; but on Saturday morning, after breakfast, she said to her mother, "What am I to do all this long day ? I wish I could earn something for my mission-circle." — "I will hire you," replied Mrs. Worth. "If you will dust the parlor and library each day for a month, I will pay you a dollar !" The child's eyes sparkled with joy ; and, singing like a busy bee, she went to work. When the month came round, punctual to the day, she said to her mother in her lively way, "Now for my dollar !"

"Well done, Jenny : you have faithfully earned the money," was the cheerful reply, as she paid her the dollar, which was quickly put in the box. Thus the little maiden started her mission-circle through self-denial and willing labor, and was never so happy in spending for herself. Yes ; and if she is really a Christian, and continues faithful to the Saviour, and at last shall meet in heaven some little ones saved from serving idols through her means, how she will rejoice, and praise God !

E. C. P.

HARRY'S STRATAGEM.

BY MISS HELEN C. PEARSON.

"I can't afford it," John Hale the rich farmer answered, when asked to give to the cause of missions. Harry, his wide-awake grandson, was grieved and indignant.

"But the poor heathen," he replied : "is it not too bad they cannot have churches and schoolhouses and books ?"

"What do *you* know about the heathen ?" exclaimed the old man testily. "Would you wish me to give away my hard earnings? I tell you I cannot afford it!"

But Harry was well posted in missionary intelligence, and, day after day, puzzled his curly head with plans for extracting money for the noble cause from his unwilling relative. At last, seizing an opportunity when his grandfather was in good humor over the election news, he said, —

"Grandfather, if you do not feel able to give money to the Missionary Board, will you give a potato?"

"A potato !" ejaculated Mr. Hale, looking up from his paper.

"Yes, sir ; and land enough to plant it in, and what it produces for four years?"

"Oh, yes!" replied the unsuspecting grandparent, settling his glasses on his calculating nose in a way that showed he was glad to escape from the lad's persecution on such cheap terms.

Harry planted the potato, and it rewarded him the first year by producing thirteen; these, the following season, became a peck ; the next, seven and a half bushels; and, when the fourth harvest came, lo! the potato had increased to seventy bushels, and, when sold, the amount realized was with a glad heart put into the treasury of the Lord. Even the aged farmer exclaimed, —

" Why, I did not feel that donation in the least ! And, Harry, I've been thinking, that if there was a little missionary like you in every house, and each one got a potato, or something else as productive, for the cause, there would be quite a large sum gathered."

Little reader, will you be that missionary at home ?

———◆———

SUNDAY SCHOLARS IN INDIA.

BY A LIFE-MEMBER.

Yesterday I heard that you had sent me some money. How much I thank you ! It takes two months for a letter to come from America ; and, although I write at once, you must be kept waiting four long months to know that it is received.

Every Sunday morning you will see our church open, and boys with their teachers coming to service. One school, numbering fifteen, comes five miles ; another of eighteen, four miles ; and one of about twelve, three miles. Still another, very near us, numbers fifty boys. They recite verses from the Bible, and also about ten questions from a catechism called " Sweet Savour of Divine Truth," and from one entitled " Divine Milk ; " the boys asking each other the questions.

After the lessons have been recited, we give them a banana, or a kind of boiled rice beaten into flakes. Many of them come so far that they need food ; and that is why we give them a little fruit, or something which they can carry in their cloths. Then they repeat the Lord's prayer in concert, and are dismissed.

Our Sunday-school boys do not look much like those in America. Their hair is shaven from their heads, except a little lock upon the crown. A white cloth is tied around the waist, reaching to the knees. This is their only clothing. Now and then a boy has a jacket. They all have very bright eyes and very white teeth. They never can forget these Bible-verses, and lessons from the catechism ; and though their parents are heathen, we hope they will become Christians. Some will repeat from one hundred and thirty to one hundred and fifty verses, giving the chapter, &c., and many will recite a hundred. Do not forget our Sunday-school children in India !

MERCY-SEATS UNDER THE CACTUS-BUSHES.

Said the missionary's little daughter to her mamma, one evening, "It seems as if it was very easy for the school-girls to pray."

On being questioned, she added, "Sometimes I find G. under a bush, and sometimes R. and K. together ; and, oh ! any time now I may see a girl praying somewhere."

A young native Christian girl, who was undressing the children, said, "This *is* a nice place : there are so many bushes all about, that we can go any time and pray."

The missionary mother further remarks, "Outside our compound walls are many clumps of the prickly cactus ; and, the ground being somewhat undulating, I can easily see how our heavenly Father has made little 'mercy-seats' for my school-girls, whom I have so longed to lead to him with a simple confiding heart. It must delight the angels, who see an idol shrine under every clump of green trees, to look down upon my school-girls here and there, by the rough cactus, offering heart-incense, however unworthy, more fragrant than the perfumed sandalwood. It would be unspeakably sweet to me to look down from heaven upon them."

The Little Hindoo.

EMILY C. PEARSON.

I.

" I am a little Hindoo girl,
　Of Jesus never heard ;
Oh ! pity me, dear Christian child,
　And send to me his Word.
Oh ! pity me; for I have grief
　So great I cannot tell ;
And say if truly there's a heaven,
　Where such as me can dwell ? "

II.

That pleading voice was borne across
　The rolling ocean wide :
Forthwith the children, touched with love
　Of Him who bled and died,
Said, " Here's our money, little girl,
　To buy God's word for you :
We wish 'twere more, a thousand fold,
　And you should have it too !

III.

" We've heard of Jesus, and we know
　The way of life full well ;
' Let children come to me,' he says,
　' And they shall with me dwell.'
Ever with him ! with hearts renewed,
　And ' badness ' all forgiven ;
For He has said, who never fails,
　' Of such the realm of heaven.'

IV.

" We'll speed Christ's gospel o'er the earth
　To each dear child so sad.
If one soul saved gives angels joy
　How will all heaven be glad !
And if at last we reach the shore
　Where sorrow is unknown,
We hope to greet thee, Hindoo girl,
　Safe, safe before the throne."

LIFE AND LIGHT

FOR

Heathen Women.

VOL. I.	MARCH, 1870.	No. 5.

TALKS WITH HEATHEN WOMEN.

BY MRS. CAPRON.

I HAVE often wondered whether many of my American sisters comprehend the difficulties attending efforts to give the ignorant heathen women, even one clear idea of what it means to be saved through Christ. You have heard encouraging things: let me tell you of some that are discouraging.

There are a few pages in " The Cross in the Cell " which I have read many times. They refer to the great question, What shall I do to secure the salvation of these souls? The work seems still more difficult, when under the depression of the feeling, that perhaps this is the only opportunity they will ever have of hearing of a Saviour. The following scene is illustrative of many in a missionary's experience.

I had just turned the blinds of my window for a little shade and rest, on the noon of a hot day, when a voice outside called to me, " You must come out, if only a few minutes: don't refuse us. We have come on purpose to see you." There had been a large gathering of Mohammedans at some ceremonies at a celebrated tomb, for two days. The day previously, I had

13   145

been visited by a company of twenty-five women, and now another party had come.

Of course, I went out to see them. One glance showed that they were of a better class; and they seated themselves on the veranda, — forty-one women, besides girls and boys. Whatever motives of curiosity brought them, there was no wish to know of Jesus. What can I possibly do to turn even one soul towards salvation? Bear in mind the foreign tongue; the glare and heat; the imperative necessity of gaining such ascendency over them as to keep them quietly listening; the noisy children; the sudden thrust at you of a question that reddens your cheek; the cool survey of yourself, as if you were an idle show: and then pray for us who stand in your stead.

I wish to convey the idea, if possible, that Christ bore our sins, and was punished for us; and therefore we are saved. So I begin : —

"Whom do you like best, — those who try to please you, or those who don't care for you?"

"Those who like us," says the woman who wears a cloth with a palm-leaf figure. You very quickly detect the more intelligent as well as the more impudent of your audience.

"If you tell one of your children not to go to the bazaar, and he goes, what do you think?"

"I beat him," says the woman with a monstrous ring in her nose.

"We all like obedient and kind servants and children," I continue. "Now, try to understand me. These are my two children. I tell the little one that she must never go out of that gate ; and one day she goes."

"Why don't you make holes in their ears?" says a woman with a white cloth. Upon this, her neighbor punches her, and says, "You fool you, — don't you know you mustn't talk?" and she goes off into a berating speech, that taxes my patience more than the question itself. As soon as possible I continue :

"This little girl goes out, and disobeys me. What must I do?"

"No matter about it. She is only a little girl," says one. "Beat her if you are angry," says another. Alas! their ideas of obedience to parental authority are sadly at fault.

"Must I not punish her for disobedience?" I said.

"Make her afraid to go again," said a woman who was nursing a baby.

Just here, three women with very dirty cloths and tangled hair, who had been sitting on the edge of the group, yawned aloud, and stretched themselves out for a nap.

"I cannot allow that," I said: "it is quite too disrespectful. You can go, but you cannot stretch yourselves out on my veranda." Two sauntered away; and one sat up, and listlessly guided her finger up and down the seam of the mat.

Having disposed of this interruption, I make another attempt. "We were talking about punishing this dear little girl for disobedience. It must be done. There is no escape. I am very sorry, but my orders must be obeyed. Now, her sister's heart is full of love and grief; and it seems ready to break. She comes weeping to me, and says, 'O mamma! don't punish my dear little sister: if you punish me, will not that do?'"

The presence of these dear children added to the effect of my remarks; and many eyes were turned towards them, with exclamations such as, "Golden child! good child! lovely child! not one in a thousand would do that!"

"Yes," I continue, "that is just the way we all feel when we see such love. I punish her, and what does the little sister do, but look on with many tears; and after that, if she has some candy or some nuts"—

"Gives half," interrupted a dozen voices at once. Now we have secured complete attention. Can we think fast enough to give them one such view of Jesus' love, and the adoring, grateful love of a saved sinner, before the mind unused to thought is gone to the ends of the earth? Oh for a thousand tongues!

"Give half! yes, indeed : more than half, and even the whole, — will she not?"

"Yes," said the woman with the palm-leaf figured cloth : "she never will forget it." This is the woman whose eye I have kept from the first, and upon whom it seems as if the strength of my soul's desire had fallen. Looking at her, I ask, "Have you ever done any thing wrong?"

"Yes, indeed. How many lies I've told! We are all sinners."

"We are all sinners,— all liars," echo many voices.

"How very sad it all is!" I reply. "God has said that the one who commits one single sin can never enter his beautiful home, but must go to be punished."

Here two nicely-dressed women, who had shown not a little haughtiness, said to the others, "We have been here long enough : come, let us go."

Not discouraged at the general moving, so long as I had the eye of that woman with the palm-leaf figured cloth, I said, with an earnestness that arrested even the children, "And will He not keep his word? You can never escape from that punishment,— never. What do you think was done up there in the glorious courts above? God's Son said, 'Let me go to that world, and be punished in their place. They will love me and let me guide them, and I will bring them here to dwell forever.' So, when God's time had come, he came. Do you know his name?"

"Jesus Christ," said the woman with the palm-leaf figured cloth. The next instant, suddenly rising, she exclaimed, "He never came ; he *never* came, — *never*."

"No, he never came," said others, the best listeners, rising.

"How do you know that?" I quietly asked.

"We never saw him," said my excited friend.

" Have you a grandfather ? "

" To be sure," she replied ; " but I never saw him : he died when I was so high."

" Then you never had a grandfather."

" Why do you say so ? "

" Because you never saw him."

" But I've heard others tell about him ; " and, turning to the others, " what does she mean ? "

" This is what I mean : I never saw Jesus; but others who have seen him, and who knew him, have told many things about him, and I believe them. Whether you believe it or not, the great truth stands, — Jesus Christ came into the world to save sinners."

" He never came : never. I don't believe it. We are going. Salaam." .

The whole were on their feet in an excited hurry to be gone. Another word was out of the question.

So they went,— forty-one women, besides boys and girls. We may have very quiet and even pleasant talks with Mohammedans, so long as we confine ourselves to other topics than that of a crucified and risen Lord. But the first approach to the great central doctrine of the cross rouses their opposition ; and we find ourselves in a tumult, from which we are only too willing to escape.

MANA MADURA, INDIA, Sept. 6, 1869.

13*

CHINA.

TUNGCHOW.

THE following extracts of a letter from Mrs. CHAPIN, cannot fail to interest our readers : —

"I think I never was happier than yesterday. Twelve women present at the services, and not one listless or uninterested! I have never seen the truth take such hold, on hearing it for the first time.

AN EAGER LISTENER.

"One, named Chii, over seventy years of age, seemed full of wonder and delight, and, while listening, burst out: 'They are indeed all false, senseless gods, the work of our hands: never again will I do them reverence. Why! I have taken the garments from my back, to get incense to burn at the temples!' In the afternoon she went to the chapel, and gave fixed attention ; and, when particularly pleased, nodded her assent, and even spoke aloud. At night, I asked what she had learned on this first day: she promptly answered, 'That there is one only true God. I shall come to hear more of this new doctrine.'

VALUABLE ASSISTANT.

"In work and prayer, our dear Mary Andrews and I are one. I wish every mission station had such a one, for the sake of the missionaries, as well as the natives.

NEW BIBLE-READER.

"I obtained a Bible-reader by Mrs. Goodrich's going home. She has been with them as servant, and is a´ member of their church. I have long coveted her, but felt that, in Mrs. Goodrich's poor health, she had a mission there. In many respects she is well fitted for her work: loves to learn, and loves to teach ; has a winning manner ; is never out of humor ; and, being a Manchu, has large feet, and so can take long walks. Directly after morning prayers, I spend an hour with her, study· ing the Scriptures. She seems to prize this opportunity, and asks many questions. She goes the rest of the day, and studies faithfully in the evening. Her heart is in the work. She does not force herself upon any one, but goes when invited, and often comes home with her face glowing, to tell of new places opened. She prays much.

[The W. B. M. have assumed the support of this Bible-reader.]

THE MOTHERS' PRAYER-MEETING.

"We have a mothers' prayer-meeting once a week, and they have become very precious seasons. The Christian women all pray, and the petitions for their families are simple and earnest. Last week, Miss Andrews read the story of the crucifixion; and we tried to make them feel that scene was for each. One woman had in her prayer, 'You died, we live!' It was the most solemn meeting we have had; and I felt, on coming out, that no circumstances which at present exist could send me to America."

FOUCHOW.

Extracts from a letter by Miss PAYSON : —

LEAVE-TAKING.

"Our school had a vacation in July, lasting until the first of September. The pupils came to bid me adieu; but the leave- taking was quite formal, as I could only say, 'Walk slowly,' which is synonymous with our 'Good-by;' and could neither shake hands nor kiss them, because it is not the custom here. In return, they desired me to 'seat myself,'— the most polite form of leave-taking on the part of the visitor. I had learned to say, 'Pray every day,' and was glad to show my interest in their spiritual welfare, even in so simple a manner. We hope the heathen homes to which most went heard much gospel truth from their lips. They sing sixty or seventy hymns, without books; and, doubtless, many strains precious with Jesus' name fall on ears unused to such utterances. We long for the conversion of these girls: they might exert such an influence for Christ in their vacations.

STRANGE CUSTOMS.

" Chinese houses are often far from inviting. In one, where a woman sat sewing near the door, we saw fourteen small black pigs sleeping on the floor near her. Air-tight coffins, containing the bodies of friends who have been dead six or eight years, often stand in the family room; as keeping them thus is an act of great respect to the departed.

E-PO.

"We rarely pass the door of E-Po, one of our most exemplary church-members, without looking in for a moment. She is a little woman, over sixty years old, and her name, E-Po, means simply 'old lady,' it being universally applied to respectable women of her age. She became interested in the truth by hearing singing at family prayers in the missionaries' houses, and was received into the church two or three years since. Every morning, unless ill, she is at school-prayers; and, though she reads but little, has a hymn-book, and sings on her own key, with great earnestness. Kiu Kok, one of the scholars, goes daily to her house, and teaches her to read the Bible. Not long since, being sick, and partially deranged, she would not permit her heathen neighbors to wait upon her, but was delighted when members of our school called, saying, 'These are God's people: they are good.'

E-PO'S HOME.

" Her home is a room eight feet square; and the rent, three dollars a year, is quite reasonable. The floor is of hard earth; a rude bedstead stands in a corner, and near it the large smoky furnace for boiling rice and frying fish; a table, two or three bamboo stools, a rack for rice-bowls and chop-sticks; while clothing, boxes, pails, jars, and baskets so fill up the rest of the apartment, that there is barely space for two persons to turn round. But here dwell the wife, husband, and a young man, an adopted son. Above, loose boards indicate a sort of loft, — the lodging-room of the youth. The husband often treats his wife very unkindly; and, either from laziness or inability to obtain work, she is barely kept from want. We praise God that his light has entered E-Po's abode, and that some day the gates of heaven may open for her admission. The darker the night, the brighter, surely, will seem the dawn.

THE LONELY WIDOW.

"Another E-Po, a widow, has more of this world's goods than the former. Her room has a floor of boards, and contains painted furniture. Its contents, however, are quite as miscellaneous as those of the other; a dozen or more baskets hung from the roof constantly coming in contact with our heads. A married son, with his wife, dwells in the same room, taking down an extra bedstead every morning, and setting it up at night. The daughter-in-law, about seventeen years of age, with a bright, pleasant face, came in while we were calling, having finished her day's work of assorting skins. She told us that her wages for ten hours or more of daily labor were not quite three cents. The elder woman seems interested in hearing the gospel. She once asked Mrs. Baldwin to give her son, who can read, a book from which he might learn filial respect, as he was not dutiful. She had been left a widow twice; and, as she sits alone sewing, the tears often roll down her cheeks. With so few comforts here, and no light for the hereafter, it is no wonder that she sometimes weeps.

SEED-SOWING.

" These are not harvest-times: many days of patient broadcasting of seed must come first. Comparatively few women have embraced the truth, though some are earnest, sincere inquirers. Mr. Hartwell baptized one lately, at an out-station, whose husband greatly persecuted her on account of her faith. He even followed her to church, one Sabbath morning, cursing and threatening her while at worship. But she paid no attention, and came in the afternoon as usual. There are a few women interested in Mr. Woodin's field, so we are not without hope. Pray that the harvest-time come quickly."

TURKEY.

THE PRIEST'S GRAND-DAUGHTER.

BY MISS MYRA PROCTOR.

[Our readers will be glad to learn that Miss Proctor reached Aintab Oct. 25, 1869. We are happy to give the following narrative from her pen: —]

"Sister Varteni has fallen from a ladder and injured herself," reported a native friend one day; and, in great fear lest we were to lose this faithful mother in Israel, I went at once to see her. She was unable to walk, and suffering severely from the casualty; but, as usual, looking on the bright side.

" I was needing something," she said; " for I had not had any sickness or pain for a long time, and was forgetting to sympathize with the feeble. True, the flesh is weak, and I cannot bear pain very well; but it is good for me, and with pain God gives comfort to his children."

As I sat with her one evening during her illness, she told me many incidents of her early life. She was the grand-daughter of a priest, who taught her to read when a child. In fact, when the missionaries first went to Aintab, in 1848, she was the only Armenian woman who could read intelligently. When about fourteen, Varteni was taken sick, and was wholly confined to her bed for three years. "But it was a blessed thing," said she; "for then God made known to me his power. Every one who called upon me would shake her head, and say, — perhaps thoughtlessly, and without any true faith in God, — 'This is from God;' but the expression, so often repeated, set me to thinking. Before this I had thought myself strong; but now I saw I was weak, and felt that God alone was powerful. My father spent a great deal for physicians, but they could not help me. I began to cry to God, — '*Ya Rabb sen pek koovveth imish sin,*'— ' O Lord, thou art very powerful, they say ; help me : if it be thy will, raise me up to health again.' There were a few cases of plague in the city, and I was taken with it. My friends thought that surely now my hour was come. Seven buboes appeared, but passed away lightly, and with them my former disease ; and I arose up healthy. I felt that God had heard my prayer; and ever after I kept the idea of his great might in my mind. I felt a friendship towards him, loved him. I did not understand about Jesus, or know the way of salvation perfectly. I learned that afterwards from the gospel, but never lost the idea of God's strength; and, when I sinned, I felt that I had a great Saviour."

I asked her what she did for her soul's welfare before she heard the gospel. She replied that she carefully kept all the rules of her church, strictly observing the fasts, and attending to the sacraments and prayers. She was not one of the very first converts ; but when her mind did perceive the idea of a Saviour's dying love, and the way of salvation through him, her heart laid hold upon it with a clinging and unyielding grasp. Her husband soon manifested his enmity, and forbade her attending the Protestant services. "I shall obey you," she replied; "but do not think you will thus lead me to forsake this new way. I've found the truth, and shall abide by it!" His opposition gradually ceased; and years afterwards, in answer to the prayers of his faithful wife, he, too, was rejoicing in the light.

Of her manifold labors for her people, I can give but the merest outline. She was a seamstress, with her home full of little sewing-girls. These she taught to read, toiling until late in the evening to make up the lost time. Many a half-day she laid aside her work to go from house to house, and read the Scriptures to those who would not attend church. Her kind, motherly ways usually secured the respectful attention of those whom she addressed; but I never saw her face brighter than when we were one day driven angrily away from an Armenian house. She rejoiced that she was counted worthy to suffer even this bit of persecution for Christ's sake. With no monthly wages, and no ceremony of laying-on of hands, she was yet a most efficient Bible-reader and an excellent deaconess. Latterly she has sometimes been employed by the church in Oorfa as their teacher and Bible-reader.

She is now about sixty-five. She will not long be a life-member of your Society; but I rejoice that her name is to be recorded on your list. How often in this life is the promise fulfilled, "He that soweth and he that reapeth shall rejoice together"!

HARPOOT SEMINARY.

In a recent letter, Mrs. Wheeler gives an interesting account of the examination of the Harpoot Female Seminary:—

"All of the twenty-two graduates were married except one. They did themselves honor in all the studies except arithmetic. In astronomy, geography, and Bible, they would be a credit to any school; and the compositions were as good as Holyoke girls write. We heard essays from those who had been in the seminary but two years, that would not have disgraced a theological student. One, entitled 'The Education of Women,' by Asneev, a woman from Bitlis, was interesting enough to be published. The following topics were discussed : 'Should the ministry be rich?' 'Should the theological student be a married man?' 'We are to preach the gospel to our own nation' and the negative, 'Go ye into all the world, and preach the gospel to every creature.' One of the class read an essay on, 'How shall we improve our nation?' When asked if she wrote it herself, she replied, 'I have spent all my spare time for six weeks upon it, often working till midnight.' She is a wife, and has a little babe to care for. But her patience and toil were rewarded by the high position given to her composition. Dear Mrs. B., I wished you were present when this class received their diplomas! It was easy to love such neat, interesting young ladies. Most are earnest Christians; and their teachers have hope that all are renewed. We believe they go forth to be bright lights among their dark sisters. We can train them in our seminary, but they can do more than we in the homes of this land. We are foreigners, but they can get close to the hearts of their sisters. We hope they will soon be able to take all this work, and we be free to go to darker regions beyond."

BITLIS.

Miss Mary A. C. Ely, giving some account of her labors among the women, says, "The privilege of working for souls is more and more delightful and encouraging, especially as we see so much need of labor, and such precious results.

MODE OF INSTRUCTION.

"The manner of giving instruction differs widely from methods adopted in our own country. A few examples will illustrate this. An old lady, physically unable to learn to read, with tears

14

streaming down her cheeks, inquired, 'Can a person be saved who does not know how to read?' To the reply, 'You can, if you believe in Christ,' she said, 'Who does not? We all believe in Christ; but I don't think we shall all be saved.' I answered, 'If you believe in him, you will love him, and try not to sin, and ask him to help you; but if you do not try to stop sinning, though you pray, he will not help you; for he will see that you love sin better than his favor.' Another asked, 'I have no money to put into the Lord's treasury: cannot I fast one day in the week instead?' I replied, 'If, to advance the Lord's work, you would rather give one day's allowance of food than to eat it yourself, do so; but do not think that going hungry will atone for your sins: Jesus has done that.' It is such a reward to have them say, as they often do, "Oh! I see it so differently! A window of light has been opened to me!"

PERSIA.

THE following from Mrs. Sarah J. Shedd of Oroomiah gives a graphic idea of missionary effort among the women : —

MOTHER MARY.

"One day, an aged woman came tottering in, pressing her way to my side through a group of younger women, who laughed heartlessly as they heard her begging for medicine. 'Her disease is old age,' sneered one. The poor, trembling creature sat on the ground close beside me, and told all her ills. I asked if she could not go to the warm sulphur-springs of Oroomiah. 'In the waters of Oroomiah is there healing for me? My son is dead.' The sad tones went to my heart; and I told her of the fountain opened on Calvary, where all might come and find healing 'without money and without price.' She could not understand. I asked, ' Who died for you ? ' — ' Nobody,' was the prompt reply: after a moment's thought, she said, ' Mother Mary.' Recounting her prayers to the Virgin, her fasts and works of merit, she added, ' What more can I do? ' In vain I labored to show her Christ the Saviour; her hope was in fasts and ' Mother Mary.'

BLIND GULY.

" An old blind woman, who lives in the churchyard, called. For thirty years she has been a regular attendant on the morning and evening worship, until she understands the services in the ancient Armenian, and has become familiar with the Bible. She professed to believe in Christ only, and to look to him for salvation ; and seemed to feel deeply her own unworthiness. I cannot but hope that poor blind Guly is one of Christ's chosen ones, whom he is calling out of darkness into his marvellous light.

MOSLEM LADIES.

" Sabbath morning, a company of Moslem ladies walked in. After the usual compliments, I remarked that our custom was to spend the Sabbath in studying God's word ; and, if they desired, instead of the usual refreshment, we would read to them. They were much pleased, and begged us to do so. Dea. Eshoo read and explained the story of Lazarus, and clearly showed Christ the way of life. They heard with interest, and said, ' If our Mullahe would only read to us in this way, how gladly we would listen ! ' Another group listened eagerly to the parable of the unjust judge. One woman seemed thoughtful and intelligent ; and I was deeply interested as the good deacon led her step by step, until she acknowledged herself a sinner in need of a Saviour, and then pointed her to Christ. Another poured out her sad story of bereavement to me. Her husband and children were dead, and she was left with no comfort. As Nazloo read to her of Lazarus, and Jesus weeping, she exclaimed, ' You must read to me every day from that book. That will comfort me ! '

" Two poor Jewish women called ; and, when I spoke of Jesus, I could but shudder at the bitter scorn and hatred exhibited by one, as she replied, ' Who is Jesus? He belongs to Armenians.' Two others showed a different spirit. I asked them the meaning of the blood which I had seen over their doorways ; and, as they told of their sacrifices, I pointed them to the Lamb slain from the foundation of the world. Quite excited, the elder repeated to her companion, ' Hear! she says the blood means the blood of Christ ! ' They were especially interested to learn, that they might pray. A Saviour who stooped to women and children was a new and welcome idea to their darkened minds. When we visited the Jewish synagogue, the women gathered around, pleased to hear that we received their Holy Book. As the sacred roll was carried about the room, receiving the adoration of the men and boys, the females — who were in a small gallery looking on — said to me, ' Do you do so to the Testament ? ' and were really puzzled by the reply, ' We worship God, and not a book.' My heart aches for them ! I have never seen any class so ignorant and neglected, and yet so susceptible to kindness. In a conversation with their chief rabbi in his house, I tried to show, that, by educating and elevating their women, they would prevent so many from becoming Moslems. He admitted it, but was careful that his wife and handsome black-eyed daughter should not hear.

AN ARMENIAN BRIDE.

" In our social meeting, before the Lord's Supper, Hanna, a girl from Miss Rice's Seminary, now the wife of a wealthy Armenian merchant, told us of the opportunities which she found to speak for Jesus, even in the seclusion in which an Armenian bride is kept. Through her influence, a little school for girls was started, which she visited every Saturday afternoon, teaching the children to sing, and reading the Testament. The priest soon scented heresy, and broke up the school; but the little pupils — now grown to maidenhood — retain their love for Hanna; and often, as she sits in a dark corner of the retired gallery appropriated to young women in Armenian churches, these girls seek her, and she reads and prays with them. The wives of wealthy Armenians meet often at each other's houses, on the Sabbath, to feast and drink wine. It is now well understood that Hanna will not join her companions; but recently some have desired to learn more of the Bible, and send for her to come and read to them."

APPEAL FOR PERSIA.

WRITTEN FOR THE ANNUAL MEETING.

MRS. WINSLOW says, "Eight hundred ladies were present at the last annual meeting."

Eight hundred ladies !

It is a privilege for a moment to have your sixteen hundred ears ! Perhaps each one of your hearts thrills now and throbs in perfect unison with the living, beating heart of Christ. Ye are the members, he is the Head. Eight hundred ladies ! each one as true and loving, as capable of self-sacrificing and faithful devotion, *till, through,* and *beyond* death, as any Mary in the Bible ! Each one has brought here an alabaster box of very precious ointment. Her own heart is a casket of inestimable value; and as, with eager love, she presses up to the nail-pierced feet to-day, to anoint them with her richest offerings, a fragrance exquisite and overpowering fills the house. He will accept and approve it all, though some may complain and murmur, "Why this waste ?" Even women and children in this land, as well as "wise men from the East," may "come into the house and

14*

fall down and worship him, and open their treasures, and present unto him gifts, — gold and frankincense and myrrh."

You eight hundred ladies are favored women. You had your birth in a gospel land, and only therefore are you ladies! What if you had been born in Persia! Your very birth would have been a calamity, and awakened commiseration. Your unhappy mother would have received condolence, instead of congratulation, that you were "only a girl." You would have grown up despised for your sex, ignorant, neglected, taught only your inferiority, your equality with the beasts of burden that perish; that you were only created for hard work, and to minister servilely to man. Your own children might have beaten and reviled you. Your spirit would have been broken to grovelling in the sphere assigned you, or rebelled against it with futile rage and all the wild and fiendish wrath and ill-temper of a loud, ungovernable woman, who is the most depraved and disagreeable object in God's universe.

You rejoice that my hideous picture is not your photograph! Why is it not? Because Christ died, and you have the benefits of his salvation: only this. Oh! be willing to disperse abroad the streams that flow from this living fountain. Let others drink as you have drank. Send to Persia, for our dark sisters there, from your excess, the blessings that so especially exalt women! It is your work, *eight hundred ladies*. It is appropriate. It is feminine. It is benevolent. It is *imperative*. Do it for Persia, do it for Christ. If my missionary sister and true yoke-fellow, Miss Rice, is with you, she can tell you, as few living (after twenty-two years' experience in arduous labor), how the work is done. Listen to her: let her charm you by her stories, which are eloquent because they are true.

May Jesus the beloved Master come up to your feast!

Yours in the labor and consecration of the gospel,

SARAH J. RHEA.

KNOXVILLE, TENN., Dec. 30, 1869.

The Master Calleth.

BY EMILY C. PEARSON.

LISTEN ! 'tis a voice from heaven :
" In my vineyard work to-day."
Christian, if thou lov'st thy Saviour,
Willingly thou wilt obey.
        He is saying,
" In my vineyard work to-day."

There is work for all who love him.
Nations perish still for light :
If thou canst not bear his message,
Send forth others with thy mite.
        Strive to rescue
All who grope in pagan night.

Said God's angel, " Curse ye, Meroz,
Curse that people bitterly." *
Lest a doom like this befall us,
Let us Christ's co-workers be :
        Ever praying
Sinners lost from wrath to flee.

To God's help against the mighty,
Lingering Christian, onward speed !
None may falter in this warfare :
None may cease God's word to heed.
        Teach all nations :
Heathen tribes to Jesus lead.

Offer freely ! God bestoweth :
A glad giver loveth he.
So shall dwell in yon blest heaven
Souls redeemed because of thee !
        Win to Jesus
Stars to shine eternally.

* Judg. v. 23.

ANNUAL MEETING.

THE second annual meeting of the Woman's Board of Missions was held in Park-street Church, Jan. 4, at 10 A.M. The meeting was called to order by the president, Mrs. Albert Bowker, and the exercises opened by singing

> " Praise God from whom all blessings flow,"

followed by the reading of a portion of Deborah's song of praise, found in Judges v., as an appropriate model of thanksgiving. As Deborah uplifted heart and voice to the Lord, who had gone before Israel working wonders for them, and moving the people to offer themselves willingly at need, so, it was suggested, had we like occasion for like thanksgiving. Prayer was offered by Mrs. Dr. Anderson, followed by singing

> " Songs of praise and glad thanksgiving
> Fill our hearts with one accord."

Allusion was made to the bereavements the board had sustained in the loss of two valued members, — Mrs. Pease and Mrs. Hubbard; and to the affliction of our recording secretary, Mrs. J. A. Copp, in the death of her husband. But we were assured, as from her own lips, that, although absent in body in a distant city, in spirit she was present with us.

ANNUAL REPORT.

The annual report was submitted by the secretary *pro tem.* The prosperous condition of the society was manifested in the fact, that the receipts for the year had reached fourteen thousand dollars, where ten thousand was scarce expected ; and that the Society are now supporting thirty-two missionaries and Bible-readers in Turkey, India, Syria, China, and Africa.

The appropriation of three thousand dollars to found a " Home " in Constantinople, for the single ladies who are to labor for the women of that city, received mention ; also that the Society has within the year found a local home in the Mission House, No. 33, Pemberton Square, where communications may !.e received, and inquiries answered with reference to the work ; and from whence is issued our periodical, entitled " Life and Light for Heathen Women." This little quarterly, having for its object the diffusion of missionary intelligence among our auxiliaries, although less than a year old, has already reached a large circulation.

TREASURER'S REPORT.

Indicated receipts, from donations, subscriptions,
and life memberships . . . $13,153.87
For quarterlies 847.74

Mrs. George Gould, one of the corresponding secretaries, then read very interesting extracts from the letters of several missionaries ; two of which, Mrs. Capron's and Mrs. Wheeler's, we publish in this number.

MORAL MAP.

A very beautiful map of the two hemispheres, drawn and painted for the use of the Board of Missions by Mrs. Miron Winslow, one of the corresponding secretaries, hung in full view of the audience, on which was plainly delineated the moral condition and religious aspect of the world, by the use of appropriately distinguishing colors, to which Mrs. Winslow thus directed attention : [A reduced form of this is given in this number].

" Let us look at the eastern hemisphere : Asia is buried in the night of heathenism and Mohammedanism. Africa about equally divided between the same ; Southern Europe is Roman Catholic; Eastern Europe is Greek Church, which also extends into Northern Asia ; a sadly small portion of Northern Europe is Prot-

estant.   Turning to the western hemisphere, how large a portion
of it we find still under the darkness of superstition ! while the
United States seems like a sun to scatter the moral darkness of
the world.   For this, God has opened the gates of mighty em-
pires that had been shut during long ages.   Two and a half
centuries since, and our New World was entirely in darkness :
now the descendants of the Pilgrims are standard-bearers of the
cross to all the benighted nations of the world.   Paralyzed by
the long lethargy that has come down through many generations,
they know not that a bright path of hope may be open to them,
until they see the light.   To bear this to them is our privilege ;
and who that has been eye-witness to the deep degradation of
our sex in heathen lands, — that has seen the highest and lowest
type of womanhood side by side, and realized the broad moral
gulf that lay between, — but would blush at our insensibility to
the great needs of mothers and children, numbering four hundred
millions, — tenfold the population of these United States."

Here is work for woman , and responsibility rests upon us
individually.

For the advance upon our feeble beginnings, we render heartfelt thanks to God.   Though cheered by progress, we call this
but the day of "small things;" for we have but begun to awake
to our duties and privileges.   Renewing our strength in the Lord,
can we not do more, that we may no longer hear the question so
often repeated, "If Christians have for so many years enjoyed the
blessings of the gospel, why have we been so long left in darkness? and why are not more teachers sent to enlighten us?"
Shall we not be stimulated to renew our efforts? and though the
shadows now so widely overspread the earth, and the enemy
presents a gigantic front, shall we not take. fresh courage, in
striving to fulfil that last command, "Go teach all nations,"
sustained by the animating promise, "Lo, I am with you alway"?
Thus may we hasten on the day when the kingdoms of this
world shall become the kingdoms of our Lord and of his Christ.

CHOICE OF OFFICERS.

A nominating committee was chosen to prepare a list of officers for the coming year; and, during its absence, a hymn entitled "The Master calleth," composed by Mrs. Emily C. Pearson, was sung by the audience. On the return of the committee, the old board was re-elected.

A DAY'S TOUR.

Miss Rice of Oroomiah was then introduced as the co-laborer for eleven years of the sainted Fidelia Fiske, and for eleven years her successor. Her very presence an inspiration to effort in the missionary work, her remarks were received with exceeding pleasure and attention. Many an eye filled with grateful tears at being privileged to look upon one who had so long borne the mantle of devoted missionary service; and in spirit the entire audience leaped the bounds of sense and space, and walked with her the familiar streets of her Persian home, or accompanied the Bible-reader on her village tour, breaking bread, sitting in the house of mourning, or listening to the well-known words of holy writ with those upon whom the glory of the Lord in Christ Jesus has but just arisen. The morning session was then closed with the Doxology.

COLLATION.

An ample and generous collation was served in the vestries of the church to the large audience, numbering from one thousand to twelve hundred; and opportunity offered for the interchange of friendly greetings between delegates, missionaries, and members.

AFTERNOON SESSION.

At 2 P.M. the meeting was again called to order by the president, and a solo and chorus was very pleasantly rendered by a large choir of children under the direction of Miss Addie Lovejoy.

REPORTS OF AUXILIARIES.

After prayer, the audience listened to an interesting report of the Fall-River auxiliary, presented by Miss Borden, who was followed by Mrs. Brackett of Jamaica Plain, Mrs. Pierson of Andover, Mrs. Page of Rutland, Vt., and Mrs. Johnson of Walpole. Many other auxiliaries were also represented by delegates. By request, the constitution was then read, to satisfy the inquiries of some present who desired to form auxiliaries. A half-hour was devoted to exercises by the children, introduced to interest mothers to form mission-circles among the young.

THANK-OFFERINGS.

At the close of the morning session, ladies intending to make contributions were advised to enclose them in envelopes provided, and forward them to the Treasurer. Mrs. Bartlett was thus enabled to report the receipt of several hundreds of dollars during the progress of the meeting.

MRS. SNOW'S ADDRESS.

Mrs. Snow of Micronesia was then presented. She unfolded, somewhat at length, the degradation of her people when she was first called to labor among them; who, though remarkable for delicacy and refinement of feeling in some particulars, were most degraded and fallen in others. Since their knowledge of the sacrifice of Christ, a similar spirit has been begotten in many of them, as illustrated in the words of a chief, when questioned as to his willingness to part with his instructor, a native preacher. "We have had the light: let Kanoah go." About to return home, she asked her people if they had any message to send to Christians in her native land. The reply was, "Yes, we want to send our love to all the Christians in America. We never expect to see them on earth, but shall meet them in our Father's house on high." She alluded to the children on Strong's Island, and made an appeal to children here.

Mrs. Dr. Anderson was next introduced, whose words of counsel and appeal commended themselves to us as eminently practical. She spoke as follows : —

"The missionary work has two aspects. We may look at it in a spiritual light, drawing us nearer to our Saviour in obeying his commands, and pray that the work may be hastened; or we may look at it in a business-light, which, if our motives are right, will be equally obeying his commands, and equally drawing us nearer to him.

"We cannot send the gospel to the heathen without money; and we cannot get the money without organization and personal effort. Even in these seemingly worldly duties, let us look at the example of our Saviour. When he was on earth, he performed many works which seemed worldly. But how did he do them? As the works which his Father had given him to do. He fed the five thousand, and purged the temple in the same spirit as when he fasted and prayed. He undertook the salvation of the world, and with it assumed all the life-duties and the humiliation involved therein. He never neglected or forgot any thing he had engaged to do. No case of healing, no word of instruction nor of comfort, was ever overlooked. He did all he had promised to do, suffered all that was appointed for him, until he could say, 'It is finished;' and then he died. He opened the way for the salvation of the world, and then left the work of making that salvation known to his people to us; and the time for us to be doing that work is now.

"What are we doing? Are we bearing this cause on our hearts, as Jesus bore it while here on earth? Or do we forget and neglect this work? Are not remarks often made like these? 'If I had thought of it, when I went into the country, I might have helped to form an Auxiliary Society;' 'If I had thought of it, when I met such a friend, I might have gained a subscriber to "Life and Light," or interested her in the cause of

15

missions;' or, 'When the sisters of our church came together, if we had thought of it, we might have devised some plan for increasing the usefulness of our society.'

"Jesus never forgot. He did not forget, though wearied, when sitting by the well, to tell the Samaritan woman of God, and how he should be worshipped; and shall we forget to send to heathen women the word of life? Jesus did not forget to say, for the comfort of all mothers to the end of time, 'Suffer little children to come unto me;' and shall we forget to send these comforting words to those who have so little comfort? Let us remember that we have a part of this work committed to us personally; and, if we neglect our part, it will remain undone. We have not merely to feel an interest in missions, and pray for the conversion of the world, but a practical part of the work to do. Perhaps you will ask, What can I do?

"There is work all around you. If there is no Auxiliary Society in your church, you can aid in forming one. If there is a society, you can increase its efficiency by gaining and imparting missionary intelligence, or by gaining subscribers to the 'Missionary Herald,' or to our quarterly, 'Life and Light.' Or you can interest the children, and lead them to form mission-circles, and enter upon duties of benevolence.

"But let no one enter upon this work merely from impulse. It is not like worldly business. If you would really work for Jesus, you must feel the worth of souls; you must come into sympathy with Jesus, and seek from him strength and wisdom, and love and zeal; then you will be a co-worker with him, and receive his blessing. And shall we not, this year, with more earnestness and perseverance, do all we can to send the gospel to heathen women?"

THE CONSECRATED DOLLARS.

The gold dollars, referred to in the December number of "Life and Light," were presented by the president to the audience, with the suggestion, that, should any lady or ladies desire to purchase them for twenty-five dollars each, or upwards, the sums thus contributed should be appropriated to the support of a Bible-reader in India, in connection with Mrs. Fairbanks.

They were taken ; and thus the prayer of her who formerly labored there, and who consecrated the first gold dollar to that work, has been visibly answered.

VOTE OF THANKS.

A vote of thanks was tendered by the corporation to the proprietors of Park-street Church, for their generosity in placing at our disposal their spacious and commodious edifice ; also to the ladies of the associated churches, who so kindly and amply provided the collation.

CLOSING EXERCISES.

Our president now assisted us to gather up the lessons suggested by the morning Scripture, urging a full consecration of all our powers to the great work committed to us ; and called us to remember, that, as in Deborah's time, various gifts were requisite for the work, so *now*, in ours, we need the daughters of Issachar to be our burden-bearers in the home department ; the daughters of Manasseh to root our auxiliaries and mission-bands ; the daughters of Ashur to :"offer willingly" gifts of gold and silver ; and the daughters of Zebulon " to handle the pen of the writer," in correspondence with our missionaries, in executing our maps, and contributing to our periodical.

We were told, also, to bear in mind the "heart-searchings" for the daughters of Reuben ; and that, while we should heed the feeblest bleating of the lambs of our flock, we should still see to it that no Deborah had cause to lament the neglect, at our hands, of God's work for our sex ; and, finally, that we also needed the daughters of Napthali to jeopardize, if necessary, their lives to the death, in foreign fields ; since

" That life is long that answers life's great end."

MRS. EDWIN WRIGHT, *Sec. pro tem.*

EARLY FRUIT.

An aged saint, whose eyes have long been sealed to earthly vision, but whose eye of faith is clear and bright as she nears the "promised land," upon hearing from her daughter an account of the last precious meeting of the Woman's Board of Missions, said, "I shall never attend a meeting, and probably shall not live to hear from another; but I should like to be a life-member : the money will be doing the Lord's work, whether I am here or not;" and, putting out her hand for the key to her treasury, her husband, sitting by, took out his pocket-book, saying, "Here is twenty-five dollars to make my wife a life-member, and twenty-five dollars to make my daughter a life-member;" which delightful New-Year's gift each sealed with the kiss of affection. And that daughter prays that the benevolent Christian heart of both parents may be her precious heir-loom.

. TREASURER'S REPORT.

BALANCE on hand Jan. 1, 1870 . . . $5,341.74
Receipts at annual meeting, and since, to Jan. 18, 1870, 2,102.80

$7,444.54

Appropriations since, to date, Jan. 18, for salaries
of additional missionaries, Bible-readers, and
support of schools $6,485.00

LABORERS NOW IN THE FIELD.

The Woman's Board now employs eighteen missionaries, and eighteen Bible-readers, and has assumed the support of the following schools : —

Mrs. Edwards's, among the Zulus.
Miss Norcross's, at Eski Zagra.
Miss Proctor's, at Aintab.
Miss Seymour's, at Harpoot.
Miss Parmelee's, at Mardin.

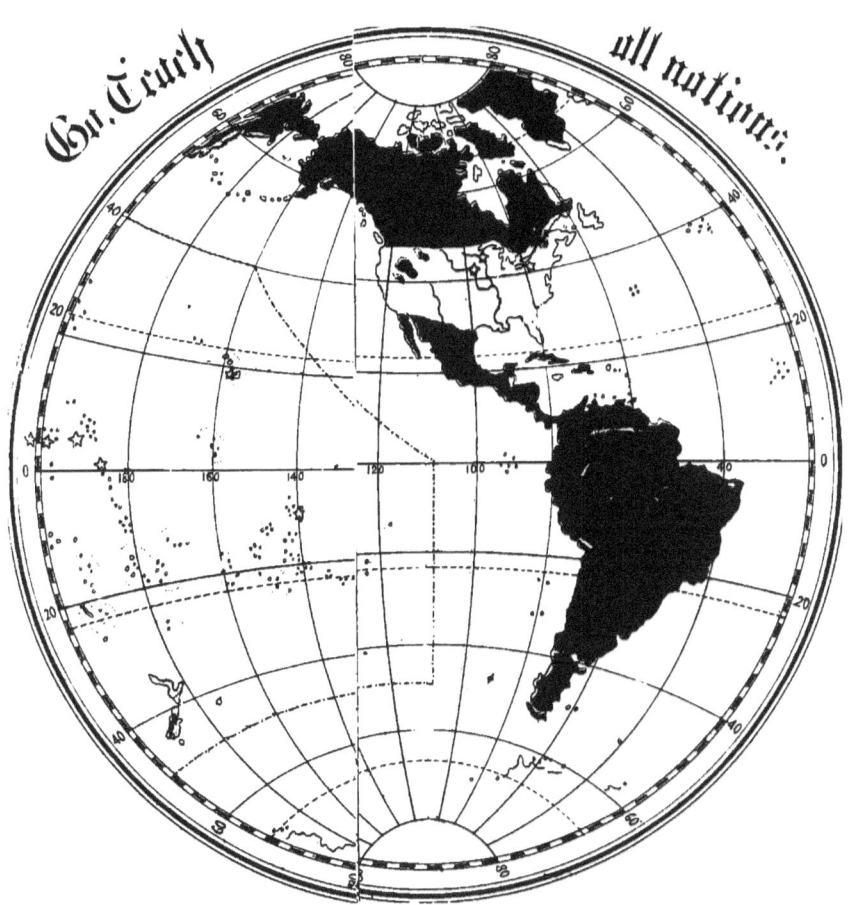

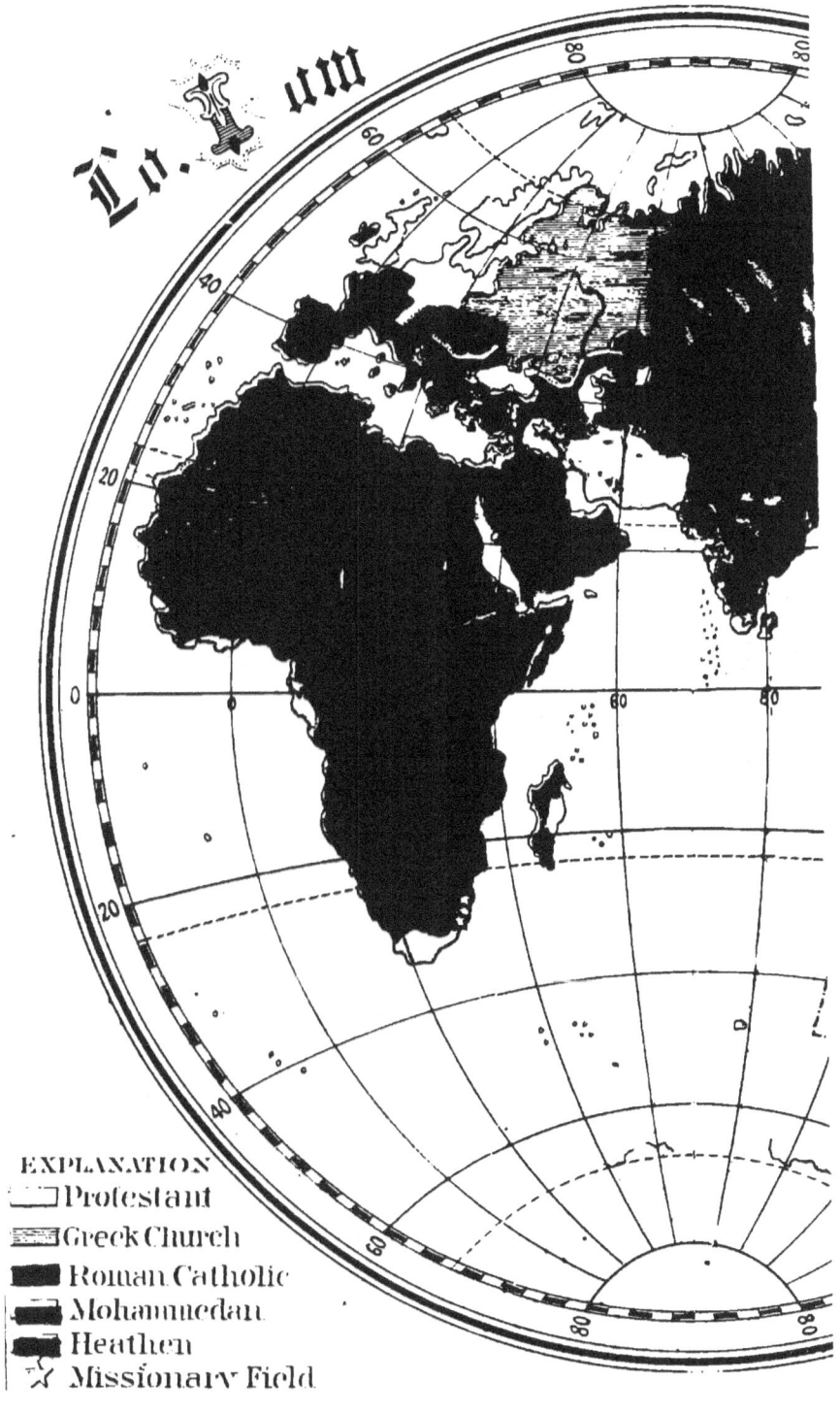

EXPLANATION
☐ Protestant
▤ Greek Church
■ Roman Catholic
▣ Mohammedan
▤ Heathen
☆ Missionary Field

Song of Praise.

BY MRS. EDWIN WRIGHT.

"Awake, awake, Deborah; awake, awake: utter a song."—JUDG. v. 12.

SONGS of praise and glad thanksgiving
　Fill our hearts with one accord,
For thy presence, wisdom, counsel,
　In the past, as now, our Lord.
With thy strength we have been girded:
　" Thou hast oped the two-leaved gate,
Loosed the loins of kings before us,
　Made the crooked places straight." *

Praise we bring for " willing offerings,"
　Warm from hearts thy love inspires ;
Praise that faith with mighty vision
　Bids us bring thee large desires.
Thou hast promised, thou hast promised,
　To thy well-beloved Son,
Heathen lands for his possession :
　Through us speed the victory on.

Lord, we plead new inspiration :
　Breathe upon us till we wake, —
Wake to yield in consecration
　All our powers for Jesus' sake.
Wake " to stretch out habitations," †
　" Lengthen cords," and "strengthen stakes,"
Till Christ's kingdom of the nations
　One unbroken household makes.

* Isa. xlv. 1, 2.　　　　　† Isa. liv. 2.
15*

Children's Corner.

CHILDREN'S EXERCISES.

My dear children, has it seemed very prosy to you to hear mother read about the great missionary meeting held lately in Park-street Church? And have you thought, "I'm glad I was not there; for I don't know any thing about business, and 'constitutions,' and '.practical needs,' and all those things"?

I don't blame you: I used to get sleepy myself over long words: but there was something that would have made you open your eyes, and drink in at your ears; and, if I tell you how it seemed to me, perhaps it will be the next best thing to having been there yourself. You see, it was impossible to invite all the little boys and girls who love missionary work, for they are scattered throughout our land, — here on the hillsides, there snugly nestled in the valleys, or almost lost amid the bustle and hurry of our big cities. Besides, there is Boreas, a rough old fellow, and his little shadow, Jack Frost, that are very apt to be abroad at this season of the year, nipping the fingers and biting the toes of the wee ones; so I think it will be altogether best that you should be satisfied with hearing about it.

Well, your mother will tell you that it was stated in the morning meeting, that, in the afternoon, there would be some *children's exercises*. Said I to myself, "Of course, children are always exercising, — hopping up and sitting down, twisting on one foot and then on the other; but that can't be what they mean;" and so, you see, I was all alive with curiosity.

When the time came, the first thing I noticed, that appeared to have any thing to do with it, was a whole lot of little girls in the gallery in front of the organ. I should think there were fifty ; but such little bodies, that they seemed almost lost in its shadow. But before I had time to think much, happening to look down among the audience near the front of the church, my breath was almost taken away by seeing what looked like a real heathen child. How could she get there ? But there she was : and I guess she was a Mohammedan ; for she was entirely covered, head and all, with what looked to me like a white sheet folded about her, with a little opening before the face. This opening was of very little use ; for a black veil, embroidered with fancy colors, hung over her face, so that not a single speck of it could be seen.

Perhaps I shouldn't have thought much about it : but I pitied her ; for she was lifting a corner of the veil, and fanning herself, as if almost suffocated. But again, before I could put two thoughts together, the organ commenced a prelude, and a sweet, youthful voice in the gallery sounded out loud and clear, —

" Over the ocean waves, far, far away,
There the poor heathen live, waiting for day."

And the other fifty little voices joined her, in

" Pity them, pity them, Christians at home :
Haste with the bread of life, hasten and come ; "

until I could almost have cried, to think of those dear children over the sea, that might die without ever having heard of our blessed Saviour. But, before I could get half-way back from those dark lands to which my thoughts had carried me, I heard something about a little Hindoo girl, and looked up to see a tiny, dark-haired mite, a truly Hindoo girl in appearance, — for she was dressed in a short, Turkey-red skirt and blue jacket,

with ample folds of the red disposed about her tiny person, —
and hear her say, —

> 'I am a little Hindoo girl,
>   Of Jesus never heard;"

and when, in most beseeching tones, she said, —

> "Oh! *pity* me, dear Christian child,
>   And send to me his word,"

away off again I went to the poor Hindoo's home, until recalled by
another musical voice, in sweetest answer of comfort; and the little
Christian and Hindoo disappeared among the crowd, just as children, here and there, are daily disappearing from the stage of life.

The next moment, I saw the heathen girl, of whom I told you
at first, representing a young woman going to mosque. As she
stood up, her tall figure enveloped in the long, white-cotton
cloak, with only small lattice-work squares for her eyes, and,
slightly throwing open the garment, disclosed the black veil,
while a missionary lady told us she might never uncover her entire face, even to her father, husband, or brother, I blessed God
that we might at all times be fanned by the sweet breeze, and
bathe in the clear sunlight of heaven.

Let us all ask Him to give us a part in putting away the veil
which covers their hearts, so that, at least, they may lift up un-
covered souls to Jesus who has died for them.

This young lady was not really a heathen, but the daughter
of a devoted missionary, and willing to wear the dress, that we
might see the outward difference between heathenism and Christianity. She permitted the white robe and the close veil to be removed, and then appeared in a bright-colored skirt and jacket,
with native jewels upon her arms, neck, and head, entirely covered and delicately draped with a richly embroidered white gauze,
which is never removed under any circumstances. Her head-
dress, which looked much like a red cap, thickly set up and down
the sides with silver coins, was originally worn by a heathen wo-

man; and we were told that often these coins had been removed to do missionary work for others more destitute than themselves. And now came three little children in Turkish costume, — a boy in tunic and pants of high-colored cloth, the little girls in the full dress and ornaments of Turkish children. Two of these children had buried their father in their foreign home, and often play "Turkey," as they call it, in memory of past days; and hope some time themselves to be missionaries of the cross.

Next in order was a dialogue, spoken by two girls, about the "promised land," and these very heathen countries that God promised his dear Son that he would give him as his own; and we were told that our dear Saviour expected us, big and little, to do the work, while he prepared our hearts and our way, and blessed our efforts; and when the little girls had come to the conclusion that "we are able to possess the promised land," the whole choir of children broke out into singing, —

"We are going, onward going,
    To possess the promised land;
Fearing not the hostile legions,
    Since we go at Christ's command.
We are able, *fully able,*" &c.

But oh! I forgot to tell you something that would have interested you very much; which was, that Mrs. Winslow, a dear missionary lady, repeated the "Lord's Prayer" in Tamil; and, although it sounded very funny to our ears, our hearts could pray it with those in far-off lands who love to call upon our Father through it. And you remember the sabbath-school song, "Joyfully, joyfully"? Mrs. Gould, another lady, who has also been a missionary, repeated this in the Arabic tongue, and so sweetly that it almost made music itself; and then our dear president kneeled down, and asked God to bless to our hearts all we had seen and heard, and to help us every one to desire very earnestly that the Holy Spirit would show us how to work, that Jesus' name might be glorified in all the nations under heaven; and as she prayed "Our Father who art in heaven," we all joined with her, asking aloud that "his kingdom might come, and his will be done on earth as it is in heaven."

And now I hope you will feel as if you wanted to be a missionary at home; and some time, perhaps, we will gather all the young missionary-workers and have a children's meeting all to ourselves.   *Secretary, pro tem.*

AN ARAB PHOTOGRAPH.

BY DR. JESSUP.

WOULD that I could frame some of these Arab children, and stand them up in the Children's Corner of your Quarterly, to be seen and prayed over by good Christian friends at home! Word has just come of new troubles and fiery trials in Safeeta, twelve hours north-east of Tripoli. A Greek mob attacked the houses of the Protestants, broke in the doors, and tried to force them to go *en masse* to worship the pictures in the Greek Church. Some of the men were forced to go: others fled. One little girl looked upon the mob with perfect coolness, and said, "Hew me in pieces if you wish; but I will not go one step." This dear child once went without her food all one Sunday, in order to keep God's day holy. Her mother told her, if she would not work on Sunday, she should not eat. So she went without eating.

WORKING CHILDREN IN INDIA.

In speaking of the school at Mandapasalie, South India, Rev. H. S. Taylor says, "All the children work around our yard every Saturday, and receive a quarter tutu (or cent) to put in the contribution-box sabbath-day. In this way they form the habit of giving. Last year, the sum thus raised went towards the support of the native catechist. This year, in addition, each has a little spot of ground to cultivate, the first fruits of which are to be given to the Lord." Little readers, cannot you do as much for Jesus as these children in heathen India?

A GOLDEN STAR.

BY MRS. MIRON WINSLOW.

WILL the dear children look at the map, which shows in how small a portion of the world the people have a true knowledge of their God and Saviour? Would it not be delightful to add a golden star, which represents a mission-field? The children of America once built a missionary ship which was the wonder and admiration of the heathen. Now, will you not support a school for the little ones who live in benighted Asia, Africa, China, or the islands far over the sea? How much could be done if all the children in New England would save their pennies for this object! They could look forward to something better than putting golden stars on the missionary map. They would be as angels of love to bear the story of Jesus to the little ones now in ignorance, and who, we hope, will become stars in our Saviour's crown.

CHILD-FAITH.

A MISSIONARY sister writes to her friends in America, —
" Our children are in perfect health. The *little one* has been praying to-night, since she got a thorn in her foot, through a rip in her little old shoe, 'that God would go all round, and get all the thorns, and carry them all to the place where he put the naughty angels when they made him so much tubble.' Her older sister said to her, ' You mustn't ask God to do so to the thorns : they are not souls, and they do just as God lets them, and God cannot punish them. It's not right to pray such a way.'
" Number two evidently felt the force of the argument; but, being naturally persistent, she was not disposed to yield, and

replied, ' I can tell God *any* tubble ; and, if he likes to help me, he may.' ' Except ye be converted, and become as little children, ye shall not enter into the kingdom of heaven.' ''

LITTLE E——'S EARNINGS.

THE following note was handed to the President during the morning session of the Annual Meeting. An enclosed gold dollar has been instrumental in forming a mission-circle : —

" After the meeting of last year, little E—— became interested in an account of the children earning pennies for the missionaries, and was delighted when told that he could do the same.

" This small sum — three dollars — was earned, when the Saviour called him to that better home, where many children from 'east and west, and north and south,' with 'voices sweetly blending, praise the heavenly King.' ''

PERAPEONE'S LETTER.

To my kind friends in America with humility I send this :

MY BELOVED BENEFACTORS, —Very thankful am I to you, that, by doing kindness, you have provided that I be able to read the Holy Book, and to learn about the loving Saviour, and what he did for leading us to heaven. While for me you provide, I beseech that for me you pray that the Holy Spirit change and renew my heart, that I become a good girl, and worthy of your kind remembrance. I a thing have not to send you ; only all the days of my life I will beseech the Saviour Jesus, that, as the reward to the one giving a cup of cold water is not lost, to you also there be a recompense.

I remain your humble girl,

PERAPEONE ENFIAZEAN.

LIFE AND LIGHT

FOR

𝕭eathen 𝖂omen.

| VOL. I. | JUNE, 1870. | No. 6. |

INDIA.

TALKS WITH CHRISTIAN WOMEN.

BY MRS. CAPRON.

I HAVE from fourteen to sixteen women at my weekly meeting, most of whom are Christians. We have been dwelling for several weeks on Christ's instructions to his disciples before he sent them out into the villages. There seemed to be many lessons applicable to our circumstances. I have been endeavoring to impress on these women that the work of reaching the hearts of their countrywomen belonged to them. At the close of one of these interviews, I said to them, "I have often told you of my visits to the women in this town, and asked you to pray for particular cases. I wish now to speak of some difficulties in my way, from which you are entirely free.

"In the first place, I must wait until five o'clock in the afternoon, on account of the sun. It is at this time that every woman begins to make preparations for the evening meal. You could go early in the afternoon, when they are comparatively free.

"Then, again, it is impossible for me to go quietly into any

house.   If I leave the bandy at a distance, I have a crowd, continually increasing, of boys and girls, who follow me to the very
doorsteps of the house I wish to enter.   If the people of the
house drive them away, there may be a few moments' quiet.   I
have sometimes thought that this crowd was allowed to remain
so as to shorten my visit.   Think how unobserved you could
enter, and how quietly and uninterruptedly you could speak of
Jesus!

" Supposing I happen to have secured a quiet spot, and, after a
few words of friendly inquiry about the family, I at once begin
to speak to the woman whom I have sought, about her total un-
readiness to die.   I have talked with her before.   She listens
attentively, and perhaps has asked some questions, when the
door suddenly opens, and two or three neighbors with children
come in, and the precious opportunity is lost.   She would not
venture to show such interest before them.   I can go on, and
talk to them all, to be sure; but the heart to heart work has
been hindered.   The whole neighborhood have heard of my
arrival, and I am soon like one preaching in a crowd.   I am
sure to be interrupted by questions about my dress and my
customs.   I am willing to talk to numbers together; but I am
convinced that it is you who should follow me with your warm
hearts, and consciousness of Jesus' presence with you, your
familiar dress, and their own language and yours.   It is you
who should seek the soul who is wishing, perhaps, she had such a
Saviour as yours, and yet who knows that her foes are those of
her own household."

This appeal reached every heart.   There were tears in some
eyes, and exclamations of "How true!"   "It is just so!"

I did not ask for any promises to daily duty of this kind, lest
there be a temptation to do what would please me; but I hoped
for good results.

The week following, I was going on as usual with the Bible-
lesson, but was asked if I would listen for a few moments.

"I have thought," said one of the older women, "much about what you said last week. It is a great blessing to us to have such instruction as you give. I never think, when you are talking to us of your different ways, and I never thought before as I do now, that it was not the same when you talk to the heathen women. We have received freely, we ought to freely give. Last week, that old woman who sells ghee, and her daughter-in-law, were passing; and I walked along a little with them, and said, —

" ' We ought to thank the great God above for such a world as this, and try to please him. He is a Father, and we are his children.'

" 'Are we all one caste, then?' said the daughter-in-law. ' What caste are you?'

" I replied that I was not going to talk about that; she knew very well what caste I was : but that I had been thinking about this old woman whose hair was white, and what would become of her when she died, if she never sought God while she lived.

" The old woman then gave me a very pleasant smile, and said, ' The stone idols are our emblems of God, and books are yours. All you Christians make homage to books. If anybody joins the Christian religion, they have to have books. Books for you, and stone idols for us : that's all the difference ! '

" I tried to tell her that we did not worship books, but only got knowledge from them. They were like letters full of news. God's Book was what told us all about himself and heaven, and what our eyes could not see. The most important part of our life was what could not be seen, only felt.

" The women both replied, ' You talk wisely and kindly : your way is good for you, and we must stay by the old way.' I had kept them waiting under the tulip-tree ; and so I said they might go on, but that, the next time they came along, I should talk with them some more. I should be very glad to see that old woman alone. I would have her know Jesus as a friend. I can pray for her."

Tears showed her earnestness of purpose. This woman also spoke of another visit. At my left sat one of our youngest Christians. Her happy face is always a beam of sunlight. She drinks in truth at these meetings, and was evidently much impressed by my appeal the week before. She also had a word to say : —

" I have thought about what you said, and have tried to say something to the women who bring wood ; but they are always in a hurry. One morning, I suddenly remembered that a woman lived next door, who knew little about Jesus, though a Romanist; and I walked right into her house, and said to her, —

" ' Do you suppose you are ready to die ? '

" She replied, ' You only are learned, and know about these things. I am ignorant. How can I know ? '

" Then I felt ashamed that I had not told her all that I knew. If we should think more about saving souls, we should find many to save, I think."

The effect of these remarks on the others was plainly seen. There was a current of feeling like courage and hope, like a consciousness of personal responsibility, like a joyful earnestness to serve a Master who never overlooks work done for him.

The preaching on the Sabbath has all been in this direction ; and it is in the personal, active service of our native Christians that my hope for success lies.

LETTER FROM MISS SMITH.

WE have been cheered by the intelligence that Miss Rosa A. Smith of Madura is convalescing. She writes from Pulney Hills, where she had gone to gain strength, and speaks gratefully of the unremitting attentions of Dr. Palmer in her severe illness : —

" While all were anxiously watching the approach of death, Dr. Palmer again asked wisdom from above to select something that should turn the feeble current of life : his eye fell upon a powerful medicine that had not been used; he tremblingly administered it; the Lord blessed the means, and my life was saved! Mr. and Mrs. Chandler cared most tenderly for me, anticipating every want; and native brethren and sisters came from distant stations with ready sympathy and aid. The English residents were very kind, supplying me with ice, which was indispensable, but could not have been otherwise obtained." While intensely longing to return to her work, she says, "I have had such precious experience of God's love during my illness, that I will follow where he points the way, believing that this trial will enable me render more acceptable service to Christ. The loving Saviour revealed himself to me so tenderly, that I feel new strength for conflict. If I may win immortal souls to him, I cannot regret that he called me back from the very gates of heaven, and will praise him for the precious view given me of the promised land. I have found Him 'faithful who has promised;' and, because of his gracious presence, seem to have entered a new world."

----◄♦►----

CHINA.

EXTRACTS FROM MRS. GULICK'S JOURNAL.

FRIENDLY GREETING.

You may remember my telling you, last year, of an elderly woman we met a few miles from Peking, who seemed much interested in learning of Christ's power and love, and who repeated most of it to those who had not heard. It is seldom we find a Chinese woman who has heart and mind enough to gain the least idea of the truth at the first interview; and when we heard her relating one of the Saviour's miracles, and talking of his love to those around, we were astonished, and a hopeful prayer went up from our hearts. As we again approached this village, we thought much about her, but did not even know her house; and how could we expect to find her? I asked God to help us, and he granted the request. No sooner had we entered the village than we met her. She gave us a friendly greeting, and asked us to stop and drink tea. We found she remembered much of what she had heard the year before. She told a person beside her that we believed in the one God who made heaven and earth; that the gods they worshipped were false; that Jesus died for our sins; and that we should daily pray to him to forgive us. We conversed with her as long as we could; and then, committing her to Him who alone can make her his, we went on our way with sorrowful hearts, fearing that this poor woman may never have another opportunity of listening to the truth.

NEED OF HELP.

The village belongs to the Peking District, being within a day's journey of the city; but Peking and the suburbs are larger than New York, and what can two or even ten missionaries do in preaching to the city people alone? Yet, so few are the missionaries in North China, that we consider Peking well supplied compared with the vast country population. The district which we, from lack of laborers, are compelled to look upon as ours, is larger in extent than the whole of England, and thickly populated. The roads are bad, and the easiest and quickest mode of travelling is on horseback. Our hearts sink within us when we think how little we can do among so many.

CURIOUS REMARKS.

It is often amusing to hear the remarks made by the country people. Our dress and saddles are very attractive objects. One laborer, wearing a hat as dirty as the ground, with only half a crown, and two-thirds of a brim, stood contemplating my brown

head-covering. At length he turned away, remarking contemptu-
ously, " What a number of years she must have worn that hat !
Just see how brown it is!" Another time, several were examining our saddles. " What are these handles for?" asked one.
" Why, don't you see?" replied another, more knowing than the
rest. "The man's saddle" (a Mexican saddle with a lasso knob)
" has only one handle, because the teacher holds on with one
hand; but the woman's has two, because she wants to hold on
with both hands." Was it not flattering to our horsemanship?

TURKEY.

HOW TO PRAY FOR MISSIONARIES.

BY MISS MYRA A. PROCTOR.

I HAVE just been reading an account of the meeting of the
American Board in Pittsburg; and am rejoiced that so much
attention was given to the subject of prayer for missions, as good
results must follow such a discussion. While in America, no remarks about the cause, even by cold and worldly professors, so
chilled and pained me as some of the prayers, — a dull routine
of words, without any intelligence or feeling manifested, and
nothing specific prayed for. The unmeaning formality of some
prayers reminds one of the following : " O Lord, bless the missionaries, who have taken their lives in their hands, and gone to
the *un*inhabited parts of the world to preach the gospel." This
is in strong contrast with another petition, rude and broken, that
has done my heart good in seasons of distress and perplexity.
It was offered by an aged Indian convert. " O Lord, bless de
missionary, and *help him to set one foot afore t'oder*, and preach
de gospel to every nation !" My heart would respond, " Yes,
Lord, —

> ' Lead thou me on :
> I do not ask to see the distant scene;
> *One step* enough for me ; '

only, dear Father, give me grace to place my foot, at each step, directly in the footprint of Jesus."

Dear sisters, let your prayers mean something. When you plead for us missionaries, look within upon your own heart-life, and remember we also are struggling, through temptations and trials, to be like Christ, and serve him here acceptably.

LETTER FROM MRS. WHEELER.

We received a very interesting letter from Mrs. Wheeler, giving an account of a tour recently made with her husband. Our limits only allow us to refer to her visit at Perchenj.

PERCHENJ CHURCH.

The Protestants there had built an expensive church, incurring a heavy debt. They thought that they had done all they could, and yet owed three hundred dollars in gold. The missionaries felt that they could not aid them, as it would establish a bad precedent. A committee went down from Harpoot to confer with them.

THE DEBT PAID.

She writes, "All seemed to feel that the Perchenj Church could not pay the debt without help. We had a prayer-meeting; and then the women retired to pray for success, and see what they could do. The brethren began to put down their names. After all had subscribed, the debt was about half paid. Just then, a sick man, who will probably lose his foot, and who lives on charity, sent in, saying, ' Put me down for fifty piastres.' Then Mr. Wheeler asked the brethren how much they would give for a foot or a leg; and that touched hearts and pockets. The missionaries said, 'We will help you on your pastor's house, if this debt is paid.' Then came word that the sisters would raise four hundred and fifty piastres. This gave a new impulse; the whole was subscribed, and they thanked God with joyful hearts.

"We staid after the committee left, and collected the money. The sisters' contribution amounted to thirty dollars. After the debt was liquidated, one hundred and forty piastres remained in the treasury. I was amazed that the women gave so much; for they had few ornaments, except brass and copper, which were almost worthless. I wish you could have seen them part with their last trinkets. They had previously given for the chapel, and had bought the communion-service by sacrificing their rings and silver coins. Gold is not often found in the villages, and little remained; but they gave that. One widow cast into the treasury ten dollars of hard-earned money; and, when she wanted a new hymn-book, had not the means to buy one. I offered to purchase one for her, and let her pay me when she could. She replied, 'I do not wish to be in debt. When I get the money, I will have one.' Ah, dear sisters! she looked noble in her coarse but clean village dress; and, as she had labored hard to collect the money, we presented her the book. Another, sixty-five years old, gave five dollars. She is learning to read, although her eyes are poor. Her name is Hajo Anna; for she has been to Jerusalem, and Hajo means pilgrim. She is now a happy pilgrim, bound for the New Jerusalem. When I bade her good-by, she took both of my hands, and said, 'Pray for me. I am weak, but I want to read God's word!' Then came a silver bracelet worth about four dollars, — the donor's last ornament. The rest was in small sums, — the children bringing one cent, half a cent, cutting off head-ornaments worth two or three cents, and taking bead bracelets from their wrists. Rings were brought, worth from one to twenty cents.

One poor widow sent three head-ornaments. Thus these indigent women gave, and ' Jesus sat over against the treasury.' It was a happy day to me and to these sisters, whose bright eyes and beaming faces told of joy that riches could not give. Be encouraged, Christian sisters. There are warm hearts under rough garments and sunburnt faces, which are laboring and praying with you."

THE MOUNTAIN TOUR.

Mrs. Schneider writes from Hazen Bile, where she had gone with her husband to visit converts. She speaks of "eyes strained by torchlight to examine the Bible," and " discussions far into the night " with Armenians awaking to a sense of new errors in their church. Quite a number had broken away from the bondage of years of sin, and many families had left the Armenian Church. She continues, —

"Five who became Protestants had been robbers and outlaws. The owner of the cabin where we stop, while plundering a man from Aintab, cut off several fingers.

CONVERTED ROBBERS.

"A gruff man with a grizzly beard, who gives evidence of change of heart, told us he once took down his gun, and threatened to kill a Protestant. But, while brigandage has been suppressed by Government, the Holy Spirit has done more effectual work. Twenty of these mountaineers wished to profess Christ. To allow this privilege to those who were waiting for it, Mr. Schneider made this toilsome journey. While crossing high mountain-peaks, I was obliged to dismount often, to keep my feet from freezing. But I felt a hundred-fold repaid for all the fatigue. So much spiritual light breaking in upon the darkness, such artless narratives of Christian experience, such intelligent convictions of truth in those who have only within a year heard

the story of the cross, and cannot read, — we have not found else-
where.

THE BRIGAND'S PRAYER.

" A famous brigand came to be examined for admission to the
church ; but it was thought best to give him a longer trial. How
do you suppose he and his accomplices quieted their consciences
when starting on a marauding excursion ? They prayed to be
kept from robbing an honest man. 'Let a covetous man be
our prey, O Lord ! Throw a bone to thy dog this day ! ' If
disappointed in plunder for two or three days, the first victim
was struck, for delaying so long to respond to their petition.
The booty taken was exchanged, to shift the guilt upon another
head.

CONDITION OF THE WOMEN.

" Here, as in every unenlightened place at the East, the women
are looked upon as inferior to the men. They eat after their
husbands have finished ; and, if a group of men wish for the
comfortable chimney-corner, they stand in the rear, shivering with
the cold. Five or more hope they have found Christ. Several
are commencing the alphabet. I have had many pleasant meetings with them. They have more of soft gentleness than one
would expect of women who toil with their husbands in the
field.

THE ZEALOUS INQUIRER.

" One Sabbath, the moistened eye and silent tear showed how
deeply they were moved by the preaching. Women were present who had never heard a sermon before. One, whose face
showed refinement and sense, interested me much. She was
bound by strong family ties to the Armenian Church, but too enlightened to remain there. Her mind was roused to learn the
truth on various points of Christian belief. She came to us with
questions and difficulties. With tearful eyes she said to me,
' We are like those in a dark well, — a little light has come

down to us : shall we not accept the help given to lift us out of the well ? ' We cannot but hope the Spirit will complete his work, and raise her up to be a power for good.

THE COMMUNION SERVICE.

"Would you could have seen that group of thirteen men and two women partaking for the first time of the Christian sacrament ! In that rustic chapel, where no silver plate was upon the table, the white mug containing the wine, and tin plate of bread, from which each lowly one took his portion, did not detract from the solemnity of the scene. The emblems of Christ's body and blood were passed amid audible sobs from those sturdy men. Several were in convulsed weeping, with their heads bowed nearly to the ground. It was a day to be remembered for a lifetime.

THE MOUNTAIN CABIN.

"I have not spent twelve happier days in the East than those passed in that half cave, half cabin. The dirt and gravel of the mountain formed two sides of our room ; the third was a rough stone wall of our neighbor's house ; the fourth faced the west, overlooking a cultivated valley ; a large fireplace extending nearly to the door, — which was without latch or bolt, — two or three rough boards, and you have the walls of our room. The ceiling was composed of trees, split, and thrown — branches, leaves and all — upon long poles, covered with a thick layer of dirt and gravel, which frequently dripped upon our beds at night ; and we felt liable to an inundation of dirt at all times. We had no windows ; and when it rained, and the door had to be closed, I crept up into the chimney-corner, to read and write by the light coming from the hole in the roof which served as an outlet for the smoke. Our floor was the disintegrated gravel of the mountains. We had no furniture, save our travelling-beds and chairs ; and yet that gloomy, leaky, comfortless home is a shrine I would gladly visit at some future time. In that fireplace, from many seated around the hearth, we heard what God had wrought in their dark souls.

THE INHOSPITABLE HOSTESS.

" Our journey home was very cold and hard. One night we lodged in the filthiest, most disagreeable place I was ever in. The hostess angrily forbade us her house, even denying us the small space occupied by our beds ; but, with the consent of the host, Mr. Schneider had our muleteers — two of whom had joined the church the day before — come in. She would not have been lonely without us, certainly ; for fifteen persons lay snoring at our feet, and thirty animals at our head, — goats cough- ing, sheep bleating, horses and oxen chewing their food : and then the vermin ! But, in that Mussulman family, Mr. Schnei- der read and explained God's word, and pastor Sarkis led in prayer. Another guest, a fine-looking man, who had been leader of fierce banditti in the mountains, listened with great earnest- ness. Pray for the work, and for all missionaries."

MISS WARFIELD'S JOURNAL.

We had received this communication before hearing of the lamented death of the writer. In November, when at Karpeh, three hours from Harpoot, she wrote, —

" There are no Protestants here ; and it has only been occupied as an out-station two years, although so near the city. The visits of the Harpoot brethren have not been welcomed until recently ; but now opposition has ceased, and the teacher is allowed to re- main. The room in which we are to spend the night has mud walls and floors, while the beams above are blackened with smoke. The fire is made in a deep hole in the floor, and the smoke escapes through an opening in the roof. Hattie Seymour re- marked that the place suggested the hymn, —

'I thank the goodness and the grace,' &c.

17

" *Friday*, 26. — Five hours' ride brought us to the teacher's house in this village. We were ushered into a stable, a corner of which — raised a little, and separated from the rest of the apartment by a railing a foot in height — is the family sitting-room. It is about twelve feet square, and is nearly half full of boxes and bags. We seated ourselves in the other end of the room, — Mr. B. on one side of the open fire-place, Miss Seymour and I on the other. The cook prepared our supper, and spread a part of it upon a little box, and the remainder upon the floor. Our repast was very acceptable, consisting of cold chicken brought from home, semilena, — similar to farina, but coarser, — cookies, and bread. After supper, some men called to see Mr. B. The cattle also came in, and the stable was quite full. One calf was tied by the railing so near me that he could easily have reached over and kissed me had he been so disposed. We could not see how we were to be accommodated for the night, with a family of five, and our two men besides.

" *Saturday*, 27. — This morning, Mr. B. talked with an old lady who appeared thoughtful and interested when I was conversing with her last night. He urged her to let her daughter-in-law learn to read; but she refused. Judge of my disappointment! Mr. B. suggested that the old lady was opposed to the reading because she feared the young woman's work would be neglected, as she was required to take care of the cattle, clean the stable, make fuel, &c. I fear our words fell on a cold heart; but the Lord is able to bless the seed.

" *Tuesday evening.* — It was past sunset when we reached here, as we were delayed in leaving M. by the escape of two horses. We enjoyed the day much, and had a good meeting with the women in the morning: several promised to commence reading. I talked to them on the parable of the fig-tree. It was a solemn meeting. I felt that the Lord was with us. We were glad to meet blind Hohannes' mother. She seemed ripe for heaven. We called afterwards at the house of a man who has recently become a Protestant. He received us cordially ; but his wife was bitter, and would not speak peaceably to us. We saw something of the strife there is in families where one member is persuaded of the truth, and the other opposed. The father decided to send his son to the seminary, although the mother stoutly objected. We spent the night with our dear little Miriam, and were treated with great kindness. We met the wife of Baron Pillibo, who was in our school three or four years. She was a dull scholar, and learned to read hesitatingly ; yet here she shone as a bright light in the midst of the surrounding darkness.

"*Dec.* 6. — There has been a church in this place for ten years or more, and it is about fifteen since the truth began to take root ; but there have been few additions to the church, and for several months they have not had the communion, on account of coldness and trouble. We held three meetings with the women, and called at several houses. I spoke to-day on the words, 'As many as are led by the Spirit of God are the sons of God ; ' and tried to make it plain, so that those trusting to false hopes might be led to examine their hearts. May the blessing of God make it effectual ! Hattie spoke yesterday upon the contrast between heaven and hell, and the duty of being prepared for heaven. A good number were present. This has been a day of fasting and prayer, and the pastor seems much encouraged. We are stopping at his house, which is very comfortable. I must tell you about our ablutions. The people here do not wash in basins, but pour the water on each other's hands : it is not considered neat to dip the hands in water and wash the face. The water is always poured by an inferior. Once, at the close of the evening meal, when the water was brought, Mr. B. offered to pour it for the pastor ; but he would not allow it. To-night I offered to do it for him, and he made no objection. This shows the different estimation in which men and women are held in this land, even by those who have been enlightened for years, and have given up many of their old customs.

" *Wednesday evening.* — This morning we went to meet the women. There were six besides Gyran, in a stable-room. After singing and praying with them, we mounted our horses and came on to A., to the meeting of the pastors and preachers of this field. Several years ago the Arabkir missionaries formed a church here ; but the work has not increased much. There are only six Protestant houses. They are just building a neat chapel, and have a preacher, who we hope will be ordained next year. There have been two sessions of the meeting to-day, for prayer and the discussion of several questions relating to the wants of the field. ' What means shall be used to awaken a revival spirit? What shall we do in regard to the new opposition? What shall a preacher do if sent to a place, and is not received?' This evening we had a meeting for the women. Quite a number are reading ; and others, we hope, will begin this winter.

"*Friday.* — Early yesterday morning we went to a village containing but ten Armenian and a few Turkish houses. They have not been visited much by the missionaries or native preachers, and but few are able to read. We visited an upper room, and talked to the women, but found most of them ignorant and careless. Two had learned to read, and seemed anxious to know the truth. After lunching with them on pilaf, bread, and cold fish, we went to M. We had a pleasant visit with one of our pupils, and were glad to find that she had entered earnestly upon the work, and held meetings for the women twice a week. She is teaching several to read, and visits from house to house. The truth has not yet taken root, and the people are not acquainted with us. Several men came to see Mr. B., and, while listening to him, made remarks about us. They were greatly astonished at the idea of girls leaving their homes and going about to teach others. One said, ' This thing is a puzzle to me ! ' They were surprised that we knew how to read. As we wrote, a man crept towards us on his hands and knees, and gazed wonderingly at the novel sight.

"*Harpoot, Dec.* 18. — We reached home after an absence of two weeks and a half. During the time, we travelled a hundred and forty miles, visited fourteen out-stations, and held thirty-four meetings, some of which were quite informal, but perhaps as profitable as the public meetings. We were well repaid for an evening's talk, if some ignorant woman showed a desire to learn of Jesus. We can with grateful hearts praise God, and say, 'Truly, goodness and mercy have followed us' all the way."

PERSIA.

WORDS OF CHEER.

Mrs. Rhea has kindly permitted us to make the following extract from a letter received by her from Mr. Coan: —

"And you, too, have gone up to the feast, and seen that great company of the good of our land, the Aarons and the Hurs, who stay up the hands of the missionaries! Did it not do your soul good? And do you not feel, 'I wish I was back again to labor for the daughters of Persia'? Oh, what a work is here to be done for poor woman! and, alas! who is there to do it? The longer I live, the more I feel the great importance of labor among the women. Woman has a deeper religious nature than man. The Marys are constant in their love for Jesus. They do not forsake him, though dead. They visit his grave with their spices and ointments. I have thought of this, these days, when unprincipled men, who care only for 'filthy lucre,' would lift up their heel against us.

"Malik Yonan's wife, Shereen, was reached but imperfectly by Miss Fiske, and mostly through Yonan. He had the full blaze of gospel light continually pouring into his mind and heart for years, under the teachings of that holy woman. Shereen
17*

caught some of these reflected rays. There are many such women in Persia. Oh, what a jewel is that Munnee wife of Priest
Karam! What another is Sarah, wife of Priest Oshana! Sisters, labor and pray that there may be many such in Persia and
the East.

AFRICA.

OPINION OF A VETERAN MISSIONARY.

THE following testimony from Rev. A. Grout cannot fail to
interest the friends of Mrs. Edwards. Referring to her school,
he says, —

"Mrs. Edwards has a definite system in all she does; and it
goes like clockwork. She allows nothing to pass that is not
understood or done right. The system in her school, of itself,
will exert a most beneficial effect on the girls. The pupils had
come from but partially-civilized homes, yet every thing in the
schoolroom was tasteful and orderly. I learned also that Mrs.
Edwards was faithful in giving religious instruction."

EXTRACTS FROM A LETTER BY MRS. LLOYD.

MRS. EDWARDS'S SCHOOL.

"Before closing, I must put in a line with regard to Mrs.
Edwards's school. The schoolroom reminds me of a New-York
public schoolroom on a small scale; but I must say, I never
saw girls more orderly or systematic, even in a New-York school.
There are now twenty-six, I believe, from eight to sixteen years
old; the youngest reading English spelling-book, and learning
easy arithmetic lessons. The most advanced are reading an
English book, and ciphering in compound numbers. The rapidity with which they work their examples, and write English spell-

ing, is quite wonderful. I felt like envying Mrs. Edwards to-day, as I saw the row of bright girls rise in such an orderly way to spell, and thought of their histories and probable future. Most of them I know in their homes, and a number of them are pet daughters in important families. It is a great experiment, and thus far a success.

APPEAL FOR AN ASSISTANT.

" These two days have convinced me that some woman should be here as soon as possible to assist Mrs. Edwards. Have you no one with a willing heart to come ? I think it is a work that pays."

SUGGESTIONS FOR AUXILIARIES.

BY MRS. Z. P. BANISTER.

THE former pupils of Mrs. B., scattered throughout our land, will be glad once more to listen to her counsel : —

" We at the present day are called by the providence as well as by the word of God to obtain by our own effort, at least in part, the answer to our daily prayer, 'Thy kingdom come, thy will done in earth as it is in heaven.'

" This kingdom, that ' the God of heaven has set up which can never be destroyed,' is in the hearts of its subjects. (Every person who with the heart has believed unto righteousness, and with the mouth has made confession unto salvation), every true disciple, is identified with this kingdom of our Lord, who would have his purchased ones give him ' life for life, and heart for heart.' 'Freely ye have received, freely give,' are words no less binding on his disciples of the present day than on those who heard them from the living voice of their author.

" We cannot afford the loss that will accrue to ourselves by remaining in ignorance or inactivity; nor the loss from the want of that spirit which prevailed after the day of Pentecost, when all classes of believers ' went everywhere, preaching the word.'

" In forming a woman's foreign missionary society, you will wish to promote your own elevation, and that of the community. You will choose to organize on such principles as will endure, and manifest greater life and vigor, after your first members shall have passed away.

" 'That the soul be without knowledge is not good.' And surely Christians ought not to be without knowledge of what has been effected by missionaries of whatever denomination or country in any part of the heathen world at the present day. Let the character and condition of the people without the gospel, and their character and condition after hearing and accepting it, be thoroughly studied and understood, and it cannot fail to inspire every candid and generous mind with missionary zeal. The people of the Sandwich Islands afford an illustration of the wonderful change here referred to. 'The Missionary Herald' for years past contains illustrations of the like kind in various countries. To this periodical we may resort as to a rich storehouse of information. It may be well to select for your attention, for half a year or more, some specific mission, where you have a personal acquaintance with some of the faithful laborers. This course can hardly fail of cultivating an intelligent interest and sympathy in the general cause. Or you can select some mission concerning which books can be obtained suited to enlighten and to elevate.

" The late *Nestorian Mission*, 'a field which the Lord has blessed,' affords means for acquaintance with devoted Christian and missionary spirits, whose meat and drink it has been to do the will of our Father in heaven ; and who, in their own experience, have proved that Christ's 'yoke is easy, and his burden light.'

" Among the hundreds of Nestorian converts are scores of young women, trophies of grace, who are qualified to be Christian teachers, blessings on generations yet to come. And such is the preparation of many to labor as preachers, or as helpers of various grades, that they are relied upon to extend the gospel not only to their own people still in unbelief, but also to the Armenians, to the Jews, and to the Mussulmans around them. The name *Nestorian Mission* is therefore merged in the more comprehensive one of *Missions to Persia.*

"There are many books which throw light upon this mission. All your members would find profitable, 'Life of Dr. Grant,' 'Missionary Life in Persia,' 'Life of Rev. David Stoddard,' 'Woman and her Saviour in Persia,' 'Life of Fidelia Fiske,' and 'Life of Rev. S. A. Rhea.'

"On the 'Eastern-Turkey Mission' all would choose to read two books written by Rev. C. H. Wheeler while on his late visit to our country, — 'Ten Years on the Euphrates,' and 'Letters from Eden;' and also one by Rev. M. P. Parmelee, — 'Life-Scenes from the Mountains of Ararat.'

"Some among you will doubtless choose to become acquainted with the Armenians from the time (1830) that Messrs. Smith and Dwight made their 'Researches' among that people. Within the last forty years, thousands of them have found Christ to be the wisdom of God and the power of God to their salvation.

"Records in periodicals and books might be studied, also, in regard to other missions ; as India, China, Africa and Micronesia.

"The small maps in 'The Missionary Herald,' and in some of these descriptive books, as well as Bidwell's large Missionary Maps, will be found a great assistance.

"'The Memorial Volume,' and 'Foreign Missions, their Relations and Claims,' by Dr. Anderson, would be a treasure in any small library for a missionary society.

"For your regular meetings, whether monthly or quarterly, let your programme, in addition to the mission you are studying, give place for other reading, and for conversation or remarks, that profit may be secured, and all things be done decently and in order. Let your selections of Scripture be suited to make a deep and permanent impression. In opening or closing these n.. etings by prayer, you will present, in the arms of faith and love, individuals, teachers, and taught, to the Great Shepherd, who cares for each, and who can supply all their need ; remembering the sure word, ' Whatsoever ye shall ask the Father in my name, he will give it you.' "

QUARTERLY REPORT.

THE Quarterly Meeting, April 5, was opened by singing, followed by a short Scripture reading from Jer. vii. and xliv., from which our President presented us a graphic picture of the unity in service of entire heathen households in their idol worship ; enforcing the lesson, that if, in idolatrous rites, it was deemed expedient that the children gather wood, and the fathers kindle the fire, and the women knead dough to make cakès to the queen of heaven, we should consider it far more important to educate our households, from the least to the greatest, to labor personally that idolatry be supplanted by the worship of the true King of heaven, even Christ our Lord.

Prayer was offered by Mrs. Johnson of Cambridge, and the Secretary's report submitted..

It presented the names of eighteen auxiliaries formed since Jan. 1, and alluded to the mission-circles springing up here and there, as tender plants, but promising to become trees, to scatter leaves of healing through the benighted nations of the earth.

Mention was made of a young lady secured as our missionary physician for the Constantinople Home, who will, we hope, ere long enter upon her duties in the field assigned her.

The Treasurer reported the total receipts of funds since Jan. 1,

as seven thousand dollars and upwards. For further particulars our readers are referred to the " Herald."

The Corresponding Secretaries read interesting extracts from
the letters and journals of our missionaries. After those from
Miss Warfield and her physician to the bereaved mother, Mrs. Dr.
Folts offered a touching prayer for the afflicted home-circle and
mission-band.

Mrs. Winslow exhibited a map in elucidation of the golden
stars upon the map issued in the March number of " Life and
Light," by which a star was seen to represent an entire mission-
field, with its stations, out-stations, schools, together with the
clustering villages attracted by its influence.

Mrs. Anderson exhibited a tract in Tamil, as a fruit of the
children's earnings in the mission-circle connected with Mrs.
Capron ; three thousand copies of which were distributed as
Christmas gifts among heathen children.

An interesting poem suggested by the Scripture in Jer. xliv.,
and prepared by Mrs. Emily C. Pearson, was read ; after which our
President again directed attention to the picture of idolatrous
families con ecrated to personal religious service, and urged us
to make it our especial purpose this year to gather the young
into mission-circles not only to secure pecuniary benefit, but with
the higher thought of systematic training in personal missionary labor, that a generation may arise, able to multiply our service a thousand fold.

Our recent anxiety and bereavement with our mission families we would not fail to chronicle, nor the way in which our
kind Father has dealt with us. Yes, we have held our breath
with theirs in watchfulness beside the sick-couch of our dear Miss
Smith ; have strained, with theirs, our listening ears to catch her
faint but sweetly conscious speech of the " dark valley " almost
past, but brightly illumined by the presence of our elder Brother
and Saviour ; have prayed, almost in agony, " Let this cup pass
from them, Father; " but with the blest refrain, " Thy will, not

mine, be done;" and again been lifted into a frame of chastened but joyous thanksgiving at the seeming miracle wrought in their experience before our wondering eyes.

She almost touched the heavenly strand, but has been lent back to earth again, fragrant with the breath of heaven in all her garments, and baptized anew of the Holy Spirit for her life-labor of self-denying love for souls.

"But one is taken, and the other left." While she has come back, we mourn our dear Miss Warfield. She has laid her armor down; she has joined the glorified ones. She has finished her work, and entered into "the rest that remaineth;" and our stricken mission-families bow their heads in chastened suffering, in spirit saying, "We are dumb, and open not our mouths, because thou didst it." May we so sorrow and pray for and with them, that God may bless it to their life-long good!

After the Doxology, the meeting adjourned to May 26, 10 A.M., at the Old South Chapel, Freeman Place.

H. C. W., *Secretary pro tem.*

TO MOTHERS.

CHRISTIAN MOTHERS, — Our hearts are burdened with the woes of perishing millions. Look out upon the spiritual night of the world, the darkness pierced only here and there by a star of hope.

Anchoring on the promises of God, we turn from the drear prospect to the nurseries of the Church, in faith. The young must be educated with missionary aims, that shortly they may kindle lights wherever brood the dark shadows of idolatry. Like the mother represented in our engraving, we must point the child to the Saviour's command, and then to the lands where shadowy forms appear, waiting for light. Tell them over and again the story of the cross, and then about the little heathen who have never heard it; and, as their hearts melt in pity, picture to them the mission-ship in which they may some day embark to carry the glad news of salvation to India, China, Africa, or the islands of the sea. Instruct them about those countries, and mission-work. Begin early to train them to self-denying efforts for these perishing ones ; and as soon as they know the worth of a penny, to gratify their taste, show them its better use, — to help the ignorant and needy.

Avail yourselves of the strong social nature of the young, and gather them in mission-circles ; some of the older reading to, guiding, and charming the younger. If truly in love with the cause of missions, various ways will occur to you of interesting your children. If you have an inspiring faith, they cannot fail to feel its influence ; and, the Lord blessing your efforts, they will be won sooner or later to do his will.

Do you sometimes sigh for a higher position, a wider sphere of usefulness? Train your offspring for the world's conversion ; remembering that she who holds the heart of a child wields the mightiest power on earth. For this be grateful to Jesus, and offer praise.

Look, then, to him, till the amazing power of his love constrains you in the work of nurturing your children to bear part in his glorious coming among the nations.

> " Oh to help these lost and wretched !
> Oh to break their fearful chain !
> Christian mother, teach thy children,
> And thou shalt not toil in vain ;
> And, wherever God shall call them,
> Consecrated let them go.
> Crowns of glory we are winning,
> If we honor Christ below."

For Treasurer's Report, see " Missionary Herald " for March, April, and May.

18

SOW BESIDE ALL WATERS.

MRS. DAY was one of those convenient helpers in a Sabbath school, who, although belonging to a Bible-class, can be relied upon as an able substitute for any absent teacher.   Recently she was requested to take charge of a class of boys, one of whom bore an unenviable reputation for bad behavior.   He came to Sabbath school because he was obliged to, and, while there, only created disturbance.   "How can I possibly interest that boy ?" thought Mrs. Day, as she stepped to the class.   She lifted up her heart for guidance.   He was, as usual, inattentive and turbulent.   The lesson led her to speak of missions.   She was herself deeply interested in the cause, and very familiar with the subject.   To her great delight, she found that she had touched the right chord.   The dull features of the lad lighted up ; and his eyes were fixed upon her, spell-bound, till the'bell struck for closing.   What a suggestive incident for Sabbath-school teachers to ponder !

AN INSPIRING MEETING.

THE first annual meeting of the Woman's Foreign Missionary Society of the Methodist Church was held in this city, April 21. Delegates were present from Brooklyn, New York, Philadelphia, Chicago, and St. Louis.   Their reports showed a deep and wide-spread interest in the organization.   The receipts of the Society for the year amounted to seven thousand dollars.   The services continued through the day.   A bountiful collation was served at the noon intermission, in the chapel.   Addresses were given by Mrs. Willing of Chicago, and Mrs. Maclay, Mrs. Butler, and Mrs. Parker, returned missionaries from India.   The ladies were deeply in earnest, and were listened to with intense interest.   The exercises throughout were a great success ; and we predict for our sisters a glorious future.

Awake!

BY EMILY C. PEARSON.

I.

WAKE from slumber, Christian mother!
Now hath come the hour of need:
Train thy children for the Saviour,
And salvation's chariot speed.

II.

Tell them how the hapless pagan
Boweth down to idols vain:
Of degraded, suffering woman,
In her joyless life of pain;

III.

Shut away in dread zenanas,
From a child a very slave,
With no glimpse of blessed sunlight,
Only wishing for the grave.

IV.

Or, if poor, an abject menial
Delving in the torrid sun,
'Neath the heel of husband-master
Crushed till life's sad course is run.

V.

Point to hosts of young immortals,
Old in crime and misery,
Who have never heard of Jesus,
Who would gladly to him flee.

VI.

Oh to help these lost and wretched!
Oh to break their heavy chain!
Christian, give to Christ thy children,
And it shall not be in vain.

In Memoriam.

The painful tidings has just reached us of the death of our beloved missionary,

MISS MARY E. WARFIELD,

WHO FELL ASLEEP IN JESUS, FEB. 12.

"We loved your daughter very much," writes Mr. Barnum, "but Jesus loved her more." We, too, had learned to love her and her work; and, now that she has reached her eternal home, we rejoice in the belief that her interest in the Saviour's cause is intensified as she enters upon the employments of the redeemed. We weep not for her promotion, but for our loss; yet in this, we "*know* but in part." Who can say that her death may not accomplish more for the daughters of Turkey than a long life of active service?

Her Christian character has ever been marked by earnest purpose, strong faith, and an unusual spirit of consecration; and these traits, with a clear and vigorous mind and thorough education, fitted her eminently for her work.

One Monday morning, three years since, her pastor told her of the want of a female teacher at Harpoot; expressing his conviction that the "Master had need" of her. Consulting with her dear mother, she promptly decided to go.

On reaching her Turkish home, she said, "It is the happiest moment of my life." And, after having grappled three years with difficulties "in the acquisition of a new language, summer fatigues, and winter touring in cold and snow," she writes, "It is a blessed work; and I rejoice that my dear Father brought me here, and gave me strength for it."

Her missionary associates testify to "her sweetness of temper, childlike simplicity, great purity of character, enthusiastic labors, warmth of affection, and nobleness of soul." Shortly after her last tour, she was attacked with measles, which, assuming a typhoid form, in a few days proved fatal.

As she neared heaven, her thoughts reverted to her native land; and she said, "If I die, write to my mother, and tell her that I am ready to go, and happy in the thought of going. Do not let her mourn for me: tell her that I am glad I came here, and I could not have had a pleasanter home."

From her glorious work she has gone hence to receive the gracious plaudit of the Saviour, "Well done!"

ECHOES from "LIFE and LIGHT."

JUNE. PUBLISHED BY THE WOMAN'S BOARD OF MISSIONS. 1870.

WORDS TO THE CHILDREN.

WE fancy that our young readers, when looking for their " Corner " in " Life and Light," will wonder why they find instead a " Children's Quarterly," and inquire what it means.

We intend, dear children, to issue your little " Corner " by itself, in new dress, that each of you can have a missionary paper of your own. We call it " Quarterly," because it will be sent out four times a year, and " Echoes from ' Life and Light,' " as it will follow it, echoing the glad tidings from our mission-work among the children.

We shall echo, too, the cry that comes to us from the krawls, cabins, and dark homes of the poor little heathen : " Come over and help us ; " " Tell us about Jesus ; " " Show us the way to heaven : " that you may pity them, and gather money to send to them God's holy word.

We shall echo, also, their grateful thanks and fervent greetings, that they may be heard in mission-circles and Sabbath schools.

18*   209

We shall echo, likewise, the cheering words that reach us from your missionary meetings, North and South, East and West.

And now we hear you say, " But what shall we do ? "

We want you to earn pennies for us ; and, that you may understand our wish, we will give a few lines from a letter just sent to the children in Maine by their missionary father, Rev. W. Warren : " One of my boys writes me, ' This makes four years that I have sent you a dollar and a quarter, to support some heathen child at school. I love to think my money has done this. I earned a part of it by sewing patchwork for my mother.' Two other noble boys took to raising eggs for this work, and thus let a nice missionary pullet into the partnership. The disciples found money for the Saviour in the mouth of the fish ; so these brothers found money for the Saviour's use in the nest of their little pullet."

We want you to call your companions together, and interest them to form mission-circles. Several have reported to us since the new year ; and it may gratify you to know some of their names : as " The Seek and Save Society;" " The Little Sowers ; " " The Pearls ; " " The Little Gleaners ; " " The Maveric Rill ; " " The Zulu Helpers."

Please remember, we shall give five copies of " The Children's Quarterly " to every circle that sends us five dollars, and ten to every one that supports a heathen child or Bible-reader.

Will each of you ask your Sabbath-school superintendent to furnish you with the little paper ? Twenty-five copies can be obtained for one dollar, or one hundred for four dollars, by sending to the Secretary of the W. B. M., 33 Pemberton Square, Boston.

Who will be voluntary agents for us ?

The Gleaners.

BY MRS. JOEL. S. BINGHAM.

WE are a little gleaning band.
We cannot bind the sheaves ;
But we can follow those who reap
And gather what each leaves.

We are not strong; but Jesus loves
The weakest of his fold,
And, in our feeble efforts, proves
His tenderness untold.

We are not rich ; but we can give,
As we are passing on,
A cup of water in his name
To some poor, fainting one.

We are not wise; but Christ our Lord
Revealed to babes his will ;
And we are sure, from his dear Word,
He loves the children still.

We know, that, with our gathered grain,
Briers and leaves are seen ;
Yet, since we tried, He smiles the same,
And takes our offering.

Dear children, still hosannas sing,*
As Christ doth conquering come ;
Casting your treasures, as he brings
The heathen nations home.

* " And when the chief priests and scribes saw the wonderful things that he did, and the children crying in the temple, and saying. Hosanna to the Son of David, they were sore displeased, and said unto him, Hearest thou what these say ? And Jesus saith unto them, Yea : have ye never read, Out of the mouths of babes and sucklings thou hast perfected praise ? " — MATT. xxxi. 15, 16.

THE BLIND MOUSE'S FOOT.

BY MISS MARY A. C. ELY.

My Dear Children, — Though I have never seen you, yet I love you very much. I think you like to hear stories, and will tell you one which happened far away, where the children have not such pleasant homes, or good parents to care for them, as God has given you.

Near a mountain village of a few houses, I spent three months last summer, breathing the pure air, and keeping away from the sickness and heat of a very old, wicked city in Turkey, where I had gone to teach the children. In this village lived several bright, pretty little ones, who used to come and take lessons in reading, and listen to us, as we tried to tell of the dear Saviour who had done so much for them.

One day, a woman came, bringing in her arms a puny girl-baby, nearly a year old. It had a pretty face, with sweet, blue eyes, but was very pale and thin. You would have felt sorry for it if you could have seen it. We inquired if it was sick. "Oh, no!" replied the mother; "but it's small!" It was her only child, and had on quite a number of ornaments, such as beads, silver and copper coin, sewed on its patched fez, or cap. There was one ornament we had never seen before, but it looked like a tiny hand. We asked the mother what it was; and she said, "My baby was small; and I inquired what I should do to make it grow, and was told to find a blind mouse, and, while it was alive, cut off a foot, and sew it on the baby's fez; and so I did it." Poor mother! she loved her baby, and wanted it to grow strong and well, that it might run about and learn to play. It was for this that she hunted till she found a blind mouse, and then cut off the poor little animal's foot, with its five tiny toes, and fastened it on the cap. Do you think the wee foot will make the baby grow, and get well? The mother said it had worn it a good while, but it had not begun to get better.

Perhaps you will say, the woman was very silly to follow such advice : if you do, I hope you will pity her too. She had never been to school ; no one had taught her to read the Bible, or told her of the blessed Saviour who loves children so dearly. I hope this story will make you think of a great many things. Think how much these ignorant people need to be taught, and how many there are who have no one to instruct them ; think how good God has been to give you your home in a pleasant land, with so many comforts and friends. You have a Bible, and are taught to read it, and have heard of a Saviour's love. And, lastly, think how much you can do to give the blessings you enjoy to those who have them not.

PRIZE ESSAY.

OUR young readers will be interested in the following extract from the prize essay referred to in this number : —

" God has so formed the plastic and unbiased mind of youth, that instruction gained in early years bears with greater force upon the character before selfishness gains its sway, and love of money dazzles the vision.

" The exercise of benevolence is important to the young, as it is a powerful element in the formation of character ; and cannot be overlooked with impunity, whether we regard our happiness and usefulness in this life or that which is to come."

> " Give strength, give thought, give deeds, give pelf,
> Give love, give tears, and give thyself;
> Give, give, be always giving:
> Who gives not is not living."

Minnie's Plan.

BY MRS. EDWIN WRIGHT.

SAYS Minnie to Kitty, " I've thought what we'll do,
And no one shall know it save myself and you ;
That is, till we get it all planned out complete,
And then we will tell all the girls in the street.
Some money I've wanted, but knew of no way,
Until I remembered to kneel down and pray,
And tell my dear Saviour, who once died for me,
About the poor heathen far over the sea, —
Ten thousands of children with souls almost dead,
Because of Christ Jesus they never have read.
I said, ' Unto others I'd do as I would
That they in my place should to me if they could.
I'd send them my Bible, but they cannot read:
Some lady to teach them how much more they need!'
' Whatsoever we ask in Christ's name we receive,
If we only are sure,' he says, ' to believe.'
And truly I believe we could get up a sale, *
If we of the labor of others avail.
John's father makes brackets : we'll ask him for one ;
I know John himself would leave nothing undone.
You and I can dress dolls ; and we'll coax little Sue
To play the ' old woman who lived in the shoe.'
Pen-wipers and rabbits, and kittens and mice,
If we met once a week, we'd get up in a trice.
And, when we are tired of work, day by day
We'll go into the woods and make believe play ;
We'll pluck tiny mosses, and gather bright leaves,
And tie drooping grasses in bunches like sheaves ;
Take ' life-everlasting ' and weave it in crowns,
Or make birch-bark houses with fairy-like grounds.
And when we have fancies enough in detail,
Of both common and rare, we'll make up our sale,
And ask in our fathers and friends not a few,
Placing clearly before them what we have in view:
That, if ever so little, do something we must
To show to those children the Saviour we trust ;

---

* We do not favor questionable fairs, but, in some cases, approve of children's
sales, suitably conducted.

That we dare not neglect it until we are grown,
For they may have passed Death's river alone.
And you know, should we sow e'er so tiny a seed,
Asking Jesus to bless it, he, seeing our need,
Might cause it to grow a big tree in his time,
O'erspreading all nations in every clime.
Now, if God moves their hearts, as I doubt not he will,
To buy up our dainties, our purses will fill.
Don't you think we could do it if we only incline?
You tell your dear mother, and I will ask mine ;
And, if they are willing, our first meeting shall be
'Neath the wide-spreading shade of our old willow-tree."

ALOHA FROM HONOLULU.

"Our girls unite in great Aloha * to your Society," writes Miss Lydia Bingham of Honolulu. And the loving message travels to us all the way from the Sandwich Islands. Gladly we find evidence of their sincerity in the receipt of thirty-five dollars, to constitute their teacher a life-member of the W. B. M. "The money was earned by the pupils in extra tasks, — house-cleaning, scrubbing floors, etc. ; receiving a dime or half-dime for their service. They also do plain sewing very neatly, and are expert with their crochet-needles in making nice edging, which finds a ready sale. Every month they deposit their earnings in the missionary-box, and are very regular in their contributions."

WORTHY OF IMITATION.

A short time since, one of our Western Sabbath schools offered a prize of ten dollars for the best essay on "The Benefit to the Young of Practical Benevolence." Miss Mary J. Tolman, a girl of fifteen, received the prize, and very modestly, through her pastor, sent the whole sum to the Treasurer of the Woman's Board of Missions. Does it not seem quite clear that she believed what through her pen she had spoken?

* Loving salutation.

Gather for Christ.

JER. vii. 18.

BY EMILY C. PEARSON.

" GATHER wood : we'll kindle fire!"
Said the mother and the sire.
" Children, ye must something do,
Or to idols ye're not true.
Make we cakes to heaven's queen
Rules she o'er the hearts of men.
Gather, all! we'll worship now:
Bring the wood, and haste to bow!"

With idolatry defiled,
Firm the parent trains the child.
Infant homage must be paid
To the idols vainly made.
Living in the gospel light,
Learn we from the pagan rite,
When we seek the Saviour's throne
'Tis not for ourselves alone.

Let our *children* oft be there,
Taught to love the place of prayer,
Taught to love the Saviour's name,
Him to praise with one acclaim;
Let us teach them day by day,
In the house and by the way,
That with us they, too, may bring
To the Lord their offering.

For Christ gather, little child;
Gather for the Undefiled;
Bring thy gifts and something do;
To thy Saviour be thou true.
Then shall kindle such a fire
As shall pale the funeral-pyre,
As shall idols cast away,
And all nations win to pray.

LIFE AND LIGHT

FOR

𝕳eat𝔥en 𝕎omen.

•

| VOL. I. | SEPTEMBER, 1870. | No. 7. |

A BEVY OF MOSLEM WOMEN.

BY MISS MYRA A. PROCTOR.

THE other morning, we were startled by the sudden appearance of a bevy of Moslem women. My mind has been much exercised in regard to my personal duty towards this portion, — by far the largest of our field. The following sketch will present some of the difficulties in the way.

Nine women were bustling around in the veranda, peeping into this door and that, holding their black veils closely about their faces, and drawing back with a horrified expression when a missionary brother passed out of the dining-room through their midst down into the yard. After satisfying themselves that there was no man about, they were persuaded to walk in. They glanced with childish curiosity at the parlor, then made a rush for the dining-room.

" Can you read ? " exclaimed one.

" Yes," I replied.

" Let us hear you ! " they said.

I went for my Turkish Testament, and brought some chairs ; but part of the company were already squatted upon the rugs.

I seated myself on a low cricket; and they gathered about me in a semi-circle, — an old lady at my right hand, who seemed to be the matron and leader of the party; another at my left, less intelligent, who constantly appealed to the first for explanations; in the centre, seven young women, giddy and thoughtless, two of whom were very rude in their manners, frequently slapping. and chasing each other like two romping boys. But they sat expectant as I opened to the sixth chapter of Matthew, and read, "Take heed that ye do not your alms before men, to be seen of them."

"What does that mean?" asked the woman at my left.

I attempted to reply, but the matron at my right took the words from my mouth.

"That means, that we must not bestow charity with a proud heart, and make a show of it."

The forbidding to pray "at the corners of the streets" excited their surprise, but the old lady's comments satisfied them that it is better to pray in-doors. "Use not vain repetitions, as the heathen do."

"That means," said she, "that you should make a short prayer and be done."

Our Lord's beautiful formula of prayer I insisted upon explaining myself; and, as usual, all agreed that it was "very good." "But thou, when thou fastest, anoint thy head . . . that thou appear not unto men to fast." Here the young women laughed, and took the old ladies to task for their style of fasting.

"Lay up for yourselves treasure in heaven."

"That means, that we should not spend our strength for this world, but should be laying up good works and meritorious deeds for the world to come," said our aged friend.

"We do not believe in meritorious works," said I; "for is it not our duty to do all the good we can?" She admitted that it was. "And have we not many deficiencies and sins?" This was also acceded. "Then, if we cannot do any more than is our duty, and, on the other hand, are guilty of so many sins, how are we going to have an overplus of good works?" There was a moment's silence. I never before had found so good an opportunity for speaking of the atoning work of Christ to any of the Mohammedan religion. "We believe," I continued, "that, because we could not by meritorious works obtain salvation, Christ came to earth, lived a holy life, kept the law, and then died for us, so that all who believe in him, and obey him, will obtain free salvation."

"What's that?" exclaimed two or three voices.

"Oh!" replied the old lady, "that's what they believe. That is not necessary. Let that go."

I resumed my reading: "'No man can serve two masters.'"

"That's evident," rejoined my commentator: "you know, 'Two water-melons can't be held in one hand!'" quoting an Oriental proverb.

They asked for another book; and I read from Isa. xlviii. 12, and onward; the old lady explaining to the younger ones that formerly there were those who used to make idols with their own hands, and then fall down and worship them. Her gesture of contempt is indescribable. Turning to me, she asked if there were still idolaters in the world; and the whole company showed the utmost astonishment when I answered, "Yes, a great many."

But they were growing listless, and wished to see the house, and hear the melodeon. As I closed the book, they wished "health" to my "tongue," and prayed again and again that God would lead me to become a true Moslem. "May God guide us all to the truth!" I replied.

"Perhaps she is a Moslem at heart," said one. "You know Varteni said that was the necessary thing."

It seems that they had called on Varteni, and bestowed the same wish upon her; and she replied, that it was necessary to be a Moslem (a true believer) at heart.

They asked if I received letters from my mother, and who brought them.

" The post," said I.

" Oh, yes ! " replied the wise old lady : " there's a telegraph now."

The physiological charts in the schoolroom they took to be pictures of Satan ; and the explanation that they represented the circulation of the blood through the lungs and body hardly satisfied them, for " Who had ever seen the inside of the body ? " However, they were so much pleased with what they saw, and with the music, that they warmly congratulated the scholars upon their privileges.

I was watching for my opportunity, and now asked, " Haven't you some little girls whom you would like to send here to school ? " That was too good a joke, and they laughed immoderately.

" Why," said one, "you could not teach them Arabo-Turkish." " Yes, we would," I replied. They laughed again at the idea of a Christian being able to teach a Moslem, and went away with many polite expressions and good wishes.

Ten thousand such women in this city, thoroughly incased in ignorance, pride, and self-righteousness.

It is indeed the " day of small things " with us ; but we can scatter the good seed, " here a little, and there a little," trusting in the promises. Pray that the bread thus cast upon the waters may yield an abundant harvest !

CHINA.

LETTER FROM MISS ANDREWS.

Miss Andrews of Tungchow writes as follows : —

" I carried out a plan of hiring a house in a part of the city where we had already done some work. I fitted it up for a

schoolroom or chapel, and commenced going there daily for teaching. It required only a very small expenditure ; the furniture
consisting of a Chinese stove, a tiny table, a few benches, and a
mat for the "kang," which is a necessity in every Chinese house.
It is a simple platform of brick, warmed by a fire underneath,
and sometimes covered with a mat, on which the family sleep at
night, and sit during the day. The room has walls of mud, a
dirt floor, and paper windows; but it is much pleasanter and
more comfortable than the houses of the majority of these poor
women. A few hymns, and the Lord's Prayer written in character, with a sheet of rude Scripture pictures, are fastened upon
the wall. Quite a number of girls came in at first, but they
were all afraid to read. I found, too, that the work of the women,
most of it, was such as could not well be taken from home. I
spend an hour or two there daily with Mrs. Wo, our Bible-
reader, teaching them to read and sing the hymns on the wall ;
reading to them from the Gospels, and illustrating the lesson by
bright-colored pictures.

ACCESS TO HEATHEN HOMES.

"Far more hopeful and interesting is the work in another quarter of the city, where I had tried at first, unsuccessfully, to obtain a room. No one had heard the truth there, save three
women from one yard, who had attended Sabbath services, and
were learning to read. They were, however, unwilling to have
us visit them ; fearing another woman in the same yard, who was
very much opposed, would make them trouble. Providentially,
one of the three, Mrs. Kung, had an attack of palsy. I visited
her as a friend, not a teacher, and, under Dr. Treat's direction,
gave her medicine. This won her heart, and also the women of
the neighborhood, who begged me to save her life. While I assured them of my inability to do that, I told them of One who
had power to heal, and who heard prayer. I then urged Mrs.
Kung to pray Jesus to heal her disease and forgive her sins.

At first, she prayed that she might recover; but, as she continued sick and feared death, she was led to pray for the salvation of her soul. She is now better, and I feel that God has used her illness to open a way for the gospel.

"Every day the neighbors come in, and sometimes the room is thronged. As soon as I found them favorably disposed, I told them of the Saviour, and read from the Evangelists, while they listened with earnest attention. Fifty women and girls have thus heard of Jesus; some of them again and again.

CONVERTS.

"Mrs. Kung professes to believe in Christ, and I have been invited to several houses in the neighborhood. Last week, Mrs. Yin, another of the three, cast away from her house her idol god, which she had long since ceased to worship; and with her husband is now asking admission to the church. She led in prayer at our last two meetings for women, and prays much in her own home, giving good evidence of real conversion."

LETTER FROM MISS PAYSON.

Miss Payson of Fouchow wrote, April 27, — .

"Our eldest pupil was married in November. Her wedding was the first I have attended, and gave me an insight of Chinese etiquette. Seuk Hiong, the bride, left for her father's house five days before the event, and there participated in the customary festivities. On the appointed day, we repaired to our little brick chapel, which we found nearly filled. The bridegroom was in readiness; and shortly a scarlet* sedan was brought into the vestibule, from which the bride emerged, leaning on the arm of an old woman, her only attendant, as Chinese custom forbids any relatives of the bride to be present at the ceremony. She was attired in scarlet, an embroidered silk. Elaborate flowers of gilt and tinsel in her hair, with a scarlet silk pocket-handkerchief,

* The bridal color.

composed her adornments. Here all ladies, on their bridal-day,
are expected to look wretched and forlorn; and our bride appeared so abject and heart-broken, as she walked up the aisle,
that I could scarcely believe it was all affectation. The officiating missionary read the ceremony from a long roll of red paper;
but no joining hands on the part of the happy pair was required,
as all staid, virtuous people would be shocked at any such pro-
cedure in public. The nuptials over, the husband went out by
one aisle, and the modest bride, with her duenna, departed by the
other. Reaching their house, we found preparations for a fine
dinner; but, following the bride into her bedroom, we beheld her
sitting in a corner, still melancholy and speechless. Having
tasted tea and cakes, we left. At these feasts, the men eat in
one apartment, and the women in another; but the bride is expected to eat none at all during the day.

SCHOOL DISCIPLINE.

" In January, our scholars had a vacation of a week; but
some of them, yielding to the entreaties of friends, remained away
two or three weeks longer than the allotted time. On their return, they were deprived of their ' pwoi ' a certain number of
days. ' Pwoi ' signifies every thing eaten as a sauce to the
inevitable bowl of rice which appears at each meal. Chicken
and pork stews, cabbage, and all sorts of greens boiled, and fish,
constitute ' pwoi ; ' and it is considered a great trial to be forced
to eat rice only for a day or two. Some of the relatives of the
culprits, hearing of their punishment, brought bowls of ' pwoi,'
but were dismissed summarily, much to the grief of the hungry
school-girls.

BANDAGED FEET.

" Two little girls, named Sai Hing and Ai Chio, entered the
school last autumn with bandaged feet; but, as we forbid this,
the unbinding process began at once. The youngest, seven years
old, acquiesced readily; but Sai Hing, twelve years old, was ob-

stinate, and has caused us trouble. Her feet were much bent under and misshapen, and at first she could not take a step without the bandages; but, by unbinding them each night, by degrees they returned to something of their original shape. Last week, she reluctantly unbound her feet entirely, and I carried away her wee shoes in triumph, Mrs. Baldwin having promised to purchase them of her as a relic. She walks, and even runs now, though not very gracefully. It is astonishing how wedded these people are to this intolerable fashion. Those living in the most squalid poverty insist on binding the feet of their daughters, though it cripples them for life.

PRAYER ANSWERED.

" In one of my letters, I requested special prayer for three pupils. King Ugi, one of them, about eighteen years old, giving evidence of faith in Christ, united with the church in February. She is to marry one of the most promising of our student helpers Mi Chio, another of our older girls, we trust is a Christian; though she is timid, and fears to offend her relatives. We are praying that the dear Lord will guide and strengthen her. Oh that all these pupils may speedily feel the Spirit's power! If Christians at home would offer fervent, effectual prayers with every dollar sent here, how manifold more would be the results!"

INDIA.

LEAVES FROM A MISSIONARY'S JOURNAL.

NUMBER FOUR.

OUR nearest neighbors are of a class known as the " salt-merchant caste." They carry grain to the sea-shore, and bring back coarse salt, using donkeys to carry the burdens. They are a " hard set." In the leisure between their trips, the men give themselves to gambling and cock-fighting. The women never seem to know me, however many favors they may have received. If we ride through their street, the children shout rudely, "There go the white-faces." For all that, I have felt that I ought to visit them, and have been wishing the way would open for me.

Saturday afternoon, the sound of wailing reached our ears ; and, as the smoke of the funeral pile went up from the river-bank, I inquired about the death. It was the youngest son of a widow, whose house is in sight from our front veranda. Sorrow, even in heathenism, softens the heart; and I quickly resolved to go to the mourning mother.

Sabbath afternoon I took with me Peri — one of my school-girls — to visit this neighborhood. Virginia and Martha, who had preceded us on their way to another part of the town, turned back to tell me that the wailing was so loud that I should fail to get a hearing.

"Jesus went to a house when there was such tumult ; and I can, at least, try to be heard," was my reply, as I kept on.

There happening to be no one to announce me, I reached the door before I was noticed ; and the astonishment that made a sudden silence rebuked me for being such a stranger.

The mother and wife of the young man, and a wife of an elder brother, were sitting on a low, square platform, on the edge of which I took my seat. The mother received me most respectfully, the wife looked wonderingly, while the other young woman at once broke into a deafening but tearless wail. Beating her breast frantically, she rocked to and fro, repeating over and over, —

"He was like forty-five kings, I-yo, I-yo."

"Forty-five kings have gone, I-yo, I-yo."

"Where is he who was like forty-five kings? I-yo, I-yo."

"Great king, great king, come back, come back ! I-yo, I-yo."

But I had not come to look on such a scene. The wife was

joining in the wailing chorus; and I drew up to the mother.
There were tears on her face, and she tried to catch my words.

"I have come to see you, because I know what your sorrow
is."

"You are very kind. Oh, how it aches here!" and she
made an expressive gesture, as if her heart were being torn in
pieces.

Others had now come in; and, with two or three children half
wild with terror, speaking was out of the question; and I asked
the mother to come out into a back yard, where was a low mud-
wall, on which I seated her, and took my seat beside her. Oh,
the pure air, and the broad, peaceful blue!

"Now tell me all about it," I said; and she told me the
whole story of the journey to the sea-shore, and of the thorn in
the foot, the weary journey home, the spasms and convulsions, and the death. The stern facts had stripped all the hollow
mockery of grief; and I had before me the mother, — quiet, sad,
and earnest. A young daughter, about eighteen, had taken her
seat at my feet; two wicked young men, her brothers, had sauntered along, and were seated at my side; five women joined my
audience; while, within the house, the wailing increased in fury.

Where, from heathenism, was I going to find consolation for
this woman? Neither could I say, "Blessed are the dead who
die in the Lord." I could only say, "Your son is gone, but
you are living. I want to tell you how you may die with the
joy of knowing you may go to the Golden City."

"Nothing that you can say will take away this ache;" and
she made the same expressive gesture.

Never was sky more peaceful and golden than on this Sabbath
evening. To bid her look above seemed like a step towards
heaven.

"Now, think what a God who can spread such a sky can do
for us," I said. "What can that Puliar (a stone idol with an
elephant's head) out there do for you?"

Respect for me mingled with utter indifference to my subject, as she pointed towards her younger son, and said, —
" Talk to him. His eyes are opened. He knows how to read. He knows how to write. His hand is clever. As for me, I can only die as all my race have died before me. ˙ What's the good of talking to me ? "

My young companion Peri stood before us. She has come out into the marvellous light of the gospel, and her face shone with serenity and beaming cheerfulness. It was a moment of joyful reward for all that I had gone through, when I could say, —

" Look at this woman : she was shut up in darkness like you ; but she came to us, as others in my school have done, and she has learned joy in the Lord, and of a Friend who even died for us to let us go to heaven."

No words could have been more eloquent than the dear girl's responsive look, and the tears of joyful assent in her eyes. The heathen mother looked at her. She will remember this witness for the truth.

With the most satisfactory attention, I went on to speak of the love of the Father manifested in the Son, and the inheritance of the redeemed sinner. The poor woman seemed to understand it all, and more than once exclaimed, " Joyful ! joyful ! good news ! " The story of the cross is so simple, — adapted to every nation. I was going to question her upon what I had said, and try to plant one thought firmly in her mind, when a woman rushed out from the house, exclaiming angrily, —

" What business have you here, and we wailing there ? What way is this for the mother to be doing ? Are you the first to forget ? "

Cruel, merciless heathenism !

" You see they are even now angry with me," said the mother. " I must go ; " and so she went, but to join less furiously, and with more tears, the evening wail for the dead.

The young men still kept their seats. I said to the one who could read, " You ought to take God's words to us, and read them carefully. Find out for yourself what they are about. Make up your mind whether this is truth or folly ; but do not make the foolish mistake of declaring a thing good for nothing, when it may be proved and found pure gold."

With the greatest deliberation, he took up a white cloth that lay on a wooden mortar near by. Carefully folding it with the same deliberation, he laid it over his shoulders, and brought it before and crossed it, as I wear my shawl, and as a native never wears a cloth. I was not suspecting any special motive in his doing so, nor was there the least lurking look of contempt on his face. Still holding it together, he said, " I am not cold. I put this on to prove it, and see if I liked the feeling of it." Then throwing it off in a twinkling, he added, " What was the use of doing all that, when I knew before that I wasn't cold, and didn't need it? "

His cool survey of the little group betrayed his consciousness of having made a fine speech. Turning to his sister, he asked for tobacco ; at which I rose, and left. To gain the street, I had to pass through the house ; and on the platform were nine women, all intent on wailing. When the rice was ready, they sat in a circle, and again bewailed the dead. After that, they ate their evening meal, and the duty of mourning on the second day was ended.

·MADURA.

THE following cheering intelligence is from Mrs. C. H. Chandler : —

" Long have we waited and prayed for ' a door of entrance ' into the homes of the higher castes. The Lord has heard us. Ten houses are open to us in different parts of the city ; and the interest is increasing.

" Since October, I have employed several Bible-readers. The

first, Gnanaperahasen, an intelligent native woman, began with fear and trembling, but found the work very pleasant, many asking her to come again. The labor increasing, I appointed another, a superior woman, the wife of a native pastor. She dresses in European style, and speaks English, which proves attractive. She relinquished higher pay from love to the cause. The third, Parkeum, mistress of a girls' boarding-school, volunteered her services during two months' vacation, and labored with a will. I am often accompanied in my visits by the scholars, who always interest the young with stories. One attentive listener repeats my remarks to the women, who crowd about the door to hear. I was invited to a place, and found fifty persons assembled, to whom I spoke of the progress of the work in other fields, and the importance of educating Hindoo females. The encouraging result was a school of eighteen high-caste girls, kept in the house ; and the pupils are making rapid progress. I have several applications for similar institutions.

" To carry on the above work, two hundred dollars are required annually. Hitherto, the expense has been defrayed from private funds; but these failing, we present the object, trusting that you will supply our want. But, most of all, we need an assistant. We would cordially welcome a young lady to our home and hearts, promising her joy in this glorious work. Miss R. Smith has returned from the mountains well and full of hope. We rejoice in the success of your Board, and feel new courage and zeal, as we think that you are working and praying for the females of India."

TURKEY

Mrs. KNAPP of Bitlis writes, at a recent date, —
" We are enjoying a powerful revival, the like of which we have never seen. The Lord is working miracles among our

people. From stones he is raising up children unto Abraham. He is breathing upon these dry bones, and they are coming to life. About the first of January, we made a special effort among the women, exhorting them with the opening of the year to begin a new life ; and we believe that many consecrated themselves anew, and others covenanted to be the Lord's.

"Last Sabbath, we sat in church six hours, till sundown. The pastor arose several times to pronounce the benediction ; but two or three were on their feet ready to speak, and he could not. He said, ' I saw that the Lord had taken this meeting entirely into his own hands.' "

Miss Mary Ely reports the revival as follows : —

"Words are inadequate to speak of the Lord's wonderful dealings with us. I am incapable of portraying, in faintest outlines, the great work that has been and is still going on. Our hearts are full, and we long to share with you the joy which has been given us in ever-increasing measure.

THE WORD OF GOD VERIFIED.

" During the last three months, we have often called to mind the predictions concerning the flourishing of Christ's kingdom in the thirty-fifth chapter of Isaiah, and rejoiced as we were permitted to see its fulfilment. Many 'ransomed of the Lord have returned and come to Zion with songs and everlasting joy upon their heads : they have obtained joy and gladness, and sorrow and sighing have fled away.' By one word of the quickening Spirit has the lame man obtained strength to leap as an hart, and the tongue of the dumb found power to sing in sweet accents the song of salvation ; literally the tongue of stammerers has been loosed to say, ' All worthy is the Lamb who was slain.' The brow, long lifted up in haughty self-righteousness, has bowed before the power of the Holy Spirit, and wears for a ' crown of glory and diadem of beauty,' that lowly spirit which rests on the new-born soul in sweetest gentleness and peace.

" Among the women and school-girls, there was a manifest awakening at the opening of the year. The week of prayer developed a marked and wide-spread interest in the community. Some of the first fruits were garnered on the 6th of March, eleven persons being admitted to the church. Six of these were women, the first time in the history of the work here that the female candidates have outnumbered the male. As, on the sweet Sabbath morning of last communion-day, I saw the sisters come in till they numbered fourteen, and remembered, that, less than eighteen months since, there was not one female member of the church, my heart was lifted up in deep thanksgiving.

" It is wonderful how, under the teaching of the Holy Spirit, these poor, ignorant women learn at once what we have failed to convince them of in months of patient instruction.

BOGHOS AND HIS MOTHER.

" A particularly interesting case is that of an elderly woman, the mother of an efficient helper (Boghos). When the call came last fall for us to send an Armenian helper to Persia, this young man seemed just the one ; but his aged father and fond mother used many persuasions to prevent his going. He, however, remained firm, and, although much moved by his mother's tears, obeyed the call he recognized as greater than her loving entreaties. The day the son left, I tearfully begged the sad mother to seek that dear Saviour her son so devotedly served ; and I cannot doubt that the voice of the Spirit was then speaking to her soul. A week or two after, she came early one morning to see us. I invited her into my room, and talked and prayed earnestly with her. At last I said, ' You often tell me, " I wish to be a Christian," but you do not say, " I give my heart to Jesus now." '. This touched the right chord. Raising her hands, the tears flowing down her cheeks, she fervently exclaimed, ' I do give my heart to Jesus *now !* ' From that moment, she was blessed and accepted. Her great difficulty then was, to pray before others

She was first led to pray with her daughter. At the next female prayer-meeting, when all were invited to take part, with sobs and groans she again bore her heavy cross. She seemed crushed in view of her sins; and it was deeply touching to hear her repeat with broken voice, ' O God ! I have sinned, I have sinned, and I knew it was sin. Oh, how can you forgive me ! I have sinned; but you shed your blood for me. I come, I come. Help me to believe. Help me henceforth to live according to thy will. Oh, I have sinned ! ' Sustained and strengthened, she visited her former home, and begged forgiveness of her old neighbors and friends. The conflict in her soul was severe but short : grace triumphed; and, at our last communion season, she sat down at the table of the Lord for the first time.

THE HUSBAND'S TESTIMONY.

" The testimony of this woman's husband is very sweet. He says, ' Our house used to be full of contention and strife : now a bright light has suddenly been kindled there. I thank God for this change.' Although for years an attendant at our chapel, he has trusted in his philosophy, learning, and good works to save him. Touched by the Spirit, he has now become a child in simplicity and meekness. He says, ' For years I have received the gospel with my intellect, now I receive it by faith in my heart.' A marked feature of this revival is, that youth and age have alike been blessed. To some gray-headed fathers, the still, small voice has come in wondrous power, showing them their sins, and revealing the mighty depth and breadth of God's grace in Christ; teaching them, in a single hour, lessons which years of preaching have failed to instil.

FINDING JESUS.

" A very aged man, with flowing, white beard, long a pillar in the Armenian Church, and widely known as a person of unusual piety and devotion, but for three years a constant attendant at our chapel, rising, tells his story briefly, ' I beg you all, young and old, to pray for me. Ever since I was a little boy I have deceived myself, thinking, that by keeping fasts, by tormenting my person, by getting absolution of sin from the priests, I should find Jesus; but I did not find him thus. Now the Holy Spirit has touched my hard heart, and I believe I have found the Saviour. He dwells in a broken and contrite heart. The work of sanctification has but just begun in my soul. Pray that I may overcome my sins in Christ's strength and for his love. I exhort you to love one another, and, when you go out, speak gently, kindly to all. Win them by love. Never dispute. Warmth attracts, cold repels. Let our hearts burn with Jesus' love, and so go forth and work for souls.' "

LETTER FROM MISS CLARKE.

In a recent letter from Miss Ursula Clarke of Broosa, she says, —

" How I wish you could know Anitra, whom I love and admire more and more ! Her patience and skill are wonderful in managing incorrigible children and unreasonable parents. This week, one of our brightest, largest girls left school; her mother fearing that being there might stand in the way of her marriage. My remonstrances had no effect; but Anitra saw the grandmother, with whom such matters rest, and so appealed to her conscience, that she promised the girl should return Monday.

TUITION PAID.

" An Armenian has just come to school. Her mother, being poor, renders an equivalent by ironing for us. The Protestants pay for each of their children at the rate of fifteen piastres a month. We shall raise it to twenty-two when practicable ; but this year the church has assumed an increase of fifty pounds on the one hundred and fifty they gave before. They have done well in taking books; and the wealthy help the poor. Sometimes I think this people generous and open-handed, and again their determination to get all they can out of the missionaries is apparent. But good Dr. S. well remarks, 'If they were what they should be, why did we come to them?'

THE BIBLE WELCOME.

"I make calls almost every day, mostly on Armenians; and at several places my Bible also is welcome. Some of the young Protestant women feel that they must learn to read it. Mariane, one of my girls, goes each day to teach a woman who pays her well; but most are careless and heedless. What is the use? they say. Their great concern is to dress."

LETTER FROM MISS NORCROSS.

Miss Norcross, in reporting the Girls' School, says, —
"I can give a better idea of what is accomplished, and how it is done, by noting individual cases.

THIRSTING FOR THE LIVING WATER.

"A girl, fourteen years old, the only female teacher in a city twelve miles distant, accompanied back to school her younger sister, who had been a pupil. She says, 'Ostensibly I came the better to be prepared for teaching; but my soul burned to come, because I discovered that my sister had learned something about the way of salvation through Christ, and I wanted to hear about it too.' Her soul was thirsting for the living water, and she soon found the life-giving fountain. Her two years' course expired last year. A few weeks before, the younger sister went to her heavenly home, and it became the lot of this one to comfort her mother. She gathered her friends and neighbors, and told them of the love of Jesus for sinners, and of the beautiful land of rest where her sister had gone, until they cried, 'Teach us more! Read to us more!' Eight of her hearers came regularly. We invited her to spend another year in school. Her mother said, 'I sent her before with joy, that she might become learned : I will send her again, though with tears, and spare her that she may learn more of this blessed truth. I know that the people will not receive her if she teaches such doctrines, but let her show us the way of salvation.' This week she wrote to her daughter, 'We cannot wait until the year is out : come to us *now* for a little while !' My heart has been much drawn to the dear girl, yet I rejoice to see her go forth to labor in the Master's vineyard.

THE AWAKENING.

" There has been an awakening in a village six miles from here. The people have converted an old mill into a school-house, which serves also for a chapel, and have called a former member of the boys' school at Phillippopolis to be a preacher, and teacher during the week. He has often a Sabbath audience of four hundred, — a great congregation for Bulgaria. The women, as well as the men, learn to read.

YAMBOUL PERSECUTION.

" At Yamboul, the women are keeping pace with the men in searching the Scriptures. Stephen, our colporter, a man full of faith and good works, became the spiritual teacher a month since. Immediately the multitude set upon him with stones, destroyed the house in which he lodged, and otherwise annoyed him. The great adversary is very active now in Bulgaria. Mr. Morse went to look after the disturbers, and returned with the intelligence that remuneration was made for the damages done, and the government and people promised that the Protestants should not be molested.

WHO WILL GIVE THE ORGAN?

"Music is a great source of attraction to native guests and callers, and almost indispensable in school. I am obliged to teach singing, and to lead the songs of praise on the Sabbath; but, on account of the weak condition of my voice, it will be difficult to get along without an instrument. Our trustees feel that we should secure one without delay. I know the Board cannot furnish it; but will not some one, for Christ's sake, supply our want?"

A WORD FROM MISS SEYMOUR.

In a communication from Harpoot, Miss Seymour says, under date of May 12, in referring to the loss of Miss Warfield, —

"Yet He, who never takes from his children an earthly blessing without supplying in its place some rich spiritual gift, has graciously led me to rejoice that in my school-duties an unerring Counsellor is ever ready to direct, and an Almighty arm to aid."

Miss Caroline E. Bush of Rochester, N. Y., sailed, May 28, for Harpoot, to take Miss Warfield's place.

MISSIONARY ITEMS.

On May 12, Miss Powers of Antioch wrote, —

"Deploring the coldness among the Protestants, I sought to revive the female prayer-meeting. At the first one, I invited the pastor's wife to pray; but she looked foolish as a bashful child, and declined. At the next, when she begged to be excused, I spoke of the privilege and duty of social prayer, and the sin of neglecting to do the work God intrusts to us, and called on her again. She began in a trembling voice, gathering courage as she went on, and never since has refused. I had a similar experience with the rest. Having attained that point, I led them forward yet another step; and, when I left for the health retreat, they were willing to take the leadership of the meeting.

A letter from Marash states, "that three Mothers' Meetings are held there monthly, on the same day and hour, well attended and very interesting. The native women take the principal parts, leading in prayer with great earnestness and propriety, — as many as twelve or fourteen being offered at each meeting. These mothers are very poor, and many have to bring their little children ; but they come with great cheerfulness, and seem to prize and enjoy their spiritual privileges."

Extract of a letter from Mrs. Edwards, Inanda, May 19 : — "You ask if I am sorry I came ? I can truly say, no. There is no peace and comfort equal to that found in the path of duty. During a recent illness, the scholars behaved beautifully. One of them acted as teacher ; and things went on as orderly and quietly as usual. I was surprised to feel so much freedom from care, while confined in a dark room. It was a great comfort to know that they sympathized with me."

Mr. Rendall writes, May 27, — "On her arrival at Madura, Mary had the pleasure of receiving a kind letter from the ladies in Chicago, offering their prayers, sympathy, and support. I believe the formation of the Women's Board is a new era in the missionary cause. How it will strengthen and encourage our hearts to know that Christian sisters at home are co-operating with us ! I think, too, that our communications will interest them in the good work."

In a recent letter, Miss Isa Baker, of Mardin, writes, — "For a long time, the land has been parched and dry. The 'early rains' did not fall, and the people saw famine staring them in the face. The pasha ordered three days to be spent in prayer, and the cattle to be driven out, that their leanness might

move the Lord to pity; but not a *woman's* face must be seen
outside the city, or God would not send rain."

In a communication just received from Rev. **J. W.** Parsons,
Nicomedia, he says, —

"The work among adult females is very inviting, and calls
for a lady who will engage in missionary labor, superintending
Bible-women, common schools, and encourage the opening of
high-schools for girls." Who will go?

PERSIA.

ADDRESS OF MISS RICE.

CHRISTIAN ladies, daughters of Jerusalem, dwelling on the
heights of Zion, in the full blaze of gospel light and privilege!
These priceless blessings are yours because our adorable Redeemer endured the cross for us. Have you ever pondered the
deep meaning, the wonderful power, contained in these precious
words "endured the cross," — *endured the cross?* Union with
Him who "endured the cross" is the secret of spiritual success. This is the power that shall renovate the world. This
the power that shall reach down into the deep, dark caverns of
humanity, in which immortal spirits lie, imbedded in darkness,
ignorance, superstition, and vice of every form, "hateful and
hating one another." In China, in Burmah, in India, in Persia,
Turkey, Syria, Africa, and in the islands of the sea, there have
been trophies of victorious grace among women who have "endured the cross," and endured it to the end. They have passed
over the dark river, singing "Thanks be unto God, who giveth
us the victory through our Lord Jesus Christ!"

Many remain ready to endure the cross. They are bright
stars in our missionary sky, on which we gaze, in the sweet

hope that in the great coronation day we shall see them shining in the radiant diadem of Him who "endured the cross, the King of many crowns."

Many of you, no doubt, are familiar with the history of the Nestorian mission. You have read the thrilling stories of "Woman and her Saviour in Persia," and the life of the now sainted Fidelia Fiske, the spiritual mother of many Nestorians. You know the condition of woman there thirty years ago, the slave, not the helpmeet and companion, of man. The customs of society were such that no young woman could go to the place of public prayer, and so degraded and dark was she that she did not desire the light. To illustrate the change wrought by the gospel, let me refer to a few examples.

About the time that I went to Persia, a little Nestorian girl, named Hoshebo, entered the Oroomiah Female School. Like other new pupils in those days, she was untruthful, dishonest, and, in addition to these traits, had an irritable temper. Self-willed and obstinate, she was at times a great trial. But, after a few months, grace was grafted on this crab-stock. The "flesh lusting against the spirit," severe were the conflicts, but many were the victories. After finishing her course of study, she engaged in teaching a few years, and then became the wife of a native pastor, an humble, earnest, godly man. They were stationed in a village, and were blessed in their labors by the gathering of women into the church. These were years, not only of success, but of discipline, to Hoshebo. "Whom the Lord loveth he chasteneth." One child after another was taken from her, till only one was left ; and then she was deprived of her beautiful stay and staff, — her husband rested from his labors ; and for nearly six years she has been a widow. Every year but one, since, she has taught in the Oroomiah Female School.

[Miss Rice then read passages from Hoshebo's letter of a recent date, showing the fruit of twenty years of discipline and labor ; which we hope to give in a future number.]

The winter before we left Persia, there was a revival of unusual interest in a neighboring village. One of the native brethren came to the school, saying that the women were deeply interested, but there was no one to lead them to Christ. "Will you go to our village?" he asked earnestly. One of our pupils was apparently very near death, and I could not leave. Arrangements were made to send Hoshebo. She went three times, and was constantly surrounded by anxious, weeping women, asking "What shall we do?" She labored day and night, sometimes forgetting to eat, in the blessed "walk from Sinai to Calvary."

I would like to tell you of another native Christian woman; and what the gospel can do for one, it can do for all. Fourteen years ago, a Nestorian school-girl gave her heart to Jesus, and consecrated herself to the work in Koordistan. She became the wife of a mountain missionary. His health failing, they were obliged to leave their field. She still smiles through her tears, and everywhere delights to labor for Christ. Winter before last, her husband was itinerating in the mountains. The Friend of little children had taken her last babe; and she came to Oroomiah to spend a few months in a missionary family, where she was a great blessing during weeks of watching and weariness with sick children. One evening, the mother went to our weekly prayer-meeting, leaving Esli in charge. The oldest child was very restless; to soothe and quiet him, she told the story of Jesus, the old, old story of Bethlehem and the cross. The child listened with eager, rapt attention. She prayed with him. The boy said, "Esli, I do not know how to pray in your language." So she taught him a sweet, childlike prayer in Syriac, and the little one slept. Under the influence of this lesson, the child soon found the stable-boy in the kitchen, and said, "Yosip, do you love Jesus?" — "No, Charlie: when I was a little boy, Miss Fiske came to our village, and told me I must give my heart to Christ, but I have not done it yet." — "I will pray for you," said the little missionary, for he believed in the power of prayer. When ill and nervous, a few months before, nothing, in his uncontrollable state, had soothed him like prayer. He would say, beseechingly, " Pray, pray ! " and was always calmed.

[A Boston mother, too old to go, and with no daughter to send to foreign missionary work, gladly assumes the support of this happy, zealous teacher and Bible-reader.]

The door is open for women in America to carry or send the blessings of the gospel to their sisters in foreign lands. The work must be accomplished mainly by native Christian females, educated by missionary ladies. As yet, there are few compared with the immense demand. A great work remains to be done. Who will do it ? Perhaps some heart here is saying, " Lord, here am I. Send me."

Beloved, is there not need of laborers ? Ask the graves of departed ones. Still voices whisper, " Who will be baptized for the dead ? " Behold weary, exhausted disciples laid aside from labor, with the whitened fields ever before them. Look at the pale, careworn missionaries, faltering under heavy burdens which they may not lay down, since there are none to fill their places. Christian sisters, you will give your prayers, sympathies, love, and money ; but He who withheld not his only Son asks *more.* Give your sons to lead the way ; your daughters to reach woman in her seclusion in heathen lands. O Christian mothers ! have you no thank-offering, no whole burnt-offering, to lay upon the altar of missions ? Have you no Samuel or Timothy, no Mary or Persis, to send away to endure the cross, and go home to wear a crown ? There is joy unspeakable in this service ; but there will be fulness of joy, and pleasure forevermore, in the glad harvest-day, when we shall be permitted to unite with " kindreds and people and tongues from all nations " in the ascription of praise, — " Worthy is the Lamb ! "

For Treasurer's Report, see " Missionary Herald " for June, July, August.

16

THE MEETING AT YARMOUTH.

In compliance with repeated invitations to hold a public meeting exclusively for ladies, in connection with the Maine Conference, convened at Yarmouth, June 21, the President of the Woman's Board, with one of the secretaries, made arrangements for such a meeting. Surely the call to go was of God. Instead of finding, as was expected, " a faithful few " who long and pray for the coming of Christ's kingdom, a crowded church waited to hear what had been and can be done to save heathen women. After brief devotional exercises, the President gave a concise statement of the formation of the Woman's Board, its relations to the American Board, the work already undertaken, and of that which remains to be accomplished, urging most tenderly upon each lady present the privilege and duty of working with the Master. Letters of thrilling interest from Turkey, China, and Armenia were read by the Secretary. Mrs. Allen of Harpoot, and Mrs. Snow of Micronesia, also addressed the audience, holding their tearful, undivided attention to the end. Already the seed sown on that occasion is bearing fruit. God grant it an abundant increase !   A. C. G., *Secretary.*

MAY MEETING.

A meeting of the Women's Board of Missions was held in the Old South Chapel, May 26, at 10 o'clock, the President occupying the chair. A large and appreciative audience of ladies was present. After devotional exercises, a report was read from the Recording Secretary, which indicated a deepened and growing interest in the work. Auxiliaries were multiplying, and a vigorous and successful effort is being made to interest the children in forming Mission Circles.

The Treasurer, Mrs. Homer Bartlett, reported ten thousand

dollars received since the 1st of January. While grateful mention was made of the increase of funds, attention was called to the growing demands of the Board, in the enlargement of its work.

Mrs. Winslow, one of the corresponding secretaries, read extracts of a letter from Philadelphia, stating that a " branch " of the Woman's Board had been established there, with the confident expectation of forming auxiliaries in that region. Mrs. Gould also read deeply interesting letters from our missionaries, several of which communications are in our columns.

Miss Rice, from Oroomiah, was introduced, and gave the address which appears in this number.

Mrs. Wilder, from South Africa, was presented, and said, " We often hear it remarked that the heathen do not need the gospel : they are better off without it. If people holding these opinions could live in Zulu land, as I have done twenty years, they would bear different testimony. Men, women, and children are there elevated, ennobled, and Christianized from the depths of idolatry and barbarism. The missionaries need just such helpers as the Woman's Board is sending out. The converted Zulus ask, ' Why have Christians kept the gospel from us so long ? ' What can we answer ? "

The audience then sang —

> " Go labor, ere your hands are weak,
>   Your knees are faint, your soul cast down:
> Yet falter not; the prize you seek
>   Is near, — a kingdom and a crown."

We thank our many subscribers to " Life and Light " for prompt remittances. There are, however, nearly three hundred whose dues are yet unpaid. Will these please remember that fifty cents retained by each is, in the aggregate, one hundred and fifty dollars loss to our treasury.

The King's Need.

BY EMILY C. PEARSON.

"Inasmuch as ye did it not to one of the least of these, ye did it not to me."—
Matt. xxv. 45.

"Go ye forth and give my gospel!"
　　Said our glorious risen Lord.
Should we, listless, disobey him,
　　And the priceless treasure hoard,
Those who might have shared salvation
　　Will arise, a judgment throng,
Us upbraiding with their mourning,
　　Thus bewailing for the wrong: —

"Oh! the summer now is ended;
　　All the harvest-time is passed!
Since no one our need befriended,
　　We have failed of heaven at last!"
"I was hungered," will the King say,
　　"Nothing gave me ye to eat;
I was thirsty, poor, in sorrow,
　　Me ye never came to greet;

"I was sick, and oft in prison,
　　Yet ye came not to my aid:
All the suffering ye could save me
　　To your charge shall now be laid!"
Thus he hungers in his offspring,
　　Thirsts he in the very least;
For the maimed and blind he bids us
　　Haste to spread the gospel feast.

Halt and maimed and blind, the millions
　　In the shadows drear and dim:
Shall we not arise and feed them,
　　Christians, for our love to him?
Thus he'll heal them, in compassion,
　　Shield them with his boundless love;
And from long-benighted nations
　　Shall be gathered hosts above.

ECHOES, from "LIFE and LIGHT."

SEPTEMBER. PUBLISHED BY THE WOMAN'S BOARD OF MISSIONS. 1870.

THE CHILD HELPER.

MRS. EMILY GULICK of China gives an interesting account of a missionary tour of herself and husband, accompanied by a little girl five years old, whom they adopted about a year since. Mrs. Gulick says, —

" Martha was generally carried on a donkey: while crossing a stream, the one she was riding made a false step, and over rolled Chenger and Martha into the water. We had to convert our steeds into clothes-horses, and laughed to see how odd they looked dressed in the wet garment. Unfortunately, my dear little girl was ill with lung-fever, caught from the damp, brick beds at the inns: her bath made her worse, and for several days we were very anxious about her.

" I thought of the time when she was given to us. Her mother's village is two days' journey from Kalgan, where we live; and, as we were bringing her home, people shook their heads, and

21*   —   245

said she was a dying child. She was so reduced by cold and hunger, that, although four years old, she could not have weighed ten pounds; and so weak that it was a fortnight before she could creep, and longer still before she learned to laugh. Poor child! her short life had indeed been one of suffering. She had had small-pox, and whooping-cough, and had often been left alone from morning till night, cold and hungry, while her mother went into the fields to gather wild roots and herbs. The father told us they thought of throwing her into the river, if we would not take her, because she cried so much, and they had so little food to give her. She is now fat, happy, and loving. I think, too, that Christ is making her one of his precious lambs. Once, when we were talking of God's goodness to her, she said, 'I want to kiss God : where is he ?' — 'He is in heaven.' — 'When I die, I shall go to heaven, then I will kiss him.'

"She is very fond of Timeus, our blind boy, and often prays that he may love Christ. One night, she stopped in the midst of her petition, and asked, 'Doesn't Timeus love Jesus?' I said, 'I hope God will teach him.' A few days after, they were playing together in the veranda, and she asked him if he loved Jesus; and, when he said he did, she ran joyfully to tell me. 'Timeus does love Jesus, mamma !'

"We spent a Sabbath in a village not far from Pekin. Mr. Gulick went into the town to preach, and Martha and I staid at the inn. We were soon surrounded by a crowd of young folks, whom I tried in vain to interest in the gospel. At length, in despair, I took up the 'Peep of Day,' to teach Martha. As I told her about each picture, she of her own accord showed it to those around, repeating the story in her touching, baby way, which so completely won their attention, that I could not help feeling that my little one had taught them more than I could have done. 'Out of the mouths of babes and sucklings thou hast perfected praise.' "

VARVAR'S LETTER FROM HARPOOT SEMINARY,

ADDRESSED TO THE CHILDREN'S MISSIONARY SOCIETY, FREDONIA, N.Y.

My very beloved and little friends in Christ, — My thankfulness I offer for your love, that, like the vernal, sweet-scented, and beautiful violets, you have blossomed in that flower-adorned plain. Oh, how sweet is your fragrance towards us! Though very great seas and high mountains keep us at a distance, one from another, nevertheless, they are not able to hinder that sweet-breathed wind, — your gush of love, — that it blew not towards us. I know that it is love for our beloved Saviour that constrains you to put your hands to such good works, viz., to give money for our education. I very much desire to be a good girl, and in the vineyard of the Lord to work, though I am weak, and do not know many things. I beseech that for me you make prayer, that I be faithful in my lessons and to my teachers. With love I salute you. Your sincere sister,

VARVAR ISAKAZIAN, *the daughter of Isaac.*

THE SCHOOL-ROOM.

IN visiting one of the villages near Harpoot, Miss Seymour says, " After stooping to enter a low door, we groped our way till we reached the stable, where it was utter darkness. A woman took hold of my hand, and piloted me between cows and donkeys, pushing them aside to clear a pathway. But, as she opened the door at the other end of the stable, my heart was touched with the picture before me. There sat more than twenty little girls and boys, most of them with the primer in their hands. Though in January, it was not cold ; for the stable-door was usually kept open, that the warmth from the animals might be communicated to this room. As the children rose to welcome us, we saw that most of them were clad only in a blue cotton shirt, or sacque, reaching nearly to the knees, while the little bare legs and feet told a story of privation."

JAMIE'S BANK.

Among the gifts Santa Claus brought to little Jamie, one Christmas Eve, was a small, brown, iron bank, with an opening just big enough to slide in pennies. St. Nick felt quite sure that the little fingers that enjoyed slipping them in could never find the "open sesame" concealed in the brown screw, which looked only like a bit of an ornament, — certainly a five-year-older could not understand it to mean any thing more, — and now the numberless pennies that burn so many holes through pockets would surely be tempted into a safe place, where they could never get out. Little Jamie was greatly pleased with his gift, and thought it fine fun to slip in his pennies, and hear them jingle as he shook the bank. But it soon became evident to him that what he was so fast slipping in would be slow coming out. Then the busy little brain and fingers began to work hard to re-gain the lost treasures: his knife in vain endeavored to cut the iron hole larger. Santa Claus, it seemed, had at last found something that would keep babies' pennies from melting into candy. But he was too sure in this case: he did not know that Jamie belonged to the "never-give-up company," and that his ten little servants called fingers knew just how to work out all Corporal Try's plans. And so it came to pass, one day, that mamma was astonished by seeing one of her nice tea-knives used as a screwdriver; and Jamie was overjoyed to find the little or-nament of a screw fast drawing out, while the bank separated on either side, like the waters of Jordan, and all the pennies rolled out.

Mamma expected to see them going for candy as before; but, to her joyful surprise, when she asked her little boy what he in-tended to do with his money, he replied, "I shall give my first bankful, mamma, to the heathen."

Jamie had always felt great pity for the heathen boys and girls, especially for the babies thrown to the crocodiles, and un-consciously obeyed the command, "Honor the Lord with thy first fruits ; " for his first bankful he freely offered. Not one of all that treasure of pennies did he keep for himself; and one bright, sunny day, he went to Boston with his papa to the "Heathen House," as he called the "Missionary House," and left his money for the heathen children.   MARY B.

Girls and boys, if you have no little "bank," you can obtain a very pretty missionary box for a few pennies, at our room, 33 Pemberton Square.

The following communication, from an unknown writer, enclosed one dollar and twenty-five cents : —

Self-Denying Charlie.

" I WISH I could do something," said little Charlie B.,
"For the poor, foolish heathen, away across the sea ;
For since mamma has shown me the map in 'Life and Light,'
And pointed out the darkness the Bible would make bright,
I long to send some money, and have another star
To tell of Christ our Saviour, and bless the isles afar.
But, oh, I am so little ! I'm only five years old ;
Although ma often tells me 'I'm worth my weight in gold.' "
Just then dear little Charlie heard mamma speaking quick :
" Now, who will fix my basket shall have five cents for it ;
And who will get some paper, down stairs within a drawer,
And bring it in a minute, shall have five pennies more."
Then, with his black eyes sparkling, his cheeks so rosy too,
Away rushed little Charlie : "Here, mamma, 'tis for you ;
And now I'll fix the basket, for, though I want to play,
And the little boys are calling, yet 'tis a better way
To get my wished-for money." Sitting upon the floor,
See self-denying Charlie the basket fixing o'er ;
And when his mother paid him, a happy boy was he.
"Now, sisters dear, and brothers, if you would happy be,
Just help me in this object ; " so Maggie brought her hoard,
James, Walter, and Louisa, and gave them to the Lord ;
And the blessedness of giving filled each young heart with joy.
Now, who will be like Charlie, the self-denying boy ?

MISSION CIRCLES.

THE girls and boys are busily at work. "Cheerful Givers," "Willing Workers," "Little Nightingales," and "Wide Awakes" have promised their aid since our June call; while Alice, Susie, and Hattie have determined to start missionary rills in their Sunday-schools.

THE NIGHTINGALES.

The annual meeting of these juveniles took place May 4, at Rev. Mr. Fisher's church in Lawrence. The pastor, superintendent, parents, and friends united in the exercises. Declamations by the boys and appropriate recitations by the girls, with piano and vocal music, made a good programme. It was a gala day for the young folks; and we were cheered by their interesting report.

THE MONATIQUOT CIRCLE.

The pupils of Miss Faxon's school, East Braintree, gave a social entertainment during the afternoon and evening of June 22. Printed invitations were sent to friends a fortnight before. Under the direction of their kind teachers, the members had manufactured many fancy and useful articles, which were sold; while the occasion was enlivened by music, speaking, and exhibiting native costumes from India and Turkey. Those present had a delightful time; and the treasurer of the W. B. M. received one hundred and twenty-six dollars for Mrs. Edwards's school as the result.

THE ZULU HELPERS.

This mission circle, under the charge of Miss Wilder, held a strawberry festival and sale at East Boston, June 29. Tickets of admission were disposed of in advance. Various attractive and serviceable things, made by the members, found ready purchasers.

A quilt for Mrs. Edwards, made by many little fingers, was bought by friends, and sent to her. A " curiosity shop," filled with articles brought from heathen lands, and a " missionary tree," laden with bags of candy, baskets of cherries, and the like, helped to raise funds. The festival passed off admirably ; and the young folks were gratified in sending to us, through their treasurer, Miss Mary Bingham, the proceeds — one hundred and eighty-five dollars — for the Zulu girls.

WILLING HELPERS.

This children's society in Fall River gave an evening entertainment, Thursday, July 26. The exercises, including songs, dialogues, and recitations, elicited great interest, and received hearty praise. The dialogues were original; and the speakers appeared in appropriate foreign costumes.

The pastor of the church, Rev. W. W. Adams, gave an interesting address, which was followed by the song, " There's work to do for Jesus." The children have added more than fifty dollars to the Lord's treasury by this effort.

Received one dollar and twenty-five cents, with the mother's sketch of " Little Nellie," which we give in verse on the next page.

Twenty-five copies of the " Children's Quarterly " can be obtained for one dollar a year, or one hundred for four dollars, by sending to the secretary of the W. B. M., 33 Pemberton Square, Boston.

Children, will not all of you ask your superintendents to furnish you with this little paper ?

Little Nellie.

BY EMILY C. PEARSON.

"Oh, I'll be a missionary!"
Loving little Nellie cried.
"Far away I'll tell the children
How our blessed Saviour died.

" Soon as I do get there, mother,
I will shut them in my room ;
Sing, and pray, and tell them Jesus
Bids 'the little children come.'

" Say, dear father, you will spare me,
Though I'm all the child you have :
Oft you've told me how our Father
Gave his Son the world to save.

" Let me go and help the children
Serving idols far away :
Seems as if I heard them calling,
' Show us, please, to heaven the way.' "

Gladly, rosy five-year Nellie
All her little fortune gave —
'Twas a dollar and some pennies —
Darkened, famished souls to save ;

For her heart was full of longing
To make heathen children good.
Precious little missionary,
She was doing what she could !

Jesus called her soon to heaven :
Finished was her mission well.
Happy Nellie! early chosen
In his glorious home to dwell.

Forth the King doth speed his herald :
."Lead them shall a little child,"
Till "the wilderness shall blossom,"
No more desolate and wild.

LIFE AND LIGHT

FOR

Heathen Women.

| VOL. I. | DECEMBER, 1870. | No. 8. |

INDIA.

THE SEED IS THE WORD.

BY MRS. S. C. DEAN.

UNDER the shade of the mango-trees, between two villages, our tent was pitched. The larger village was about one-third of a mile distant on our left ; and the other close by at our right, on the opposite side of a small stream. I had been into the latter, and had a talk with a company of women at the house of a " Joshee," the village astrologer, who had invited me to come ; but as yet I had not been able to get access to the women in the town. I had, however, made my way into the fields, and talked with some of the poorer classes, who were digging peanuts.

One day, a company of travellers passed along the road, going to the town. There were two vehicles drawn by oxen, closely curtained, concealing those within. The oxen were ornamented with bells, tassels, and small blankets of turkey-red cloth. Two or three horsemen rode alongside. After they had gone on several rods, they stopped ; and one of the horsemen galloped back to the tent with a message from the principal personage in the party.

1

The wife of a petty rajah had been on a pilgrimage to the shrine of an idol to perform a certain vow; and now she was returning home to a distant city, but intending to stop a few days with an aunt in the village. She sent her compliments, and wished to know when she might call upon me. I named an hour the next day. She arrived at the appointed time, accompanied by her aunt, the "Baee Sahib," a title of respect, and many followers from the town. The ladies came in the covered cart, and were closely veiled till they got into the tent. I showed them pictures, books, my sewing-machine, played and sang some of our hymns translated into Mahratta, all which seemed to please them very much. I then alluded to the pilgrimage, and tried to impart some religious truth to them; but the priest who came with them arose, and said they had made a long call; and so the visit ended.

Baee Sahib urged me to call upon her very soon. I took an early opportunity and went. Her niece had gone, but she met me at the door, and led me to the veranda of the inner court, where mats were spread for us to sit upon. Her aged mother, having a very pleasing face, was presented to me, and I was hopeful that I might do them some good. The priest who came with her was there, — I learned afterward that he was the family priest, — and annoyed me by interrupting our conversation, and trying to prejudice the women against any thing I said in favor of Christianity. The interview was not satisfactory. I wanted a private talk, but caste prejudice prevented them from asking me into their private apartments.

We left the place without seeing them again. The year after, when the mission-house was completed, we went there to reside. Baee Sahib was among the first to send me a message of welcome, and ask me to come and see her. I went, taking my New Testament; but the house being full of visitors, I again came away, thinking that very little, if any, good had been done.

A few months later, we were obliged to leave our chosen field of labor on account of my husband's continued ill health. As soon as Baee Sahib heard this, she sent word by one of our people that she intended to make me a stealthy call on a certain evening. She came, and I took her by a side door into my bedroom. As soon as we were seated, she took hold of my hands and said, "How can I let you go? Who will tell me of what I wish to know? Tell me again of the name of the one to whom you pray?" "Jesus Christ," she repeated after me; and then said, "How do you pray in his name? 'For Jesus Christ's sake,'" she slowly repeated after me. Tears came into her eyes.

My friends, you who have never tried to lead a soul to Jesus cannot know the joy I felt that a spirit of inquiry had sprung up in that dark heart. I told her that she must watch for opportunities to learn of Jesus, and pray for light, and the Saviour would show her what to do.

Is it wholly in vain that we go to the heathen? or give to the cause of missions as the Lord prospers us? The seed is the Word. Be it ever so small, the power of the Spirit can cause it to grow in the heart, and bring forth abundant fruit to the glory of God.

KURAPPAI'S NEW NAME.

BY MRS. CAPRON.

WE invited our Christian people to come on New Year's, and spend the Sabbath, and help us dedicate the "Hartford Tent." Jewel of Life came, and how good she looked! Kurappai came, and how her face beamed! Mariammal came, moving about with such quiet dignity and grace, that I loved to look at her. The very thought of her as conducting women's meetings, and showing consistency of character, is inspiring. "Nothing can ever take from me the wealth that I have found here," was her testimony to the worth of this school to her. Elizabeth came, free from the tyranny of her mother-in-law for a while. And Irulai came. So did Kurappai's mother-in-law; and a lovable woman she is. It was a pleasant greeting.

Kurappai, Elizabeth, and Peri joined the church on the Sabbath. The previous examination was conducted before all the church-members; and when the vote respecting Kurappai was to be called, her mother-in-law was asked if she had any objection to make concerning her fitness for the step. She ventured to say, that, when Kurappai was angry, she wouldn't speak. This was infinitely amusing to me; for I had drilled it into the girls to shut their mouths under provocation, and Kurappai had learned the lesson well while she was here. This was not regarded as a disqualification.

I had a new lesson on this very point the other day. When reproved for some neglect of duty, my sweeping-woman, a quiet, gentle body, broke forth into such a storm of words that I was astonished.

"My good woman," I exclaimed, "you need not rave so!"

Throwing down her broom, she put on an air of offended dignity.

"Don't you know, that, if we don't scold when we are angry, the people call us idiots? If we scold, they think we are brave, and have sense."

This view of the subject of fierce quarrelling will serve me some future day.

"Sabbath noon, just before church-time, Kurappai came to me and said, —

"I don't want to be baptized with such a heathen name. I want a better name."

Dismayed at the want of time for counsel on so important a subject, I asked her if she had any choice.

" None at all, only to have a name suitable for a Christian woman."

" And I will write upon him my new name." Yes, it must be the Lord's will to give Kurappai a new name ; so I sent for the father-in-law, and the mother-in-law, and the sisters Martha and Nyannammal, and the brother Samuel. The husband, Solomon, could not be spared from his home.

" Kurappai wants a new name : do you approve ? " I said to the father-in-law.

" It is better to change it. Her present name is heathenish. It is the name of a heathen goddess."

" Will you mention something ? " I asked.

We now had quite a gathering about us, all intensely interested in a " new name " for Kurappai.

" Call her Annal," said Vetham : " she was a good Bible woman."

" Call her Parkium," said Mariammal. Parkium means " happiness."

" Call her Lydia," said Virginia.

" Let the mother-in-law give us a name. She is the proper person," said I, turning to her as she sat close by my side.

" Let her name be Rebecca." Promptly and distinctly she said it, and the murmur of approval sealed the decision. The father-in-law repeated it, and nodded a positive assent. The brother and sisters were told to say " Rebecca." The school-girls echoed " Rebecca."

" Neither shall thy name any more be called Kurappai, but thy name shall be Rebecca. May the Lord our God bless thee evermore ! "

Thus it was that she was baptized Rebecca.

CHINA.

WE give below the last letter of Miss Mary E. Andrews of Tung-Chow, the beloved missionary, concerning whose fate Mrs. Chapin expressed much anxiety in her remarks at the Brooklyn meeting : —

" The temple Tieu Chung Sy, in which we spent the summer, is situated in a beautiful gorge of the mountains; and the road is so steep and rocky, that we can only go up to it on foot.   The first day, on our way up the hill, we stopped at a little temple by the roadside to rest ; while there, a poor woman came to see us, carrying a sick child, who for four years had been unable to walk.   Of course, we could not help the poor child ; but, while the mother rested, we talked to her of Jesus, and his power to heal the sickness of the soul.   She listened eagerly, and seemed to take in the meaning of the Saviour's wonderful sacrifice, and of the way of salvation through him.   A few days after, she came up to the temple to see us, bringing other women from the village. Again we spoke of the Saviour, and read from the Gospels, and sung to them.   They invited us to go to the village, and talk to those who had not heard.   At our first visit, they begged us so earnestly to teach them more, that we went again and again, until nearly all in the village had heard the truth, and many seemed to understand the way of salvation.   One poor woman said she had no sin, and needed no Saviour; another told us, that, if this doctrine would only tell them how to get riches, they would all follow it ; and a third said this teaching was very good, but it was hard to change."

BIBLE-WOMEN.

" I have a Bible-class each Sabbath, composed of five women, who will, I hope, become Bible-readers.   One of them, Mrs. Ysua, is an earnest Christian, and is very much interested in learning to read.   We are studying the Gospel of Mark."

CEYLON.

LETTER FROM MISS TOWNSEND.

Miss Townsend, of Oodoopitty, Ceylon, writes us very encouragingly of her work. We give from her pen the following account of a heathen festival.

PULIAR'S FESTIVAL.

Last month I witnessed the ceremonies of the Puliar's temple at Manepay on the day of the annual feast, and gained such an idea of Satan's power over the minds and hearts of men as I never before received; and, painful as the sight was, I will try to tell you of it, that you, too, may know and weep.

The temple at Manepay is across the road from our church. Our oldest missionaries remember it as consisting of a simple hut and a stone Puliar under the tree from which the temple takes its name. Private individuals have erected buildings, added courts and resting-houses, covering a large piece of ground; so that, from the little temple under the tree, it has become one of the seventy-seven large temples of Jaffna, which hold great annual festivals, attended by crowds of people, with much display and expense. A festival usually lasts ten or fifteen days. Puliar is the oldest son of the chief god and goddess of the Sivites. His face is that of an elephant; and, having four hands besides the trunk, he is called the " five-handed god." He has three eyes ; and many of his worshippers are seen with a spot between the eyebrows, on the forehead, in imitation of him. He is a bachelor, and once made his mother very angry by replying to her advice to choose a wife, that he should not marry until he could find a wife equal in all respects to herself. For punishment, she caused him to sit by the roadside to choose a spouse from the passers-by. Therefore Puliar's temples, and even little stone Puliars, are found by the roadside. His father, for a misdemeanor, once cuffed him and pulled his ears. Though chagrined at this treatment, he asked his father to grant that persons should invoke his aid before undertaking any business, and that his worshippers should cuff their own heads and pull their own ears, in honor of the treatment he had received. This was granted, and he is worshipped accordingly. The invocation begins with the breaking of a cocoanut.

At eight o'clock in the morning, people were flocking to the temple ; some on foot, some in carts, parents carrying children, and all bringing a bag of rice, with the pot and wood with which to boil it, and other offerings of fruit, vegetables, &c. The wide plain on three sides of the temple was already covered with people engaged in rice-boiling to the gods. The steam or flavor only is acceptable ; and the cooked rice is carried home, or given to the religious mendicants who are sure to be present. By this act of charity, the givers lay up a certain amount of merit in a future world.

At eleven, I went up into the tower of our church, where I could look down upon the scene, and watch the entire proceedings, except what transpired within the temple buildings. An intelligent native Christian explained the proceedings I could not understand. The crowd was very large, forming little companies over the plain, making rice offerings, or gathered about the temple in great numbers, filling the rest-houses, standing about, lounging under the trees, or running wherever there was any excitement. One shed, which was much crowded, was erected for the occasion, by a private individual, to supply water and sour milk to the people. In a tank, which seemed nothing more than a large, irregularly-shaped pond, many tardy ones were still bathing, drinking the muddy water, and washing their cloths, in order to purify themselves preparatory to making their offerings. Apart from these, in an arm of the same tank, the heated oxen which had drawn the carts were being refreshed by standing in the water, and having their bodies washed by their owners.

The wall, or outer enclosure, of the temple had covered sheds on each side, with raised floors forming resting-places for the pilgrims. Within this wall we could see the low roof of the temple itself, and the tree which is also considered sacred from its locality. Many people were within this enclosure; some merely gazing, others offering religious homage to the tree, while the passage-way was filled with men rolling on the ground, and then rising and stepping forward with uplifted hands to place their feet in the spot where their hands had been, and again prostrating themselves. In this way, these men and women, in performance of a vow, made the circuit of the temple, all going from left to right, in order to enter the temple from the right side. As I turned from this sight, I saw a nicely-dressed woman in the road in front of us, making the long circuit of the entire temple wall in the same manner. She was accompanied by two attendants, and was most punctilious to place her feet exactly in the spot marked by her hands. Remember the broiling sun of a tropical noon, the dust, the publicity, which is the greatest of trials to a heathen woman, and get some idea, if you can, of how Satan cheats God of his due; for there is no doubt that the prayer which led to the performance of this vow was that of Hannah's in the temple.

From the early morning until the ceremonies closed, companies of cavady-bearers were coming in, and bringing their offerings to the god. The cavady is an ornamental arch of wood, covered with tinsel, peacock-feathers, and any thing that can add to its gaudy appearance; and is carried on the shoulders of the individual from his home to the temple, in performance of a vow usually made in sickness. Preparation is made for the ceremony by some days of fasting; and the bearers come whirling and dancing, as if possessed with a spirit, under the excitement of the crowd which follows, and the sounds of timbrels, drums, flutes, hautboys, and cymbals. The more he dances, and consequently the slower he advances, the more approbation he receives from the crowd.

Many of the cavady-bearers were so overcome by the heat,

the previous fasting, the fatigue of the burden, and the exertion of whirling and dancing with such an unwieldy affair on their shoulders, as to faint continually, and require the almost constant attendance of their companions to relieve them of the weight for an instant, and revive them by throwing water over them, and giving them drink.   How my heart moved me to call to them in the words of Jesus, " Come unto me all ye that are weary and heavy-laden.   Take my yoke upon you."   Some who bore cavadies were quite small ; and one or two were boys not more than five or six years old, attended by their fathers to see that they made no mistake.   Some performed an additional penance by having hooks in their backs, held tight by a string in an attendant's hand, or spears through their cheeks.   But it is doubtful whether these last are not fixed there by some mechanical contrivance ; for there was no appearance of soreness or blood ; and we never see men with holes in their cheeks, as there would be if they had been really pierced.   The people consider it done by a miracle.   The bearer makes the circuit of the temple, and, going within, makes his offering of milk or camphor, which he has brought in a brass pot attached to the arch.

About one o'clock, the car which stood at the further end, in front of the temple, began to move around the walls, being drawn with two thick ropes by some forty men on either side, and followed by rolling devotees and bowing women.   The idol in the centre of the car, attended by three or four priests, was too small to be seen ; but the whole company stood with bared shoulders, to do it reverence.   The car stopped once, to enable a man to present an offering of the milk of young cocoanuts, which were broken on a stone ; then it was drawn on, until it stood just beneath us, and before a pile of a thousand cocoanuts.   A young blacksmith, who was about to make an offering of these, occupied a small shed or booth opposite, which he had erected for the purpose, and where he had been performing preparatory ceremonies.   A plantain-tree ornamented each side of the doorway ; and a bunch of the ripe fruit hung on the pole overhead. This annual ceremony of breaking a thousand young cocoanuts before the god was in performance of a vow made by his uncle years ago, in a time of distress, and, since his death, continued by the nephew, who was the inheritor of his property. As soon as the car stopped, the man came from the booth, and carried forward his offering of a cocoanut, mango, and portion of a jack-fruit to the officiating Brahmin, who received it, and gave him in return sacred ashes, which he rubbed on his forehead, neck, and breast. After acts of adoration, he retired backward, until he stood by the heap of nuts. Two stones had been provided, and four men occupied themselves in handing him the nuts ; while he hurled them, one by one, against the stones with his right hand, as fast as he could raise it.

They were young and easily broken ; and the ground was speedily soaked with the milk, and heaped with the fragments. Only two or three times was the aim false ; but the work was hard, and lasted nearly two hours. When the last nut was broken, the crowd of poor pariahs, who stood watching for the expected spoil, were let in, to gather up the pieces for themselves. Such a furious scramble then ensued, that, in two minutes, there was not a fragment visible.

The men again seized the ropes ; and the awkward, heavy car moved on, followed by the crowd of devotees, who had kept their places, lying on the ground all the while the ceremony was being performed. A few brisk ones kept up with the car, to enjoy its shade ; others, more weary, followed far behind : while some were very slow in making the circuit, imposing additional tortures. Some of the women wiped their faces, first on one side and then on the other, in the dust, at each prostration ; and some of the men rolled, with their feet in their hands. As soon as the devotees had made their circuit, they rushed to the tank to bathe. When the car-drawing was over, the crowd dispersed ; and all was as quiet as usual.

TURKEY.

JOURNAL OF MISS VAN DUZEE.

CAMP-LIFE.

June 6, 1870. — We arose early this morning, and hurried to finish all the preparations for our journey. We were ready to start from Erzroom at nine o'clock, but were detained by the tardiness of the Cartigees [muleteers], who finally made their appearance at three. Our party consisted of Mr. and Mrs. Pierce, baby Arthur, five weeks old, and myself. After riding an hour, we were overtaken by a heavy shower, which called into requisition all our rubber goods.

June 7. — I slept last night in the taktravan [covered wagon], and found it very comfortable. We rose this morning at half-past three, so as to start early; but our Cartigees pretended that they had lost their horses, and did not appear with them until eleven. The day was a very fine one for travelling; yet scarcely three hours had passed when the Cartigees were determined to stop, and we had a high altercation to make them go on. The Turkish soldier who was with us for protection struck one of the men two or three times, and it was half an hour before they could be coaxed and made to proceed.

Meanwhile the clouds had gathered in heavy masses, and presaged a coming storm. We hurried on to a village, intending to camp just outside, but were hardly dismounted when we were overtaken by rain, thunder, lightning, and hailstones as large as peas. I stood and held my horse, while puddles of water gathered around my feet, and the hailstones beat upon my head and back. My riding-skirt was wet and muddy three inches deep; and my hat fell into the mud, white muslin side down. We cover our hats with white to reflect the rays of the sun. I afterwards wore the hat in a storm to wash it. The ground being too wet to pitch our tent, we sent to the village to engage a room, and rode there as fast as possible.

We passed through a long hall into a stable, and opening from that, without a door, was our apartment. It was small, with only two little panes of glass in the top; quite dark, as you may imagine, and rendered worse by the smoke of the fire, which found no outlet. Mrs. Pierce was very tired, yet she and the baby slept soundly. Just think of a five-weeks-old baby out in such storms; but they seemed to agree with him. The fleas were troublesome, and the room so hot and full of stable-air that I could not sleep at all. Only five feet from me stood a mule, and beyond him, horses, mules, and calves, numbering fourteen.

June 7. — We are camped in a beautiful spot upon the side of the mountain, surrounded by singing birds, flowers, and rippling brooks. All day we have been wandering among the mountains, looking down into the valleys, and enjoying some splendid views. This mode of travelling is pleasant, but hazardous, as we are in constant danger from robbers.

June 9. — We started and went on our mountainous route, ascending slopes so steep and long continued that my saddle slipped back two or three times, although strapped tighter than usual. After journeying some distance, we overtook a caravan stuck in the snow, horses down, and altogether in a sad plight. Our party was obliged to dismount; and we all walked up the snowy road, with the exception of Mrs. Pierce, who rode on Whitey, clinging to his mane, a man leading him.

June 10. — This morning the travelling was on a plain, and good. We crossed the Araxes River, which was very deep. A man waded through, leading our horses, and afterwards the tak-travan. Ascending and descending, we were very tired before we reached a camping-place.

June 11. — After a long, hot ride, we came to the village of Chevermeh about ten, A.M. Our tent was pitched by the river, a short distance from the pastor's house. Here we were among friends. In the afternoon, Mrs. Pierce and I made eight calls,

2

carrying the baby with us. The houses all looked alike; no windows, but a hole in the roof for light; and the fireplace being immediately under it, the smoke went out of the same hole. The women nearly pulled our hair down examining it, and wondered why I didn't get married. Most of them were friends of my scholars.

Sunday, June 12. — Mr. Pierce and I went with two natives to a village two miles distant. As soon as I had alighted, I was greeted with a hug and a kiss from the mother of one of my girls, and in the yard was saluted in like manner by another. The women assembled to meet me at the home of one of my pupils, and I held a personal conversation with seven of them; after which Mr. P. and I were provided with a good dinner, consisting of bread and eggs, bread and madzoon [sour milk], and bread with sweet cooked fruit. It was eaten without knife, fork, or spoon. In the afternoon, we went to the chapel, which was crowded. Mr. Pierce preached; and, at the close of the service, I held a meeting with sixty women and children. I read, explained, sang, and prayed with them, and then called on the women to follow. Five responded who had never before taken part in public. I obtained from them a pledge to revive their prayer-meeting; and fourteen promised me that they would attend every week. Thus ended our work there; and, after our return to Chevermeh, I assisted Mrs. Pierce in conducting a large meeting for women in that village, and afterwards attended a general chapel service. The day had been crowded with work, and I was very tired, but trusted good seed had been sown.

June 13. — We find ourselves camped to-night on the top of a mountain, tired and sleepy. The most eventful occurrence of the day was crossing the Euphrates. On reaching the river, several men met us, and said that there was no raft, but that we could cross without one. They wanted Mrs. Pierce to get down from the taktravan. Asking why, they said, " The waters will come into it." — " How will she cross ? " — " On our shoulders."

" How deep is the water? " — " Up to our necks." Think of our fording such a river on horseback. The object of their proposition was to extort money. Just then a person came along who told us that there was another crossing, which we found after travelling an hour. A raft was provided, and all went over dry except the horses. Their saddles were removed, and a man swam across with each horse. Mr. Pierce's horse was large and heavy, and he could but just keep his nose above water.

June 15. — The day was fine ; and, as we rode along, we were reminded of the garden of Eden run to waste. There were great varieties of beautiful flowers, — beds of red tulips, blue grape, hyacinth, mille-fleur, yellow and white roses, gorgeous lil ies, sage, pie-plant, and mints.   •

June 16. — To show you how unskilful I am as yet in the use of my new language, I must tell you what an awkward blun-der I made yesterday. On seeing a small lake, I attempted to say, " How blue it is ! " but instead, said, " How red it is ! " And again, " The horse took the bits in his ears," in place of he took them in his teeth.

June 17. — We reached the ruins of what is called a bon (or hotel) for horses and men. We rode within all around on horseback. The walls, built perhaps hundreds of years ago, were of stone, twenty feet high, arched, and must have been very fine when new.

RECEPTION AT BITLIS.

June 28. — We arrived in Bitlis this morning about eleven o'clock, and were met by Mr. Parmelee. On reaching the mis-sionary grounds, we were greeted by Mr. and Mrs. Knapp, Mr. Burbank, the Misses Ely, Messrs. Barnum, and Dr. Reynolds. Then came the cry, " The Labarees (of Ooroomiah) are com-ing ; " and soon they were there. In the bustle of meeting them, Mr. Andrews of Mardin slipped in, no one knew when or where. It was a happy, happy time.

ANNUAL MEETING OF THE MISSION.

On Saturday morning, we met to organize our annual meeting. Mr. Knapp of Bitlis was chosen chairman; and Mr. Pierce of Erzroom secretary. The meetings throughout were of deep interest. On Thursday afternoon, we had a sweet communion season; and, at that time, Mr. H. N. Barnum of Harpoot baptized Arthur Pierce. A half-hour prayer-meeting was held every morning before business commenced, and we felt the Holy Spirit was present. The meetings closed on Thursday evening, but we remained until after the following Sabbath. On that day, at the communion, ten natives joined the church.

RETURN HOME.

Our journey back was very pleasant until the last day, when we had a combination of rain, hail, snow, wind, cold, scanty food, with insufficient clothing, and a hard mountain road. Some places seemed almost perpendicular; and such was the violence of the tempest, that our horses with difficulty kept their way. However, we reached home safely, although much fatigued.

LETTER FROM MISS S. A. CLOSSON.

Miss Closson wrote from Talas, May 25 : —

"I thank the Woman's Board for assuming my support. From the first, I have been deeply interested in the work, and rejoice in your success. It is easier to labor, knowing that such a noble band are praying for us.

"There are about forty Protestant women in Cesarea. Were you to attend their Sabbath school, you would find them in the gallery of our church, seated on mats, around the teachers, reciting from the Shorter Catechism. On Tuesday, sometimes forty or fifty are assembled in the prayer-meeting; and they are greatly interested in the mothers' meeting. Ten women could be employed among the Armenians and Greeks. We hope the sisters will do this work in time. We have two Bible-readers: one in Nigdi, who is seeing the fruits of her faithfulness; and another, who spends most of her time in Cesarea. She is a noble woman, entirely devoted, and wins the love and esteem of all in the great work she is doing. We have been at Talas — which is four miles from Cesarea — over two years. At first, we had from seventy-five to one hundred visitors a day, and still have a goodly number. We seek to interest them by showing the house, the sewing-machine, and playing the organ ; then, as the way opens, read the Scriptures, and tell of Jesus' love. A great change has been wrought among this people : their consciences are becoming enlightened and quickened. The priests are watchful, and keep many away. Once a large number gathered, and begged to be read and prayed with ; but a priest appeared, and ordered them away, standing by the door till all had passed out. In one out-station, where the work has just commenced among the women, several are learning to read, they are regular at church, and appear anxious to have the helper's wife read with them. One year ago, we spent a Sabbath in the place, and were impressed with the moral courage needed by this people to keep them faithful to Christ. Numbers put their hand to the plough, and, overborne by persecution, turned back. A mother had her three children taken from her because she married a Protestant teacher. She feared to come out on the Lord's side, lest she should never have them again. We spent a night at another village, where, two years before, they were more interested in our dress than in their souls' salvation. Twenty women collected, beseeching us to come to them, and several were learning to read. If middle-aged women, who have said 'they had no souls,' were 'broken wood,' learn for the sake of reading the Bible, our labor is not in vain.''

LETTER FROM MISS PARMELEE.

MISS PARMELEE, writing under date of July 1, thus pleasantly sketches some of her pupils : —

MISSIONARY PUPILS.

"We have five scholars, who are supported by the Mission, and pledged to the work. Three are wives of theological students. Of the two dear girls, Fareeda, especially, is a great comfort, because she illustrates the class coming up in these Protestant communities. Her father and mother were the first Christian couple Mr. Williams married in Mosul, so that from her birth she has been under happy influences. She has refined, pleasant manners, is bright and intelligent, and we hope the grace of God has renewed her heart. She is anxious to learn, and equally eager to impart to those less favored. Ahdool, also from Mosul, is a good reader, and takes hold of her studies with much interest. Miriam, from Kullaat, is again with us, grateful that she can come. Both she and little Miriam engage in study much better than last year : their winter's attempt at work has taught them what they need. Little Miriam has been greatly waked up in heart and soul. The third married woman, Alie, is a ripe Christian. It is a pleasure to teach this earnest, loving spirit. Although outside the simple range of Bible truths, her powers are very feeble, yet she has done a good work for Christ these years. Her influence in school is worth much : the others respect her earnest piety.

"You ask how I get on with the Arabic. The women understand me perfectly, and our meetings are becoming very precious. The Lord is blessing some souls."

BROOKLYN MEETING.

The third public meeting of the W. B. M., held in connection with the Annual Meeting of the American Board, met in Brooklyn, in the Church of the Pilgrims, on Thursday, Oct. 6, at 9½, A.M., Mrs. Albert Bowker, of East Boston, presiding.

The exercises were commenced by singing the Doxology.

The President read from the thirty-fifth chapter of Isaiah, accompanying the reading by a few very concise and pertinent remarks. She also read an extract from a letter from Miss Ely of Bitlis, Turkey, giving an account of a revival in that mission-station, quoting the passage read, and citing illustrations of its remarkable fulfilment.

After prayer, an original hymn, written for the occasion, was sung.

REPORTS.

The minutes of the meeting at Pittsburg were read by Mrs. Geo. Gould. Mrs. E. W. Blatchford of Chicago, representing the W. B. M. I., offered a report, from which we give brief extracts : —

BOARD OF THE INTERIOR.

"In nine of our Western States, auxiliary societies are already formed. It is our ideal, towards which we are constantly working, to have a woman's society in every church contributing to the American Board. We delight in the fact, proved by the statistics of these two years, that the regular contributions to the Board have been in no way diminished, but rather increased, since our work began.

"One hundred and four of these societies now pour their contributions into our treasury, each giving according to its own ability.

"A feeble, struggling, home-missionary church on the prairie, by strenuous effort, may send us five or six dollars, while a large, strong, city church may contribute with ease five or six hundred : but such churches are not numerous with us ; and we sometimes feel that the little gifts, the fruit of painful self-denial and consecrated by earnest prayer, are indeed our richest gifts. It is wonderfully sweet, the interest and attachment which gradually and naturally grow up between us and these little bands of Christian women.

" This year, up to September (and our financial year does not close until November), the amount contributed is seven thousand dollars; and we count on our list of missionaries, fourteen.

" But the attempt were vain to measure our work by statistics, unless, indeed, we count the links in the golden chain of love that binds so closely together the hearts of all these home-workers, and stretches away over the sea to our sisters who have gone to teach the gospel to the heathen ; yes, and to those heathen sisters too, bowed down by the cruel bondage of ignorance and sin. Who shall count the links ? Bright angels may ; but our poor arithmetic does not suffice."

The report of the Boston Board was given by the Recording Secretary *pro tem.*, showing a prosperous condition, both in the home and foreign departments. The receipts of the Treasurer, since January, had been upwards of sixteen thousand dollars.

JACKSON AUXILIARY.

Mrs. Hough of Jackson, Mich., gave a spirited account of the formation of an auxiliary in that place. The ladies composing the society agreed to pay a certain amount weekly, the sums promised ranging from two to fifty cents per week. The result of this effort, the first year, was upwards of $600.00 ; and the second year did not show any material diminution, either of funds or interest.

Mrs. Hartt of Philadelphia detailed briefly the formation of the Branch in that city, which has the promise of co-operation from churches in Washington and Baltimore, besides various others in neighboring States.

Mrs. Clark, President of the Albany Branch of the Woman's Union Miss. Society, was next introduced. After speaking of the passage of Scripture read at the devotional exercises as sounding in her ears like a bugle-note of triumph for the joyful flourishing of Christ's kingdom, she added, "I do not belong *o your Board; yet, while I owe to another entire loyalty and enthusiastic devotion, I do congratulate this society on the success already attending its efforts for heathen women. The world waits for *woman's* agencies. Herein is your Father glorified, that ye bear much fruit."

Mrs. Rhea of Ooroomiah was then presented, and spoke of the sweetness of dwelling on Christ's words, quoting the passage, "The kingdom of heaven is like unto leaven, which a *woman* took and hid in three measures of meal till the whole was leavened." In a few words she described the utter degradation of woman without the gospel; made her hearers feel that the world is lost without Christ; and when every heart was ready to ask, "What can be done?" bid us remember the Master's own words: "The kingdom of heaven is like unto leaven, which a *woman* took and hid in three measures of meal till the whole was leavened."

She spoke of the instruction in the Female Seminary at Ooroomiah, where she had spent four years of widowhood, trying to hide this gospel leaven, as eminently biblical. When asked to tell how much of the teaching was from the Bible, she replied that it was the first study in the morning, the last at night, and occupied much of the intervening time. With great eloquence and pathos she illustrated the power of the simple gospel to civilize and Christianize, and begged, if we would suffer the Bible to be excluded from our schools, never, never to let the heathen know what we Christians had done; for, "if the foundations be destroyed, what can the righteous do?"

FIFTEEN YEARS IN TURKEY.

Miss West, for fifteen years in Turkey, eight of which were spent in Constantinople, said, on rising, —

"My dear Christian Sisters and *Mothers*, — It is good to be here. It is worth crossing the mountains and plains of Mesopotamia and Armenia, sleeping, or rath.r not sleeping, in mud-khans and stables by the way, fording the Rivers Tigris and Euphrates, and passing over the Black Sea, the Mediterranean, and the Atlantic, to be present on this occasion.

"As I look upon this assemblage of more than a thousand Christian women, and think of all that is here represented, both for the home and the foreign field, I am strongly reminded of the words of a gifted English lady, ' This is, of all others, the age of sanctified female talent.' Truly we are living in times foretold by the prophet. God has indeed poured out his Spirit upon his handmaidens; and they prophesy, i.e., *teach*.

"Towards the close of my second year, I visited, with Mrs. Dwight, a Protestant Armenian family, living in the old city, where once it was death for a foreigner to enter. We were speaking of the death of a friend, when one of the women said, with much feeling, ' Oh how dark was the grave to us once! How we shuddered at the thought of dying, and going, we knew not whither! But now, thank God! there is light shed upon the grave. We bless God that he has sent you missionaries to bring it to us. When our dear ones die in the Lord, we know where they have gone, and our separation is not forever.'

"At the close of my third year of missionary life, I visited Bithynia (where Paul was not permitted to go, and *I*, the least of saints, was permitted to teach Christ). A missionary family had recently been stationed at Bagchejuk, but had not yet acquired the language. On Monday, Mrs. Parsons went with me from house to house; and we invited the women to a meeting that afternoon in the chapel. Forty women came, and many of them heard for the first time the words of life. There was a law in that village, that no woman should enter the church till she was the mother of two children !

"Thus many had never enjoyed even the dim light of a religion so overlaid with superstition. How they listened ! many of them bending forward, in their eagerness, with open lips ; and not unfrequently I saw the tears gather, and fall over some wrinkled face. After the meeting, they lingered, reluctant to depart; and, at last, one aged woman clasped me in her arms, saying, ' You are an angel sent from God to teach us ! '

"Many a time I was asked, ' Have you a mother ? ' and, when I replied, ' Yes, indeed, a blessed mother ! ' the next question was, ' How could she give you up to go so far away ? ' ' Because she loved your souls, and wanted you to get to heaven : she prays for you every day.' This never failed to touch the heart of even the most indifferent. They would look at each other as if to say, ' If *she* cares for our souls, why should not we ? ' My mother was the text for many a sermon to those poor women. ' Can she read ? ' they would ask : and then I could tell them how her Bible comforted and sustained her in her widowhood and many afflictions ; how she said to me, when she gave me up for that work, ' If *one soul* is saved through your instrumentality, my child, it will repay me for the sacrifice I make in parting with you.'

"In the providence of God, I was subsequently called to Harpoot, on the Euphrates, to superintend the Training School, for women as well as girls. The wives of the men under training for the work of preaching and teaching were to be prepared for help-meets in that relation. There, too, the Bible was the basis of our instruction. It was inwrought into almost every lesson.

"Never did I see any thing so wake up intellect, quicken and refine and ennoble all the faculties, as the teachings of this blessed book.

"It was wonderful to watch the change, and mark the contrast, in some of those women who came to us so stupid, — mere clods of earth; to see how the soul began to shine out of their eyes, how their countenances would kindle and glow with new life and light, as they fed upon and were nourished by the 'Bread which cometh down from Heaven.'

"The great Harpoot plain, with its hundreds of villages and cities, was a moral gymnasium to those schools.

"Not long before leaving Turkey, I went to Malatia, a city on this plain.

"On the Sabbath the pastor gave notice that all the women must stay at home on Monday to receive 'the teacher.' Going from house to house, I found in many cases fifteen or twenty of my own sex, waiting to learn from my lips the way of life.

"Many were melted to tears by the simple story of the cross, and, following me to the door, begged me to tell them 'just a little more.' The result of that day's visit cannot be computed by numbers alone. Scores of women began at once to learn to read the word of God for themselves; and he blessed the spoken word to the conversion of not a few." At the close of Miss West's remarks, which were listened to with eager interest, the audience rose and sung the hymn commencing,

> "Christian, slumbering, canst thou stay
> From the ripening fields away."

PLEA FOR CHINA.

Mrs. Chapin of Tung Chow, China, followed, saying that she owed more to the W. B. M. than any other person; for it had given her Mary Andrews. She bore glowing testimony to Miss Andrews's character as a Christian worker, and spoke with deep feeling of the invaluable aid afforded to her by so efficient a helper. She carried the enthusiasm of the audience with her; nor did she fail to elicit their warmest and even tearful sympathy for herself and the station she represented, when she spoke with choked utterance of a telegram that morning received, bringing intelligence that the lives of our missionaries in Northern China were in great peril, the late massacres at Tientsin having served to arouse hostility towards all foreigners.

She begged all present to pray for deliverance from these dangers for the loved ones in China, and also urged, that, should her beloved associate lose her life, the Woman's Board would heed the call of the four hundred millions in China, and fill up the broken ranks.

As Mrs. Chapin took her seat, numerous requests were sent to the platform, that prayer might be offered then for the safety of Miss Andrews; and all hearts united in the fervent petitions sent up to Him who has not said in vain, "Ask and ye shall receive."

A VOICE FROM THE PACIFIC.

Mrs. Snow of Micronesia was then introduced by the President, who said that this was probably the last occasion on which she would meet with us before returning to her island home. She bore noble testimony to Christ's faithfulness to his last promise during eighteen years of service, which her audience knew had been marked by peculiar trials and privations.

Her stirring appeal, "Let us put away all superfluities, and *work* for Him," reached every heart. Her two children, whom she will leave behind, she commended most tenderly to the prayers of Christian mothers. In closing she said, —

We shall meet again, but not here. Meanwhile we have a *work to do, — each of us,* for

" We are living in a grand and awful time."

The President, in a few closing remarks, spoke with warm interest of other organizations doing a work similar to our own, and bade them, in the name of the Board she represented, a hearty God-speed.

She alluded to the quarterly, " Life and Light," sent out by the Boston Board, saying that the great hinderance to Christian activity is the lack of sanctified Christian intelligence; and urged every lady to help swell its list of subscribers, that its light and life might be diffused through the world.

She referred also to the valuable publications sent out by other societies, — " The Female Missionary Intelligencer," from England; " The Missionary Link," from the Union Miss. Society, New York; " The Heathen Woman's Friend," by the ladies of the Methodist Church; and expressed the wish that their circulation might be very greatly increased.

The singing of the hymn, —

> " The heathen women wait to know
> The joy the gospel will bestow,"

concluded exercises, which, in point of thrilling interest, have rarely been excelled. A large and appreciative audience remained to the close; and then the question was asked, " Can we not have another meeting this afternoon?" God grant that the good impressions there received may lead every one who listened to ask, " Lord, what wilt thou have me to do?"

A. C. GOULD,
Rec. Sec., pro tem.

For Treasurer's Report, see " Missionary Herald " for September, October, and November.

DECEMBER.   PUBLISHED BY THE WOMAN'S BOARD OF MISSIONS.   1870.

LITTLE CARRIE.

BY MISS NORCROSS.

A YOUNG man, from a village near by, applied some months ago for the admission of a pupil in our school in Eski Zagra. He was told that the girl was too young, and that the house was already full ; and, after visiting the school, returned home. A few weeks later, he appeared at the door, leading his little sister with one hand, and carrying her bundle of clothing with the other. Calling for the smallest girl in school, he exclaimed, with a comical expression of countenance, "See, she is as large as that little girl!" Our pupils were greatly amused, and began so heartily to arrange for the fulfilling of the various duties that would fall upon the new-comer, that we concluded to smile too. I gave one corner of my room for a sleeping apartment, and we all enjoy the little one very much. Her name is Carrie ; and I wish I could give you a picture of her.

279

Imagine a child ten years old, with bright black eyes, dark complexion, nut brown curly hair, head thrown back, and figure slight and erect as an Indian. She is clad in a striped brown woollen dress, just low enough in the neck, and long enough at the feet, to reveal the edges of the heavy cotton undergarments, which are embroidered with colored woollen yarn, — sometimes wearing stockings and shoes. But, best of all, Carrie's counte-nance is radiant with the realization of the truth, that she is one of Jesus' little lambs. Only a few weeks after her arrival, I said to her one evening, " My lamb, it seems you are not sleepy to-night. Why do you not go to sleep?" — "Because I am thinking." — "Thinking of what?" — "O teacher! I do not know whether Jesus loves me or not." — "Did he ever invite little children to come to him?" She repeated the passage, "Suffer little children." "Well, who is this for?" Rising from her couch, she exclaimed, "It is not for you, is it? You are not a child. No : these words are for me, *for me !* " Jesus did not leave dear Carrie long to wonder if he loved her; and when, two weeks later, she knelt in the little girls' prayer-meet-ing, and poured out her soul in thanksgiving to the precious Saviour, every heart was gladdened. The next day she went to the little girl whose short stature seemed to be her passport into school, and, putting her arms around her, said, "Why don't you come into our meetings?" A reason was given. "Oh!" she replied, "Satan gives you that reason, but Jesus won't listen to it. I love you very dearly, and want you to come to meeting; won't you?" She could not withstand the simple, earnest en-treaty; and, a few days after, I found her alone, reading with tears the eleventh chapter of Luke.

I have never seen a mind unfold and expand under the sun-light of the gospel more beautifully than Carrie's. It was worth coming to Turkey, to hear her earnest inquiries about Jesus.

AFRICAN CHILDREN.

Mrs. WALKER of the Gaboon mission, in a letter to our Treasurer, says, —

"The youth and children under our care are much help and comfort. Out of school, the boys keep the premises in order; the girls do the washing, ironing, house-cleaning, and are skilful with the needle. When confined to the bed, in a late illness, I feared it would be necessary to go home. A large pile of sewing lay near at hand. I said to the four eldest girls, 'When can you do that work? It is waiting for you.' In two days it was neatly finished. We gave them one week in which to sew for themselves, and each fitted and made nicely a new dress. These dusky maidens are tasty, and take pride in fashioning their garments in the latest style. Three hours each day are occupied with studies. In the evening they commit verses of Scripture, and on the Sabbath recite fourteen or twenty passages apiece. Two elder girls and one boy assist in teaching."

YOUTHFUL SYMPATHY.

EXTRACT OF A LETTER FROM MISS SEYMOUR.

"In a Turkish village, where few Protestants are found, a woman read to a group of children the story of Samuel. A little Armenian girl, nine years old, strayed into the room, and for the first time heard a Bible narrative. Directly she obtained and mastered a primer, and then wanted a Bible. Her father refused to buy one, saying, "What do you want of a Bible?" "I want to learn to read, so that I can go to the girls' school at Harpoot." He angrily replied, "I'll put your head into the fire, before you shall go there!"—"You can only burn my body, father," she replied; "for my soul would go to Jesus!" Hearing of this, the pupils collected money among themselves, to buy her a Bible and hymn-book, and of their own accord sent her a letter of encouragement.   The following is the translation : —

" *Our beloved sister in Christ, Miriam,* —

   " We greatly rejoiced when we heard your history.   By writing this to you, we make known our desire that you remain established in the love of Christ, and we hope that more information we shall hear about you.   We love you very much, though with the eye we have not seen you.   This holy book with much love and pleasure we present to you, that, by reading the promises of Christ, you may love him more.   We have heard that you suffer trouble for the love of Jesus.   It is hard, the enduring of affliction ; but in heaven you will be joyful that you suffered for Christ's sake, for he for us endured great tribulation, that he might save us.   Paul the apostle suffered much for Christ ; but now how joyful is he !   Read II Corinthians, eleventh chapter, and you will see how much-trouble he endured.

                  We remain your sincere friends,
       THE GIRLS BOARDING IN HARPOOT FEMALE SEMINARY."

CEYLON SEWING–SCHOOL.

   IN a letter from Mrs. DE REIMER, after telling us of a pleasant ride to Thunevy to visit one of her sewing-schools, she says, —

   " On my arrival at the Christian woman's house, I found the little girls on the veranda.   The arrangement showed more order than is usual here.   Those who could only sew patchwork were seated on one side of the door, and on the other were the pupils who were making jackets.   All were seated on nice ola mats, and had on clean cloths, and hair nicely braided.   As I entered, they rose and said, together, 'Salaam, Ammah !'   They looked bright, and pleased to see me.   I examined all the work, and asked the name of each child : some were very pretty, such as 'Pure Gold,' 'Pearl Mother,' and so on.   After talking to them a little while, I showed them how the children practised their gymnastics, which delighted them very much."

WIDE-AWAKE BOYS.

Two eager childish faces peeped into our room in Pemberton Square. Then the elder boy entered gravely, with a worn copy of the "Echoes" in his hand. He carefully studied a passage he had marked with his chubby thumb, before he said earnestly, —

" Is this the place to get the missionary boxes it tells about in ' Jamie's Bank ' ? "

His companion followed, with the money clasped in his little palm ; and each bought one of the pretty bronze and gilt boxes. The children had walked from a distant part of the city, and were brim-full of missionary zeal.

" You'll see us again," said one, with an emphatic nod, as they left. " Mother makes rosettes for slippers ; and I can help her out of school, and earn fifty cents a week ! "

" I'm not rich," added the other, tucking his treasure lovingly under his arm ; " but I guess I can run errands, and shovel sidewalks next winter, enough to fill this. There's plenty ways of earning money ! "

We know these little men will bravely carry through their enterprise ; but where are the rest of the boys ?   H. C. P.

Oh, let me Ring the Bell!

A MISSIONARY far away,
    Beyond the Southern Sea,
Was sitting in his house one day,
    With Bible on his knee ;
When suddenly he heard a rap
    Upon the chamber-door,
And opening it, there stood a boy
    Of some ten years, or more.
He was a bright and happy child,
    With cheeks of ruddy hue,
And eyes that 'neath their lashes smiled,
    And glittered like the dew.

He held his little form erect
    In boyish sturdiness ;
But on his lips you could detect
    Traces of gentleness.
"Dear sir," he said in native tongue,
    "I do so want to know
If something for the house of God
    You'll kindly let me do."
"What can you do, my little boy ? "
    The missionary said ;
And, as he spoke, he laid his hand
    Upon the youthful head.
Then bashfully, as if afraid
    His secret wish to tell,
The boy in eager accents said,
    "Oh, let me ring the bell !
Oh, please to let me ring the bell
    For our dear house of prayer :
I'm sure I'll ring it loud and well,
    And I'll be always there."
The missionary kindly looked
    Upon the upturned face,
Where hope and fear and wistfulness
    United left a trace.
And gladly did he grant the boon,
    The boy had pleaded well ;
And to the eager child he said,
    "Yes, you shall ring the bell ! "
Oh, what a proud and happy heart
    He carried to his home,
And how impatiently he longed
    For Sabbath-day to come !
He rang the bell, he went to school,
    The Bible learned to read ;
And in his youthful heart was sown
    The gospel's precious seed.
And now to other heathen lands
    He's gone of Christ to tell ;
And yet his first young mission was
    To ring the Sabbath bell.
                    Heathen Woman's Friend.

MISSION-CIRCLES.

THE BUSY WORKERS.

THE 17th of August was a joyous day for our mission-circle, " The Busy Workers " of Swampscott. The weather was delightful. The sun, peeping from beneath the clouds, smiled upon the little ones as they wended their way to the vestry of the Congregational Church with their flowers, cake, or handiwork. They found their good pastor, Rev. J. Thompson, changed to a skilful upholsterer, arranging curtains for the Missionary Museum, which proved quite an attraction.

The tables were handsomely furnished with fancy and useful articles. The wife of the pastor had met her Sunday-school class once a fortnight during the year to aid them in preparing for the occasion ; and their contributions were a valuable acquisition. Refreshments were abundant; ice-creams, delicious; and the day passed off to the satisfaction of all.

The proceeds, fifty-seven dollars, it is hoped will stimulate to future effort. L. F. B.

FAITH MISSION-CIRCLE.

This class of a Sabbath school in Madison, N.J., held a festival, and sent twenty-eight dollars for the support of a pupil in Miss Rice's school, Ooroomiah. Something more than faith, little workers !

LITTLE MISSIONARIES.

Received from the mission-circle connected with the Chambers-street Chapel, Boston, eighty-one dollars. Our young friends are earnestly at work, and we entertain much hope from them in the future.

Twenty-five copies of " The Children's Quarterly " can be obtained for one dollar a year, or one hundred for four dollars, by sending to the secretary of the W. B. M., 33 Pemberton Square, Boston.

Ellen's Penny.

BY EMILY C. PEARSON.

"Now I have a penny, I know what I'll do!"
Cried pouting pet Clara, in pretty dress new.

"I'll buy nuts and candy, a nice little doll,
If only my money will pay for them all."

"I'm glad I've a penny!" said Ellen more grave:
"I'll give it to help a poor child to save.

"I know it is little, but 'tis all I have!"
So to the mission-box thus saying, she gave.

From the far-away land I hear a child's cry,
"Oh tell me of Jesus! — in darkness I die."

In mansions of glory, where happy ones dwell,
"I was saved by a penny," a cherub will tell.

Blithe Ellen gave wisely, wealth storing in heaven:
To her the dear Saviour's approval was given.

Which will you do, children, which way will you live?
Be selfish, as Clara, or, like Ellen, give?

We were pleased to receive seventy-five cents from little
Eddie Brown, his "first savings and earnings."

Go forth, little pennies,
    Gifts of willing hands,
Blest to work for God
  · In far heathen lands.
Where death's shadow broodeth,
    Spread of truth the light;
Make the tearful valley
    With Christ's radiance bright.

INDEX TO VOLUME I.

AFRICA, 50, 120, 198:—The Pioneer to the Zulus, 50; Mrs. Edwards and the Zulu, 52; First Impressions, 52; Honesty of the Zulus, 53; An Appeal for the Zulu Women, 53; Letter from Mrs. Edwards, 120; Need of Sympathy, 120; Second School Term, 121; A Happy Old Woman, 121; Opinion of a Veteran Missionary, 198; Letter from Mrs. Lloyd, 198; Mrs. Edwards's School, 198; Appeal for an Assistant, 199.
ACT OF INCORPORATION, 71.

CHILDREN'S CORNER, 25, 67, 101, 137, 174, 209, 245:—Light on the Dark River, 25; Our Missionary Boys, 27; A Heavy Subscription, 30; Little Sowers, 30; The Mother's Jewel, 31; What can Children Do? 67; Little Arab Girl, 69; Our School Girls, 101; Our Young Friends, 104; Children singing, 105; Celia's Sacrifice, 106; A Beautiful Sum in Addition, 137; Jennie's Mission Circle, 139; Sunday Scholars in India, 142; Harry's Stratagem, 141; Mercy-seats under the Cactus-bushes, 143; Children's Exercises, 174; An Arab Photograph, 178; Working Children in India, 178; A Golden Star, 179; Child-faith, 179; Little E——'s Earnings, 180; Perapeone's Letter, 180; Words to the Children, 209; Blind Mouse's Foot, 212; Prize Essay, 213; Aloha from Honolulu, 215; Worthy of Imitation, 215; The Child-helper, 245; Varvar's Letter, 247; The Schoolroom, 247; Jamie's Bank, 248; Mission Circles, 250; Little Carrie, 279; African Children, 281; Youthful Sympathy, 281; Ceylon Sewing-School, 282; Wideawake Boys, 283; The Busy Workers, 285.
CHINA, 50, 76, 113, 150, 185, 220:—Letter from Miss Payson, 50; Women in Temples, 76; Letter from Miss An-

drews, 113; A Successful School, 113; Village Work, 114; Conversion of a Teacher, 114; Letter from Miss Payson, 115; A Useful Graduate, 115; An Aged Scholar, 115; Tungchow, 150; An Eager Listener, 150; Valuable Assistant, 150; New Bible-reader, 150; Mother's Prayer-meeting, 151; Letter from Miss Payson, 151; Leave-taking, 151; Strange Customs, 152; E-po, 152; Lonely Widow, 153; Seed-sowing, 154; Extracts from Mrs. Gulick's Journal, 185; Friendly Greeting, 185; Need of Help, 186; Curious Remarks, 187; Letter from Miss Andrews, 220; Access to Heathen Homes, 221; Converts, 222; Letter from Miss Payson, 222; School Discipline, 223; Bandaged Feet, 223; Prayer Answered, 224; Letter from Miss Andrews, 258.
CEYLON:—Letter from Miss Townsend, 259; Pullar's Festival, 259.

DONATIONS, 34.

IN MEMORIAM:—Mrs. Giles Pease, 66; Mrs. Samuel Hubbard, 136; Miss Mary E. Warfield, 208.
INDIA, 77, 116, 181, 224:—A Visit to Hindoo Women, 77; Kurappal, 79; Letter from Miss Smith, 116; "We'll Try!" 116; Talks with Heathen Women, 145; Talks with Christian Women, 181; Letter from Miss Smith, 184; Letter from Mrs. Chandler, 223; The Seed is the Word, 253; Kurappai's New Name, 255.

LEAVES FROM A MISSIONARY JOURNAL, 37, 73, 109.

MISSIONARY ITEMS, 236.
MISSIONARIES, Departure and arrival of, 33.
MEETINGS, Annual, 2, 164–171; Pittsburgh, 126; May Meeting, 242; Yarmouth, 242; Brooklyn, 271.

MISCELLANEOUS: — A Word to our Readers, 1; After many Days, 13; A Privilege, 24; A Suggestion, 37; A Morning's Work, 55; A Model Auxiliary, 91; An Inspiring Meeting, 206; Bible-women in India, 10; Bread cast upon the Waters, 92; Bridget's Comment, 97; Call for Auxiliaries, 65; Consecrated Gold Dollars, 122; Effectual Prayer, 12; Earnestness in professing Christ, 17; Extension of our Work, 94; Early Fruit, 172; First Fruits of the Annual Meeting, 9; How we formed our Auxiliary, 61; Letter from Kohar, 14; Moslem Women, 217; Mrs. Anna Maria White, 20; Our Work, 62; Our Missionary-room, 98; Our Methodist Sisters, 98; Soul-loving Society, 18; Self-denial, and its Reward, 63; Suggestions for Auxiliaries, 199; Sow beside all Waters, 206; Triumph of Grace, 15; Talk about It, 89; To Mothers, 204; Value of Early Christian Instruction, 76; Word to Subscribers, 135; Woman's Board of Missions for the Interior, 64.

NESTORIA: — Report of Hânée, 58.

PERSIA, 158, 198, 238: — Letter from Mrs. Shedd, 158; Mother Mary, 158; Blind Guly, 159; Moslem Ladies, 159; Jewish Scoffer, 160; An Armenian Bride, 160; Appeal for Persia, 161; Words of Cheer, 197; Address of Miss Rice, 238.

POETRY, 54, 70, 93, 100, 124, 144, 163, 173, 207, 211, 214, 216, 244, 249, 252.

QUARTERLY REPORT, 59, 90, 125, 202.

SYRIA, 56: — Letter from Miss Everett, 56; The School, 57; Need of Woman's Work, 58.

TURKEY, 41, 81, 117, 154, 187, 229: — Miss Parmelee's Letter, 41; The Glad Welcome, 41; A Happy Home, 41; Sara of Mardin, 41; Week of Prayer, 42; Letter from Broosa, 43; Passages from Mrs. Knapp's Manuscript, 46; Women of Bitlis, 46; School at Bitlis, 47; Contributions of the Women, 48; Marrying a Blind Man, 49; Aintab School, 80; Semi-annual Examination, 81; The Changed Shoe, 82; Letter from Miss Ely, 83; Sketch of Sarkis, 83; Need of a New Schoolroom, 85; Letter from Miss Parmelee, 86; First Labors, 86; Adult Pupils, 87; Letter from Miss Ely, 117; Description of the City, 117; Buildings, 118; Boarding-school, 119; Only a Girl, 120; The Priest's Granddaughter, 154; Harpoot Seminary, 156; Letter from Miss Ely, 157; Mode of Instruction, 157; How to pray for Missionaries, 187; Letter from Mrs. Wheeler, 188; Perchenj Church, 188; The Debt Paid, 188; Mountain Tour, 190; Converted Robbers, 190; The Brigand's Prayer, 191; Condition of the Women, 191; Zealous Inquirer, 191; The Communion - service, 192; The Mountain Cabin, 192; The Inhospitable Hostess, 193; Miss Warfield's Journal, 193; Revival Intelligence from Mrs. Knapp, 229; Letter from Miss Ely, 230; The Word of God verified, 230; Bodhos and his Mother, 231; The Husband's Testimony, 232; Finding Jesus, 232; Letter from Miss Clarke, 233; Tuition Paid, 233; The Bible Welcome, 234; Letter from Miss Norcross, 234; Thirsting for the Living Water, 234; The Awakening, 235; Yamboul Persecution, 235; Who will give the Organ? 236; A Word from Miss Seymour, 236; Journal of Miss Van Duzee, 264; Camp Life, 264; Reception at Bitlis, 267; Annual Meeting, 268; Return Home, 268; Letter from Miss S. A. Closson, 268; Letter from Miss Parmelee, 270; Missionary Pupils, 270.

TREASURER'S STATEMENT, 99, 172.

FIRST ANNUAL REPORT

OF THE

WOMAN'S BOARD OF MISSIONS,

PRESENTED AT ITS

ANNUAL MEETING,

In the Mount Vernon Church, Boston,

JANUARY 5, 1869.

————◆————

BOSTON :
GEO. C. RAND & AVERY, 3 CORNHILL.
1869.

OFFICERS.

ANNUAL REPORT.

In presenting the first Annual Report of the Woman's Board of Missions, we naturally refer to the meeting in the beginning of 1868, which led to the formation of the Society.

Looking back upon it under the light of a year's experience, we cannot doubt that the Christian women then assembled were moved by the Holy Ghost, and were really come to ask in all earnestness, " Lord, what wilt thou have us to do ? "

The lessons of the past had not been unheeded by these women. They had learned during the mighty conflict of preceding years, which had called forth all the energies of our country, that there was work for woman also; and, quite within her own sphere, she might find ample scope and pressing need for her unwearied labors, watchings, and prayers. These she gave; and they were not in vain, but, though subordinate and unobtrusive, were felt, and had their humble share in hastening on the day of our country's deliverance.

The day of deliverance ! — and now she asks what she may do to hasten the day of deliverance to the

4

multitudes who are in the thraldom of Satan, and under the dominion of the very powers of darkness.

We trust one answer to this question has been found in the impulse which gathered strength in that meeting, and resulted in the organization of this Society; and, indeed, it should be devoutly acknowledged that God was manifestly present by His Spirit to lead his children in the way he would have them go.

At this meeting, statements were made, by returned missionaries and others, in regard to the degradation and wretchedness of heathen women, and the great obstacle thus interposed to the complete success of the missionary work; while the encouraging fact was also mentioned, that, through the gradual breaking-down of prejudices which have in many places rendered them inaccessible, "a wide and effectual door" is now being rapidly opened for their elevation and Christianization.

Propositions from the Prudential Committee of the American Board were also read, by which a woman's society could co-operate with theirs, availing itself of their long experience, and avoiding at the same time the perplexing details incident to an independent organization. In view of these considerations, it was thought to be the solemn duty of the Christian women of our land to engage earnestly and unitedly in some direct efforts for the benefit of their sex abroad; and it was therefore unanimously resolved, "That this meeting will proceed to the formation of a Woman's Board of Missions,* whose object shall be, by extra funds, efforts, and prayers, to co-operate with the

* Organized under the name of N. E. W. F. M. Society.

American Board in its several departments of labor for the benefit of the degraded of our sex in heathen lands."

The solemnity of that moment will never be forgotten by any who were present. The felt presence of the Holy Ghost consecrated and sanctioned the act; and some were baptized with a new baptism of missionary zeal, which, it is humbly hoped, may be productive of results, the value of which eternity alone may disclose.

It is matter of thankfulness to Almighty God that we who were permitted to inaugurate this missionary enterprise are all alive to meet this day to renew and strengthen the sisterly tie which binds us together, and, with encouragement and hope, to press forward in the good work of aiding in the world's conversion to our blessed Redeemer.

Aside from the great object we have in view, it is due to the grace of God to record that our meetings during the past months have been seasons of refreshment and strength to ourselves as Christians. While devising and consulting together for the good of our perishing sisters in heathen lands, God has revived and comforted our own hearts. Thus it has pleased him to fulfil his own most gracious promise, — " The liberal devise liberal things, and by liberal things shall they stand; " and it ought never to be forgotten that every charity or effort put forth from love to Christ for the benefit of others becomes a means of grace to the benefactor.

It is a grateful and cheering consideration, for which we should return thanks to God, that the effort which we have been permitted to make has already awakened an extensive interest among our sisters of New England and the West, in behalf of the cause of Christ in the world; and to-day we joyfully welcome to the same work of faith, and labor of love, a kindred society recently organized in Chicago, its constitution identical with our own, and, while occupying a different field laboring to precisely the same end.

With what promises to be so efficient a coadjutor, having the resources of the Great West within its reach, enlisting the enterprise and activity of that young and vigorous people, it requires no great exercise of faith to believe that "the day of small things" for our cause will soon be past, and that the Woman's Board of Missions for the Interior, in the growing prosperity with which a beneficent Providence has crowned her, will soon lead her elder sister of the East in the abundance of her offerings to the Lord.

MEETINGS.

The stated monthly meetings of our committee have been faithfully sustained, and have been, as before intimated, seasons of spiritual refreshing.

The quarterly meetings of the Society have been regularly observed and well attended. Some of them have been favored with the presence of one or more missionaries, whose earnest appeals, and touching narrations of missionary life, while they have excited strong personal sympathy and regard, have also deepened the interest already felt in missionaries and their work.

At the meeting in June, Mrs. Wheeler (wife of Rev.
C. H. Wheeler) from Harpoot made an earnest address,
urging mothers to devote their children to the missionary work, and calling upon the younger women to
give themselves to it. She also besought them to consider whether it is not their duty to adopt a plainer
style of dress for themselves and their children, that
the time and money thus saved might be consecrated
to Christ and his cause.

Mrs. Cyrus Stone, returned long since from the
Mahratta Mission, on account of the failure of health,
gave her testimony to the personal enjoyment result-
ing from missionary labor; and now, as she was near-
ing the close of a long life, and looked back upon the
work, she felt, that, had she a thousand lives, they
should all be given to it.

Farewell services have also been held in one or two
instances with missionaries on the eve of embarkation
and too much cannot be said of the exceeding interest
of these occasions. While listening to their recitals,
given in the confidence of sisterly affection, we were
led to feel, that, if this Society had accomplished no
more than to bring our missionaries into sympathy with
Christian sisters here, its work had not been in vain.
Indeed, the cordial testimony of each of them was,
that nothing could more strengthen and encourage
them, as they went forth alone, than this bond of union
to our Society, by which they were assured, not only
of the general sympathy of the Church, but of the
lively personal interest and prayers of their sisters at
home.

One of them remarked, just before sailing, that the

precious influence of these interviews encircled her like
an atmosphere, and would be her abiding comfort and
joy; and another, that she would not on any account
have been deprived of the privilege which this opportunity had afforded, adding that it had met a want in
her own heart not before supplied.

A special meeting of the Society was held during
the sessions of the American Board at Norwich in
October last. Of that meeting it is not too much to
say, that, in point of interest and numbers, it is doubtless without a parallel in the history of female missionary effort in this country. The Second Congregational
Church in that city was well filled with an audience
of cultivated and intelligent Christian ladies from all
parts of our land; and the earnest and often tearful
attention universally exhibited left no room to doubt
that the cry of heathen women,

" Rolling sadly through the sky,"

had reached their ears and touched their hearts; and it
is hoped, that, as they scattered to their homes far and
near, they carried with them an influence which shall
be extensively propagated, and result in a great increase of missionary zeal.

This meeting derived additional interest from the
presence of several missionaries. Mrs. Snow, of Micronesia, stood before us careworn and jaded by the anxie-
ties and privations incident to her trying field; and
yet she spoke not a word of privations and sacrifices,
but only of the privilege and rewards of her work, con-
straining all who heard her to feel that her lot, though

one of toil and self-denial, was, *with her supports*, one
to be envied.

Miss Proctor of Aintab, Mrs. Green of Broosa, and
Mrs. Ladd of Constantinople, with some others, made
interesting remarks; and the meeting, though long, was
yet too short to give full expression to the fervor of the
occasion.

STATE OF THE WORK.

The state of our work is encouraging and hopeful.
Several of our missionaries have arrived at their respec-
tive fields, and are already engaged in their preparatory
work. Letters from missionary families with whom
these single ladies are domesticated speak of them as
being treasured blessings to their homes, as well as
valued assistants in their missionary labors. We quote
from one received from Mrs. Chapin of Tung Chau,
China, soon after the arrival of Miss Andrews, who left
Boston early in the spring. She says, "I must tell you
how happy I am in the dear young lady you have sent
to labor with me. She is all I could have asked, — full
of love for these heathen souls, and longing to tell
them of Jesus. She has taken hold of study most
earnestly, and goes out with me among the women,
and has also begun to help in the school. Her gentle,
winning manner has drawn our boys to her with love
and respect; her deep, earnest piety, and fresh, vigorous faith, have helped my own faith much. We feel
that we have much to encourage us in this our first
work among the women of this city: they are far
more accessible than they were at Tientsin. We only

2

go where we are invited, and cannot keep pace with our invitations."

While speaking of our laborers, we would take occasion to express our thankfulness for their decided religious character, and moral adaptation to their work, which the intimate relations we sustain have brought to our knowledge.

While listening to their experience from their own lips; following the leadings of divine Providence, varied in each; noticing in some instances the gradual growth of seed implanted in the infantile mind by devoted Christian parents, and witnessing the alacrity with which they obey the call of their Master, even though it requires them to give up father and mother, "and count not their lives dear," — we have felt that they were Heaven-called and Heaven-sent. Indeed, the divine supports acknowledged by all in the hour of separation from friends and home made us feel that they had meat to eat which we knew not of, and caused us almost to envy them their privilege.

Christian sisters, let us, from this time henceforth, so labor with them in this cause as to prove that "she who tarries at home," as well as she who goes, "shall divide the spoil."

Our missionaries, at present, number seven, located as follows: —

Mrs. MARY K. EDWARDS, in charge of the first female boarding-school among the Zulus, South Africa.

Miss MARY E. ANDREWS, with Mrs. Chapin, at Tung Chau, China.

Miss OLIVE L. PARMELEE, at Mardin, Eastern Turkey.

11

Miss Rebecca D. Tracy, at Siras, Western Turkey.

Miss Adelia M. Payson, at Foochow, China.

Miss Maggie Webster, to assist Miss Agnew in boarding-school for girls, Oodooville, Ceylon.

Miss Ursula E. Clark, to have charge of boarding-school for girls in Broosa, Western Turkey.

These, with eleven Bible-readers, are all whose support thus far we have been able to assume; but, if spared to the close of another year, we trust a fuller treasury will enable us to report a much larger number.

The Society would gratefully acknowledge their obligations for facilities afforded them by the American Board, whose long experience and acknowledged wisdom fit them so eminently to be guides and directors in this great work. They would also notice the kind care of our heavenly Father in providing us with Corresponding Secretaries who have shown their love for the missionary cause by giving themselves to it, and who have only relinquished its duties at the call of Providence. While they regret the temporary absence of both from this country (one of them in affliction), they congratulate themselves that they have been able to secure a substitute, who has testified in like manner her love for the heathen.

The work of raising funds to sustain not only the missionaries and Bible-readers already employed, but, we hope, a large additional number, is committed to all those women in New England and the Middle States who love our Lord Jesus Christ in sincerity, and whose ecclesiastical relations bring them into sympathy with the American Board. We earnestly beg all such, as they value the blessings of our religion, and recognize their obligations to Christ its founder, that they will cause themselves to be represented in our Society (yet not ours, but theirs) by their dollar a year, more or less, as God hath given them ability. And, as the female membership in these churches is probably more than a hundred thousand, is it too much to expect that as many thousands of dollars shall be brought each year to the treasury of the Board, as the gift of women saved by grace, and living in the light of the gospel, to their sisters upon whom this light hath never shined?

In concluding this Report, we would allude to the fact, that one great object in the formation of this Society was the increase of missionary interest, and consequent elevation of the tone of female piety. To some extent, this has been realized ; but much remains to be done. Fashion and extravagance still hold their sway even to a great degree among Christians; and the wants of a world that lieth in sin are therefore too often forgotten.

Oh for a baptism of the Holy Ghost, which shall consecrate ourselves and our families to Christ, which shall take off our eyes from beholding the vanities of this life, and, instead of sacrificing our children on the altars of this world, shall bring them an offering to the world's Redeemer !

MRS. J. A. COPP, *Secretary.*

13

Dr. The Woman's Board of Missions in Acct. with Mrs. Homer Bartlett, Treas. **Cr.**

1868.		
Dec. 31.	To paid to the American Board of Commissioners for Foreign Missions, for support of the following persons, viz.:—	
	Mrs. Mary K. Edwards, Natal, South Africa	$400 00
	Miss Mary E. Andrews, Tung-chow, China	500 00
	Miss Olive L. Parmelee, Mardin, Turkey	350 00
	Miss Rebecca D. Tracy, Sivas, do.	350 00
	Miss Adelia M. Payson, Foo-chow, China	500 00
	Miss Maggie Webster, Ceylon	700 00
	Miss Ursula E. Clarke, Broosa, Turkey	400 00
	Ten native "Bible Women," in Turkey and Persia	420 00
	Marianne Doodoo, Bible Reader, Constantinople	76 65
	Girl in Seminary at Foo-chow, China	40 00
	" paid for printing Constitution, Certificates of Membership, Circulars and Notices, and for Blank Books and Stamps	185 63
	Balance to new account	1,110 85
		$5,033 13

1868.		
Dec. 31.	By Donations, as acknowledged monthly in "The Missionary Herald"	. $5,033 13
		$5,033 13
1869.		
Jan. 1.	By Cash in hand	. $1,110 85

L. F. BARTLETT, *Treasurer.*

BOSTON, January, 1869. — In the absence of the Auditor, Hon. Alpheus Hardy, I have examined the accounts of Mrs. Homer Bartlett, Treasurer, and found them correct, showing a balance due the Society as above stated.   GEORGE ATKINSON.

LIFE MEMBERS.

Mrs. Miron Winslow.
Mrs. Freeman Allen.
Mrs. Albert Bowker.
Mrs. Homer Bartlett.
Miss Mary Fowler.
Mrs. S. N. Stockwell.
Mrs. Alpheus Hardy.
Mrs. Benj. E. Bates.
Mrs Cragin.*
Mrs. Luther Wright.
Miss Elizabeth Hammet.
Mrs. H. B. Hooker.
Mrs. Henry Durant.
Miss C. Newman.
Miss Vida Scudder.
Mrs. Samuel Hubbard.
Mrs. H. H. Hyde.
Mrs. Frederick Jones.
Mrs. Wentworth.
Mrs Avery Plummer.
Mrs Daniel Safford.
Mrs. W. T. Eustis.
Mrs. J. C. Howe.
Miss E. Davis.
Mrs. Frederick Allen.
Mrs. Chas. Stoddard.
Mrs. Samuel Johnson, Jr.
Mrs. A Wilkinson.
Mrs. J. W. Kimball.
Mrs. John Duff.
Mrs. J. F. Baldwin.
Mrs. James S. Stone.
Mrs. Jeremy Drake.
A Friend. H. H.
Mrs. Ezra Farnesworth.
Mrs. M. H. Simpson.
Mrs. Jacob Mitchell.
Mrs. Chas. Freeland.
Mrs. Wm. S. Grover.
Mrs. Linus Child.
Mrs. E. Kendall.
Mrs. E B. Huntington.
Mrs. A. Sweetser.
Mrs. S. E. Herrick.

Mrs. J. A. Copp.
Mrs. Richard Borden.
Mrs. Nathan Durfee.
Mrs. Hale Remington.
Mrs. Robert K. Remington.
Miss Carrie Borden.
Mrs. N. G. Clark.
Mrs. A. Pierce.
Mrs. J. N. Fiske.
Mrs. Wm. B. Wright.
Mrs. Sarah E. Holland.
Mrs. E. C. Parkhurst.
Mrs. Wm. R. Lovejoy.
Mrs. Wm. Bates Lovejoy.
Mrs. Jeremiah Kittredge.
Mrs. Julius A. Palmer.
Mrs. Elizabeth E. Taylor.
Mrs. Horatio Bardwell.
Mrs. Caroline S. Hubbell.
Miss Eliza S. Josselyn.
Mrs. Barna Snow.
Mrs. Ellen E. Manney.
Mrs. E. B. Webb.
Mrs. S. M. Lane.
Mrs. Newman Clark.
Mrs. Edward J. Thomas.
Mrs. Joel S. Bingham.
Mrs. Rufus S. Frost.
Mrs. Joseph Fales.
Miss Mary E. Fales.
Mrs. Nathaniel D. Wellesley.
Mrs. Alexander Strong.
Mrs. F. M. Bean.
Miss Caroline C. Kent.
Mrs. Eliza W. Merrill.
Mrs. M. A. Smith.
Mrs. Maria W. Smith.
Mrs. Mary Gorham.
Mrs. J. O. C. Smith.
Miss Caroline Sutton.
Mrs. A. D. Webber.
Mrs. G. G. Phipps.
Miss Eunice B. Knight.
Mrs. James R. Bates.

Mrs. R. B. Smith.
Mrs. Mary F. Ellis.
Mrs. Julia M. Tolman.
Mrs. Mellen Chamberlain.
Mrs. Charles B. Wilson.
Mrs. S. M. E. Fay.
Mrs. Luther L. Dutcher.
Mrs. Charles Wyman.
Mrs. Henry M. Stevens.
Mrs. John W. Newton.
Mrs. James Bates.
Mrs. Harriet T. Newton.
Mrs. Luther Bodman.
Miss Susan Kimball Jones.
Mrs. Moses Day.
Mrs. J. G. L. Colt.
Mrs. George F. Betts.
Mrs. Julia P. Carrington.
Mrs. A. W. Porter.
Miss Lucinda Chapin.
Mrs. Dorus Clarke.

Mrs. Daniel Winson.
Mrs. Clara E. Schauffler.
Mrs. Elizabeth W. Labaree.
Mrs. Lucy C. Lincoln.
Mrs. James G. Vose.
Mrs. Harriet W. McEwen.
Mrs. Amos H. Hubbard.
Mrs. Margaret S. Wood.
Mrs. E. S. Brayton.
Mrs. F. B. Perkins.
Mrs. C. H. S. Williams.
Mrs. Wm. P. Wastell.
Mrs. Eliza Root.
Mrs. E. C. Cummings.
Mrs. Henry Fairbanks.
Mrs. Daniel Ladd.
Mrs. Stephen Hubbell.
Mrs. Sarah B. Capron.
Mrs. N. M. Field.
Mrs. Dr. Keep.*

CONSTITUTED SINCE JAN. 6, 1869.

Mrs. M. Fearing.
Mrs. A. Ramsay.
Mrs. A. W. Grant.
Mrs. John Smith.
Mrs. George W. Coburn.
Miss Martha T. Clarke.
Mrs. J. B. Wheeler.
Miss E. S. Tappan.
Mrs. Chas. H. Wheeler.
Mrs. Greenwood.
Mrs. Charles Noble.
Mrs. C. F. Foucher.
Mrs. A. W. Tufts.

Mrs. A. H. Plumb.
Mrs. I. P. Langworthy.
Mrs. A. W. Crittenden.
Miss A. Newman.
Mrs. Louise Powers Gordon.
Mrs. S. T. Armstrong.
Mrs. Alfred B. Ely.
Mrs. Augustus Fuller.
Mrs. Stephen C. Damon.
Mrs. Julia A. Grinnell.
Mrs. Susan H. Morgan.
Mrs. Almena Morgan.
Miss Myra A. Proctor.

SECOND ANNUAL REPORT

OF THE

WOMAN'S BOARD OF MISSIONS,

PRESENTED AT ITS

ANNUAL MEETING,

In Park Street Church, Boston.

JANUARY 4, 1870.

———◆———

BOSTON:
PRINTED BY RAND, AVERY, & FRYE,
No. 3, CORNHILL.
1870.

'CONTENTS.

ANNUAL REPORT - - - - - - - - - - - - - - 3

NUMBER OF LABORERS - - - - - - - - - - - - 7

LIST OF MISSIONARIES - - - - - - - - - - - 7

TREASURER'S REPORT - - - - - - - - - - - - 8

ADDITIONAL STATEMENT - - - - - - - - - - - 10

PRACTICAL HINTS - - - - - - - - - - - - 10

LIST OF CONTRIBUTIONS FOR 1869 - - - - - - - - 12

LIFE MEMBERS - - - - - - - - - - - - - 32

LIFE AND LIGHT

Will be published quarterly, by the WOMAN'S BOARD OF MISSIONS, at the subscription price of FIFTY CENTS a year, payable in advance. It may be obtained on application to Mrs. LINUS CHILD, 5 St. James Avenue, Boston, or Mrs. HOMER BARTLETT, 25 Marlborough Street, Boston.

We trust our friends will interest themselves in obtaining subscribers for us.

ANNUAL REPORT.

COMPLETING, as we do to-day, the second year of the Woman's Board of Missions, and contemplating its results, we are led to exclaim, " What hath God wrought ! "

Our success has been greater than our expectations, and is manifestly due to that Providence which has called us to our work, and which has graciously prepared the way before us.

The twofold object of the society, which seeks to bless woman at home and abroad, has been measurably gained, by awakening and developing the Christian zeal of the former, and by presenting to the latter the priceless boon of the gospel of our Lord and Saviour Jesus Christ.

At this hour, there is many a heart that acknowledges augmented joy in serving the Master through the new channels which this society has opened ; and we have reason to believe that numberless closets have witnessed thanksgivings to God from those who have been waiting to learn his will, that they have heard his voice, saying, " This is the way, walk ye in it."

The sanction of fathers in Israel, — the prayers and contributions of aged saints, just catching the light coming down from the opening gates, which they were soon to pass through, — the warm interest of missionary sisters, who have, upon beds of sickness, laid down their work, but not their love, — the thankful acknowledgment of help and increased hope from those who are laboring in foreign lands, all of whom we believe have the mind of the Spirit, — are sufficient to remove doubt, if we had any, of the divine origin of our society.

This being conceded, it is to be expected that our record will be one of progress. It is not surprising that our receipts for the year should have been upwards of fourteen thousand dollars, when we scarcely dared hope for ten. It is not strange that the future opens upon us still more brightly, and that every week brings to us new promises of effort for our cause. It is not strange that our meetings should increase in numbers and interest, when, we reverently say it, there is " One walking with us whose form is like unto the Son of God."

It is not strange that the hearts of our large membership are knit together in love, and that invisible but powerful bonds reach over the seas, and bring missionary sisters, who are planting in their far-off fields, into direct communication with us who are seeking by our prayers to bring down upon the seed they sow the refreshing showers of grace.

In a word, as God, we believe, has begun the work, it is not strange that He should carry it on ; and we think we are warranted in believing that this goodly tree, planted just two years ago, will yet " shake like Lebanon."

Oh, what happiness may be ours, if we, being found faithful, shall be permitted to share in binding up those sheaves from heathen lands which are yet to be laid at the feet of our Redeemer!

Our missionaries now number fifteen, eight of whom have been added during the year.

A new enterprise, and a large one for us, is the founding of a home in Constantinople, to accommodate three single-women, one of whom is to be a physician ; the other two are to engage in teaching, and such other labors as may be practicable.

This enterprise has been undertaken at the urgent recommendation of missionaries long resident in the city, and is handed over to us by the American Board, as belonging legitimately to our work.

An appropriation has also been made of four hundred and twenty-five dollars towards a school-room for the Misses Ely at Bitlis; themselves also being contributors to the same object.

An undertaking which seemed formidable in the beginning was commenced in March last, and has thus far been successfully carried on. We allude to the publication of "Life and Light for Heathen Women," which is issued quarterly, and is designed to be our organ of communication with our membership ; and, more especially, to meet our constitutional pledge to furnish auxiliaries with intelligence respecting the progress of our work.

Under the blessing of God, it has found favor in the eyes of many, so that its subscription-list is already encouragingly large; and it is hoped that during the present year its circulation may be greatly extended.

The hand of the Lord also moved before us in the kind provision of a business-room when the work — commenced in supplication and cherished as an aspiration rather than as a success, — had so grown as to render necessary a place where communications could be received, inquiries answered, and the publishing of the quarterly attended to. A room was kindly offered on the lower floor of the Mission House, No. 33 Pemberton Square, and gratuitously furnished by the members of the Board ; and so enlarged has been the work, and increased the public interest in it, that, during some days, there have been upwards of sixty calls made upon the secretary on matters of business.

Thus has this provision, made without expense to the organization, proved itself a necessity, and been an evident means of enlarging our operations.

It should be mentioned, that, since the annual meeting in January, our society has been placed on a permanent footing by becoming a corporate body.

The act of incorporation was granted in March, by the legislature of this State ; and in April, at a meeting legally called, the society was re-organized under the act, and the officers chosen at the annual meeting re-elected.

The way is now open for those who may wish, living or dying, to bestow permanent funds, the income of which they may desire should be perpetually appropriated to the objects of the society.

In this connection, we may be pardoned if we allude to a form of permanent fund which has given us peculiar satisfaction.

A friend in Philadelphia has for some time fulfilled her pledge, which she gave unsolicited, of twenty-five dollars monthly, to our treasury, concealing her name under the initials, " C. A. L."

Though we may not penetrate the privacy of those initials, we may be forgiven if we insert them with significance ; and while to ourselves " C. A. L." represent only an " unknown friend," to the heathen do they not appropriately signify " Christ And Life " ?

To complete the record of the year, we must, alas ! make mention of the ravages of death.

In the month of April, one of our directors, Mrs. GILES PEASE, closed a life of great usefulness, and was admitted to her reward. The sufferings of her protracted illness did not quench her confidence in God, and, having waited patiently his time, she went joyfully to her rest.

Mrs. SAMUEL HUBBARD, another director, who, for many years, wore so beautifully the mantle of her departed husband, himself a Prince in Israel, and who was for a long time identified with every good word and work, received her summons in a foreign land, and was called thence to her heavenly home.

> " The Christian lives a pilgrim, lives to roam ;
> But die where'er he may, he dies at home."

Christian sisters ! let us be admonished to perform with our might what our hands find to do   Already the same messenger may be preparing his despatch for some of us : let us seize the golden moments as they fly, and load them with acts of beneficence and self-denial, so that death shall be cheated of half his victory ; and Christ for whom we labor, and for whom we would suffer if need be, shall say to us, " Well done, good and faithful servants ! "   MRS. J. A. COPP, *Rec. Sec.*

LABORERS NOW IN THE FIELD.

The Woman's Board now employs eighteen Missionaries and eighteen Bible-readers, and has assumed the support of the following schools : —

Mrs. EDWARDS', among the Zulus.
Miss NORCROSS', at Eski Zagra.
Miss PROCTOR's, at Aintab.
Miss SEYMOUR's, at Harpoot.
Miss PARMELEE's, at Mardin.

MISSIONARIES SUPPORTED BY THE WOMAN'S BOARD.

Mrs. MARY K. EDWARDS, Zulu Mission, South Africa.
Miss MARY E. ANDREWS, Tungchow, China.
Miss ADELIA M. PAYSON, Foochow, China.
Miss HARRIET E. TOWNSHEND, Oodoopitty, Ceylon.
Miss HATTIE G. POWERS, Antioch, Central Turkey.
Miss MYRA A. PROCTOR, Aintab, Central Turkey.
Miss OLIVE L. PARMELEE, Mardin, Eastern Turkey.
Miss ISABELLA C. BAKER, Mardin, Eastern Turkey.
Miss HATTIE SEYMOUR, Harpoot, Eastern Turkey.
Miss MARY E. WARFIELD, Harpoot, Eastern Turkey.
Miss CHARLOTTE E. ELY, Bitlis, Eastern Turkey.
Miss MARY A. C. ELY, Bitlis, Eastern Turkey.
Miss URSULA C. CLARK, Broosa, Western Turkey.
Miss SARAH A. CLOSSON, Cæsarea, Western Turkey.
Miss ROSELTHA A. NORCROSS, Eski Zagra, European Turkey.
Miss ELIZA FRITCHER, Marsovan, European Turkey.
Miss ROSELLA A. SMITH, Madura, India.
Miss MARY SUSAN RICE, Oroomiah, Persia.

8

Dr.   *The Woman's Board of Missions in Acct.*

1869.

Dec. 31. To incidental expenses............................ $41 80
            Salary of Secretary Missionary Room.......... 192 00
            Stationery, stamps, and publishing notices..... 65 46
            Printing annual report, certificates of member-
              ship, and circulars........................... 114 30 $413 56

          To publishing and stereotyping quarterly......... 738 52
          Stamps and stationery for   do. 14 82
          Printing receipts for same...................... 7 00
                                                                ———
                Total for quarterly........................   760 34

APPROPRIATIONS AND SALARIES.

Wellesley Auxiliary Society, for support of a girl in
  Miss Smith's school, Madura mission... $25 00
  Miss Edwards' School.................... 30 00
  For a Bible-reader in Cæsarea........... 45 00
  To support a pupil in Miss Fritcher's school
    at Marsovan............................ 25 00
Wellesley S. S. To support a pupil in Miss
    Clark's school at Philippopolis........ 40 00   165 00

St. Johnsbury, Vt. To support a Bible-woman at
    Broosa, and for mission-work among the Zulus 173 00
Boston, Chambers-street Chapel, for missionary
    purposes.................................... 112 25
          To educate a pupil at Marosh seminary by
            Mrs. Deborah Fuller's donation.......... 30 00
          To support a scholar at Miss Proctor's school,
            Aintab, Turkey, Mrs. Coggswell's donation. 25 00
Chelsea. By a member, from retrenchment....... 35 00
  Miss Proctor, for missionary tours........... 10 00
Madison, N.J., Auxiliary. For a native Bible-reader
    at Oodoopitty, Ceylon mission.............. 50 00
Salary of Misses Charlotte E. and Mary C. Ely at
                Bitlis............................... 425 00
    "   " Miss Myra A. Proctor, Aintab.......... 444 00
    "   " Miss Sarah A. Closson, Cæsarea........ 400 00
    "   " Miss R. K. Norcross, Eski Zagra....... 400 00
    "   " Miss Rosa A. Smith, Madura............ 700 00
    ⸱   School at Bitlis..................... 425 00
                Home at Constantinople.............. 3000 00
Salary of Mrs. Edwards, Natal, South Africa...... 436 50
    "   " Miss Andrews, Tungchow, China....... 480 00
    "   " Miss Parmelee, Mardin, Turkey........ 360 00
    "   " Miss Payson, Foochow, China.......... 480 00
    "   " Miss Clark, Broosa, Turkey........... 396 00
                Ten Bible-readers in Turkey and Persia 400 00   8,946 75
                                                                ———
                To balance to new account.....................   5,341 74
                                                                ————
                                                                $15,462 39

with Mrs. Homer Bartlett, Treasurer.   Cr.

1869.

Jan. 1.	By balance from last account, on hand....................	$1,110 85
	Am't refunded by A. B. C. F. M., for Miss Tracy's salary	350 00
Dec. 31.	By total receipts to date for subscriptions and donations....	13,153 80
	By total receipts to date for quarterlies....................	847 74

$15,462 39

Dec. 31. By balance on hand...................... $5,341 74

BOSTON, Jan. 3, 1870. In the absence of the Auditor, Hon. Alpheus Hardy, I have examined the accounts of Mrs. Homer Bartlett, Treasurer, and found them correct, showing a balance due the Society as above stated.

GEORGE ATKINSON.

ADDITIONAL STATEMENT.

Balance on hand Jan. 1, 1870................$5,341 74
Receipts at the annual meeting, and since, to Jan.
  18, 1870....................................$2,102 80
                                        $7,444 54
Appropriations since, to date (Jan. 18), for salaries
  of additional missionaries, Bible-readers, and
  support of schools.......................$6,485 00

PRACTICAL HINTS.

We are very grateful for life-memberships, and hope they will continue to be generously made, and in great numbers ; but for our main reliance we must depend upon our annual subscribers. We hope, therefore, that the coming year will be one of general effort in all our churches to form auxiliary societies, and in our sabbath schools mission-circles. And as we are all voluntary laborers, any one who will, can do something to promote this good work.

In some churches the objection is made that so many societies now exist, it is undesirable to form a new one. To this we would say, that an auxiliary society can easily be grafted upon a sewing-circle, or a stated female prayer-meeting, and the duties of secretary and treasurer be performed by one person ; and, with efficient collectors, all the work can be easily done.

It has been often stated in missionary papers and circulars, that the expense of supporting a girl in one of the mission boarding-schools is from thirty to fifty dollars a year. The expense of a native Bible-reader is about the same, — sometimes less, sometimes more ; while the cost of living for a female missionary varie, from four hundred to eight hundred dollars, according to the place of residence.

There is a peculiar pleasure in *individualizing* effort, and thus being able to know for whom we are laboring, and what is the result of our efforts. Acting on this principle, many of our patrons and auxiliary societies send in their donations as " For a Bible-reader," or " For a girl in —— female boarding-school ; " hoping thus to secure a special correspondence with that Bible-reader or pupil.

Good friends, " suffer a word of exhortation." Our principal item of expense is, of course, the support of our *missionaries,* both because their expenses are greater, and because Bible-readers and boarding-pupils are, to a certain extent, supported by native Christians.

Again : it is no small embarrassment for a teacher to select particular girls from a school of thirty or more, and keep them in correspondence with their supporters in America. There is about it a tinge of partiality which every teacher wishes to avoid. But chiefly the officers of the Board at home are embarrassed when the greater part of their funds come in for *specified objects,* when they are perhaps needed immediately for some other department of our work.

As far as possible, please send your donations *without* specifications, that those who stand at the centre of operations, and know the wants of the whole field, may be able to use the funds without restraint, just where they are most needed.

CONTRIBUTIONS

Received by the Woman's Board of Missions for the year 1869, *as reported monthly in "The Missionary Herald."*

Mrs. HOMER BARTLETT, *Treasurer.*

DONATIONS RECEIVED AT ANNIVERSARY.

MAINE.

Wells — Miss Sarah Lindsey, $1; Mrs. I. B. Simmons, $1 . . . . $2.00

NEW HAMPSHIRE.

Mendon — Miss Mary A. Bryant 2.00

MASSACHUSETTS.

Arlington — Mrs. Henry Mott 1.00
Andover — Mrs. John Smith, to constitute herself and Mrs. George W.
    Coburn Life Members 50.00
Boston — Mrs. D. C. Scudder, $5; Mrs. M. Fearing, L. M., $25; Mrs.
    Richmond, $2; Mrs. A. Ramsay, L. M., $25; Mrs. Case, $1;
    Mrs. Hooker, $1; I. R. Stacey, $5; Miss Rebecca Reed, $1 . 65.00
Boston Highlands — Mrs. Munger 2.00
Brighton — Mrs. D. T. Packard, $1; Miss Chadwick, $5; Miss I. M.
    Noble, $1 . . . . 7.00
Cambridge — Mrs. Stevens 1.00
Charlestown — Mrs. A. W. Grant, L. M. 25.00
Jamaica Plain — Congregational Church, by Mrs. Perkins . . . 2.00
Lynn — Mrs. James Flint 5.00
Newton Corner — Mrs. Snow and sister, $2; Miss Ida L. Sears, $20;
    Mrs. Baldwin, $2; Mrs. Stephen Stackwell, $50 . 74.00
Somerville — Mrs. Oakman, $1; Mrs. B. W. Eldridge, $1 . . . 2.00

CONNECTICUT.

Colchester — Mrs. Joshua Clark, to constitute Miss Martha T. Clark L. M.,
    $25; Mrs. Wm. S. Curtis, $1; Mrs. Joshua B. Wheeler, $25, 51.00

IOWA.

Dubuque — Mrs. George R. Ransom 1.00

$290.00

RECEIPTS FROM JAN. 7 TO FEB. 5.

NEW HAMPSHIRE.

Bedford — Ladies in Presbyterian Church, a part to constitute Mrs.
Stephen C. Damon L. M. $31.75
Hollis — Mrs. F. B. Day, to constitute Mrs. Julia A. Grinnell, of Grin-
nell, Iowa, L. M. 25.00

MASSACHUSETTS.

Boston — Hon. John Tappan, to constitute Miss E. S. Tappan L.M., $25;
"Persis," to constitute Mrs. C. H. Wheeler, Harpoot, Turkey,
L. M., $25; Mrs. Greenwood, to constitute herself L. M., $25;
Mrs. A. W. Tufts, to constitute herself L. M., $25; annual
sub., $1; Mrs. E. A. R. Winslow, $10; Miss S. Farrington, $2;
Mrs. Wilson, $1; Miss Amy Foster, $1; Mr. Cragin, " In
Memoriam," $10; "A Friend," $100; Miss A. Newman, to
constitute herself L. M., $25; I. C. Gordon, to constitute Mrs.
Louisa Powers Gordon L. M., $25; Mrs. S. T. Armstrong, to
constitute herself L. M., $25; Mrs. Freeman Allen, $100; Mrs.
C. M. Putnam, $5; Mrs. Hale, annual sub., $1; additional from
Mt. Vernon Church, for collation, $0.30; Homer Bartlett, to
constitute Mrs. Almena B. Morgan L. M., $25; Mrs. Homer
Bartlett, to constitute Mrs. Susan H. Morgan and Miss Myra
A. Proctor L. M's., $50; Miss Mary Fowler, annual sub., $5;
Mrs. William S. Houghton, to constitute herself L. M., $25;
annual subscription, $20; Miss Lillie, $2; Mrs. J. C. Tyler,
annual subscription, $5; Miss Esther S. and Miss Cutler, $2;
Mrs. Joseph Sweetser, to constitute herself L. M., $25; Miss
Rebecca Reed, annual subscription, $5; Shawmut-av. Cong.
Church, $80, and to constitute Mrs. John Erksine L. M., $25 ; 675.30
Charlestown — Mrs. William Abbott 6.00
Chelsea — Chestnut-st. Church, to constitute Mrs. Albert H. Plumb and
Mrs. I. P. Langworthy L. M.'s. 50.00
East Randolph — Young Ladies and S. S. to constitute Mrs. Louisa S.
Russell L. M., and the whole to be appropriated to
educating a native girl in Mrs. Edwards' school . 30.05
Ipswich — First Church ladies' prayer-meeting, " New-Year's Offering,"
$10; Ipswich Seminary, $9.50 . . . . 19 50
Littleton — Ladies' Benevolent Society Cong. Church 10.00
Newton Corner — Mrs. Alfred Ely, to constitute herself L. M. . . 25.00
Northampton — C. E. L. 1.00
Pittsfield — Mrs. A. C. Morely 10.00
Stockbridge — Mrs. Anna I. Whitney, to constitute herself L. M. . 25 00
South Amherst — Ladies' Benevolent Society, to constitute Mrs. Clara B.
Hutchings L. M. 25.00
Townsend — Cong. Church Ladies' Benev. Soc. to make themselves aux. 10.00
Williamstown — Mrs. Prof. Tattock 4.50

2

Wellesley — Ladies' Miss. Soc. to constitute Mrs. Augustus Fuller L. M.,
and to support a pupil in Miss Fritcher's school, Marsovan,
$25; S. S. for support of a pupil in Mr. Clark's school,
Philippopolis, $40 . . . . $65.00
Westhampton — Mrs. Newman Clark, $10; Miss Hattie F. Clapp, $5;
Mrs Ansel Clapp, $2; Mrs. Clark Bridgeman, $1; Mrs.
Submit Bridgeman, $1; Mrs. Lucas Bridgeman, $1;
Mrs. Alfred Montague, $1 . . . . 21.00
West Amesbury — Cong. Church Ladies' Social Circle 38.25

CONNECTICUT.

Bolton — Mrs. Talcott Carpenter, Mrs. Henry Alvord, Mrs. E. C. Ruggles,
Mrs. William Loomis, Mrs. E. B. Moore, $1 each . . . 5.00
East Haddam — A. H. 1 00
Norwich-town — Cong. Church additional, by Mrs. E. S. Gilman . . 3.00
North Woodstock — Mrs. Peleg Child, to constitute herself and Mrs. T.
H. Brown L. M.'s. 50.00
New Haven — North Church Ladies' Society 25.00

NEW YORK.

New - York City — Mrs. E. W. Chester, annual subscription . . . 5.00
Poughkeepsie — Vassar College, Miss Hannah W. Lyman, to constitute
herself L. M. 25.00
Sand Lake — Mrs. W. H. Seram, to const. Mrs. Isabella Brooks L. M. 25.00
Utica — Mrs. A. W. Crittenden, to constitute herself L. M. . . . 25.00

OHIO.

Belpre — Congregational Society 11.63

MICHIGAN.

Concord — Presbyterian Church, to constitute Mrs. C. M. Foucher, Ho-
mer, Mich., L. M., and for the support of Miss Dean of the
Nestorian Mission 25.00
Detroit — Mrs. Charles Noble, to constitute herself L. M. . . . 25.00

Total for the month $1,297.48

RECEIPTS FROM FEB. 5 TO MARCH 5.

VERMONT.

East Rutland — Ladies' Aux. Soc. of Cong. Ch., by Mrs. John B. Page, $25.00
Georgia — Mrs. C. C. Torrey 5.00

MASSACHUSETTS.

Boston — Essex-street Church, Miss E. Keep, L. M., $25; a friend, $2;
by Mrs. Scudder, from Wm. D. Coit, Esq., N.Y., to constitute Miss Bessie M. Scudder L. M., $25; a friend, $2; Mrs.
Selah B. Treat, $5; Mrs. Henry F. Durant, to constitute
Mrs. C. M. Hyde of Brimfield L. M., $25; Mrs. Geo. White
and Miss White, $1 each 86.00
Mt. Vernon Church, Mrs. J. G. Tappan 5.00

Old South Church, Miss Briggs, collector (of which, from Mrs.
Bancroft, $25, and Mrs. Gray, $25, to constitute themselves
L. M.'s; Mrs. Chas. Morse, $5, and six subscribers, $1 each) $61.00
   Miss Brewster, collector (of which, from Mrs. Samuel
Johnson, Jr., to constitute Mrs. G. W. Blagden L. M., $25;
Mrs. B. F. Kimball, $5; nine subscribers, $1 each)   .   .   34.00
   Mrs. S. E. Goodale, collector (of which, from Mrs. J. Haw-
kins, Mrs. G. Lane, Mrs. Ware. Mrs. Wetherbee, Mrs. S. E.
Goodale, $2 each ; four persons, $1 each ; one 50 cents)   .   14.50
   Miss C. Coverly, collector (of which, from Mrs. Charles
Stoddard, to constitute Mrs. J. M. Manning L. M., $25;
Mrs. J. Thayer and daughters, $10; Mrs. Chas. Browne,
$7; Mrs. C. A. Jellison, $3; Mrs. E. C. Milliken, Mrs. F.
Jellison, and Mrs. E. Coverly, $2 each; four subscribers,
$1 each) 55.00
   Miss A. Walley, collector (of which, from Miss Elizabeth
Davis, $100, Mrs. J. R. Payson, $10, Miss Payson, $5, an-
nual subscriptions ; Miss Walley, donation, $5; Mrs. L.
Child, subscription, $1) 121.00
   Miss H. S. B. Walley, collector (of which, all being annual
subscriptions, from Mrs. Wentworth, Mrs. Chas. Blake,
Miss Jane Houghton, the Misses Hill, $10 each; Mrs. N. B.
Gibbs, $5; Miss Goodnow, $2; four, each $1; donation
from Miss F. Houghton, $3) 54.00
Park-street Church, by Mrs. Hubbard, from Mrs. J. H.
Field, and Mrs. Lemuel Shattuck, each $25, constituting
L. M.'s ; Miss Florence L. Hubbard, constituting L. M., $25 ;
Mrs. Hubbard's annual subscription, $5; from Bible Class,
$5; six annual subscribers, $1 each, $6; additional from
Mrs. Coburn, $2; Miss Martha A. Quincy, to constitute her-
self L. M., $25   .   .   .   .   118.00
Shawmut Church, additional subscriptions 37.00
Salem-street Church 10.00
Central Church, Mrs. Joshua Davis, annual subscription   .   5.00
   Miss Myra B. Child, collector: Mrs. Benj. E. Bates, to
constitute Mrs. H. M. Clark, Gilbertsville, N.Y., and Mrs.
John E. Todd L. M.'s, $50; Mrs. James White, constituting
herself L. M., $25 ; Mrs. Thos. H. Russell, constituting her-
self L. M., $25; Mrs. William O. Grover, annual subscrip-
tion, $25; Mrs. Wiswall, $5; Mrs. Joseph White, $5; Mrs.
William M. Flanders, $2; Mrs. N. P. Sargent, $1   .   .   138.00
   Miss Gordon's subscription 2.00
Boston Highlands — Eliot Church 5.00
Cambridgeport — Prospect-street Cong. Church subscription .   .   .   7.00
Chelsea — Broadway Church, by Mrs. J. A. Copp (of which, by ladies of
church, to constitute Mrs. Ira B. Cheever L. M., $25; Mrs.
Alonzo C. Tenney, to constitute Mrs. Elizabeth C. Tenney
L. M., $25; infant class, $5) 145.00
Danversport — Miss E. P. Putnam, annual subscription .   .   .   10.00

Dorchester — Second Cong. Church, aux. (of which, from Mrs. Walter Baker, Mrs. John H. Brooks, Mrs. Elbridge Torrey, Miss E. Cornelia Shaw, and Miss E. A. Wales, $25 each, to constitute themselves L. M.'s; and $128 from annual subscribers, including one dollar in *pennies, the savings of a little girl*) $253.00

East Boston — Maverick Church, from Miss Elizabeth Hammett, annual subscription, $10, and to constitute Mrs. Snow, Micronesia, L. M., $25; Mrs. Luther A. Wright, to constitute Mrs. K. C. Loyd of Zulu Mission, So. Africa, L. M., $25; Mrs. Albert Bowker, to constitute Miss Sarah F. Bowker and Miss Mary F. Bowker L. M.'s, $50; subscriptions from Mrs. Paul Curtis, Mrs. Nelson Curtis, and Mrs. Daniel Gregory, $10 each, ($30); Mrs. Edwin Wright, $5; Mrs. Luther Hall, $3; Mrs. John A. Brown, $3; Mrs. Thos. Demond, $3; Mrs. Gilman Collamore, $5; twenty-one subscribers, of $1 each ($21) 170.00

East Cambridge — Miss L. Munroe, subscription, $10; donation, $2 . 12.00

Falmouth — Mrs. Oliver C. Swift, to constitute herself L. M. . . . 25.00

Ipswich — With sums previously acknowledged, to make Mrs. T. Morong L. M. 6.00

Lancaster — Aux. Society, by Mrs. H. C. Kendrick, $10; Ladies' Industrial School, to constitute Mrs. Jane A. Ames L. M. . 35.00

Monson — Mrs. Reuben A. Chapman, constituting herself L. M. . . 25.00

Newburyport — Mrs. Edward W. Hooker 2 03

Taunton — Mrs. Alvah Cobb 10.00

Waltham — A few ladies, to constitute Mrs. Elnathan Strong L. M. . 25.00

Wrentham — Mrs. Jemima Hawes 10.00

RHODE ISLAND.

Coventry — Five subscribers, of $1 each 5.00

CONNECTICUT.

Columbia — Miss Emily C. Williams, annual subscription . . . 1.00

Colchester — Aux. Society, by Mrs. J. B. Wheeler, treasurer (of which, by ladies of the church, to constitute Mrs. S. G. Williard L. M, $25; Mrs. Mary Ann Hyde, to constitute herself L. M., $25; Mrs. C. B. McCall, to constitute herself L. M., $25) 90.00

New London — A lady in First Cong. Church, to constitute Mrs. Abby E. Brown and Mrs. Abba W. Smith L. M.'s . . 50.00

Orange — "Unknown" 50.00

NEW YORK.

Brooklyn — Plymouth Church, Mrs. J. W. Hayes, to constitute herself L. M. 25.00

New York — Mrs. Wm. E. Dodge, to constitute Mrs. Geo. L. Prentice and herself L. M.'s 50.00

Spencerport — Mrs. S. Weare, for China 10.00

Syracuse — Mrs. E. W. Leavenworth, to constitute herself L. M. . . 25.00

NEW JERSEY.

Vineland — Mrs. G. M. Bartlett and Miss Clara P. Bartlett, $1 each . $2.00
Received for quarterlies 6.00

$1,914.50

RECEIPTS FROM MARCH 5 TO APRIL 5.

MAINE.

Lewiston — Mrs. A. D. Lockwood, to constitute herself L. M. . . $25.00

NEW HAMPSHIRE.

Claremont — Mrs. Edward L. Goddard, to constitute herself L. M. . 25.00

VERMONT.

Burlington — Ladies of White-street Cong. Church 21.50
Cambridge — Mrs. Mary C. Turner, in part L. M. 5.00
Peacham — Mrs. D. S. Chamberlain, to constitute herself L. M. . . 25.00

MASSACHUSETTS.

Boston — Mrs. G. W. Crockett, L. M., $25: Mrs. Sam'l Wells, subscription, $1; Mrs. Alvan Perry, subscription, $1 . . . 27.00
Essex-street Church, additional. Miss Lee, $2; Mrs. and Miss French, $1 each; Mrs. W. A. Wingate, $3; Mrs. Hall, $2; two subscribers, $1 each; Mrs. Charles Scudder, to constitute herself L. M., $25; Miss L. J. Brown, to constitute herself L. M., $25; five ladies, to constitute Mrs. S. B. Treat L. M., $25 . . . . 86.00
Old South Church, Miss Blagden, collector: Miss Harris, $10; Mrs. James F. Baldwin, $5; Mrs. Ewd. C. Johnson, $5; Mrs. Ward, $5; Mrs. David Buck, $5; Mrs. Thomas Palmer, $2; five of $1 each . . . . . . - . . 37.00
Mount Vernon Church, Mrs. Woodford 1.00
Mission Circle of Chambers-street Chapel 105.60
Park-street Church, Little May's Life Membership . . 25.00
Central Church, Miss Myra B. Child, collector (of which, from Mrs. E. B. Bigelow, Mrs. Lewis Child, Mrs. Isaac Kendall, $10 each; Mrs. H. B. Nash, $1), 31. Miss Rollins' collection (of which, from Mrs. James Bird, L. M., $25; Miss Abbie Pearson, $20; annual subscriptions, Mrs. James Bird, Mrs. Edward Page, Mrs. A. Brimckcome, $5 each; Mrs. N. Carr, $3, and thirteen of $1 each), 76. Miss Abbie Herman, collector: Mrs. J. W. Tyler, Misses Herman, $5 each; Mrs. L. Herman, Mrs. Cyrus H. Hale, Miss L. Fowler, $2 each, and nine annual subscribers, $1 each, $25. Miss L. E. Francis, collector: Mrs. Francis, $3; Miss Francis and Mrs. Geo. O. Sears, $2 each, and nine annual subscribers, of $1 each, $10. Miss Wheeler, collector: nine subscribers, of $1 each, $9 . . . . 157.00

Brookline — Harvard Church, by Miss M. G. Stoddard, subscriptions (of which, from Mrs. Horatia Burditt, Mrs. A. De Puyster, Mrs. C. W. Scudder, Mrs. Moses Withington, Mrs. W. T. Eustis, $5 each; Miss M. C. Bancroft, $4; Mrs. C. P. Bancroft, Mrs. Frank White, Mrs. Elbridge Mason, Miss S. Studley, Mrs. Seville, $3 each; Mrs. G. W Merritt, Mrs. Z. F. Brett, Mrs. Oliver Hay, Mrs. Otis Withington, Mrs. Colby, $2 each; and twenty-one subscribers, $1 each) $75.00

Braintree — Rev. S. Storrs, to constitute Mrs. Ann S. Storrs, Miss Eunice C. Storrs, and Mrs. Mary Sugden L. M.'s . . 75.00

Dennysville — Mrs. P. E. Vose, annual subscription 1.00

East Boston — Maverick Church, additional, Mrs. Rebecca Laud, and Mrs. Nehemiah Gibson, $5 each; five annual subscribers, $1 each 15.00

Falmouth — A friend 2.00

Groton Junction — Aux. Society, by Mrs. H. F. Frye 10.00

Jamaica Plain — Central Church, by Miss M. A. B. Brackett, annual subscriptions . . . . 77.50 ·

Lowell — Mrs. E. R. Stevens 1.00

Marblehead — Mrs. Wm. Fabens, and Mrs. S. G. Knight, Boston, $1 ea. 2.00

North Leominster — The Misses T—— 2.00

South Boston — Phillips Church, by Mrs. Jeremy Drake (of which, from Mrs. Jeremy Drake, to constitute Mrs. E. K. Alden L. M., $25; Mrs. C. C. Conley, constituting herself L. M., $25; Miss E. N. Vinton, constituting herself L. M., $25; Mrs. Edwin Briggs, $10; Mrs. E. K. Alden, Mrs. G. M. Amsden, Mrs. C. Burnham, Mrs. S. B. Conley, Miss Alice Cooper, Mrs. William Eaton, Miss Mary E. Fox, Mrs. M. C. Lang, Mrs. C. Shepard, Miss S. Shepard, Miss Kate Burnham, $5 each; Mrs. Willis Howes, Miss A. B. Jewell, Mrs. A. King, Miss H. N. Vinton, $3 each; Miss H. M. Baker, Mrs. G. W. Ellis, Mrs. J. C. Howes, Mrs. Nickerson, Mrs. Pierce, Mrs. S. A. Stackpole, Mrs. A. J. Wright, Jr., Miss Eliza L. Darling, and Miss Bell C. Darling, $2 each; and thirty-five subscribers, of $1 each) . 205.00

Whitinsville — Auxiliary, by Miss F. A. Bachelor, treasurer (of which, from Mrs. C. B. Whitin, constituting Mrs. L. F. Clark L. M., $25; Mrs. Paul Whitin, to constitute herself L. M., $25; forty-two subscribers, $1 each) . . . 100.00
Mrs. Freeman Allen, additional, to constitute Mrs. Charlotte L. Reed, L. M. 25.00

Weymouth — Miss Sarah M. Bailey, L. M. 25.00

Westhampton — Mrs. David Montague, to constitute R. Louisa Montague L. M. 25.00

Westmoreland — Mrs. A. Noyes 2.00

RHODE ISLAND.

Providence — Aux. Central Cong. Church, Miss Anna S. White, treas.
(of which, $100, to constitute Mrs. Wm. J. King, Mrs.
H. Lathrop, Mrs. A. Sprague, and Mrs. J. L. Snow,
L. M.'s) $182.50
Richmond-street Church (of which, $100, to constitute
Mrs. S. S. Sprague, Mrs. J. N. Nason, Mrs. Isaac Cady,
and Mrs. M. A. Merrill, L. M.'s) 152.50
Beneficent Church (of which, $100, to constitute Mrs. H.
W. Wilkinson, Mrs. B. M. Jackson, Mrs. George T.
Spicer, and Miss Ann S. White, L. M.'s) . . . 158.00
High-street Church, Mrs. B. B. Knight, L. M. . . 25.00
Charles-street Church, subscriptions 20.00
Free Church 25.00

CONNECTICUT.

Andover — Charlotte E. and Sarah A. Hyde, $5 each 10.00
Norwich — Mrs. Wm. W. Williams, to constitute Miss Emeline Palmer
and herself L. M.'s 50.00

NEW YORK.

Westport — Mrs. V. C. Spencer, $3; Mrs. B. H. Nash, $1 . . . 4.00

OHIO.

Oberlin — Mrs. Henry Viets 10.00

CANADA.

Sherbrooke — Mrs. Duff, of Cong. Church, by Rev. Mr. Duff . . . 0.58

TURKEY.

Cesarea — Miss Sarah A. Closson 26.20
For quarterlies 196.00

Total 2,047.78

RECEIPTS FROM APRIL 5 TO MAY 5.

NEW HAMPSHIRE.

Bennington — Mrs. Chas. P. Whittemore 5.00
Claremont — Mrs. Edward L. Goddard, annual subscriber . . . 1.00
Exeter — Ladies' Missionary Society, to constitute Mrs. I. T. Otis L. M. 26.00

VERMONT.

Bennington — Mrs. Hubbard 1.00
East Dorset — Ladies Aux. Society, to constitute the wife of Rev. F.
W. Olmsted L. M. 25.00
St. Johnsbury — Additional by Mrs. A. L. Cummings 3.50
Union Village — Mrs. John Lord, over eighty years old 1.00

MASSACHUSETTS.

Auburndale — Mrs. Samuel Cutler, annual subscriber 1.00
Boston — Miss Adams, Miss Anna Apthorp, and Mrs. Martin Moore,
subscribers, $3; to constitute Mrs. Giles Pease L. M., $25 . 28.00
Salem-street Church, additional 4.00

Park-street Church, Mrs. Garratt, and Mrs. Chase, $5 each;
Mrs. Farley, $2, Miss Hobart, $3, and five annual subscribers,
$5; by Mrs. Hubbard, Mrs. J. H. Wiggin, to constitute
herself L. M., $25. Annual subscribers, Mrs. M. H. Simpson,
$10, Miss Susan M. Jones, $5, and by Miss Lincoln, col-
lector, $21 . . . . $81 00
Chambers-street Chapel Mission Circle 12.65
Shawmut Cong. Church, subscribers, $5; additional, $35; Mrs.
Mary A. Blaney, to constitute M. L., $25; additional, $1.50 . 61.50
Central Church, additional, Miss Dennison, collector: Mrs.
and Miss Southwick, $10; Mrs. G. Dennison $5; Miss L.
Thompson, $5; Mrs. Elisha Vinton, $2; nine annual sub-
scriptions of $1 each, $31; Miss Sarah A. Ullman, collector:
Miss Topliff, $8, and six subscriptions of $1 each, $14 . 45.00
Essex-street Church, Mrs. W. H. Dunning, L. M., $25, addi-
tional from Mrs. Scudder, avails of work, $1.12 . . . 26.12
Mount Vernon Church, Mrs. John J. Tappan, $5; Mrs. Kim-
ball, $2; and twenty-three subscribers of $1 each . . . 30.00
Boston Highlands — Ladies of Vine-street Church, to constitute Mrs.
J. O. Means L. M., $25; ladies of Eliot Church, to
constitute Mrs. Rufus Anderson L.M., $25; High-
land Church, $20 . . . . 70.00
Brookline — Harvard Church, additional, Mrs. H. McG. Noyes . . 5.00
Barre — Mrs. Arnold Adams 5.00
Cambridgeport — Miss Julia Bridges 1.00
Charlestown — Mrs. S. B. Goldthwait, annual subscription . . . 1.00
Chelsea — Chestnut-street Church, by Mrs. J. H. Sweetser, $17; by Mrs.
A. H. Plumb, $34 . . . . 51.00
Broadway Church, by Mrs. J. A. Copp, from Rev. E. Pason
Thwing, to constitute his wife L. M., $25; four annual sub-
scribers, $1 each 29.00
Cambridge — Chas. G. Green, Esq., to constitute his mother, Mrs. G.
M. Green, L. M. 25.00
Dorchester — Mrs. Chas. Plaisted 5.00
East Cambridge — Five subscribers, $1 each 5.00
East Braintree — Mrs. J. H. Holbrook 3.00
East Somerville — Ladies' Maternal Association of Franklin-street
Church, to constitute Mrs. E. Davis L. M. . . 25.00
Lunenburg — Ladies' Aux. Society 10.00
Lowell — Mrs. Owen Street 2.00
Milton — Mrs. Lucy Wadsworth 25.00
Malden — Ladies' Benev. Society, to constitute Mrs. Chas. E. Reed L.M. 25.00
Newburyport — By Mrs. H. A. Ingraham, treasurer Woman's Foreign
Mission Society 100.00
Newtonville — Twelve subscribers of $1 each; and Miss E. A. Goodale,
L. M., $25 . . . . 37.00
Plymouth — Mrs. Dr. T. Gordon, to constitute herself L. M. . . . 25.00
Pittsfield — Mrs. Ewd. Clapp and Miss Sarah Martin, $5 each . . 10.00
South Boston — Miss S. A. Holt, annual subscriber 1.00

Stratham — Aux. Society $12.00
    Eddie and Henry, who send their all to heathen children,
    that they may hear of Jesus 1.85
West Newton — By Mrs. B. F. Whittemore, from Mrs. L. H. Valentine
    and Mrs. J. B. Whitmore, $5 each; eleven subscribers,
    $1 each, $21; Mrs. J. A. Newell and Mrs. B. F. Whit-
    temore, L. M.'s, $50 . . . . 71.00
Worcester — By Mrs. Anna F. Washburn, from Mrs. Albert Curtis, Mrs.
    Richard Ball, and Mrs. P. L. Moen, $25 each, constitut-
    ing themselves L. M.'s; Mrs. C. Washburn, to constitute
    Miss Ellen H. Washburn L. M., $25; and $185.25 from
    subscribers, all of Union Church 285.25
Woburn — Accompanying order for twenty-five copies L. and L. . . .75

CONNECTICUT.
Colchester — Mrs. Henry Burr, $1.50; Miss Eliza Day, to constitute her-
    self L. M., $25; eleven annual subscribers, $1 each . 37.50
New Haven — Mrs. M. S. Ferguson, by A. P. F. 10.00
Willimantic — A subscriber 2.00

NEW YORK.
Jewett — Ladies' Benevolent Society, by Mrs. Buck 6.00

OHIO.
Cleveland — Mrs. Elizabeth E. Taylor 24.00

TENNESSEE.
Lookout Mountain — Educational Institutions, a part to make Miss
    Mary A. Wilson L. M., $30; C. C. Carpenter,
    Esq., to make Mrs. Feronia R. Carpenter L. M.,
    $25 . . . . 55.00
    Also for quarterlies 223.85

$1,545.97

RECEIPTS FROM MAY 6 TO JUNE 1.

MAINE.
Brunswick — From Prof. J. B. Sewall, to constitute his wife L. M. . $25 00

NEW HAMPSHIRE.
Henniker — Mrs. R. H. B. Cogswell, to support a pupil in Miss Proc-
    tor's school at Aintab, Turkey 25.00

VERMONT.
Rutland — "Persis 2d," $25, Mrs. Morse, $1 . . . . . . 26.00
Middlebury — Aux. By Miss Julia Beckwith, treasurer 36.00
Grafton — Mrs. E. B. Barrett, $5, Mrs. S. B. Pettingill, $3, Mrs. C. B.
    Aiken, $1 . . . . 9.00

MASSACHUSETTS.
Falmouth — Mrs. Cornish, $3, E. S. Atwood, to constitute Mrs. Joseph
    H. Gray L. M, $25 . . . . 28.00
Long Meadow — Aux. By Miss Mary Lawton, to constitute Mrs. M. L.
    Harding L. M. 26.50

West Newton — Mrs. Thomas E. Graves, to constitute herself L. M. . . $25.00
Northampton — "A Thank-offering" 25.00
Fitchburg — By a friend, to constitute Mrs. John Lowe L. M. ' . . 25.00
Cambridge — Shepard Church Aux. A part to constitute their pastor's
wife L. M. 30.00
Mount Holyoke Seminary — A part of which to constitute Miss Helen
M. French, Miss Mary Ellis, Miss Julia E.
Ward, Miss Lydia W. Shattuck, Miss M.
Elizabeth Childs, Miss Harriet E. Ses-
sions, Miss Elizabeth Blanchard, Miss
Elizabeth D. Ballantine, Miss Anna C.
Edwards, Miss Hannah Noble, Miss
Ellen P. Bowers, Miss Lucy J. Holmes,
Miss Susan M. Clary, Miss Frances M.
Hazen, and Miss Elizabeth B. Prentiss,
Life Members 400.00
Waltham — A friend 5.00
Monson — From Mrs. Otis Bradford, to constitute Miss Sarah E. Brad-
ford L. M. 25.00
Stockbridge — A Life Membership for Mrs. S. B. Brown 25.00
Ashby — Aux. A part to constitute Mrs. Ellen S. Parker L. M. . . 43.80
Bradford Female Academy — Aux. By Miss Sarah Johnson, treasurer 58.85
Beverly — From a true friend, R. W. G. 5.00
Southbridge — Mrs. S. M. Lane 5.00
Haverhill — $1, and from a friend, $1 . . . . 2.00
Billerica — Aux. By Mrs. William Bossom 20.00
Boston — Miss D. Carleton 5.00
Subscribers of $1 each '. . . . .' . 5.00
Donation . . · 1.25

RHODE ISLAND.

Providence — Aux. Anna S. White, treasurer. From Mrs. J. L. Draper,
Beneficent Church, to constitute herself L. M., $25;
Central Church, $3, High-Street Church $1 . . . 29.00
Coventry — Four annual subscribers 4.00

CONNECTICUT.

Deep River — H. Wickes, to constitute his wife L. M. 25.00
Groton — The Misses Copp, annual subscription of $1 each . . . 3.00

NEW YORK.

Watertown — By Mrs. Susan Morgan, subscriptions used to constitute
pastor's wife L. M. 25.00
Rome — From "M." 5.00

NEW JERSEY.

Vineland — Mrs. G. M. Bartlett 5.00

PENNSYLVANIA.

Philadelphia — Mrs. C. A. Lynde, to constitute herself L. M. . . . 25.00

MARYLAND.

Frederick City — E. H. Rockwell, Esq., to constitute his wife L. M. . 25.00

OHIO.

Granville — Mrs. Deborah Fuller, to constitute herself L. M., and to
educate a pupil in Marash Seminary $120.00

Total for subscriptions and donations $1,147.40
Also for Quarterlies 86.25

Total $1,233.65

RECEIPTS FROM JUNE 1 TO JULY 1.

MAINE.

Cumberland Centre — Rev. E. S. Jordan, to constitute his wife L. M. . $25.00

NEW HAMPSHIRE.

Littleton — Ladies' Mission Circle, by A. S. Whipple, Secretary . . 25.00

VERMONT.

St. Albans — Aux. To constitute Mrs. Eunice L. Janes of San Francisco, Cal., Mrs. S. Wells Williams of Pekin, China,
Mrs. Laura Seymour, and Mrs. A. J. Samson, L.M.'s . 100.00

MASSACHUSETTS.

East Taunton — From ladies, to constitute Mrs. Frederick A. Reed L.M. 25.00
Dedham — First Church, to constitute Mrs. J. Edwards and Mrs. A. B.
Whitney, L. M.'s 50.00
Auburndale — Mrs. Susan F. Shedd, L. M. 25.00
Randolph — Miss Abby W. Turner 5.00
South Boston — Mrs. S. P. Austin, annual subscriber 1.00
Boston Highlands — Eliot Church, annual subscription, by Mrs. Dr.
Anderson, $31; from Mrs. Hodges, to constitute
herself L. M., $25; Vine-street Church, subscrip-
tion, $1; Sunday-school Class, $5 . . . 62.00
Boston — A friend, $100; Mrs. Louisa Thompson, to constitute herself
L. M., $25; Mrs. William Willett, $1; Shawmut Church,
additional, $1; at quarterly meeting, subscriptions for stock-
ings knit for the "Woman's Board of Missions," by Mrs.
Nancy Philbrick, of Epping, in her 97th year, and her last
work ($10 having been subscribed), the total to constitute
her granddaughter, Mrs. Nancy P. Moore, L. M., $27; Park-
street Church, annual subscription, additional, from Mrs.
Joseph Bell, $5; Mrs. C. L. Bartlett, $5; six subscribers, of
$1 each; Mrs. Pratt, $25; Mrs. Whiting, $3; and thirteen
subscribers, of $1 each; Mount Vernon Church, "M. P. C.
H.," to constitute Roxy C. Cowles, of Ipswich, L. M., $25 . 236.00
Leominster — Missionary Society, by Miss S. M. Haskell 31.73
Newton — Mrs. I. A. Hatch, to constitute herself L. M. 25.00
Cambridgeport — Prospect-street Church, additional 1.00
Lawrence — $1, and from Ipswich, two Church members, $2 . . . 3.00
Newburyport — F. M. S., which, with $100 acknowledged in June No.,
constitute Mrs. William B. Banister, Mrs. Sarah W.
Hale, Mrs. Y. C. Tyler, Mrs. Newman Brown, Mrs.
Anthony Jones, and Mrs. Herbert A. Ingraham,
L. M.'s 50.00

Westfield — Ladies of 1st Cong. Church, by Mrs. Greenough . . . $52.00
Southampton — Aux. Soc. By Jane Z. Judd, treasurer 58.00
Pittsfield — William G. Harding, to constitute his wife L. M., $25 ; M.
      P. Le Bosquete, $1 . . . . 26.00
Whitinsville — Aux. Additional, by Miss F. A. Batchelor . . . 2.00
Chelsea — Chestnut-street Church, by Miss E. Temple, to constitute
      wife of Rev. Thos. Laurie, D.D., L. M., $25; Broadway
      Church, from Mrs. J. Q. Gilmore, $10 . . . . . 35.00
Billerica — Aux. Additional (which makes a total of $22.50 from a con-
      gregation averaging fifty) 2.50

CONNECTICUT.

Guilford — Mrs. Alvan Talcott, to constitute herself L. M. . . . 25.00
Griswold — Ladies, by E. C. B. Northrop 12.00
Norwich — Mrs. Coit, by E. S. G. 5.00
Burnside — Mrs. Dorcas Elmore, $5; M. Janette Elmore, to constitute
      herself L. M., $25 . . . . 30.00
New London — Mrs. Henry O. Ames 5.00
Bozrah — Aux. To constitute Mrs. Wm. C. Abell L. M., and from Mrs.
      Fannie Raymond, constituting herself L. M. 51.00

RHODE ISLAND.

Providence — Aux. Central Church, $2; Beneficent Church, addit'l, 50c. 2.50

NEW YORK.

Poughkeepsie — From Mary H. Sterling 10.00

PENNSYLVANIA.

Philadelphia — A *monthly* contribution from Mrs. C. A. L. . . . 25.0

                                    $1,005.73
     For quarterlies 65.90
     Total $1.071.63

RECEIPTS FROM JULY 1 TO AUGUST 1.

MAINE.

Wells — Auxiliary Society 2d Cong. Church, annual subscription . . $30.00
Bangor — "A friend " 10.00
Lewiston — By S. H. Murray, treasurer, Pine-st. Cong. Ch., from Mrs.
      A. D. Lockwood, to const. Miss Sarah L. Danielson L. M., 30.00

NEW HAMPSHIRE.

Hollis — From " friends," to constitute Mrs. Cyrus Burge L. M. . . 25.00
Milford — From Mrs. C. Juliette Gibson, for Miss Parmelee's work, $16;
      and from " little Willie, in pity for heathen children," $2.10, 18.10

VERMONT.

Worcester — "A friend " 5.00

MASSACHUSETTS.

South Amherst — Ladies' Benevolent Society, by Mrs. C. B. Hutchings,
      to constitute Mrs. E. C. Miller L. M. 25.00

Andover — " A friend: member of Free Christian Church " $5.00
Randolph — Ladies of 2d Congregational Church 15.00
Ware — By Mrs. William Hyde, from annual subscribers, $13, and to
     constitute Mrs. O. Sage, Miss S. R. Sage, Mrs. William
     Hyde, and Miss H. S. Hyde L. M.'s, $100 . . . . . 113.00
Westfield — From Miss Mary A. Leonard, to const. herself L. M., $25;
     Miss Ella E. Catlin, to constitute herself L. M., $25 . 50.00
Grantville — " A friend," to const. wife of Rev. W. S. Smith L. M. . 25 00
Lawrence — Aux. By a friend, to constitute wife of Rev. Mr. Fisher
     L. M., $25; Lawrence-st. Church, to constitute Miss Phebe
     A. Maddock L. M., $25; ten annual subscribers, $10 . . 60.00
Upton — Mrs. Sadler 1.00
Fitchburg — Ladies of Rev. Alfred Emerson's Society, to constitute his
     wife L. M. 25.00
Woburn — C. S. Adkins, annual subscriber 3.00
Newton — " From friends " . . . . . . '. 3.50
Boston — From sale of jewelry, in part 80.00
     Park-st. Church, Mrs. Peter Hobart, to constitute herself
     L. M., $25; one annual subscriber, $1 . . . . . 26.00
     Mount Vernon Church, Mrs. C. Laud 1.00
     From Miss E. H. Ropes 10.00
South Boston — Phillips Church, Mrs. R. J. Wheelwright, $25, to const.
     herself L. M., and eleven subscribers, $1 each . . 36.00
Boston Highlands — By Mrs. Anderson 15.00

CONNECTICUT.

Norwich — Ladies of 1st Congregational Church, by E. S. Gilman . 15.00
Colebrook — Two subscribers 2.00
Southbury — Ladies of Cong. Church and Society, to constitute Mrs.
     Harriet E. Smith L. M. 27.70
New Britain — From M. M. Davis 5.00

NEW YORK.

Bergen — Mrs. E. B. Talcott 10.00
Meriden — Mrs. T. R. Townsend, $10; a friend, 50 cents . . . 10 50
Rochester — Aux. Miss Caroline Starr, treasurer, from Mrs. P. H. Cur-
     tis, $5; Miss Tlerr, $4; Infant Department, Central
     Church S. S. $5; subscribers of $1 each, $40 . . . 54.00

PENNSYLVANIA. .

Philadelphia — From " G. A. L ," monthly contribution . . . 25.00

OHIO.

Belpre — From Mrs. Sophia Browning, to const. Mrs. A. T. Bates L. M., 25.00

                                         $785.80
Received for Quarterlies, ... 73.50
Total $859.30
3

RECEIPTS FROM AUG. 1 TO SEP. 1.

MAINE.

Chesterfield — A thank-offering $1.00

VERMONT.

Middlebury — By Mrs. Ladd, from Miss Martha Hough, to constitute
herself and Miss L. Simmonds L. M.'s. 50.00

NEW HAMPSHIRE.

Stratham — Mrs. Olivia Lane, to const. Mrs. Fannie D. Sinclair L. M., 25 00

MASSACHUSETTS.

Boston Highlands — Eliot Church, annual subscription, additional, by
Mrs. Anderson, $14; also later, $2 . . . 16.00
Boston — " A friend " 5.00
Chelsea — Broadway Church, Mrs. C. Powers, annual subscriber, $1; for
A. B., from retrenchment in dress, $35 . . . . 36.00
Auburndale — From ladies, to constitute wife of Rev. Calvin Cutler
L. M., $25; Mrs. N. A. Alden, to const. herself L. M., $25, 50.00
Barre — Mrs. Arnold Adams, to constitute herself L. M. . . . 25.00
North Chelmsford — Rev. and Mrs. B. F. Clark, to constitute Mrs. B. F.
Clark L. M., $25; Fanny Munger's missionary-
box, being pennies saved, $1 . . . . . 26.00
Monson — Aux. Of which, from Mrs. Dea. Porter, $25, to constitute
Mrs. Hadassah Deney L. M., and $25 from Society, to con-
stitute Mrs. John Packard L. M. 63.00
Falmouth — " A friend," to constitute Mrs. James P. Kimball L. M. . 25.00
Sale of jewelry, in part 7.00
Uxbridge — Aux. By E. L. Biscoe. 36.00
Webster — " A friend," to constitute Mrs. Parmenas Keith L. M. . . 25.00
Upton — By " friends,' to constitute Mrs George P. Claflin L. M. . . 25.00
Newton Centre — Mary H. Cornelius 3.00
Wellesley — Aux. Soc. By Mrs. H. F. Durant, to constitute Miss Asa
Baker, Mardin, Eastern Turkey, L. M., $25; by Mrs.
A. D. Webber, to constitute Mrs. M. Watkins L. M.,
$25; by Mrs. N. Dana, to constitute Mrs. G. N. Dana,
Boston, L. M., $25; by Mrs. C. B. Dana, to constitute
herself L. M., $25: by annual subscription, used to con-
stitute Mrs. E. G. Little, Miss. M. S. Webber, and Miss
Hannah Rollins L. M.'s, $75 . . . . . . 175.00
Winchester — To constitute Mrs. Stephen Cutter, Mrs. Henry Cutter,
and Mrs. N. W. C. Holt L. M.'s. 75.00
Cambridgeport — Mrs. Russell L. Snow, to constitute herself L. M. . 25.00
Andover — Miss Sarah A. Dole, to constitute herself L. M. . . 25.00
Marshfield — Mrs. Sarah L. Bourne, to constitute herself L. M. . . 25.00
South Boston — Phillips Church, Miss Mary Lincoln, to constitute her-
self L. M. 25.00

CONNECTICUT.

East Haddam — Mrs. Sarah B. Parsons, to constitute herself L M. . 25 00

Colchester — Mrs. William Stebbins $1.00
West Woodstock — Mrs. H. E. Carpenter 5.00

NEW YORK.

Syracuse — Mrs. Hibbard, $2; Mrs. Britton, $1 . . . . . 3.00
Penn Yann — Mrs. Charles C. Shepperd, to const. herself L. M. . . 25 00
Buffalo — Westminster Ch. Aux. By Mrs. F. Gridley, treasurer . . 75.00
Watertown — Mrs. James K. Bates, annual subscription . . . 2.00

PENNSYLVANIA.

Philadelphia — "C. A. L.," monthly subscription 25.00

DELAWARE.

Glasgow — Mrs. Ed. Webb, to const. Miss Mary E. Webb L. M. . . 25.00

OHIO.

Cincinnati — Mrs. B. E., wife of Rev. B. P. Aydelott, to constitute herself L. M. 25.00
Edinburg — Mrs. A. M. Bingham 2.00
$981.00

For Quarterlies 26.00

Total $1,007.00

RECEIPTS FOR SEPTEMBER.

MAINE.

Amherst — Mrs. H. S. Loring $3.00
Holden — Mrs. D. Harrington 1.00

NEW HAMPSHIRE.

Atkinson — Rev. Jesse Page, to constitute his sister, daughter, and
niece L. M.'s 75.00
Pelham — Mrs. H. C. Wyman, and Mrs. E. W. Tyler, to constitute
themselves L. M.'s 50.00

VERMONT.

Brandon — Cong. Church, a ring from a lady, and from the Society . 25.00
Montpelier — Aux. By Mrs. A. J. Howe, treasurer, fourteen subscribers
of $1 each, and $19 in smaller amounts, a part to con-
stitute Miss Mary A. Eustis L. M.; Mrs. A. J. Howe,
to constitute herself L. M., $25 . . . . . . 58.00
St. Albans — Aux. By Mary A. Smith, treasurer, to constitute Mrs. J.
Q. Bittinger, Mrs. Worthington C. Smith, and Miss
Frances M. Brainerd L. M.'s 82 00

MASSACHUSETTS.

Pittsfield — Stephen Reed, to constitute Mrs. Sarah E. Reed L. M. . 25.00
Townsend — "M. E. H.," weekly 1.04
Proceeds of a few foreign curiosities 3.00
Boston — "D. M. C.," $5; Mrs. S. Farrington, $2; jewelry proceeds,
$10; last earnings of a deceased friend, $2.40; "S. L. R.,"
$10; jewelry proceeds, from Mrs. B., $15 . . . . 44.40

Boston Highlands — Eliot Church, infant class S. S. $7.50
    (Fanny Munger's missionary-box, being pennies
    saved, $1, by mistake acknowledged in October
    Herald as from North Chelmsford, should have
    been from Boston Highlands.)
South Boston — E-street Cong. church 28.75
Allston — " A friend " 2.00
Littleton — Mrs. L S. R. Houghton's S. S. class, for Miss Clark's school,
    Turkey 5.00
Newton — Miss Hitchcock, to constitute herself L. M. 25.00
Auburndale — Mrs. Calvin Cutler 1.00
Woburn — " H." 5.00
Lanesboro' — Cong. Church and Society, to constitute Mrs. Isabella Lyon
    of New York L. M. 25.00
Winchester — Miss Lizzie Chapin, to constitute herself L. M. . . . 25.00

CONNECTICUT.

Hebron — Mrs. Jasper Porter and Miss Anna Porter. 2.00
Middletown — Mrs. Eliza H. Goodrich, to constitute herself L. M. . . 25.00
Bolton — Ladies of Cong. Church and Society 13.00
West Hartford — " J. P. C. " 1.50
Norwich — 2d Cong. Church Aux., of which from Mrs. H. P. Williams,
    $25, to constitute Mrs. Alvan Bond L. M. 150.00
Harwinton — Mrs. Sarah B. Hayes, to constitute herself L. M. . . 25 00

NEW YORK.

Coeymans — Albany Co. Miss Catharine Ten Eyck, to constitute her-
    self L. M.. . . . . 25.00
Waverly — Rev. J. B. Beaumont (of which from Mrs. Larned, 16.15), to
    constitute Mrs. H. N. Beaumont L. M. 25.00
New-York City — J. T. Leavitt, to constitute his wife L. M. 25.00
Buffalo — Westminster Church Aux., additional 2 00
Fayetteville — Onondaga Co. Aux., by Harriet S. Todd, secretary, of
    which $50 is to constitute Mrs. Katharine H. Bigelow
    and Mrs. Jane Pratt L. M.'s 70.00
Champlain — Mrs. P. Moore 5.00

PENNSYLVANIA.

Philadelphia — " C. A. L.," a monthly contribution . . . 25.00

OHIO.

Toledo — " A friend," to constitute Mrs. W. E. Parmelee L. M. . . 25.00

MICHIGAN.

North Star — 1st Presbyterian Church 2.00

MINNESOTA.

Winona — Mrs. H. F. Hatch 20.00
                                932.19
For quarterlies 23.14

Total for the month $955.33

RECEIPTS FOR OCTOBER.

MAINE.

Holden — Two friends $2.00

NEW HAMPSHIRE.

Portsmouth — By C. L. Martin, from Miss Mary Rogers 5.00

MASSACHUSETTS.

North Cambridge — M. L. S. 2.50
Cambridgeport — William H. Pratt, Prospect-street Church, to consti-
    tute his wife L. M. 25.00
Monson — Aux. Additional 12.00
Lexington — Mrs. John Davis, Senior, to constitute herself L. M. . . 25.00
Dedham — Mrs. G. M. Farrington 2.00
Bridgewater — Miss S. H. Wasgatt 2.00
Lawrence — By Mrs. Stedman, five subscribers, $1 each 5.00
Hinsdale — Mrs. N. Emmons 1.00
Swampscott — Cong. Church S. S., by Miss Fowler 4.20

CONNECTICUT.

West Hartford — Mrs. L. W. Selden 5.00
Putnam — Village Church contributions 17.00

NEW YORK.

Fredonia — Gold chain and pencil, from a lady, by Rev. C. Bush.
Buffalo — Westminster Pres. Church, additional (which, with previous
    subscriptions, constitutes Mrs. Eliza N. White, Mrs. Ellen
    Wilkes, and Mrs. C. O. Sawyer, Life Members) . . 2.00

PENNSYLVANIA.

Philadelphia — "C. A. L.," monthly subscription $25; Mrs. Charles
    Burnham, to constitute herself L. M., $25 . . . 50.00

OHIO.

Troy — Franklin-street Pres. Church, Mrs. Hannah Grosvenor, to con-
    stitute herself L. M. 25.00
Salem — Columbiana county. Mrs. David A. Allen, to constitute her-
    self L. M. 25.00

                                    209.70
For quarterlies 73.75

Total for the month $283.45

RECEIPTS FOR NOVEMBER.

VERMONT.

Dorset — Aux. A part to constitute Mrs. P. S. Pratt and Mrs. John
    Moore L. M.'s $50 00

MASSACHUSETTS.

Oxford — Mrs. B. F. Bardwell, annual subscription 5.00
Plymouth — Mrs. Betsey Cobb, Mrs. Sarah F. Harlow, Mrs. Susan D.
    Edes, and Miss Alice Bradford, $1 each 4.00
Housatonic — Miss Sophia Perry 5.00
Townsend Harbor — From Misses Myra A. and Lucy Proctor, to consti-
    tute their mother L. M., the first-named being
    one of our missionaries at Aintab, Turkey . . 25.00

Salem — " A friend " $5.00
Williamstown — Ladies, to constitute Mrs. Albert Hopkins L. M., $25;
    Mrs. Emma Bascom, to constitute Mrs. Jennie T.
    Safford L. M., $25; "a friend," $2 . . . . 52.00
Plympton — Miss Hannah S. Parker, to constitute herself L. M. . . 25.00
Falmouth — A few ladies, to constitute Mrs. William Bates L. M. . 25 00
Springfield — Mrs. Louise T. Frary, to constitute Mrs. Mary C. Gay L. M. 25.00
Newton Centre — Balance of jewelry of a deceased friend, sold according
    to her last wishes (total received, $145) . . . 50.00
Boston — Amount received at Quarterly Meeting, to constitute Mrs.
    Cyrus F. Stone and Mrs. McClelland L. M.'s (names omitted,
    because not given in all cases), $56.80; Mrs. Cornell, spring-
    field street Church, $5 . . . . 61.80
Chelsea — By Mrs. J. Sweetser, Chestnut-st. Church, Mrs. Hamlin, Mrs.
    Palmer, and Mrs. Hall, $1 each annually, $4; Broadway Ch.
    Mrs. Howard, Mrs. Punchard, and Mrs. Pike, annual, $3 . 7.00

CONNECTICUT.

Berlin — Aux. L. H. Hallock, treasurer (of which $25 to constitute Mrs.
    Mary G. Gilbert L. M.) 40.00
New Haven — E. T. Foote, M.D., to constitute his wife and step-daugh-
    ter L. M.'s 50.00
Colchester — By Mrs. Wheeler, from Miss Eliza M. Day, to constitute
    Mrs. Miranda M. Day L. M. 25.00
Groton — " A friend," to constitute Miss Kate B. Copp L. M. . . . 25.00
Lisbon — By Mrs. Matthewson, from ladies of Newcut Society, for the
    Mahratta Mission 22.70

NEW JERSEY.

Madison — Ladies of Missionary Association, for the support of a native
    Bible-reader in Ceylon 50.00

PENNSYLVANIA.

Philadelphia — " C. A. L.," monthly subscription 25.00

TENNESSEE.

Lookout Mountain — Educational Institution, Rev. C. F. P. Bancroft,
    $15; Mrs. Bancroft, $10, to constitute Mrs. F.
    K. Bancroft L. M. 25.00

MINNESOTA.

Winona — From Mrs. H. F. Hatch, additional, to constitute her L. M. . 5.00

CALIFORNIA.

Benicia — Ladies of Congregational Church 10.00
    Subscriptions $623.50
    For quarterlies 50.85
    Total for the month $674.35

RECEIPTS FOR DECEMBER.

MAINE.

South Berwick — —— —— $1.00

NEW HAMPSHIRE.

Montpelier — " A friend," to constitute Mrs. Mary J. Hubbard L. M. . 25.00

Pittsford — Mrs. A. Hammond, $2; Mrs. S. H., 50 cents $2.50
Rutland — Aux. Society, by L. P. Flack, treasurer 111.75
St. Johnsbury — From " F. A. F." 10.00
South Merrimac — Miss Rhoda Converse 2.00

MASSACHUSETTS.

Assabet — Earnings of " Missionary Rill," a class of young ladies, by
    Mrs. Stone 5.00
Brookline — Joshua Conant, Esq., to constitute Mrs. Rebecca Conant
    L. M. 25.00
Boston — Mrs. Simpson, $5; Miss Hooper, $1; Mrs. Ira Greenwood,
    " A Memorial," $25; Mrs. Sam'l Johnson, Sen., L. M., and
    $5 annual subscription, $30; Mrs. Cyrus Hale, to constitute
    herself L. M., $25; " a friend," to constitute Mrs. Sibel Blan-
    chard, Concord, N.H., L. M., $25; child's chain, sold for
    $13 . . . . 124.00
Boston Highlands — Three subscribers, at $1 each, and one of 50 cents . 3.50
Chelsea — J. Q. Gilmore, Esq., to constitute S. M. Gilmore L. M. . . 25.00
Falmouth — Mrs. Thomas Lewis, a L. M., by Rebecca, deceased, and
    the other children 25.00
Long Meadow — Mrs. Susan M. Pynchon, a L. M. 25.00
North Wilmington — Three subscribers, of $1 each 3.00
Southbridge — A donation from Miss Fannie C. Mason's S. S. Class . 5.00
Salem — South Church Ladies' prayer-meeting, to constitute Mrs. E. M.
    Atwood L. M. 25.00
    Aux. Society Tabernacle Church, a part to constitute Mrs.
    Charles Ray Palmer L. M. 79.00
South Boston — E-street Cong. Church, by F. A. Gilbert 13.00
Winchester — Ladies, to constitute Mrs. Lydia B. Dodd of Marsovan
    L. M., $25; also, 16 subscribers 41.00
Westhampton — Ladies of 12.50
Weymouth — Union Cong. S. S., Miss M. N. Blanchard's class, to con-
    stitute Mrs. A. A. Ellsworth L. M. 25.00

CONNECTICUT.

Columbia — By Rev. F. D. Avery, four subscribers of $1 each . . . 4.00
Guilford — Mrs. Joel Tuttle, to constitute Miss Clara I. Sage L. M. . 25 00
Griswold — Ladies of First Church 14.50
New London — Second Cong. Church, first offering, of which to consti-
    tute their pastor's wife L. M. 75.00
South Windsor — " A friend," to constitute Mrs. Ernestine Lord Bow-
    man L. M. 25.00
West Woodstock — —— 3.00

NEW YORK.

Buffalo — " A friend," $5; Mrs. Wm. G. Bancroft, $5 . . . . 10.00
Brooklyn — Mrs. James M. Whiton, to constitute herself L. M. . . 25.00

PENNSYLVANIA.

Philadelphia — " C. A. L.," a monthly subscription 25.00

CANADA.

Fergus (Ontario) — " A friend " 1.35
    For quarterlies 17.50
    Total for month. $821.60

LIFE MEMBERS

OF THE WOMAN'S BOARD OF MISSIONS.

MAINE.

Brunswick. — Sewall, Mrs. J. B.
Cumberland Centre. — Jordan, Mrs.
  E. S.
Lewiston. — Danielson, Mrs. Sarah L.
  Lockwood, Mrs. A. D.
Yarmouth. — Shepley, Mrs. M. N.

NEW HAMPSHIRE.

Atkinson. — Page, Abigail Little
  Page, Mary Ann
  Page, Susan Elizabeth
Bedford. — Damon, Mrs. Stephen C.
Claremont. — Goddard, Mrs. Edw. L.
Concord. — Blanchard, Miss Sibel
Epping. — Philbrick, Mrs. Nancy
Exeter. — Otis, Mrs. I. T.
Fisherville. — Moore, Mrs. N. P.
Hollis. — Burge, Mrs. Cyrus
Henniker. — Cogswell, Mrs. R. H. B.
New Ipswich. — Fay, Mrs. S. M. E.
Pelham. — Wyman, Mrs. H. C.
  Tyler, Mrs. E. W.
Stratham. — Sinclair, Mrs. Fannie D.

VERMONT.

Dorset. — Moore, Mrs. John
  Pratt, Mrs. P. S.
E. Dorset. — Olmstead, Mrs. F. W.
E. Rutland. — Page, Mrs. J. B.
  Page, Miss Helen L.
  Page, Persis, 2d.
Middlebury. — Hough, Miss Martha
  Simmonds, Miss Laura
Montpelier. — Eustis, Miss Mary A.
  Howe, Mrs. A. J.
  Hubbard, Mrs. Mary J.
Peacham. — Chamberlain, Mrs. D. S.
St. Albans. — Bittinger, Mrs. J. Q.
  Brainerd, Miss Frances M.
  Dutcher, Mrs. Luther L.
  Gorham, Miss Mary
  Merrill, Mrs. Eliza W.
  Newton, Mrs. John W.
  Smith, Mrs. Worthington
  Smith, Mrs. M. A.
  Smith, Mrs. Maria W.
  Stevens, Mrs. Henry M.

St. Albans. — Seymour, Mrs. Laura
  Samson, Mrs. A. J.
  Wyman, Mrs. Charles
St. Johnsbury. — Cummings, Mrs. E. C.
  Colby, Mrs. J. R.
  Fairbanks, Mrs. Henry
  Fairbanks, Mrs. Horace
  Ladd, Mrs. Daniel
  Thayer, Mrs. W. W.

MASSACHUSETTS.

Auburndale. — Alden, Mrs. N. A.
  Cutler, Mrs. Calvin
  Cutler, Mrs. Sarah
  Shedd, Mrs. Susan F.
Andover. — Coburn, Mrs. Geo. W.
  Dole, Miss Sarah A.
  Jones, Mrs. Susan Kimball
  Pearson, Mrs. Emily C.
  Smith, Mrs. John
  Smith, Mrs. Joseph
  Smith, Mrs. Caroline L.
  Smith, Miss Carrie R.
  Taylor, Mrs. H. B.
  Taylor, Miss Adelaide B.
Amherst. — Lewis, Mrs. Harriet E.
  Ballantine, Mrs. Henry
  Cooper, Mrs. J. S.
Amherst. — Stearns, Mrs. William A.
  Jenkins, Mrs. J. L.
Ashby. — Parker, Mrs. Ellen S.

BOSTON CHURCHES.

Old South. — Armstrong, Mrs. S. T.
  Allen, Mrs. Frederick D.
  Blagden, Mrs. Geo. W.
  Baldwin, Mrs. James F.
  Bartlett, Mrs. Homer
  Bancroft, Mrs. Jacob
  Cragin, —— Mrs.*
  Davis, Miss Elizabeth
  Fowler, Miss Mary F.
  Fearing, Mrs. M.
  Gordon, Mrs. Louise Powers
  Gray. —— Mrs.
  Howe, Mrs. J. C.
  Hardy, Mrs. Alpheus

* Deceased.

Old South. — Johnson, Mrs. S., Sen.
Johnson, Mrs. S., Jr.
Manning, Mrs. J. M.
Plummer, Mrs. Avery
Stoddard, Mrs. Charles
Wentworth, —— Mrs.
Essex St. — Brown, Miss L. H.
Durant, Mrs. H. F.
Dunning, Mrs. Wm. H.
Fiske, Mrs. J. N.
Hooker, Mrs. H. B.
Hooper, Mrs. H.
Holland, Miss Sarah E.
Keep, Mrs. Dr. *
Keep, Miss E.
Newman, Miss C.
Newman, Miss A.
Pierce, Mrs. A.
Pease, Mrs. Giles *
Ramsay, Mrs. A.
Scudder, Mrs. Charles
Scudder, Miss Bessie M.
Scudder, Miss Vida
Strong, Mrs. Alex.
Treat, Mrs. Selah B.
Tappan, Miss E. S.
Wilkinson, Mrs. Arthur
Central. — Bates, Mrs. Benj. E.
Bird, Mrs. James
Child, Mrs. Linus
Freeland, Mrs. Charles
Grover, Mrs. Wm. S.
Houghton, Mrs. W. S.
Hale, Mrs. Cyrus K.
Kendall, Mrs. Elizabeth
Russell, Mrs. Thos. H.
Todd, Mrs. John E.
White, Mrs. James
Park St. — Eustis, Mrs. Wm. T.
Farnsworth, Mrs. Ezra
Field, Mrs. John W.
Hubbard, Mrs. Sam'l *
Hubbard, Miss Florence M.
Hobart, Mrs. Peter
Kittredge, Mrs. Jeremiah
Manning, May
Pratt, Mrs. G. W.
Quincy, Miss Martha A.
Simpson, Mrs. M. H.
Shattuck, Mrs. Lemuel
Wiggin, Mrs. J. K.
Mt. Vernon. — Coit, Mrs. Dan'l T.
Crockett, Mrs. G. W.
Kimball, Mrs. J. W.
Parkhurst, Mrs. S. E.
Palmer, Mrs. Julius A.
Safford, Mrs. Dea. Dan'l

Mt. Vernon. — Tufts, Mrs. A. W.
Winslow, Mrs. Miron
Shawmut Av. — Blaney, Mrs. Mary A.
Duff, Mrs. John
Erskine, Mrs. John
Greenwood, Mrs. Ira
Hyde, Mrs H. H.
Jones, Mrs. Frederick
Stone, Mrs. James S.
Webb, Mrs. E. B.
Wilson, Mrs. Chas. B.
Berkeley St. — Snow, Mrs. Barna
Snow, Mrs. Franklin
Wright, Mrs. Wm. B.
Salem St. — Lovejoy, Mrs. Wm. R.
Lovejoy, Mrs. Wm. Bates
Maverick. — Bowker, Mrs. Albert
Bowker, Miss Sarah F.
Bowker, Miss Mary F.
Bingham, Mrs. Joel T.
Fales, Mrs. Joseph J.
Hammett, Miss Elizabeth
Josselyn, Miss Eliza I.
Stockwell, Mrs. S. N.
Wright, Mrs. Luther A.
Phillips, S.B. — Alden, Mrs. E. K.
Conley, Mrs. C. C.
Drake, Mrs. Jeremy
Lincoln, Miss Mary
Vinton, Miss Eliza
Vinton, Mrs. Laurinda R.
Wheelwright, Miss R. J.
Eliot, Highlands. — Anderson, Mrs.
Rufus
Day, Mrs. Moses
Huntington, Mrs. E. B.
Hodges, Mrs. A. D.
Vine St. — Means, Mrs. J. O.
Boston. — Allen, Mrs. Freeman
Gray, Mrs. Joseph H.
Thompson, Mrs. Louisa
Brookline. — Conant, Mrs. Rebecca
Thomas, Mrs. Edward I.
Belchertown. — Root, Mrs. Eliza
Brimfield. — Hyde, Mrs. C. M.
Knight, Miss Eunice B.
Bradford. — Kingsbury, Mrs. J. D.
Braintree. — Storrs, Mrs. Ann S.
Storrs, Miss Eunice C.
Sugden, Miss Mary
Barre. — Adams, Mrs. Arnold

CHELSEA CHURCHES.

Broadway. — Copp, Mrs. J. A.
Cheever, Mrs. Ira
Gilmore, Mrs. Sarah M.

Broadway. — Herrick, Mrs. S. E.
Sweetser, Mrs. Joseph
Sweetser, Mrs. A.
Tenney, Mrs. Elizabeth C.
Thwing, Mrs. E. Payson
Chestnut St. — Chamberlain, Mrs. M.
Frost, Mrs. Rufus S.
Langworthy, Mrs. I. P.
Laurie, Mrs. Ellen A.
Mitchell, Mrs. Jacob
Plumb, Mrs. Albert H.
Cambridge. — Green, Mrs. C. M.
McKenzie, Mrs. A.
Cambridgeport. — Pratt, Mrs. W. H.
Snow, Mrs. Russell
Charlestown. — Grant, Mrs. A. W.
Concord. — Williams, Mrs. C. H. S.
Dorchester. — Baker, Mrs. Walter
Brooks, Mrs. John H.
Shaw, Miss E. Cornelia
Torrey, Mrs. Elbridge
Wales, Mrs. Elizabeth A.
Dedham. — Edwards, Mrs. J.
Whitney, Mrs. A. B.
E. Cambridge. — Munroe, Miss L. S.
E. Randolph. — Russell, Mrs. Louisa S.
E. Somerville. — Davis, Mrs. E.
E. Taunton. — Reed, Mrs. Fred A.
Fitchburg. — Emerson, Mrs. Alfred
Lowe, Mrs. John,
Fall River. — Borden, Mrs. Richard
Borden, Miss Carrie
Durfee, Mrs. Nathan
Remington, Mrs. Hale
Remington, Mrs. Robert K.
Falmouth. — Bates, Mrs. Wm.
Bourne, Mrs. S. P.
Kimball, Mrs. Jas. P.
Lewis, Mrs. Thomas
Swift, Mrs. Oliver C.
Grantville. — Smith, Mrs. E. M.
Ipswich. — Cowles, Rox. C.
Mozong, Mrs. T.
Jamaica Plain. — Capen, Mrs. S. B.
Gould, Mrs. George
Perkins, Mrs. F. R.
Longmeadow. — Harding, Mrs. M. L.
Pynchon, Mrs. Susan M.
Lancaster. — Ames, Mrs. Jane A.
Leominster. — Batt, Mrs. Wm. J.
Lexington. — Davis, Mrs. John, Sen.
Lawrence. — Fisher, Mrs. Mary H.
Maddock, Miss Phebe A.
Marshfield. — Bourne, Mrs. Sarah T.
Milton. — Wadsworth, Mrs. Lucy
Monson. — Bradford, Miss Sarah E.
Chapman, Mrs. Reuben A.

Monson. — Deney, Mrs. Hadassah
Field, Mrs. N. M.
Porter, Mrs. A. W. *
Packard, Mrs. John
Malden. — Reed, Mrs. Chas. E.
Mt. Holyoke Seminary.
French, Miss Helen M., *Principal.*
Ellis, Miss Mary } *Associate*
Ward, Julia E. } *Principals.*
Blanchard, Miss Elizabeth
Ballantine. Miss Elizabeth D.
Bowers, Miss Ellen P.
Childs, Miss M. Elizabeth
Clary, Miss Susan M.
Edwards, Miss Anna C.
Holmes, Miss Lucy J.
Hagen, Miss Frances M.
Noble, Miss Hannah
Prentiss, Miss Elizabeth B.
Shattuck, Miss Lydia W.
Sessions, Miss Harriet E.
Newton Corner. — Ely, Mrs. Alfred B.
Newtonville. — Goodale, Mrs. E. A.
Newton. — Hatch, Mrs. I. A.
Reed, Mrs. Charlotte L.
Kidder, Mrs. Isaac L.
No. Somerville. — Hodgkins, Mrs. W.
H.
Virgin, Mrs. Samuel H.
Newburyport. — Banister, Mrs. W. B.
Brown, Mrs. Newman
Hale, Mrs. Sarah W.
Jones, Mrs. Anthony S.
Ingraham, Mrs. Herbert A.
Tyler, Mrs. T. C.
No. Chelmsford. — Clark, Mrs. B. F.
Oxford. — Bardwell, Mrs. Horatio
Plympton. — Parker, Miss Hannah S.
Plymouth. — Gordon, Mrs. Dr. T.
Pittsfield. — Harding, Mrs. Wm. G.
Reed, Mrs. Sarah E.
Southbridge. — Lane, Mrs. S. M.
So. Malden. — Bean, Mrs. F. M.
Salem. — Atwood, Mrs. E. M.
Palmer, Mrs. Chas. Ray
Stockbridge. — Brown, Mrs. S. B.
Whitney, Mrs. Anna J.
So. Amherst. — Hutchings, Mrs. C. B.
Lyman, Mrs. Maria P.
Miller, Mrs. E. C.
Springfield. — Gay, Mrs. Mary C.
Townsend. — Proctor, Mrs. Lucy
Upton. — Clafflin, Mrs. Geo. B.
W. Roxbury. — Clark, Mrs. N. G.
Ellis, Mrs. Mary F.
Hubbell, Mrs. Caroline S.
Labaree, Mrs. Susan F.

W st Roxbury. — Smith, Mrs. R. B.
Tolman, Mrs. Julia F.
West Newton. — Graves, Mrs. T. E.
Hitchcock. Miss
Newell, Mrs. J. A.
Whittemore, Mrs. B. F.
Weymouth. — Bailey, Miss Sarah M.
Ellsworth, Mrs. A. A.
Waltham. — Clark, Mrs. Dorus
Strong, Mrs. Elnathan E.
Williamsburg. — Bodman, Mrs. Luther
Winchester. — Cutter, Mrs. Stephen
Cutter, Mrs. Henry
Chapin, Miss Lizzie
Holt, Mrs. N. W. C.
Manney, Mrs. Ellen E.
Westhampton. — Clark, Mrs. Newman
Montague, Miss R. Louisa
Williamstown. — Hopkins, Mrs. A.
Lincoln, Mrs. Lucy C.
Stone, Mrs. Cyrus
Safford, Mrs. Jennie T.
Wellesley. — Dana, Mrs. Nathaniel
Dana, Mrs. G. N.
Dana, Mrs. Charles B.
Fuller, Mrs. Augustus
Little, Mrs. E. G.
Phipps, Mrs. G. T.
Rollins, Miss Hannah
Webber, Mrs. A. D.
Watkins, Mrs. M.
Webber, Miss Mary S.
Whitinsville. — Clark, Mrs. L. F.
Whitin, Mrs. Paul
Walpole. — Kimball, Mrs. Geo. E.
Theuber, Mrs. E. G.
Worcester. — Ball, Mrs. Richard
Curtis, Mrs. Albert
Moen, Mrs. P. L.
Washburn, Miss E. H.
Westfield. — Catlin, Miss Ella C.
Leonard, Miss Mary A
Webster. — Keith, Mrs. Parmenas
Ware. — Hyde, Mrs. Wm.
Hyde, Miss H. S.
Sage, Mrs. O.
Sage, Miss S. R.

RHODE ISLAND.

Providence. — Cady, Mrs. Isaac
Draper, Mrs. J. L.
Jackson, Mrs. B. M.
King, Mrs. Wm. J.
Knight, Mrs. B. B.
Lathrop, Mrs. H.
Mason, Mrs. J. N.
Merrill, Mrs. M. A.

Providence. — Sprague, Mrs. A.
Sprague, Mrs. S. S.
Spicer, Mrs. Geo. T.
Snow, Mrs. J. L.
Vose, Mrs. James G.
Wilkinson, Mrs. H. W.
White, Miss Anna S.

CONNECTICUT.

Berlin. — Gilbert, Mrs. Mary G.
Bozrah. — Abell, Mrs. Wm. C.
Raymond, Mrs. Fannie.
Burnside. — Elmore, Mrs. M. Janette
Colebrook. — Carrington, Mrs. J. P.
Colchester. — Clarke, Miss Martha T.
Day, Mrs. Maranda M.
Day, Miss Eliza M.
Fiske, Mrs. H. M.
Gillet, Mrs. Russell
Hyde, Mrs. Mary Ann
McCall, Mrs. C. B.
Newton, Mrs. Harriet T.
Wheeler, Mrs. J. B.
Willard, Mrs. S. G.
Deep River. — Wickes, Mrs. Henry
East Haddam. — Parsons, Mrs. S. B.
Groton. — Copp, Miss Kate B.
Guilford. — Sage, Miss Clara I.
Talcott, Mrs. Alvan
Harwinton. — Hayes, Mrs. Sarah B.
Middletown. — Goodrich, Mrs. E. H.
New Haven. — Foote, Mrs. Emily W.
Foote, Mrs. Amelia Leavitt
New London. — Brown, Mrs. Abby E.
McEwen, Mrs. Harriet W.
Smith, Mrs Abba W. S.
Wilcox. Mrs. G. B.
Norwich. — Arms, Mrs. Hiram P.
Bond, Mrs. S. Ann W.
Hubbard, Mrs. Amos H.
Palmer, Mrs. Emeline
Williams, Mrs. W. W.
New Britain. — Davis, Mrs. Mary M.
So. Windsor. — Bowman, Mrs. Ernestine Lord
Southbury. — Smith, Mrs. Harriet E.
Woodstock. — Brown, Mrs. T. H.
Child, Mrs. Peleg
West Stonington. — Hubbell, Mrs. S.

NEW YORK.

Albany. — Brayton, Mrs. Elizabeth S.
Wood, Mrs. Margaret S.
Brooklyn. — Whiton, Mrs. James M.
Hayes, Mrs. J. W.
Buffalo — Sawyer, Mrs. Charlotte O.

Buffalo. — White, Mrs. Eliza N.
  Wilkes, Mrs. Ellen
Coeymans. — Ten Eyck, Miss C.
Fayetteville. — Bigelow, Mrs. K. H.
  Pratt, Mrs. Jane
Gilbertsville. — Clark, Mrs. H. M.
N. Y. City. — Be ts, Mrs. George F.
  Dodge, Mrs. Wm. E.
  Lyon, Mrs. Isabella
  Leavitt, Mrs. J. T.
  Prentice, Mrs. George L.
  Smith, Mrs. J. V. C.
  Sutton, Miss Caroline
Poughkeepsie. — Lyman, Harriet W.
Penn Yan. — Sheppard, Mrs. C. C.
Rochester. — Chapin, Mrs. Lucinda
Springfield. — Winson, Mrs. Daniel
Schenectady. — Brooks, Mrs. Isabella
Syracuse. — Leavenworth, Mrs. E. W.
Utica. — Crittenden, Mrs. A. W.
Waverly. — Beaumon, Mrs. H. N.
Watertown. — Bates, Mrs. James
  Bates, Mrs. James R.
  Morgan, Mrs. Almena B.
  Morgan, Mrs. Susan H.
  Porter, Mrs. J. J.

PENNSYLVANIA.

Philadelphia. — Burnham, Mrs. C.
  Lynde, Mrs. C. A.

DELAWARE.

Glasgow. — Webb, Miss Mary E.

MARYLAND.

Frederick City. — Rockwell, Mrs. R.

OHIO.

Belpre. — Bates, Mrs. Sarah A. T.
Cincinnati. — Aydelott, Mrs. B. E.
  Brown, Mrs. S. B.
Cleveland. — Taylor, Mrs. Elizabeth E.
Granville. — Fuller, Mrs. Deborah
Salem. — Allen, Mrs. David A.
Toledo. — Parmelee, Mrs. W. E.
Troy. — Grosvenor, Mrs. Hannah

ILLINOIS.

Galena. — Kent, Mrs. Caroline C.

MICHIGAN.

Detroit. — Noble, Mrs. Charles
Homer. — Foucher, Mrs. Charles
St. Clair. — Wastell, Mrs. Wm. P.

IOWA.

Grinnell. — Grinnell, Mrs. Julia A.

TENNESSEE.

Lookout Mt. — Bancroft, Mrs. F. K.
  Carpenter, Mrs. C. C.
  Wilson, Miss Mary A.

KANSAS.

Topeka. — McClelland, Mrs. H.

CALIFORNIA.

Oakland. — Bigelow, Mrs. Anna E.
  Mooar, Mrs. Sarah A.
San Francisco. — Janes, Mrs. E. L.

MISSIONARIES.

WESTERN TURKEY.

Constantinople. — Schauffler, Mrs. C.F.
Marsovan. — Dodd, Mrs. Lydia B.

EASTERN TURKEY.

Harpoot. — Wheeler, Mrs. Crosby H.
Mardin. — Baker, Miss Isabella C.

CENTRAL TURKEY.

Aintab. — Proctor, Miss Myra A.

MICRONESIA.

  Snow, Mrs. L. V.

PERSIA.

Oroomiah. — Labaree, Mrs. E. W.
  Rice, Miss Mary S.

SO. INDIA.

Madura. — Capron, Mrs. Sarah B.
  Herrick, Mrs. Elizabeth H.
  Washburn, Mrs. G. T.
  Taylor, Miss Martha S.
  Taylor, Mrs. Martha S.
  Burnell, Mrs. T. S.
  Chandler, Mrs. Charlotte H.
  Chester, Mrs. Sophia

CEYLON.

  Spalding, Mrs. Mary C.

AFRICA.

  Lloyd, Mrs. K. C.
  Edwards, Mrs. Mary K.
  Walker, Mrs. William

CHINA.

  Williams, Mrs. S. Wells
  Andrews, Miss Mary E.

THIRD ANNUAL REPORT

OF THE

WOMAN'S BOARD OF MISSIONS

PRESENTED AT ITS

ANNUAL MEETING,

In Mt. Vernon Church, Boston,

JANUARY 3, 1871.

———◆———

BOSTON:
PRINTED BY RAND, AVERY, & FRYE.
1871.

CONTENTS.

ANNUAL REPORT · · · · · · · · · · · · 3

REPORT OF BIBLE-WOMEN · · · · · · · · · · 12

REPORT OF TREASURER · · · · · · · · · · - 16

AUXILIARY SOCIETIES · · · · · · · · · · · 18

MISSION CIRCLES · · - · · · · · · · · · 23

MISSIONARIES SUPPORTED BY W. B. M. · · · · · · · 25

SCHOOLS   "   "   · · · · · · - 26

BIBLE WOMEN   "   "   · _ - · · · 27

CONTRIBUTIONS FOR 1870 · · · · · · · · · · · · 28

LIFE-MEMBERS · · · · · · · · · · · · · 55

LIFE AND LIGHT

Is published quarterly, by the WOMAN'S BOARD OF MISSIONS, at the sub-scription-price of FIFTY CENTS a year, payable in advance. It may be obtained on application to Secretary W. B. M., at Missionary House, 33 Pemberton Square, Boston.

We trust our friends will interest themselves in obtaining subscribers for us.

ANNUAL REPORT.

WE assemble to-day to review the past year, and from its records and successes obtain a stimulus to increased activity as a society, and renewed sacrifice and effort as individuals, to speed the coming of Christ's kingdom in heathen lands.

We have cause for grateful thanksgiving in the spared lives of the members of our board, in the energy and efficiency with which they have prosecuted their labors, and in the diffusion and expression of a missionary spirit among the women of our land.

When we realize with what fear and trembling this society, but three years since, was organized, and how deeply it is now rooted in the hearts of our people ; when we consider the enthusiasm which our missionaries have carried to their work, and the warmth and strength of the ties that bind us; when we compare the present financial returns to our treasury with the meagreness of our most sanguine hopes, — we feel humbled and encouraged beyond measure. Humbled, that we had and have so little faith, and encouraged, because God's manifest guidance and support become to us an undoubted earnest of exceeding blessing to come.

We find another occasion for thanksgiving in the efficiency of our sister society, the Woman's Board of Missions for the Interior, and in the entire unanimity and affection subsisting between us. Our delegate, at its late annual meeting in Detroit, did indeed, as she said, "bear in her hand the jewelled casket of heart-sympathies from sisters in the East." Most nobly did this society respond to the call of Dr. Clark, that the Christian women of our churches should assume the expense of especial labors in behalf of women in our mission-fields. This he estimated at about thirty thousand dollars. To his question, "Will you try to lift one-third of the burden?" the response was a pledge to make strenuous effort to raise the half; viz., fifteen thousand dollars. Glorious co-workers these!

In May last, the ladies of Philadelphia also organized themselves into a society, denominated the Philadelphia Branch of the Woman's Board of Missions, to be a nucleus around which the churches and communities of the Middle and Southern States might gather, to work with our society, guided by the large experience and wisdom of the Prudential Committee of the A. B. C. F. M.

Who could have believed that the first stone dropped, three years since, into the dead sea of apathy on the subject of woman's mission to woman, would have moved its waters to such widely-extended and extending circles!

Shall we not bless God, and take courage?

ENCOURAGEMENTS.

But to return to our immediate labors.

Our receipts have the past year been twenty-one thousand dollars and upwards. By late legacies we shall also receive fifteen thousand three hundred dollars for our permanent fund. Our life-membership has reached nearly a thousand, and our subscribers to "Life and Light," three thousand six hundred ninety-eight; and to its "Echoes," four thousand thirty-six.

Our auxiliaries, one hundred and forty-eight, have more than doubled in number within the past year; and our fifty-two mission circles among the young have sprung up here and there, like wayside flowers, sweet with the perfume of cheerful sacrifice, and outgushing desire to do something for Jesus. May there not be born and nurtured in many of these a missionary spirit that shall develop into life-work in heathen lands? Should it be in the heart of your home-darling, sister, will you nurse it for Jesus?

5

Our missionaries a year since numbered fifteen ; our Bible-women, fifteen ; and our schools, five. Now we support twenty-five missionaries, thirty Bible-women, and eight schools.

With reference to our Home in Constantinople, we are able to report two missionaries already on the ground, and the third as having nearly completed her medical studies. Miss Rappleye, whose especial duty will be teaching, is devoting herself to the acquirement of the language.

Miss Laura Bliss has for the past two months been engaged in visiting from house to house among the native women. Miss Nye, in her capacity of physician, will undoubtedly win an interest and place in many a home, both for herself and companions in labor. A daughter of Dr. Dwight has recently announced her earnest desire to devote herself to this field. This fact we notice with peculiar gratitude ; for often have we asked ourselves, Why such delay in appropriating this field, and inability to secure suitable persons to occupy it? But, to the praise of Him to whom our work is all committed, we can now say that the time seemingly lost is more than made up in the unusual capabilities these young ladies are able to carry to the work.

Miss Bliss and Miss Dwight are both daughters of missionaries long resident in that field, familiar with the language, habits, and customs of the people, and also able to avail themselves of the large experience of their fathers.

Thus much for the instrumentalities of our work. What of its results? What has been wrought?

The gathering of hundreds of girls into our schools. The reduction of this uncivilized and often degraded material into classes, comparing favorably in discipline and mental acquirement with schools in our own land, and redeemed not only to habits of neatness, order, and domestic thrift, but kindled to

1*

earnest desire to know Christ in personal communion and appropriation.

In many of these schools and stations connected with our missions, there have been gracious outpourings of the Holy Spirit. At Bitlis, Turkey, the field of the Misses Ely, there has been a most remarkable revival. It commenced with the week of prayer ; and soon large numbers were under conviction, and scores converted. Our missionaries experienced a joy almost too intense to be sustained. By night they dreamed of those with whom they had labored by day, often weeping in their sleep, and waking to find their faces bathed in tears of sympathy or joy. From a congregation of a hundred and fifty, forty-two, or about one in three and a half, were added to the church.

In a field in Persia a revival has also occurred, the fruits of which have been thirty-seven converts ; among them several aged women.

In Miss Townsend's school at Ceylon, the influences of the Spirit have also been felt. Of fifty-two pupils, fourteen are members of the church. During a vacation of three weeks, many, both unconverted and Christians, daily read the Bible, and prayed with their families ; never retiring until family worship had been thus regularly conducted. Is not this both fruit and seed-sowing ? — Christian courage and devoted service ?

Fruitage also we recognize in the testimony the heathen themselves bear to the value of our missionaries' work. From Madura, a teacher writes, " Parents from a certain village brought their daughter to me to keep until she was like *that* girl," referring to a recent graduate, who was apparently a faithful, conscientious girl, of decided character. They themselves acknowledge that now they have " wives and companions," where once they had only " donkeys."

In China also, a revival commenced with the week of prayer, in the very village where, soon after, occurred the fearful massacre which has placed our missionaries in peril of their lives.

This is the scene of Miss Mary Andrews's labors. In great

danger in the past months, and present patient waiting, perhaps, for an opportunity to labor, we doubt not that the form of the Son of God has been visible in the furnace through which she and her associates have been called to pass; and that as silver they will be refined for future service. The testimony is, that " the native Christians have grown stronger in being compelled to ask their hearts if they were willing to suffer for Christ."

Missionaries who have spent years in Southern India inform us that the Zulus of South Africa, in comparison with the people of India, are sunk in ignorance and barbarism; and yet (precious fruit again!) we see in Mrs. Edwards's school a wonderful success. The discipline and mental progress are so excellent, that it seems hardly possible that the families of these girls are still living in kraals, and just out of heathenism. During the week of prayer, they united with the station-people (sixty in all), in a six-o'clock morning prayer-meeting, in which many of the girls took part, although they do not profess to be Christians.

In Central Turkey, in Miss Proctor's school, numbering thirty, all but four 'have given themselves to Christ. All of the graduating-class are Christians, and are earnestly hoping to teach; some in their own villages, and others in newer places where more needed.

In Miss Fritcher's school at Marsovan, West Turkey, there has been great progress. " The diligence of the pupils in study, general faithfulness in discharging their various household duties, love for teachers and each other, conscientiousness, prayerfulness, and general deportment, and earnest endeavor to lead others to Christ, has afforded great encouragement." In this school also, a religious interest dates from the week of prayer. Two by two, the pupils divided up their classmates among themselves, conversing and praying with them in private and in little bands.

Nor has the testimony from Harpoot and Eski Zagra been of less interest. Three female prayer-meetings are held weekly at Harpoot, in which the native women take active part; and in

Eski Zagra not only is there a thirsting for living water among the pupils, but an impatient desire in the hearts of some of the mothers to have their daughters return to show them the way of salvation.

Have we not, dear friends, in these cheering items, great occasion for rejoicing, and glorious results of our instrumentalities? But into the midst of our joy comes a sorrow that touches a world-wide circle.

DEATH OF TWO MISSIONARIES.

Turkey has been called to mourn two of her faithful, devoted laborers, in Miss Warfield and Miss Norcross; and the tide of grief which surged most wildly among those they called "their children," tempered into Christian resignation in the hearts of their associate helpers, recoils with fearful refluent wave into the homes of their childhood. The parents whose hearts have been almost riven in giving their daughters a cheerful sacrifice to such a work, in the midst of the billows that now roll over them, yield to the Father's will in entire submission. Enthusiastic and joyous in their work, these young sisters counted it a privilege to have been permitted, even for a brief period, to serve the Master in a foreign field, never for a moment regretting their going; and when the summons came, quietly awaited in loving trust their Saviour's appearing.

In a late letter, Miss Norcross asked if some one would not for Christ's sake supply her with an organ; music being a great source of attraction. In response, one was almost immediately sent; but, ere it reached its destination, the beloved teacher had joined the heavenly choir. Although her fingers may never evoke its sweet harmonies, we trust, as its rich, full tones accompany songs that speak of heaven and the Friend of sinners, it may be associated in the minds of her pupils with her memory, and ever recall her faithful love and service.

In view of this twofold sacrifice of life, shall *we* say, " Wherefore all this waste ? "

Rather would we echo the words of another : —

"But *is* their earthly mission closed forever ?
 Warm hearts that yearned
To cull such golden fruitage for the Master,
 Has Jesus spurned ?

Ask of each wave that washeth fair Mauritius,
 Each airy breath
Fresh from the grave where Harriet Newell sleepeth
 Mighty in death.

Mark well the lesson : Christ's true martyrs, dying,
 Are precious seed,
Buried, to rise, with forces still increasing,
 A host indeed.''

INDIRECT RESULTS.

Besides these manifest results, there are those that are indirect, but powerful.

Under Paganism, woman is a cipher. Hence the labor of Christian women, both in schools and visitations, assumes in the minds of heathen men a humble character. It neither stirs pride nor gives occasion for alarm ; and the benevolence that prompts it disarms opposition. Our work is among the women ; to teach them that they are of importance and interest to Jesus, if not recognized by their own households, — that they have souls, and that there is a Saviour and a heaven for them. This wonderful news, once received and believed, spreads with light-ning-like rapidity from one to another, arousing an eager desire for knowledge. Christ, accepted, brings a gentle refinement that unconsciously ennobles the recipient ; and the men, too, are blest, before they have thought to recognize the cause.

In our schools also are some two hundred girls, many of them of mature understanding, and some of them of "high caste," who are being educated in the most careful Christian manner. The civilizing ideas of cleanliness, order, and thrift, added to their mental acquirements, immediately mark them as

superior to the rest of their race. The words of Holy Writ
are being implanted in their minds, and the melody of sweet
Christian songs is permeating their souls, each and all to be reproduced in every-day life in their several households; each
pupil and each household working as leaven, until woman's
influence shall produce a mighty uprising of the whole mass.

HOW TO INSURE THE GREATEST EFFICIENCY OF MISSIONARIES.

Let us diligently and interestedly inform ourselves respecting
our several fields, that we may come into the closest sympathy
with our workers.   Let us often make spirit tours among them ;
sit for a season under India's burning suns with our beloved sister Mrs. Capron, and mark how, like her Saviour, she embraces
every passing opportunity to attract attention to the way of life.
Listen to Miss Proctor as she attracts an audience of Moslem
women to Christ's Sermon on the Mount; smile at their running
comments on her explanations, while at the strange mixture of
truth and falsehood, she whispers aside to us, " Ten thousand of
such women *in this city*, thoroughly incased in ignorance, pride,
and self-righteousness."   Tour with our young teachers into the
villages suburban to Harpoot, sleeping and teaching in stables ;
riding often on the sides of mountains or rocks whence a fall
from a horse would precipitate one hundreds of feet.

Wander about Fow-Chow, with its population of from five
hundred thousand to six hundred thousand, in city and suburbs,
in which there are sixty organized churches, and nine hundred
and sixty baptized Chinamen, where, fourteen years since, neither
church nor Christian were to be found; or, after a visit of in-
spection to the villages and kraals of the degraded Zulus, enter
the mission compound, and mark the contrast in Mrs. Edwards's
school, — a model Mt. Holyoke Seminary, where intelligence
beams in every dusky face, and where the discipline, order, and
domestic management rival that of many of our best schools.
Surely the beautiful musical instrument donated by a lady at
our last annual meeting has here found an appreciative home,

11

and may well enter into the refining influences that shall render these pupils the exponents of civilization and Christianity to their race. Thus shall we know how to pray for them ; and we must pray for them, that we may " multiply the seed sown," and sustain their frequently-drooping faith, by ours, that embraces their work in its results, unclouded by its discouraging details.

NEED OF AUXILIARIES.

If we would continue the support of the missionaries, Bible-women, and schools already adopted, and continue to occupy new fields as God drives out the " Hivites and Hittites" from before us, our society must be established on a more secure basis. The funds received since our organization have amounted to a sum total of forty-two thousand dollars, twenty-five thousand of which stands accredited to life-memberships. Can we in the future depend upon life-memberships sufficient to defray half of our expenses ? Rather should the women of our churches form auxiliaries, upon which we may fall back as a pledge that each new year shall be to us as the last, — only much more abundant.

The rooting of auxiliaries, and forming of mission circles, was suggested at our last annual meeting, as the special work of the year. We are very grateful to those who have responded to the call; but we hope our need in this respect will make the duty of all our churches imperative.

MEMORIAL FUND.

In closing our Report, we refer with peculiar pleasure to our memorial fund ; the initial figure of which was three hundred dollars, bequeathed by Mrs. Peleg C. Child of North Woodstock, Conn. May the love and prayer that prompted and accompanied the gift cause it to be multiplied in blessing a thousand-fold !

We have since had a bequest of fifteen thousand dollars from Mrs. Sarah J. Baldwin, the income of which will be yearly appropriated to the purposes of the society, and known as the Sarah Baldwin Fund.

How blessed for the living thus to perpetuate the memory of their beloved who have died in the Lord! and how blessed for the dying whom he has gifted with the gold and silver, — which are his, — thus "to put their money to the exchangers," and at the last great day to point to the hosts redeemed through this instrumentality, and the uncounted multitudes added through the efforts of those thus saved, as the multiplication of the talents delivered to them!

MRS. EDWIN WRIGHT, *Rec. Sec., pro tem.*

OUR BIBLE–WOMEN.

NATIVE Christian women are working for us in many foreign lands, teaching the Bible to their own sex, in more than a dozen different languages. Delivered from the deep moral darkness which surrounds them, they, better than others, can carry the Word of God to those who are in still darker depths. In a spirit of love and sympathy, they read to sad and weary hearts those pages luminous with hope.

They speak effectively, often using the keenest sarcasm in setting forth the absurdities of idolatry and a false faith. By their tact, and aptness in drawing from their own customs illustrations which none but a native woman would ever think of, they excite a lively interest among their hearers.

Missionaries testify to the fidelity of these women in the service of the Master, and to their self-denying offerings in their deep poverty. The late Dr. Perkins of Persia writes, "I am more and more impressed with the value of this agency. Some of the native preachers have told us that the Bible-women accomplish more than they themselves can." Often entering upon the work with timidity, they gain courage and zeal by their unexpected success. They may not speak with the wisdom of the cultured ; but with a fervent, affectionate spirit, taught of Him who " giveth grace unto the lowly," they plead earnestly, and win the closest attention.

In the fields, women and children lay aside their implements of husbandry to listen for a brief moment ; their toilsome labors during the day leaving them only the evening hours for longer instruction. Others are well educated, and speak fluently in two or more languages. They are gladly welcomed in the zenanas, those secluded, prison-like abodes of women of the highest social position. Gradually, the dull, aimless existence of the inmates is quickened into a new life.

Enter the hospitals of India. In an apartment by themselves, the women, seated upon the floor, await advice and the distribution of medicine. Borne, or wearily dragging themselves, hither, while suffering under the diseases peculiar to the country, they present a sad spectacle. Daily in their midst is the Bible-woman ; and many among them, for the first time, hear of Him who healeth the leprosy of sin. Says one, " Some would never have had the offer of salvation pressed upon them, had not the Bible-woman brought it to them in the hospital."

These labors, so acceptable to the recipient, often provoke the most bitter opposition from the old, fossilized life which has come down unchanged through the ages. To such, it is a reproach that woman should break through the superstitions which forbid her to act as a responsible being. Enemies, like wolves, surround these lambs as they go from house to house, from village to village.

Even the training for this work by a Christian education has been attended with much suffering, with annoyances in many ways, with fines, persecutions, rude assaults, and threats of greater cruelties. Not infrequently, their only resting-place at night is the stable, with the beasts of the stall ; their only quiet place for prayer, the haystacks of the field ; and oft the midnight hour has found them alone upon the cold house-top, looking unto God for strength.

2

Two raging persecutors, high in authority, threatened the extinction of every Christian work in the city. Speedy and inevitable destruction seemed near; but He who is mighty to save covered his own with the shadow of his hand, staying the fury of the oppressor. The more hostile of the two, just as his mandate was about to crush, was suddenly laid low in death; the other became a preacher of the faith which he had sought to destroy.

Each Bible-woman is under the superintendence of a female missionary, whose aim is to make this largely a work of love. The teachers and older pupils in the higher schools are nearly all voluntary Bible-readers, going out, two and two, after the school-hours, holding meetings with the women in their homes, and spending their vacations in more extended efforts.

In large cities, as Constantinople, where the ground is unbroken, or in wide districts, where they travel from place to place, and are regularly employed, their expenses must be met. Some of these women have no regular support.

In Turkey, women who can earn but two cents a day contribute to the support of a Bible-woman for their own city.

The Rev. S. B. Fairbanks of India says, in reference to this work, " We have made a beginning in a department too long neglected."

The Woman's Board of Missions in Boston assumes the support of thirty native Bible-women abroad; about three-fourths of whom have been adopted by auxiliary societies, sabbath schools, classes, and individual contributors. The society is relieved by this aid, which is most gratefully received. Thirty more readers are now needed to meet the present calls from the various mission-fields.

We have here but a glimpse of our Bible-readers and their work. In their deep gratitude, they " bless the very dust of America," which sent to them the knowledge of salvation, thus irradiating their souls with bright hopes, and filling their hearts with glad thanksgivings.

Old obstacles are being removed ; and opportunities, as never before, are ours now to aid the women of heathen lands. In the harem of the Turk, in the zenanas of India, in the hospitals and the dark recesses of heathenism, are mothers and tender little ones to whom we may send the word of life.

The lowest alleys and corners of London have learned to bless the name of Bible woman. May this joy be extended to the Mohammedan and heathen cities of farthest East !

A countless throng, who cannot here present their own need, urge us to plead for them. Earnest Christian hearts must surely be touched by their unuttered sorrows.

Shall there be lack of Bible-readers, or of schools in which to train them ? Is it not a privilege to share the life and labors of these lowly ones ; to know them by name, and sustain them in their work ? The knowledge of sight may not be ours ; but we may greet them among the saved, and rejoice together when working and watching shall be exchanged for a glorious fruition.

Mrs. Miron Winslow, *Cor. Sec.*

TO SABBATH SCHOOLS.

We are happy to state that Sabbath-school classes have in several instances individually pledged themselves to the support of a Bible-reader. This they secure by the weekly payment of a small stipulated sum.

As such classes are entitled to the original letters or journals of their Bible-readers, a feeling of personality and interest in the work of missions is secured.

TREASURER'S REPORT.

EXPENDITURES OF THE WOMAN'S BOARD OF MISSIONS FOR THE YEAR ENDING DEC. 31, 1870.

ZULU MISSION.

Salary of Mrs. Mary K. Edwards, for 1871,	$420 00	
" " Miss Gertrude R. Hance, for 1871,	420 00	
School of Mrs. Edwards at Iwanda, for 1870 and 1871,	1,560 00	
		$2,400 00

MISSION TO WESTERN TURKEY.

Salary of Miss Flavia L. Bliss, for 1871,	$308 00	
" " Miss Ursula C. Clark, for 1871,	369 60	
" " Miss Sarah A. Closson, for 1871,	308 00	
" " Miss Eliza Fritcher, for 1870 and 1871,	633 00	
" " Mrs. Elizabeth Giles, for 1871,	369 60	
" " Miss Ardelle M. Griswold, for 1871,	308 00	
" " Miss Julia A. Rappleye, for 1871,	616 00	
School of Miss E. T. Maltbie, at Eski Zagra, for 1870 and 1871,	2,333 44	
		5,245 64

MISSION TO CENTRAL TURKEY.

Salary of Miss Hattie G. Powers, for 1870 and 1871,	$719 60	
" " Miss Myra A. Proctor, for 1871,	369 60	
" " Miss Sarah L. Wood, for 1871,	369 60	
School of Miss Proctor, for 1870 and 1871,	940 48	
" at Kessab, for 1871,	50 00	
		2,449 28

MISSION TO EASTERN TURKEY.

Salary of Miss Isabella C. Baker, for 1870 and 1871,	$699 36	
" " Miss Caroline E. Bush, for 1871,	339 36	
" " Misses C. and M. Ely, for 1871,	339 36	
" " Miss Olive L. Parmelee, for 1871,	339 36	
" " Miss Hattie Seymour, for 1870 and 1871,	689 36	
" " Miss Mary E. Warfield. for 1870,	350.00	
School of Misses Parmelee and Baker, at Mardin, for 1870 and 1871,	666 56	
School of Misses Seymour and Bush, at Harpoot,	1,645 32	
" " Misses Ely, at Bitlis, for 1871,	232 00	
Support of girl in Erzroom, for 1871,	30 00	
		5,350 68

MISSION TO PERSIA.

Salary of Miss M. S. Rice,	$555 00	
		555 00

MISSION TO MAHRATTA.

School of Mrs. Mary E. Bissell, at Ahmednuggur, for 1871,	$588 00	
		588 00

Amount,	$16,588 60

MISSION TO MADURA.

Amount brought forward,		$16,588 60
Salary of Miss Rosella A. Smith, for 1871,	$560 00	
School of Mrs. Chandler, high-caste girls, for 1871,	50 00	
		610 00

MISSION TO CEYLON.

Salary of Miss Eliza Agnew, for 1871,	$560 00	
" " Miss Harriet E. Townshend, for 1870 and 1871,	1,160 00	
		1,720 00

FOOCHOW MISSION.

Salary of Miss Adelia M. Payson, for 1871,	$448 00	
		448 00

NORTH CHINA MISSION.

Salary of Miss Mary E. Andrews, for 1871,	$448 00	
School and mission of Miss Porter, for 1871,	115 00	
		563 00
Support of Bible-readers in above missions,	$717 13	
" " Pupils in female seminaries,	697 80	
		1,414 93
Salary of Miss Fannie A. Nye, medical missionary to Constantinople,	$300 00	
		300 00

HOME DEPARTMENT.

Salary of Secretary at room in Missionary House,	$434 00	
Stamps, stationery, and printing notices,	98 37	
Miscellaneous expenses,	39 74	
Maps,	166 37	
Cost of the " Life and Light " and " Echoes,"	1,017 77	
" " Annual Report,	205 54	
" Mrs. Anderson's circular, with envelopes and postage for same,	79 80	
	$2,041 59	
Deduct amount received from " Life and Light " and " Echoes,"	1,989 34	
		52 25
		$21,696 78
Balance carried to credit of new account for outfit and salaries of missionaries under appointment,		2,762 44
		$24,459 22

RECEIPTS OF THE WOMAN'S BOARD OF MISSIONS FOR THE YEAR ENDING DEC. 31, 1870.

Subscriptions and donations to date,	$19,117 48	
Balance in the Treasury, Dec. 31, 1869,	5,341 74	
		$24,459 22

Mrs. HOMER BARTLETT, Treas.

BOSTON, Dec. 31, 1870. — In the absence of the auditor, Hon. Alpheus Hardy, I have examined the accounts of Mrs. Homer Bartlett, treasurer, and found them correct, showing a balance due the society as above stated.

GEO. ATKINS.

2*

SOCIETIES AUXILIARY TO THE W. B. M.

Ashby, Mass. — Mrs. Ellen S. Parker, Sec'y.

Andover, Mass. — Old South Church, Mrs. Emily C. Pearsons, Sec'y and Treas.

Auburndale, Mass. — Mrs. Alvah Kittredge, Sec'y and Treas.

Assabet, Mass. — Mrs. L Maynard, Sec'y; Mrs. S. M. Stone, Treas.

Amherst, Mass. — Miss S. G. Ayres, Sec'y.

Amherst (South), Mass. — Ladies Benevolent Society.

Amherst (West), Mass. — Congregational Church Sewing-Circle.

Appleton, Wis. — Lawrence University.

Boston, Mass. — Old South Church, Mrs. Charles Stoddard.

Boston, Mass. — Central Church, Miss Myra Child.

Boston, Mass. — Park-street Church, Mrs. M. H. Simpson.

Boston, Mass. — Shawmut Church, Mrs. J. S. Ambrose.

Boston, Mass. — Mt. Vernon Church, Mrs. Miron Winslow.

Boston, Mass. — Union Church, Mrs. Charles Scudder.

Boston (Highlands), Mass. — Eliot Church, Mrs. Rufus Anderson.

Boston (Highlands), Mass. — Highland Church, Mrs. E. L. Howell.

Boston (Highlands), Mass. — Vine-street Church, Mrs. J. O. Means.

Boston (East), Mass. — Maverick Church, Mrs. L. A. Wright, Sec'y; Miss E. Hammett, Treas.

Boston (South), Mass. — Phillips Church, Mrs. Jeremy Drake.

Boston (South), Mass. — E-street Church, Mrs. Daniel F. Wood, Treas.

Brookline, Mass. — Harvard Church, Miss Mary G. Stoddard, Treas.

Bedford, N.H. — Presbyterian Church, Mrs. Charles Gage.

Belpre, O. — Congregational Church.

Barre, Vt. —

Burlington, Vt. — White-street Congregational Church.
Braintree and Weymouth, Mass. — Miss Helen P. Vickery.
Buffalo, N. Y. — Lafayette Church, Mrs. Mary A. Ripley,
   Sec'y and Treas.
Buffalo, N. Y. — Westminster Presbyterian Church.
Bangor, Me. — Miss Sarah Holt, Sec'y ; Mrs. E. G. Thurston,
   Treas.
Braintree (East), Mass. — Monatiquot School, Miss R. A. Faxon.
Baltimore, Md. —
Bozrah, Conn. — Mrs. Albert G. Avery, Sec'y ; Miss A. A.
   Maples, Treas.
Billerica, Mass. — Mrs. Sarah B. Work, Sec'y and Treas.
Bradford, Mass. — Academy, Miss Mary G. Giles, Sec'y.
Berlin, Conn. — Miss Lena Woodruff, Treas.
Belle Valley, Penn. — Mrs. George J. Russell, Sec'y.
Chelsea, Mass. — Chestnut-street Church.
Chelsea, Mass. — Broadway Church, Mrs. J. A. Copp.
Colchester, Conn. — Mrs. J. B. Wheeler, Treas.
Concord, Mass. — Second Congregational Church, Miss Mary
   Munroe, Sec'y.
Concord, Mass. — S. S. Missionary Association.
Cambridge (East), Mass. — Miss L. Munroe.
Cambridge, Mass. — Sheppard Church, Mrs. E. S. Johnson,
   Sec'y.
Concord, Mich. — Miss Ida Keeler, Treas.
Clearwater, Minn. — Mrs. L. M. Stearns, Sec'y.
Craftsbury North, Vt. — Mrs. R. S. Wild, Sec'y.
Cumberland Centre, Vt. — Miss Mary Rideout, Treas. ; Mrs.
   M. E. Small, Sec'y.
Castile, Wyoming Co., N. Y. — Miss Kittie V. Cochrane,
   Sec'y.
Cleveland, O. — First Congregational Church.
Dorchester, Mass. — Miss E. C. Shaw, Sec'y ; E. H. Preston,
   Treas.
Dedham, Mass. —

Dorset, Vt. —

Everett, Mass. — Mrs. Charles Atwood, Sec'y; Miss E. Whittemore, Treas.

Exeter, N.H. — Mrs. L. J. Chickering, Sec'y.

Fall River, Mass. — S. J. Brayton, Treas. ; Miss C. Borden, Sec'y.

Fredonia, N.Y. — Miss Martha L. Stevens, Sec'y.

Fayetteville, N.Y. — Miss Alice Orr, Sec'y.

Freeport (South), Me. — S. S., Mrs. H. Ilsley.

Franklin, Mass. —

Franklin, N.Y. —

Groton Junction, Mass. — Mrs. H. F. Frye, Sec'y.

Georgia, Vt. — Miss L. M. Gilbert, Sec'y.

Granville, O. — Congregational S. S., E. C. Blanchard, Treas.

Greenwich, Conn. — Miss Lizzie H. Cristy.

Granby, Mass. — Mrs. John Church, Treas.

Hinsdale, Mass. — Mrs. Ephraim Flint.

Hebron, Conn. — Mrs. John Porter, Treas.

Hadley (South), Mass. — Mt. Holyoke Female Seminary.

Hampton (East), Mass. — Mrs. G. W. Andrews, Sec'y and Treas.

Hartford, Conn. — Mrs. Dr. Thompson, Pres. ; Mrs. C. A. Jewett, Treas. ; Mrs. C. C. Dutton, Sec'y.

Ipswich, Mass. — First Congregational Church

Ipswich, Mass. — Female Seminary.

Jamaica Plain, Mass. — Central Congregational Church, Miss M. A. B. Brackett, Treas.

Jewett, N.Y. — Presbyterian Church, A. Montgomery, Treas.

Jersey City, N.J. — Mrs. L. A. Candie.

Keene, N H. —

Littleton, Mass. — Mrs. George H. Ames.

Lancaster, Mass. — Mrs. Dr. H. C. Kendrick.

Leominster, Mass. — Mrs. William Batt, Pres. ; Miss S. M. Haskell, Sec'y.

Lexington, Mass. — Mrs. Levi Prosser, Pres. ; Miss E. A. Baker, Sec'y and Treas.

Lawrence, Mass. — Eliot Church, Miss Ellen A. Brown, Sec'y and Treas.

Lincoln, Mass. — Mrs. George Hartwell, Treas.

Long Meadow, Mass. — Miss Mary Lawton, Treas.

Middlebury, Vt. — Mrs. C. W. Ladd.

Mt. Morris, N. Y. — Laura H. Ford, Sec'y.

Middletown, Conn. — First Congregational Church, Miss M. B. Hazen, Treas.; Miss Sarah Tappan, Sec'y.

Madison, N.J. — Mrs. J. C. Potts.

Malden, Mass. — Miss Phebe Marsh.

Montpelier, Vt. — Mrs. E. J. Howe.

Monson, Mass. — Mrs. N. M. Field, Treas.

Norwich, Conn. — Mrs. N. M. Williams,. Pres. ; Miss Jane Ripley, Sec'y ; Ellen G. Coit, Treas.

New Bedford, Mass. —

New Haven, Conn. — North Church, Mrs. J. W. Fitch, Treas. ; Mrs. H. D. Hume, Sec'y.

New London, Conn. — Mrs. R. P. McEwen.

New Ipswich, N.H. — Mrs. M. F. Taylor, Treas.

Newton Centre, Mass. — Miss Hattie J. Kingsbury, Treas.

Norton, Mass. — Wheaton Female Seminary.

Newburyport, Mass. — Mrs. H. A. Ingraham, Treas. ; Miss S. N. Brown, Sec'y.

Newtonville, Mass. — Miss Eliza A. Goodell.

Newton (West), Mass. — Miss Helen F. Clarke, Sec'y.

Oakland, Cal. — Mrs. R. E. Cole, Treas.

Old Colony. — S. S., J. W. Davis, Sec'y and Treas.

Pittsburg, Penn. — Mrs. Mary Veeder, Sec'y and Treas.

Prentissvale, Penn. — Mrs. M. A. Briggs, Sec'y.

Philadelphia, Penn. — Branch Society, Mrs. J. D. Lynde, Treas.

Providence, R.I. — Miss Anna T. White, Treas.

Roxbury (West), Mass. — Mrs. C. S. Hubbell, Treas.

Reading, Mass. — Mrs. Mark Temple.

Randolph (East), Mass. — Miss Carrie L. Russell.

Rutland, Vt. — Mrs. J. B. Page.

Rochester, N.Y. — Mrs. L. Chapin, Sec'y ; Miss C. Starr, Treas.

Rutland (East), Vt. — L. S. Flask, Treas.

St. Alban's, Vt. — Mrs. Mary A. Smith, Treas.

St. Johnsbury, Vt. — Miss Helen M. Kittredge, Sec'y.

Stonington (North), Conn. — Miss Emeline S. Miner.

Spencerport, N.Y. — Congregational Church.

Stratham, Mass. — Miss Carrie M. Sinclair, Sec'y.

Southampton, Mass. — Miss Jane Q. Judd, Treas.

Salisbury, Mass. — Mrs. A. E. Colby, Treas.

Shelburne, Mass. — Mrs. Elihu Smead, Treas.

Swampscott, Mass. — Mrs. Wheeler, Treas.

Stratham, N.H. — Miss Olivia Lane, Sec'y.

Salem, Mass. — Tabernacle Church, Mrs. C. R. Palmer.

Townsend, Mass. — Ladies' Benevolent Society.

Topsfield, Mass. — Mrs. Louisa Leach, Pres.

Townsend Harbor, Mass. — Mrs. Lucy Proctor, Sec'y and Treas.

Uxbridge, Mass. — Mrs. Lorin Taft, Treas.

Westhampton, Mass. — Miss Hattie F. Clapp, Sec'y and Treas.

Wellesley, Mass. — Mrs. Charles B. Dana, Treas.

Wells, Me. — Mrs. Samuel Lindsay, Treas.

Williamstown, Mass. — Miss E. Pierce, Sec'y ; Mrs. C. Stone, Treas.

Walpole, Mass. — Mrs. Loring Johnson, Treas.

Whitinsville, Mass. — Miss F. A. Batchelor, Sec'y and Treas.

Woburn, Mass. — Mrs. Derne, Pres. ; Mrs. C. S. Adkins, Sec'y and Treas.

Waterbury, Vt. — Mrs. Dr. O. W. Drew, Sec'y.

Worcester, Mass. — Union Church, Miss Anna F. Washburn, Sec'y.

Winsted (*West*), *Conn.* —

Winchendon, Mass. — Mrs. C. L. Beals, Sec'y ; Miss S. R. Upham, Treas.

Windham, Portage Co., O. — Miss Julia E. Treat, Sec'y.

Westfield, Mass. — First Congregational Church, Miss Fannie E. Vining, Treas.

Winchester, Mass. — Elizabeth D. Chapin, Treas.

Whiting, Me. — F. S. Peamy, Treas.

Wapping, Conn. — Mrs. Abbie A. Hawkes, Sec'y.

Warsaw, N. Y. — Mrs. E. J. Gates, Pres.; Miss S. H. Bates, Sec'y ; Miss G. Darling, Treas.

Wrentham, Mass. — Emily S. Shepard, Treas.

Youngstown, O. — Mrs. P. I. Caldwell, Treas.

MISSION CIRCLES.

Assabet, Mass. — Missionary Rill.

Boston. — Chambers St. Chapel.

" Cheerful Givers.

" Early Sowers.

" Onward and Upward.

" Morning-Glories.

" Rays of Light.

" Penny Weeklies.

" Upholders of the Right.

" Spring Flowers.

" Willing Hands.

" Noble Followers.

" Jewels.

" Swift Messengers.

" Youthful Heralds.

" Fragment-Gatherers.

" Open Hearts and Hands.

Boston. — SUNBEAMS.
"   CHAPEL RAYS.
"   REAPERS.
"   SUNDAY-SCHOOL CADETS.
"   TENDER BRANCHES.
"   GOSPEL TRUMPETERS.
"   EARNEST WORKERS.
"   "I WILL TRY" COMPANY.
"   "SEEK ME EARLY."
"   GOSPEL BOATMEN.
"   ROSEBUDS.
"   BRIGHT BEAMS.
"   EMULATORS.
"   GOSPEL-BEARERS.
"   GIVERS IN TRUST.
"   EARLY BIRDS.
"   ARMOR-BEARERS.
"   LAMBS OF THE FLOCK (infant class).
"   BUDS OF PROMISE (infant class).
"   STANDARD-BEARERS.
"   VINE-TRIMMERS.
"   HARVESTERS.
"   MORNING STAR.
"   LITTLE MISSIONARIES.
"   MAVERICK RILL (East Boston).
"   ZULU HELPERS.   "   "
"   LITTLE SOWERS (Highlands).
Cambridge, Mass. — WILLING WORKERS.
East Braintree, Mass. — THE MONATIQUOT CIRCLE.
Fall River, Mass. — THE WILLING HELPERS.
Hopkinton, Mass. —
Jamaica Plain, Mass. — THE WIDE-AWAKES.
Lawrence, Mass. — THE FLORENCE NIGHTINGALES.
Lincoln, Mass. — CHEERFUL GIVERS.
Lynn, Mass. —

Madison, N. J. — FAITH CIRCLE.
New Haven, Conn. — TRUTH-SEEKERS.
"   "   "   GROVE-HALL CIRCLE.
Swampscott, Mass. — BUSY WORKERS.
Walpole, Mass. — LITTLE GLEANERS.
Winchester, Mass. — SEEK AND SAVE.
Weymouth, Mass. — MRS. J. W. LOUD'S S. S. CLASS.

MISSIONARIES SUPPORTED BY THE WOMAN'S BOARD.

SOUTH AFRICA.

Mrs. Mary K. Edwards, Zulu Mission.
Miss Gertrude R. Hance, Zulu Mission.

CHINA.

Miss Mary E. Andrews, Tungchow.
Miss Adelia M. Payson, Foochow.

CEYLON.

Miss Eliza Agnew, Oodooville.
Miss Harriet E. Townshend, Oodoopitty.

CENTRAL TURKEY.

Miss Hattie G. Powers, Antioch.
Miss Myra A. Proctor, Aintab.
Miss Sarah L. Wood, Antioch.

EASTERN TURKEY.

Miss Isabella C. Baker, Mardin.
Miss Caroline E. Bush, Harpoot.
Miss Charlotte E. Ely, Bitlis.

3

Miss Mary A. C. Ely, Bitlis.
Miss Olive L. Parmelee, Mardin.
Miss Hattie Seymour, Harpoot.

WESTERN TURKEY.

Miss Flavia L. Bliss, Marsovan.
Miss Ursula C. Clark, Broosa.
Miss Sarah A. Closson, Cæsarea.
Miss Eliza Fritcher.
Mrs. Elizabeth Giles.
Miss Ardelle M. Griswold.
Miss Julia A. Rappleye.

INDIA.

Miss Rosella A. Smith.
Mrs. Mary E. Bissell.

PERSIA.

Miss Mary S. Rice, .

SCHOOLS SUPPORTED BY THE W. B. M.

Mrs. MARY K. EDWARDS's, among the Zulus.
Miss ESTHER T. MALTBIE's, at Eski Zagra.
Miss MYRA A. PROCTOR's, at Aintab.
Misses SEYMOUR and BUSH, at Harpoot.
Miss OLIVE L. PARMELEE's, at Mardin.
Misses ELY's, at Bitlis.
Mrs. BISSELL's, at Ahmednuggur.
Mrs. CHANDLER's, at Madura.

BIBLE WOMEN.

Names.	Stations.	Persons in charge.
Marianne Doodoo,	Constantinople,	Mrs. E. E. Bliss.
Favaria,	Broosa,	Mrs. Schneider.
Nigdi,	Talas, ⎫	Mrs. Giles and
Name not rec'd,	Cæsarea, ⎭	Miss Closson.
Name not rec'd,	Aintab,	Mrs. Marden.
Martha,	Oroomiah,	Miss Dean.
Hoshebo,	Oroomiah,	Miss Dean.
Jes-amine,	Bootan,	Mrs. J. G. Cochran.
Miriam,	Bootan,	Mrs. J. G. Cochran.
Nazloo,	Salmas,	Mrs. J. G. Cochran.
Khanee,	Dizza-takka,	Mrs. J. G. Cochran.
Nargis,	Tergawer,	Mrs. J. G. Cochran.
Esli,	Tergawer,	Mrs. J. G. Cochran.
Hatoon,	Gulpetalykhan,	Mrs. J. G. Cochran.
Rahibai,	Ahmednuggur,	Mrs. Bissell.
Ahilabai,	Ahmednuggur.	Mrs. Bissell.
Ramabai,	Ahmednuggur,	Mrs. Bissell.
Drupatabai,	Wadale,	Mrs. Atkinson.
Yarmonabai,	Barharpur,	Mrs. Fairbank.
Kasubai,	Satara,	Mrs. Wood.
Zaibai,	Sholapoor,	Mrs. Hazen.
Guanaperahasen,	Madura,	Mrs. Chandler.
Harriet Tilva,	Madura,	Mrs. Chandler.
Parkeum,	Madura,	Miss R. Smith.
Name not rec'd,	S. India,	Not rec'd.
Name not rec'd,	S. India,	Not rec'd.
Name not rec'd,	So. India,	Not rec'd.
Sarah R. White,	Oolooville, ⎫	Misses Agnew and
Mary Smith,	Oolooville, ⎭	Hillis.
M s. Woo,	Tungchow,	⎰ Mrs. Chapin and ⎱ Miss Andrews.

CONTRIBUTIONS

Received by the Woman's Board of Missions for the year 1870, as reported monthly in "The Missionary Herald."

MRS. HOMER BARTLETT, *Treasurer.*

RECEIPTS FOR JANUARY.

VERMONT.

Danville—"A. G. F." $10.00
St. Johnsbury — Ladies, by Mrs. J. Bacon, $10; Auxiliary, North
  Church, $74.25 (of which from Mrs. Henry Fairbanks, $25, to constitute Mrs. W. W. Thayer L. M.); South Church, $56.85 (of which
  from Mrs. Horace Fairbanks, $25, to constitute herself L. M.; So-
  ciety, $25, to constitute Mrs. J. R. Colby L. M.) 141.10

MASSACHUSETTS.

Auburndale— Mrs. Sarah Cutler, to constitute herself L. M., $25; Mrs.
  Ramlett, $1; Mrs. Tuttle, $2; Mrs. M., $1; Mrs. Howes, 2 . . 31.00
Andover— Mrs. H. Taylor, $5; M. and L. Beck, $2; Mrs. John Smith, $5;
  annual subscription, John Smith, Esq., to constitute Mrs. Joseph W.
  Smith L. M., $25; Ladies' Auxiliary, Old South Church, $176 (of
  which from Mrs. Caroline L. Smith, to constitute herself and Miss
  Carrie R. Smith L. M.'s, $50; from Mrs. H. B. Taylor, to constitute
  her daughter, Miss Adelaide B. Taylor, and Miss Mary M. Davis of
  New Britain, Conn., L. M's., $50; Society, constituting Mrs. H. B. Tay-
  lor L. M., $25; Miss Jackson, $6; other subscribers, $46) . . . 213.00
Amherst— Aux., to constitute Mrs. Harriet E. Lewis, Mrs. Henry Bal-
  lantine, Mrs. J. S. Cooper, Mrs. W. A. Stearns, and Mrs. (Rev.) J. L.
  Jenkins, L. M.'s. 132.85
Amherst, South — To constitute their pastor's wife, Mrs. Maria P. Ly-
  man, L. M. 25.00
Arlington—Mrs. S. L. B. Field 100.00
Braintree—A widow's mite 1.00
Bradford—First Cong. Church, to constitute Mrs. J. D. Kingsbury L. M. 25.00
Beverly— Young ladies' prayer-meeting, Dane Street 2 40
Barre — Mrs. Arnold Adams 5.00
Bedford — By Rev. Edward Chase 10.00
Boston — From Mrs. Freeman Allen, to constitute Mrs. Spalding, the old-
  est missionary, and Mrs. and Miss Taylor, and Mrs. Burnell, all of the
  Madura Mission, L. M's., $100; Mrs. Charles Scudder, to constitute
  Mrs. J. F. Herrick and Mrs. G. Washburn, both of the Madura Mis-

sion, L. M's., $50; the Misses Newman, to constitute Mrs. C. H. Chandler and Mrs. Chester L. M's., $50; Miss Mary Fowler, to constitute Miss M. S. Rice of Oroomiah, Persia, L. M., $25; Mrs. D. C. Scudder, $5; annual subscriber, a friend, $1; Persis, $1; Mrs. Wetherbee, Mrs. Bryant, Mrs. Royce, Miss Wasgatt, each $2; M'ss Lillie, $5; Miss Rebecca Reed, $5; Mrs. Samuel Johnson, Jr., $9; Mrs. M. V. Hooker, $10; a silver dollar; a silver quarter; M. Cragin, in memoriam, $10; Miss Lydia Cook, $2.50; Mrs. Storrs. Mrs. Hale, Miss Worcester, Miss Farrington, each $1; Mrs. Bishop, $1 50; two friends, $1 each; little E.'s contribution, $3.20; Mrs. S. J. M. Homer to constitute herself L. M., 25; Mrs. J. W. Field, donation, $25: blank envelope at annual meeting, $5; a friend on missionary ship. 50 cts. $348.95

Boston Highlands — Eliot Church, $5; Miss Soran, $2; five of $1 each; an Episcopal friend, $5; "We are Seven," $5 . . . . . 22.00

Boston, South — Rev. J. A. Vinton, to constitute Mrs. Laurinda R. Vinton L. M. 25.00

Boston, East — Mrs. Albert Bowker, to constitute Mrs Mary K. Edwards, of the Zulu Mission, South Africa, and Mrs. Emily C. Pearson, L. M.'s 50.00

Cambridge, East — By Miss L. S. Munroe, fourteen subscribers of $1 each; and from Mrs. E. Munroe, $25, to constitute Miss Louisa S. Munroe L. M. 39.00

Cambridge — Mrs. William H. Dunning, $19; Mrs. Moor, $2; Mrs. Wood, $1 . . . . 22 00

Cambridgeport — Mrs. Mary M. Gilbert, $5; nine subscribers of $1 each. 14.00

Charlestown — Mrs. Tufts and Mrs. Flint, $1 each 2.00

Concord — Aux., Miss Mary Munroe, secretary 30.00

Chelsea — Gold dollar, purchased at annual meeting by Mrs. Rufus S. Frost 25.00

Danvers — Miss E. C. Lawrence, $4; Miss C. W. Lawrence, $1; and subscriber, $1 . . . . 6.00

Falmouth — S. P. Bourne, Esq., to constitute his wife L. M . . 25.00

Fall River — Aux , salary of Miss Seymour of Harpoot. Turkey . 350.00

Groton — Miss Elial Shumway, to constitute Miss Elizabeth C. Williams L. M. 25.00

Hyde Park — Mrs. and Miss Coverly 2.00

Ipswich and Essex — One dollar each 2.00

Jamaica Plain — S. B. Capen, Esq., to constitute his wife L. M., $25; "A Friend," to constitute wife of James H. Merrill of Andover L.M., $25 . . . . 50.00

Lawrence — Mrs. S. F. Howe 3.00

Littleton — Ladies' Mission Circle 20.00

Medford — Deacon Galen James, to constitute his wife, Amanda J., and daughter, Mrs. Matilda T. Haskins, L. M.'s 50.00

Medway Village — Mrs. M. A. Richer 1.00

Marshfield, South — Ladies, to constitute their pastor's wife, Mrs. E. Alden, L. M. 25.00

Malden — "A Friend" 5.00

Newton — Mrs Isaac L. Kidder, to constitute herself L. M., $25; Mrs. Allen, Mrs Day, Mrs. Horton, and a friend, $1 each . . . 29.00

Newton, West — Mrs. S. H. Newell, to constitute Mrs E. H. Newell L. M. 25.00

3*

Newton Centre — Aux., Miss Hattie Kingsbury, $5; other subscribers,
   $5; and from Mrs. Warren Ellis, to constitute herself L. M. $25 . $35.00
Newburyport — "A Friend " 5.00
Quincy — A Friend, R. H. B. 5.00
Salem — "A Friend " 1.50
Salisbury and Amesbury — Aux., A. E. Colby, treasurer . . . 21.00
Somerville, North — Broadway Church, to constitute Mrs. Samuel H.
   Virgin and Mrs. W. H. Hodgkins L. M.'s 52.00
Somerville, East — Young ladies' prayer-meeting 2.50
Southbridge — Mrs. John March 4.50
Walpole — Aux., to constitute Mrs. E. B. Thurber and Mrs. George E.
   Kimball L. M.'s, $50; mission circle, "Little Gleaners," $5 . . 55.00
Wellesley — Auxiliary 7.25
Woburn — Mrs. C. S. Atkins, annual subscription 5.00
Windsor — "A Friend " 2.00
Williamstown — Mrs. M. Prindle 1.00
Waltham — L. L. Mitchell 1.00

RHODE ISLAND.

Coventry — Seven subscribers of $1 each 7.00
Providence — "M." 5.00

CONNECTICUT.

Colchester — By Mrs. Wheeler, from Mrs. Russell Gillett, L. M. . . 25.00
Hartford — "A Friend " 10.00
New London — Ladies of First Cong. Church, of which $50 from Mrs. T.
   McEwen, to constitute Mrs. C. C. Field and Miss Lucretia Latimer
   L. M.'s; $15 from Mrs. McEwen's Sabbath-school class, and $35 sub-
   scriptions 100.00
Norwich — Ladies of First Cong. Church, by E. S. Gilman . . . 15.00

NEW YORK.

Brasher Falls — E. L. Hurlburd 1.50
Rochester — Aux., by C. Starr 11.00
Sand Lake — From Mrs. W. H. Scram 10.00
Utica — Mrs. S. W. Crittenden 5.00
Watertown — Mrs. A. B. Morgan 1.00

NEW JERSEY.

Beverly — Eunice E. S. Lord 5.00
Madison — Mission Band 5.00
Vineland — Mrs. G. M. Bartlett 5.00

PENNSYLVANIA.

Philadelphia — "C. A. L.," monthly subscription 25.00
Pittsburg — Aux., by Mrs. Mary Veeder 110.00

OHIO.

Cleveland — Mrs. Elizabeth E. Taylor 24.00
Windham — Mrs. James Shaw 5.00

MISSOURI.

Independence — Miss Harriette N. Pixley $14.00

CALIFORNIA.

Oakland — By T. B. Bigelow, Esq., First Cong. Church, to constitute
Mrs. Sarah A. Mooar L. M., $25; "A Friend," to constitute Mrs. Ann
E. Bigelow L. M., $25 . . . . 50.00

PERSIA.

A missionary in the East, to constitute Mrs. Susan F. Labaree L. M. . 25.00

Subscriptions and donations for the month $2,548.55
Received for quarterlies 446.25

Total $2,994.80

RECEIPTS FOR FEBRUARY.

MAINE.

Bangor — A friend, "W. S. D." $5.00

NEW HAMPSHIRE.

Bedford — Ladies of Presbyterian Church, to constitute Mrs. Charles
Gage L. M. 29.20
Conway, North — Mrs. E. Merrill, in part to constitute Mrs. S. N. East-
man L. M. 10.00

VERMONT.

Cambridge — Mrs. Mary C. Turner, additional, towards L. M. . . . 5.00
Greensborough — Mrs. A. W. Wild, subscriber 1.00
Rutland — By L. S. Flack, treasurer 5.00
Wallingford — Mrs. Aldace Walker, to constitute herself L. M. $25; Mrs.
Button and Mrs. Marsh, $1 each 27.00

MASSACHUSETTS.

Brimfield — Mrs. C. M. Hyde, $5; Miss E. B. Knight, $5; Mrs. T. W.
Knight, $15; total, to constitute Mrs. Therza Knight L. M. . . 25.00
Boston — Ladies' Missionary Society, by Mrs. Hooker, treasurer, to
constitute Mrs. Hiram Bingham L. M., $25; Mrs. L. E. Caswell, $5;
Mrs. Dr. Morland, $5: Essex-street Church, by Mrs. Charles Scud-
der, a friend, $2; Miss Holland, $5; Miss Newman, to constitute Miss
Adams L. M., $25; Mount Vernon Church, from Mrs. Daniel Saf-
ford, to constitute Mrs. Helen A. Safford, New York, L. M., $25;
Mrs. Coit, collector, from Mrs. J. G. Tappan, $5; Mrs. Holbrook,
Mrs. Foster, Mrs. Price, Mrs. Kimball, Mrs. Nazro, Mrs. Hazelton,
$1 each 103.00
Boston Highlands — Eliot Church, S. S. Class, "Little Sowers" . . 5.00
Chelsea — Broadway Church, by Mrs. Edwin Carr, $80 50; Chestnut-
street Church, five annual subscribers, $5 . . . . . 85.50
Dedham — Ladies of First Congregational Church, for 1869, additional . 20.00

Dorchester—Aux., by E. H. Preston, treasurer, from subscribers, $110.02; Mrs. James H. Means, to constitute herself L. M., $25; Mrs. William Wales and Mrs. Eliza Clapp, to constitute themselves L. M.'s, $50; Mrs. Elbridge Torrey, to constitute Mrs. James C. Sharp L. M., $25; Miss E. C. Shaw, to constitute Mrs. Henry E. Mann L. M., $25; Mrs. Henry Smith, to constitute herself L. M., $25 . . $260.02

Davensport— Miss E. P. Putnam, annual subscriber. 10.00

Ipswich— South Parish Church, S. S. class of girls 2.50

Medford— Deacon Galen James (second contribution 1870), to constitute Miss Hannah James and Miss Louisa Stinchfield L. M.'s . . 50.00

Newton— Mrs. D. B. Jewett, to constitute herself L. M., $25; Mrs. Trowbridge and Mrs. Jenison, $1 each 27.00

Plymouth— Miss Mary A. B. Dyer 10.00

Southbridge— Mrs. S. Marsh 1.00

Stoneham— By Mrs. L. R. Vinton, " A Friend," $5; Miss A. Richardson, $1 . . . . 6.00

Townsend Harbor— Aux., by Mrs. Lucy Proctor, from Mrs. Mary A. Berham, $20 (the Society contributing $5), to constitute her L. M.' total sent 37.00

Ware— Aux., by Mrs. William Hyde, "S. R. S.," to constitute Mrs. William S. Hyde L. M., $25; Mrs. Perkins, Mrs. and Miss Cummings, Mrs. L. Chapin, Miss Hitchcock, Mrs. Lane, Mrs. Field, Mrs. Tuttle, Mrs. Demond, Mrs. Winslow, Mrs. Walker, $1 each . . 36.00

Worcester— By G. E. Gladwin's S. S. class of seven young ladies, Central Church, to support " Martha " of Oroomiah 40.00

Winchendon— Ladies of North Winchendon Congregational Church, to constitute Mrs. Davis Foster L. M., $25; O. Mason, to constitute his wife, Mrs. C. A. S. Mason, L. M., $25; Mrs. M. D. Butler, to constitute Miss Clara H. Dole L. M., $25 . . . . . . 75.00

RHODE ISLAND.

Providence— Mrs. H. P. Hoppin 10.00

CONNECTICUT.

New Haven—" Unknown," by Rev. F. T. Perkins, to constitute Miss E. C. Prudder and Miss Anna Bradley L. M.'s 50.00

Farmington— Pupils of Miss Porter's school, a donation to Miss Mary Porter, China 75.00

Thompson—" C." 2.00

NEW YORK.

Watertown— Mrs. James R. Bates, to constitute her niece, Miss Mary S. Boalt, L. M , $25; two annual subscriptions of $1 each; Miss P. F. Hubbard, $2.50; Mrs. R. Lansing, $1 . . . . . 30.50

NEW JERSEY.

Jersey City— Mrs. G. B. Wilcox 9.00

PENNSYLVANIA.

Philadelphia — " C. A. L.," monthly subscription, $25; Mrs. A. P. Good-
ell, $▲ $20.00

Total of subscriptions and donations $1,077.72
For quarterlies 230.50

Total $1,314.22

RECEIPTS FOR MARCH.

MAINE.

Dennysville — Mrs. P. E. Vose $5.00
Portland — " B. E. M." 1.00

NEW HAMPSHIRE.

Chester — Mrs. Greenwood and Mrs. Hill, subscribers 2.00

VERMONT.

Barre — Ladies of Cong. Church 10.00
Grafton — Mrs. Barrett and Mrs. Pettengill, $3 each; Mrs. Aiken, $2;
others, $2 . . . . 10.00
Georgia — Aux., Woman's Missionary Society, by L. M. Gilbert, secre-
tary 14.00
Vershire — Mrs. S. B. Colton 5.00

MASSACHUSETTS.

Arlington — " A Friend " 5.00
Assabet — Ladies' Benevolent Society, Aux., $10.00; Young Ladies' Cir-
cle, $1.75 . . . . 11.75
Allston — Widow's mite 50
Brighton — Mrs. W. C. Strong 18.50
Boston — Mrs. A. C. Garratt, to constitute herself L. M., $25; Mrs. E. B.
Richmond, $1; Mrs. Mary G. E. Leavitt, subscriber, $10; little
Johnnie's first gift to Persia, 20 cents; " L. H. F.," to support Esli,
$30; Mrs. Freeman Allen, to constitute Mrs. Samuel Warren L. M.,
$25; ladies of Dr. Adams's Church, $21.05; ladies of Park-street
Church, to constitute Mrs. A. L. Stone and Mrs. William H. H. Mur-
ray L. M.'s, $50 . . . . 162.25
Shawmut Cong. Church, Miss L., for girls' school, Aintab, $9; by Mrs.
Ambrose, collector, — Mrs. C. Galloupe, Mrs. J. Duff, and Miss
Knapp, $5 each; Mrs. A. Leland, $4.50; Mrs. M. Richardson, $4;
others, $1 each 138.50
Old South Church, collected by the Misses Walley, — Mrs. Charles
Blake. Mrs. S. R. Payson, Mrs. James Haughton, the Misses Hill,
Mrs. Wentworth, " A Friend," $10 each; Mrs. N. B. Gibbs, Mrs.
Warren Fisher, Mrs. E. C. Johnson, Miss Payson, $5 each; Mrs. R.
L Lane, $4; Miss F, Haughton, $3; the Misses Walley, $2; Miss
Haughton, $2. Miss Briggs, collector, — Mrs. J. B. Kimball, $5;

Mrs. Barry, $3; Mrs. Eastman, $2; eleven of $1 each ; with $4.84 from noon Bible-class, and one of 50 cents. Mrs. Tead, collector, — Mrs. George Lane. $10; Mrs. Samuel Johnson, Jr., Mrs. Thayer, Miss Goodnow, $5 each; Mrs. Ware, $3; Mrs. Porter, $2; Mrs. Hawkins, $2; eleven of $1 each; one of 35 cents. Miss C. Coverly, collector, — Mrs. C. M. Brown, $8; Mrs. Bent, $5; Mrs. Jellison and Mrs. Coverly, $3 each; Mrs. Milliken and Miss Jellison, $2 each; Mrs. Cowdin, to constitute herself L. M., $25, and $1 subscription; Mrs. Charles Stoddard, to constitute Miss Juliette Noble L. M., $25. Miss Brewster, collector, — Miss E. Gray, $10; Mrs. Hilton and Miss Allen, $5 each; Miss Crocker, $2; and three of $1 each. Mrs. C. M. Brown, collector, — Mrs. L. F. Bartlett. $100 (to constitute Miss Mary E. Andrews of Tungchow, Mrs. Walker of the Gaboon Mission, Mrs. (Rev.) John Thompson of Swampscott, and Miss Helen C. Pearson, secretary W. B. M., L. M.'s); Miss Tead, $1.50; three of $1 each. Miss Blagden, collector, — Mrs. J. C. Howe, $200; Mrs. J. F. Baldwin, $15; Mrs. David Buck and Miss Mary Harris, $5 each; Mrs. Gorham Rogers, $3; Mrs. G. W. Blagden, $2; Mrs. Thomas Palmer, $2; four of $1 each; Chambers-street Chapel Sabbath school, $25 . . $625.19
(Previously acknowledged, $51; total, since January, $676.)
Central Church, Miss Child, collector ($136); namely, from Mrs. Benjamin E. Bates, $50 (the same to constitute Mrs. Cox and Mrs. Tenair L. M.'s); Mrs. W. V. Grover, $25; Mrs E. B. Bigelow, Mrs. Jos. Whiten, Mrs. Linus Child, $10 each; Mrs. C. W. Freeland, Mrs. E. W. Chester, Mrs. James White, Mrs. T. H. Russell, Mrs. J. Kendall, $5 each; Miss Wiswall, $3; and three of $1 each. Miss Clara Dennison, collector ($56); namely, from Mrs. John Dennison, to constitute herself L. M., $25; Mrs. and Miss Southwick, Mrs. L. Thompson, and Mrs. Carleton, $5 each; Mrs. S. E. Clapp, $3; Mrs. E. Vinton, $2; and six subscribers of $1 each. Miss Rollins, collector ($63); namely, from Mrs. W. S. Houghton, $20; Mrs. Dawes, Mrs. Bird, Mrs. Page, Miss Pearson, $5 each; Mrs. Carr, Mrs. Kelly, $3 each; Mrs. Brinckhom, Mrs. C. Rollins, Mrs. Topliff, $2 each; and sixteen subscribers of $1 each. Miss Herman, collector ($38); namely, Mrs. L. Herman, to constitute herself L. M., $25; Misses Herman, $3 ; Mrs. Brett, Mrs. Towle, $2 each; and six subscribers of $1 each. Miss Wheeler, collector ($20); namely, eighteen subscribers of $1 each; Mrs. N. Wheeler, $2 . . . . 318.00
Bradford Academy, by Miss Giles, secretary, for support of a pupil in Miss Porter's school 40.00

Brookline — Harvard Church Aux. (Miss M. G. Stoddard, secretary). Mrs. William T. Eustis, Mrs. M. Withington, Mrs. H. McG. Noyes, $5 each; Mrs. Bancroft, Miss Bancroft, Mrs. C. W. Scudder, Miss S. Studley, $4 each; Mrs. Wason, Mrs. Sweetser, Mrs. Saville, $3 each; Mrs. Burditt, Mrs. Colby, Mrs. Hall, Mrs. O. Withington, Mrs. Taylor, $2 each; eighteen subscribers of $1 each; and "additional," $4 72.00

Cambridge — A gold sovereign 5.60

Cambridgeport — Miss A. Wheeler 1.00

Chelsea — Mrs. E. G. Hurter, $1; Chestnut-street Church, additional, $3. 4.00

Charlestown — Mrs. Daniel Lewis $1,00
East Boston — Maverick Church, Oroomiah Aux., Mr. Folts, to constitute
   his wife L. M., $25; by Mrs. Bowker, $225 . . . . 250.00
   ($50 previously acknowledged; since January a total of $300 from this
   auxiliary.)
Hadley — Mrs. M. H. Williams, towards L. M. for Mrs. Ayres . . . 10.00
Hinsdale — Aux. (O. H. Flint, secretary), for support of Nazloo, at Sal-
   mas 32.75
Lexington — Hancock Church, Aux., Ella A. Baker, treasurer . . . 10.00
Medford — Mrs. Goldthwaite, subscription 1.00
Medfield — The Misses Ellis 2.00
Melrose — Ladies of Cong. Church, to constitute Mrs. A. G. Bale L. M. . 25.00
Newburyport — Aux. (Mrs. Ingraham, secretary), to constitute Mrs.
   Dr. Fisk and Mrs. Alice L. March L. M.'s, $50; Juvenile Society, to
   support a Bible-reader in Persia, $60 . . . . 110.00
Newton Centre — Aux., $30 (of which $25, to constitute Mrs. Daniel Fur-
   ber L. M.); Miss L., donation, 50 cents. 30.50
Newton — Received by Mrs. Ambrose from Mrs. Hatch, to constitute Miss
   L. E. Hatch L. M. 25.00
Northampton — J. O. Williston, Esq., to constitute Mrs. C. L. Williston
   L. M. 25.00
Seekonk — Miss A. H. Carpenter, to constitute herself L. M. . . . 25.00
Shelburne — Missionary Society, by Mrs. Elisha Smead 11.35
Southbridge — Mrs. S. M. Lane . . . . 5.00 .
Swampscott — " Circle of Pearls," additional 5.20
Worcester — A widow's thank-offering 5.00
Woburn — Aux., Ladies of Cong. Church, by Mrs. Adkins . . . 50.00

CONNECTICUT.

Burnside — Miss Elmore 1.50
Colchester — Aux., Cong. Church, by Mrs. Wheeler, secretary . . . 69.19
Norwich — Mrs. H. P. Williams, to constitute Mrs. Charles Coit and Mrs.
   M. M. G. Dana L. M.'s, $50; ladies, to constitute Mrs. William Tracy
   of Madura Mission L. M. 82.50
New Haven — Mrs. Mary Pitkin, donation 9.50
Wilton — Catharine E. Hayes 4.00

NEW YORK.

Albany — Mrs. Margaret S. Wood, to constitute Mrs. William C. Hall
   L. M., $25; Mrs. Isaac Brayton, annual subscription, $5 . . . 30.00
Fredonia — Aux. (Miss Martha L. Stevens, treasurer), constituting Mrs.
   Lucia E. Wright and Miss M. L. Stevens L. M's. 55.00
Jewett — Ladies of Pres. Church, by A. Montgomery 30.00
Union Falls — Mrs. F. D. Duncan, $8; Miss D. and M. B. D., $1 each . 10 00
Spencer — Mrs. Austin 1.00
Watertown — Mrs. O. V. Brainerd and daughter 2.00

PENNSYLVANIA.

Philadelphia — " C. A. L.," monthly contribution 25.00

NORTH CAROLINA.

Raleigh — E. P. Hayes, a teacher of freedmen $1.00

ILLINOIS.

Fowler — A. S. McCormick, annual subscription 10.00

TURKEY.

Harpoot — Rev. Herman N. Barnum, to constitute his wife, Mrs. Mary E.
Barnum, L. M. 25.00

From subscriptions and donations $2,428.78
Quarterlies 334.50

Total $2,763.28

RECEIPTS FOR APRIL.

MAINE.

Bangor — Aux., by Mrs. E. G. Thurston, treasurer $10.00

NEW HAMPSHIRE.

Stratham — Aux., by Carrie N. Sinclair, treasurer. 12.10

VERMONT.

Rutland — Mrs. A. H. Post, subscriber 1.00

MASSACHUSETTS.

Abington — Rev. Frederick R. Abbe, to constitute his wife, Mary T.,
L. M. 25.00
Amherst, South — Aux., by Mrs. C. B. Hutchins, to constitute Mrs. M.
A. Dana L. M. 25.00
Beverly — " Friends," to constitute Mrs. F. W. Choate and Mrs. Charles
H. Odell L. M's, both being of Dane-street Church, $50; young la-
dies of Dane-street Church, to constitute Mrs. Mary E. Lanphear
L. M., $25 . . . . 75.00
Beverly, North — Miss Rebecca Conant, $5; Richard P. Waters, $10 . 15.00
Braintree, East — Mrs. H. J. Holbrook 3.00
Boston — Old South Church, additional, Miss Elizabeth Davis, $100;
Mrs. David Buck, to constitute herself L. M., $25 ; Hon. Avery Plu-
mer, to constitute his little daughter, Hattie Mason, L. M., $25 . . 150.00
(A total, since January, from Old South, of $326.)
Shawmut Congregational Church, Mrs. Mary S. Bishop and Mrs. Sa-
rah B. Putnam, to constitute themselves L. M.'s 50.00
(A total, since January, from this church, of $188.50.)
Mount Vernon Church, by Miss Celia Houston, $39.50; by Mrs.
Hall, from Mrs. James Cutler, to constitute herself L. M., $25; Mrs.
Winslow's subscription, $10; Mrs. A. B. Hall, to constitute Mrs.
E. C. Cowles of Ipswich, L. M., $25; Mrs. M. C. Grower and Mrs. J.
Stacy, $2 each; five of $1, and three of 50 cents each; by Mrs. Coit,
additional, five subscribers of $1 each 115.00
(A total from this church, since January, of $155.50.)

Union Church, Miss Lee, $2; Mrs. H. B. Hooker, to constitute Annie Hooker Capron L. M., $25; " L. J. B.," to constitute Mrs. Augustus Walker L. M., $25; four subscriptions of $1 each $56.00

(A total from this church, since January, of $250.05)

Park-street Church, additional, Mrs. E. C. Cutler, $5; Miss Susan W. Jones, $5. . . . . 10.00

Charlie B.'s contribution, $1.25; Mrs. Harriet M. Ayer, $2; Old Colony S. S., to support a student in Mrs. Edwards's school, $30 . . 33.25

Boston, East — Mrs. Dimock and Mrs. Franklin, $1 each 2.00

Boston, South — Phillips Church, by Mrs. J. Drake, of which $25 to ⁓ constitute Mrs. C. Shepard L. M.; Mrs. C. C. Conly, to constitute Mrs. E. S. Winchester L. M., $25; Miss Alice Cooper, to constitute Mrs. Jane R. Meins L. M., $25; Mr. King, to constitute his wife L. M., $25; Mrs. Jeremy Drake, to constitute Miss Olive E. Parmelee of Eastern Turkey L. M., $25; Mrs. Alden, Mrs. Burnham, Mrs. Angier, Mrs. Darling, Mrs. Harlow, Mrs. S. Shepard, each $5; Mrs. Amsden, Mrs. Jones, Mrs. Winchester, Mrs. Burrage, Mrs. Howes, $3 each; Mrs. Ellis, Mrs. Gordon, Mrs. W. Howes, Mrs. Jones, Mrs. Holt, Mrs. Pierce, Mrs. Hilton, Mrs. Nickerson, Mrs. Harrington, Mrs. Doherty, Mrs. Preckle, Mrs. Vinton, Mrs. Faxon, Miss E. Darling, Miss B. Darling, Miss Nickerson, Miss Dickson, $2 each, and forty subscribers of $1 each 249.00

Boston Highlands — Eliot Church, Mrs. C. F. Bray, to constitute herself L. M., $25; five ladies, to constitute Mrs. L. B. Rockwood L. M., $25; Mrs. Upton, $5; Mrs. Kittredge, $2; seven subscribers of $1 each 64.00

Highland Chuch, by Mrs. J. H. Howell ($25 of which to constitute Mrs. C. L. Mills L. M.) 54.00

Cambridgeport — Miss Bridge's subscription 1.00

Chelsea — Aux., Chestnut-street Church, by Mrs. J. Sweetser ($25 of which to constitute Mrs. Mary Stone L. M.) 47.00

Charlestown — Mrs. E. A. Trowbridge, to constitute herself L. M., $25 ; Mrs. W. Abbott, $1 . . . . · 26.00

Falmouth — " A Friend," to constitute Mrs. S. D. Robinson L. M., $25; Miss Lucy Lawrence, to constitute herself L. M., $25 . . . . 50.00

Fitchburg — Almira F. Hartwell 1.00

Groton Junction — Aux., Congregational Church 10.00

Hopkinton — Mrs. Mary Putnam's S. S. class 10.00

Jamaica Plain — Aux., by Miss M. A. Brackett 96.50

Leominster — Aux., by Miss S. M. Haskell, to constitute Mrs. Myra Burrage and Mrs. S. T. Haskell L. M.'s. 50.00

Milton — Mrs. Ruggles 1.00

Newton — " From a friend " 4.00

Newton, West — Aux., for Miss Ursula Clark's school 62.00

Newtonville — Aux., by Miss E. A. Goodell, secretary ($25 of which from Mrs. B. F. Whittemore, to constitute Mrs. J. Clark L. M.) . 52.00

Williamstown — Aux., by Mrs. C. Stone 4.50

Williamstown, South — By G. F. Mills, for support of a girl in school at Erzroom 30.00

Westhampton — A friend 2.00

4

Worcester — Union Church, Aux., by Mrs. A. F. Washburne ($25 of which to constitute Miss Seymour, of Harpoot, L. M.), $207.20; Mrs. E. C. Swift, $12 . . . . $219.20

Whitinsville — Aux., Miss F. A. Batchelor, secretary (of which $25 from Miss Annie L. Whiten, to constitute herself L. M.) . . . 44.00

CONNECTICUT.

Burnside — Mrs. A. D. Pratt 5.00

Manchester — Mrs. Emily Pitkin, to constitute Mrs. Esther W. Sherman, of Naugatuck, L. M. 25.00

Poquonnock — "A Friend" 2.00

Washington — "M. A. N." 8.00

West Winsted — Aux., to constitute Mrs. William Lawrence and M. E. Beardsley L. M's. 60.00

Westport — Mrs. M. R. 10.00

Waterbury — Aux., by Mrs. Dr. O. Drew, secretary 40.00

NEW YORK.

Buffalo — "Thank-Offering," by which to constitute Mrs. Mary Whiton Calkens L. M. $25.00

Malone — Mrs. S. C. Wead 20.00

Poughkeepsie — Pres. S. S., to educate a girl at Mardin Seminary . . 30,00

Watertown — Three subscriptions of $1 each, by Mrs. Wardwell . . 3.00

PENNSYLVANIA.

Edinborough — Pres. S. S., to constitute Mrs. Amelia Leonard of Marsovan, Turkey, L. M. 30.00

Philadelphia — "C. A. L." monthly contribution 25.00

Philadelphia, West — "A Mite" 1.00

OHIO.

Coolville — Mrs. M. B. Bartlett, to constitute Miss Mary Bartlett and Mrs. Fanny Tidd L. M's 50.00

Toledo — Prize Essay, by Miss Mary Jane Tolman 10.00

FOREIGN LANDS.

Ceylon, Oodooville, Jaffna — Miss Eliza Agnew, to constitute herself L. M. 25.00

Sandwich Islands, Honolulu — From teachers and pupils in Miss Bingham's school ($25 of which to constitute Miss Lydia Bingham L. M., the residue in part for L. M. of Miss E. Bingham) $35.84; from Mrs. B. W. Parker, 4.94 . . . . 40.78

Subscriptions and donations $2,064.58
For quarterlies 249.65

Total for month $2,314.23

RECEIPTS FOR MAY.

MAINE.

Ellsworth — Mrs. and Miss Phelps, for support of a pupil for one year in
Miss Dean's school, Oroomiah $28.00
Otisfield — Mrs. W. 2.00

NEW HAMPSHIRE.

Tamworth — " A Friend " 1.00

VERMONT.

Brattleborough, West — From " F." 5.00
Rutland — Aux., by S. B. Flack, $5; a friend, by Mrs. J. C. Tyler, $5 . 10.00

MASSACHUSETTS.

Andover — Aux., by Mrs. E. C. Pearson 12.50
Barre — Rhoda A. Dickinson 4.50
Boxford — Mrs. H. T. Park, constituted L. M. by her son 25.00
Boston — Park-street Church, by Mrs. Simpson ($25 of which, from Miss
Adeline Lincoln, to constitute her mother L. M.). $125; Phillips
Church, additional, by Mrs. Drake, $3; Mount Vernon Church, Mrs.
Bradley and Mrs. Dommett, $1 each, $2; Shawmut Church, Mrs.
Munger, $1; Union Church, by Mrs. Charles Scudder, $25; Highland
Church, additional, by Mrs. Howell, $4.50 . . . . . . 160.50
Cambridgeport — Mrs. Tilton, subscription 1.00
Cambridge — Shepard Church, Aux., to constitute Mrs. Stephen Farwell
and Mrs. William Bates L. M.'s 54.50
Chelmsford, North — Rev. and Mrs. B. F. Clark, to constitute Miss Em-
ma F. King, of Cambridgeport, L. M. 25.00
Everett — Mrs. Albert Bryant, to constitute herself L. M. . . . 25.00
Fitchburg — Mrs. Stephen W. Dole, to constitute Clara A. Clark L. M. . 25.00
Groveland — To constitute Miss Sarah Tuttle L. M. 25.00
Hadley — First Congregational Church, S. S. donation to mission fund for
Miss Porter's school, China 30.00
Hadley, South — Mt. Holyoke Seminary Aux., to constitute Miss Mary
C. Townsend, Miss Annie Dearborn, Miss E. M. Bardwell, Miss Lou-
ise F. Cowles, Miss Susan Bowen, Miss Alice W. Gordon, Miss Helen
M. Savage, Miss Anna M. Hood, Miss Mary P. Burgess, Miss Mary O.
Nutting, Mrs. Mary A. Foster (all of Mt. Holyoke Seminary), Mrs.
Esther E. Thompson of Amherst, Mrs. L. F. Garvin of Lonsdale,
R. I., Miss Elvira Cole of Stark, N. H., Miss Mary L. Carpenter of
Monson, Miss Mary T. Carter of Lowell, Miss Mary C. Gore of La
Harpe, Ill., Mrs. Ithiel Lawrence of South Hadley, also Mrs. William
F. Draper of Andover, by a friend, and Mrs. James W. Gordon of
Auburndale, by her daughter, Miss Alice W. Gordon, L. M.'s . 505.00
Lawrence — Eliot Church, Aux., to constitute pastor's wife, Mrs. H. E.
Snow, L. M. 25.00
Lincoln — " The Cheerful Givers," $5; " Silver Wedding " present, to
constitute Mrs. A. H. Farrar L. M., $25 . . . . 30.00
Longmeadow — From S. Pynchon, $10; Sabbath school, to support a girl
at Marsovan school, Miss Bliss teacher. $35 . . . . . . 45.00

Lynn — Mrs. James D. Farnsworth $5.00
Peabody — Mrs. Mary A. Gardner, to constitute herself L. M. 25.00
Plymouth — Mrs. Jane B. Gordon 25.00
Pittsfield — South Congregational Church S. S., for Mrs. Edwards, Natal,
  Africa 15.00
Quincy — Mrs. G. Hollister 1.00
Truro — Mrs. Blake and Mrs. Noble, $1 each 2.00
Uxbridge — Aux., Young Ladies' Missionary Society, for pupil at Oroo-
  miah 25.00
Weymouth — Aux., by Miss H. P. Vickery, treasurer 30.00
Wellesley — Mrs. Nathaniel Dana, to constitute Mrs. George M. Adams of
  Portsmouth, N. H., L. M. 25.00

CONNECTICUT.

Colchester — Aux., by Mrs. Wheeler, additional, $3, and 35 cents by two
  little children 3.35
Eastford — Rev. S. Clark, to constitute Mrs. William H. Brown, of Chicago, L. M. 25.00
Greenwich — Aux., Miss Lizzie H. Cristy, secretary 50.00

NEW YORK.

Bergen, North — Mrs. E. B. Talcott, with $10 previously acknowledged,
  to constitute herself L. M. 15.00
Mount Morris — Aux., Miss L. H. Ford, secretary 11.50
Poughkeepsie — Mary H. Sterling, with $10 previously given, to consti-
  tute herself L. M. 15.00
Rochester — Aux. ($55 of which from Mrs. Samuel Hamilton, to support
  a pupil in Miss Seymour's school at Harpoot, and to constitute Miss
  Julia A. Hamilton L. M.) 60.50
Spencerport — Congregational Church, Ladies' Society, for girl at Har-
  poot Seminary 30.00
Western New York. — "A Friend," for one girl three years, at Harpoot
  Seminary 100.00

PENNSYLVANIA.

Philadelphia — Branch society, of which from twelve ladies, $1 each;
  Mrs. Mary B. Coan, $4; Mrs. C. Burnham, $4; grandchildren of Mrs.
  (Rev.) Joel Fisk, to constitute her L. M., $25; Deacon James Smith,
  to constitute Mrs. John Edmands L. M., $25; Mrs. John McLeod,
  $10, Mrs. B. Hart, $5, Mrs. C. C. Fisk, $5, Mrs. J. N. Southworth, $5,
  to constitute Mrs. John McLeod L. M.; " C. A. L.," $25, to constitute
  Mrs. (Rev.) William Goodell L. M.; Mrs. Edward Webb, Glasgow,
  Delaware, $5 . . . . 125.00
Patterson — Mrs. M. H. Foley 5.00
Pittsburg — Welsh S. S., to support a girl at Oroomiah 29.00

OHIO.

Springfield — M. Mowatt, for mission fund 2 00
Windham — Aux., by Miss J. E. Treat, to constitute Mrs. James Shaw
  (who had given $5 previously) L. M. 20.00
Youngstown — Aux., by Mrs. P. T. Caldwell, treasurer 15.35

MICHIGAN.

Concord — Ladies of Pres. Church, to constitute Mrs. A. M. Shaw L. M. $25.00

SANDWICH ISLANDS.

Honolulu — Donation from Mrs. Henry Dimon, to constitute Mrs. L. H.
Gulick, Miss Margaret Flaxman, Miss C. F. Atherton, and with $10
previously given by seminary, to constitute also Miss Elizabeth F.
Bingham, L. M.'s 91.80

Subscriptions and donations for month $1,815.50
Quarterlies 134.72

Total $1,950.22

RECEIPTS FOR JUNE.

MAINE.

Washington — Calvin Starrett, Esq., to constitute Mrs. P. W. Starrett L. M. $25.00
Yarmouth — Mrs. Jacob J. Abbot 2.00

NEW HAMPSHIRE.

Exeter — Aux., to constitute Mrs. John Gordon L. M. 25.00
Salisbury — Abba S. Corser 2.00

VERMONT.

East Dorset — Aux., by Mrs. J. F. Goodrich 15.00

MASSACHUSETTS.

Belmont — Mrs. J. S. Frost 1.00
Boston — "A Friend," $5; Mrs. Samuel Wells, sen., $5; Union Church,
additional, $2; Mrs. M. H. Baldwin, $1; "A Thank-Offering," $1;
Shawmut Church, from Miss L., for girls' school, Aintab, $14 . . 28.00
East Boston — Maverick Church, "Zulu Helpers," by Miss Mary K. Bing-
ham, treasurer, proceeds of Fair 185.00
Cambridge — Mrs. E. S. Johnson's S. S. class, "The Willing Helpers," . 5.00
Granby — Cong. S. S., for girl in Miss Porter's school, Pekin, China . 40.00
Newton — A friend of missions 1.00
Peabody — Ladies of Congregational Church, to constitute Mrs. (Rev.)
George N. Anthony L. M. 25.50
Southampton — Aux., by Miss Jane Z. Judd, treasurer 50.25
Westfield — Ladies of First Congregational Church, by Miss Fannie E.
Vining, treasurer 58.00

RHODE ISLAND.

Providence — Aux., by Miss Anna T. White, treasurer 116.00

CONNECTICUT.

Colebrook — Mrs. A. Corbin 1.00
Guilford — Mrs. A. W. Chittenden, to constitute Mrs. Alice L. Kitchell
L. M. 25.00

4*

Middletown—Aux., Miss Mary B. Hazen, treasurer (of which from Mrs. Linus Coe, to constitute herself L. M., $25) $40.00

NEW YORK.

Honeoye Falls—Sabbath school, for Mrs. Bissell's school 1.10
Meridian—Mrs. S. R. Townsend, donation 10.00
Westville—Miss P. Fobes 10.00

PENNSYLVANIA.

Philadelphia—"Branch" Society, by Mrs. J. D. Lynde, treasurer—
twenty ladies, $1 each; "The Hawes Bible Class," to constitute Mrs. Edward Hawes L. M., $25; Mrs. Samuel Holmes, to constitute herself L. M., $25; "C. A. L.," to constitute Miss Emma L. Goodell L. M.,$25; Mrs. P. S. Horner, contribution, $5 . . . . . . 100.00

OHIO.

Granville—Congregational Church S. S. Missionary Society, by E. C. Blanchard, treasurer 22.50

INDIANA.

Dayton—Mrs. "C. B. C.'s" S. S. class 2.00

Total from subscribers $790.35
"Life and Light" quarterlies 68.00
Children's quarterlies 28.21

Total for the month $886.56

RECEIPTS FOR JULY.

MAINE.

Castine—Ladies of Trinitarian Society, by Mrs. Samuel Adams (of which $25 to constitute Mrs. A. E. Ives, their pastor's wife, L. M.) . $45.50
Portland—Mrs. N. Brown, a thank-offering, $5; from High-street Church, Miss H. T. Fenn's S. S. class, for a girl at Marsovan, care of Mrs. Edw. Riggs, Sivas 33.30
Wells—Aux., Mrs. Samuel Lindsay, treasurer, Second Cong. Church . 30.00
Whiting—Aux., for Bible-reader in Mrs. Bissell's school 25.00

NEW HAMPSHIRE.

Derry—Mrs. P. B. Day, to constitute herself L. M. 25.00
Danbury—Mrs. J. LeBosquet 1.00

VERMONT.

Bakersfield—Mrs. E. M. Barnes, for support of a girl in Harpoot Seminary 30.00
St. Alban's—Aux., by Mrs. M. A. Smith, treasurer (of which $125 to constitute Mrs. Emily B. Safford, Mrs. Mary F. Whiting, Mrs. Eliza C. Farrar, Miss Adeline E. Riggs, Miss Sophia Brainerd, L. M.'s; $25

43

from Mrs. John G. Smith, to constitute herself L. M.; $25 from Mrs. A. J. Samson, to constitute her daughter, Miss Henrietta L. Samson, L. M.; $25 from Mrs. Maria W. Smith, to constitute Miss Helen Lynde Brainerd L. M.) $200.00

MASSACHUSETTS.

Andover — Abbott Academy, for support of scholars at Harpoot, Oroomiah, Oodoopitty, Inanda, and Foochow, — one at each place, — in part 137.25
Amherst, South — Mrs. "M. P. L." 5.00
Athol — Mrs. Phœbe M. Thorp, $15; Miss Jennie L. Case, $1; Temple ,Cutler, Esq., to constitute his wife L. M., $25 . . . . . 41.00
Allston — For " W. B. M." 1.00
Boston — Anonymous, $5; two Friday evening earnings, $3; premium on silver dollar, 13 cents; sale of jewelry, $40; Central Church, Miss Louisa Thompson, $50; Shawmut Cong. Church, Mrs. J. S. Stone, to constitute Miss Martha A. Willard L. M., $25 . . . . 123.13
Boston, East — A thank-offering from a lover of missions . . . 10.00
Boston Highlands — Eliot Church, Aux., by Mrs. Anderson (of which $25 from Mrs. Stephen J. Bowles, to constitute herself L. M.) . . 47.00
Bradford Academy — Aux., to support a pupil in Miss Proctor's school, Aintab, Turkey 20.00
Braintree, East — " Monotequot Young Ladies' School," the proceeds of a sale of their handiwork, with $25 contributed by the principal, Miss R. A. Faxton, to constitute herself L. M. 126.00
Chelsea — " A Friend " 5.00
Dedham — " A Friend of W. B. M." 5.00
Dorchester — Second Cong. Church, a friend, to constitute Miss Eliza Withington L. M. 25.00
Hadley South, Falls — " A " 5.00
Jamaica Plain — Central Cong. S. S., by B. W. Williams, for Mrs. Edwards's school 50.00
Lawrence — Lawrence-street Church, Aux., by Mrs. J. L. Partridge, treasurer (of which $50 to constitute Mrs. C. M. Cordley and Mrs. W. A. Kimball L. M.'s) 100.00
Lincoln — George M. Baker, Esq., for pupil in Oroomiah . . . 28.00
Petersham — Mrs. L. Whitney, for a scholar in Mrs. Edwards's school . 30.00
Springfield — Galen Ames, Esq., to constitute his wife L. M. . . 25.00
Wilkinsonville — Mrs. W. R. Hill, $5; Miss Carrie W. Hill, $5 . . 10.00

RHODE ISLAND.

Providence — Aux., by Miss Anna T. White, treasurer (of which $75 to constitute Mrs. W. J. Cross, Mrs. William J. King, and Mrs. George Claflin, L. M.'s, $137); " In answer to Prayer," $25 . . . . 162.00

CONNECTICUT.

Bozrah — By Mrs. Albert G. Avery, of which to constitute Mrs. Nathan S. Ghent L. M., $25 . . . . 36.25
Poquonnock — From " A Friend " 5.00

NEW YORK.

New York — Annual contribution of D. B. Hixon, Esq., for the "Warfield Scholarship," Harpoot, Turkey $30.00
Buffalo — Lafayette-street Pres. Church, by Miss Mary A. Ripley, treasurer (of which $50 to constitute Mrs. Joseph G. Cochran of Oroo-
miah, and Mrs. Grosvenor W. Heacock of Buffalo, L. M's.) . . 154.75
Candor — Cong. S. S., for Harpoot Seminary 30.00

MICHIGAN.

Homer — Pres. S. S., by Miss L. Gurish, for a pupil at Oroomiah . . 28.00

MINNESOTA.

Chatfield — Sabbath school, for support of " Gita," in Mrs. Bissell's school, •
Ahmednuggur 22.00

SANDWICH ISLANDS.

Honolulu — " One of the Cousins " 1.00

ENGLAND.

London — Miss E. H. Ropes, $20; Miss S. L. Ropes, $10 . . . . 30.00

Total of subscriptions and donations $1,687.18
For quarterlies 20.00
Children's quarterlies 14.50

Total for the month. $1,721.68

RECEIPTS FOR AUGUST.

MAINE.

Holden — Mrs. Farrington $2.00
Lewiston — Pine-street Cong. Church, by S. H. Murray, treasurer, to con-
stitute Mrs. Annie L. Balkam and Miss A. D. F. Lockwood L. M.'s . 50.00
Mechanics Falls — " A Woman " . . . , ... 5.00
Portland — Miss A. C. M. Foxcroft, to constitute herself L. M. . . 25.00

VERMONT.

North Bennington — A Friend 2.00
Union Village — Mrs. John Lord 1.00

MASSACHUSETTS.

Billerica — Aux., by Mrs. Sarah B. Work, treasurer 21.50
Barre — Mrs. Arnold Adams 10.00
Boston — A widow, $100; " A Friend," to constitute Miss Elizabeth D.
Robinson, of Falmouth, L. M., $25; Mrs. Patch, for support of Kha-
nee, a Bible-reader in Persia, $30 . . . . 155.00
Boston, South — E-street Cong. Church, Auxiliary 23.00
Cambridgeport — Miss Susan Sparrow 4.00
Cambridge, East — William Wyman, Esq., to constitute his wife, Ruth
E. Wyman, L. M. 25.0

Falmouth — Mrs. Thatcher Lewis, to constitute herself L. M. . . . $25.00
Fitchburg — Mrs. L. A. Lowe, to constitute Mrs. Calvin M. Lowe of
    Paint Creek, Michigan, L. M. 25.00
Granville, West — Mrs. Mary L. Treat 1.00
Hadley, South — Mt. Holyoke Seminary re-union, from a few of the
    " Oria " of '55, for support of one pupil two years in Female Semi-
    nary, Oroomiah, Persia 50.00
Ipswich — " A Friend," 10.00
Lincoln — Cong. Church S. S., for support of " Jessamine," a Bible-
    reader in Persia 30.24
Malden — Aux., Cong. Church, for support of Hoshebo, in Oroomiah . 40.00
Montague City — Mrs. L. B. Bradford 2.00
Newton Centre — Mrs. A. F. Wardwell and Miss Hattie Kingsbury, to
    constitute themselves L. M.'s 50.00
Newburyport — Aux., by Mrs. H. A. Ingraham, treasurer ($25 of
    which to constitute Mrs. Hannah Tyler L. M.), $100; Mrs. Albert
    Currier, by Mrs. Page, $2 . . . . 102.00
Northampton — Mrs. C. L. Williston 100.00
Swampscott — S. S. Aux., additional, by Rev. J. Thompson, $7.02; pro-
    ceeds of Fair held by mission band, " The Busy Workers " S. S.
    class of Mrs. J. Thompson, $57 . . . . 64.02
Wellesley — Mrs. (Rev.) J. N. Parsons's dying gift to the women of India,
    and to constitute her sister, Mrs. Charles Herrick, L. M. . . . 25.00
Williamstown — Ladies, by L. J. Safford, to constitute Mrs. Elizabeth
    Pierce L. M., $25; " A Friend," $3 . . . . 28.00
Wilmington — Mrs. Charlotte C. Buck, to constitute herself L. M. . . 25.00
Woburn — " A Friend " 5.00
Anonymous 4.50

CONNECTICUT.

Easthampton — Aux., by Mrs. G. W. Andrews, treasurer . . . 10.00
Norwich — Second Cong. Church, Aux., by E. G. Coit, treasurer (of which
    $50 from Mrs. H. P. Williams, to constitute Mrs. Samuel C. Dana of
    the S. Islands, and Mrs. George Coit of Norwich, L. M.'s) . . 161.51
New Milford — Henry Ives, Esq., to constitute Mrs. L. S. Ives L. M. . 25.00

NEW YORK.

Clinton — " Ada," for woman's fund 10.00
Corning — Pres. Church, Mrs. C. G. Dennison's class, for girl at Harpoot
    Seminary 25.00
Elmira — Young Ladies' Christian Association of Female College, for
    " Hooshe," Harpoot, $30; for Constantinople, $40 . . . . 70.00
Poughkeepsie — Mrs. M. J. Myers 10.00
Fayetteville — By Miss Alice Lee, secretary, to constitute Mrs. Hunting-
    ton Beard and Mrs. N. Chipman L. M.'s 53.25
Whitney's Point — Ladies' Society, by Rev. J. W. Marsh . . . 14.00

PENNSYLVANIA.

Corry — Mrs. A. S. Nash 5.00

OHIO.

Coolville — Mrs. Margaret B. Bartlett, to constitute Mrs. Lucy B. Adams
of Freestone, O., and Mrs. Margaret C. Oscar of Missouri, L. M.'s . $50.00

Portsmouth — Pres. S. S. (of which $30 for a girl at Harpoot, and $20 for
a Bible-reader in Persia), $50 . . . . 100.00

TENNESSEE.

Lookout Mountain — Educational Institution, for little Miriam of Mardin, Turkey 10.00

CANADA.

Montreal — Mrs. Henry Lyman, for Oroomiah Female Seminary . . 43.65

SANDWICH ISLANDS.

Honolulu — Kawaiahao Seminary, by Miss Lydia Bingham (of which to
constitute Miss Sallie B. Small of York, Penn., L. M.). . . . 26.23

From subscriptions and donations 1,473.90
For quarterlies, "Life and Light" 35.00
For quarterly "Echoes" 7.77

Total for the month. $1,516.67

RECEIPTS FOR SEPTEMBER.

MAINE.

Upper Gloucester — Mrs. Clara S. Jordan $5.00

NEW HAMPSHIRE.

Westmoreland — Mrs. A. Noyes 1.00

VERMONT.

Burlington — Third Cong. Church S. S., by B. L. Benedict, superintendent 25.10
Charlestown, West — Mrs. Lavinia Barnard. 2.00
Georgia — Aux., by L. M. Gilbert, secretary, $9.50; from Mrs. A. L.
Torrey, a thank-offering, $10.50 . . . . 20.00
Newbury — Freeman Keyes, Esq., to constitute Mrs. Keyes and Miss
Hattie Keyes L. M's 50.00
Norwich — Mrs. Harriet A. Dutton 1.00

MASSACHUSETTS.

Andover — Old South Church, Aux., Miss Dow 10.00
Boston — Mrs. Celia C. Turner, to constitute herself L. M., $25; "A
Friend," to constitute Miss Louisa J. Rice L. M., $25 . . 50.00
Boston Highlands — Elliot Church, additional, by Mrs. Anderson . 20.00
Bradford — First Church, by B. D. Kingsbury, constituting Mrs. Caroline
Ordway L. M. 42.82
Chelsea — Broadway Church, by Mrs. Copp, Mrs. J. Q. Gilmore, $1.50;
Mrs. C. Powers, $1 . . . . 2.50

Groton Centre — Mrs. Eliel Shumway and S. S. class, to constitute Mrs.
  J. K. Aldrich, their pastor's wife, L. M. $25.00
Hingham, South — "From M. A. H." 1.00
Hadley — Mrs. Mary H. Williams, to constitute her pastor's wife, Mrs.
  Jane E. Ayres, L. M. ($10 having been sent in March last) . . . 15.00
Hadley, South — Mt. Holyoke Seminary re-union Orla, class of '55, to
  constitute Mrs. Mary B. Fairbank of the Mahratta Mission, Mrs. Sa-
  rah J. Rhea of the Nestorian Mission, and Mrs. Eliza W. Morse of the
  Bulgarian Mission, L. M.'s ($50 having been previously acknowledged) 25.00
Swampscott — Cong. S. S. Aux., additional, by Rev. John Thompson. . 6.76
Worcester — David Whitcomb, Esq., to constitute Mrs. M. C. Whitcomb,
  Miss Ellen M Whitcomb, Mrs. G. Henry Whitcomb, and Miss Ruth
  Peckham, L. M.'s 100.00
Whitinsville — Mrs. Charles P. Whitin, to constitute Mrs. Daniel Bliss of
  Beirut, Syria, L. M., $25; Mrs. George Gibbs, $5 . . . . . . 30.00
Winchester — Aux., by Miss Elizabeth D. Chapin (of which from Mrs. H.
  Cutter and Mrs. N. W. C. Holt, $25, to constitute Miss Nellie B. Holt
  L. M., and from six friends "$25 to constitute Mrs. Hannah Patten
  L. M.") 62.00
Williamstown — Ladies, by "E. P." 10.00

CONNECTICUT.

Hartford, East — Cong. S. S., by David L. Williams, treasurer, for sup-
  port of a pupil at Oroomiah, Persia 28.00
Hartford, West — "From Friends," by Mrs. George M. Carrington . . 10.00
Hebron — Ladies of Cong. Church, by Mrs. Jasper Porter . . . 22.00
New Britain — Mrs. Louisa Nicholls 10.00
New Haven — Aux., by Mrs. John W. Fitch, treasurer 300.00
Woodstock, North — H. E. Carpenter, additional 3.00

NEW YORK.

Auburn — Mrs. S. E. G. Boardman 5.00
Brooklyn — Mrs. C. E. Loomis and Miss C. A. Pratt, annual contribution
  for support of Amy, the Koord girl, at Harpoot 30.00
Fulton — Missionary Society of Pres. S. S., by B. J. Dyer, for girl in
  Miss Fritcher's school, Marsovan, $30; and to clothe one from Fe-
  male Seminary, $4 . . . . 34.00
Westport — Mrs. Augusta M. Spencer 3.00

PENNSYLVANIA.

Philadelphia — Branch, by Mrs. J. D. Lynde, treasurer, Mrs. Sarah C.
  Seaver, $5; Dea. David Fiske, to constitute Mrs. Burdett Hart L. M.,
  $25; "C. A. L.," quarterly contribution, $75 . . . . . . 105.00

OHIO.

Toledo — "Cash" to constitute Mrs. Anna J. Williams L. M. . . . 25.00
Windham — Aux., by Julia E. Treat, to constitute Miss A. M. Wales
  L. M. 25.00

MICHIGAN.

Grand Haven — Mrs. A. W. Ferry, to constitute Miss Mary A. White
  L. M. 25.00

48

MINNESOTA.

Clear Water — By L. M. Stearns, secretary $14.00

MISSOURI.

Ironton — Mrs. W. A. Delano, $1; Mrs. C. E. Markham, $1 . . . 2.00

CALIFORNIA.

Oakland — Aux. (being the first auxiliary of the Woman's Board of Missions on the Pacific coast), $25, to constitute Mrs. Julia A. Bacon L. M.; and from Oakland Young Ladies' Seminary $25, to constitute Miss Julia A. Rappleye L. M. . . . . 50 .00

SCOTLAND.

Glasgow — Mrs. A. F. Stoddard, to constitute Mrs. E. W. Noble of Truro, Mass, L. M. 25.00

EASTERN TURKEY.

Harpoot — " A Friend," to constitute Miss Katie Barnum L. M. . . 25.00

Total of donations $1,245.18
Quarterlies 44.50
" Echoes " 18.32

Total for the month $1,308.00

RECEIPTS FOR OCTOBER.

MAINE.

Bangor — Aux., by Mrs. E. G. Thurston, treasurer ($25 of which from " friends " to constitute Miss C. M. Pond L. M.) $62.00
South Freeport — Aux. (of which from Miss Illsley's class, $10) . . 14.50

VERMONT.

Craftsbury, North — Ladies' Missionary Association, by Rev. E. P. Wild, to constitute Mrs. R. S. Wild L. M. 25.00
Norwich — An aged disciple 1.00
Westminster, West — Miss Laura Stevens 5.00

MASSACHUSETTS.

Auburndale — Mrs. E. H. Walker 1.00
Boston — " S. F. L." of Shawmut Church, one dollar a week of her earnings 17.00
Bradford — Academy; Young Ladies' Miss'y Society, for support of a pupil in Miss Proctor's school, Aintab 20.00
Cohasset — Ladies of Second Cong. Church, by Miss M. A. Stoddard, to constitute Mrs. Calvin R. Fitts L. M. 25.00
Fitchburg — " For Woman's Board " 2.00
Falmouth, North — By Mrs. H. B. Hooker, Mrs. Francis Nye, to constitute herself L. M., $25; also from Miss S. Lawrence, $2 . . . 27.00
Granby — Aux., by Mrs. John Church, treasurer ($25 of which to constitute Mrs. Asa Pease L. M.) 55.20

Lincoln — Aux., by Mrs. George Hartwell, treasurer (of which $25 to constitute Mrs. H. J. Richardson L. M.) $35.00

Monson — Aux., by Mrs. N. M. Field, treasurer 75.00

Quincy — Mrs. George Hollister, to constitute Miss Harriet N. Ayres, of North Brookfield, L. M. 25.00

Townsend — Aux., by Mrs. Lucy Proctor 38.00

Uxbridge — Aux., by Mrs. Lorin Taft, secretary and treasurer . . . 44.00

Webster — Cong. Church S. S., by J. C. Pearson, superintendent, for support of a pupil in Miss Van Duzee's school, Erzroom, Turkey . . 34.25

Woburn — Aux., by Mrs. C. S. Adkins, treasurer. 7.50

RHODE ISLAND.

Little Compton — Isaac B. Richmond, Esq., to constitute Mrs. Abigail B. Richmond L. M. 25.00

CONNECTICUT.

Hartford — Ladies of, by Mrs. C. C. Dutton, to repair the mud walls of Oroomiah Female Seminary 107.00

Middletown — "A Friend " 5.00

Norwich — By Mrs. D. T. Coit, from Mrs. A. H. Hubbard, to constitute Mrs. J. F. Slater and Mrs. F. Bartlett L. M.'s, $50, and from Mrs. H. P. Williams, to constitute Mrs. Charles Lee, of Norwich, L. M., $25 75.00

Woodstock, North — Eddie Brown's first savings and earnings 75

NEW YORK.

Buffalo — Ladies of Westminster Pres. Church, by Mrs. F. Gridley, treasurer 69.55

New York — Alice Mather 1.00

North Evans — Mrs. H. S. Jones, in memoriam of her daughter, Fannie R. Harrington, and towards support of a pupil 15.00

Watertown — Mrs. James K. Bates, annual subscription 2.00

Williamsburg — Mrs. L. Diana Carter, to constitute herself L. M. . . 25.00

NEW JERSEY.

Madison — "Faith" Mission Circle, Lountaka S. S., by Mrs. Potts, for support of a girl in Oroomiah Seminary 28.00

PENNSYLVANIA.

Philadelphia — Branch, by Mrs. J. D. Lynde, treasurer, eight ladies, $1 each; "A Friend," $5; "C. A. L.," to constitute Mrs. Sarah J. Rhea, L. M., $25; "A Friend," $1; Coll. at Cong. Plymouth Church, when addressed by Mrs. Rhea, $10.57; "A Friend," $1; Franklinville, N. J., Aux., $10; Vineland, N. J., Aux., $15 . . . . 75.57

Anonymous, at the Brooklyn Meeting, $5 gold, $1 currency . . . 6.65

OHIO.

Troy — First Pres. Church, by E. Holden, treasurer, to apply on two scholarships in Mrs. Edwards's school 60.00

Youngstown — Aux., by Miss Julia Caldwell, secretary 18.00

ILLINOIS.

Chicago — Ella G. Ives, M. L. Parrington, and S. S. class, part payment
for Horepsima, in Miss Fritcher's school, Marsovan $8.00
Virden — Cong. S. S., towards support of a girl in Mrs. Edwards's
school 13.23

TENNESSEE.

Jonesborough — Pres. Church S. S., for Female Seminary at Oroomiah . 7.25

Total of donations $1,055.45
Quarterlies, " Life and Light " 41.63
" Echoes " 16.95

Total for month $1,114.03

RECEIPTS FOR NOVEMBER.

MAINE.

Bangor — Aux., by Mrs. E. G. Thurston, treasurer; a friend, to constitute Mrs. Thomas Smith, and " friends " to constitute Mrs. M. G.
Low, L. M.'s $50.00

VERMONT.

Cumberland Centre — Aux., by Mrs. M. E. Small, first-fruits . . . 12.10
Middlebury — Aux., by Mrs. C. H. Ladd 72.00
St. Alban's — Aux., by Mrs. Mary A. Smith, treasurer 28.50

MASSACHUSETTS.

Anonymous. " A Friend " 5.00
Boston — Ladies of Salem-street Church, by Mrs. Bates Lovejoy, $25;
Mrs. George N. Dana, $5; Mrs. Alvan Perry, $1; Chambers-street
Chapel mission circles, to be applied to the education of heathen
children in missionary seminaries, $81; by Mrs. Miron Winslow,
from Mrs. Freeman Allen, to constitute her grand-daughter in New-
ton, two weeks old, L. M., $25 . . . . 137.00
Brighton — Mrs. N. E. Willis 5.00
Beverly — Rebecca W. Groce 2.00
Beverly, North — Mrs. Rebecca Conant 5.00
Chelsea — Chestnut-street Church, by Mrs. J. Sweetser 6.00
Charlestown — Miss S. S. Tufts, to constitute herself L. M. . . . 25.00
Everett — Aux., by Miss Esther Whittemore, treasurer 20.00
Ipswich — Mrs. Cushing's S. S. class, First Parish 5.00
Lee — Ladies of Congregational Church, for support of a pupil in Mrs.
Edwards's school, South Africa 33.25
Lynn — First Church Sabbath school, J. F. Patten's class, first quar-
terly payment for support of a Bible-reader, Aintab, Central Tur-
key 12.50
Milton — Mrs. Lucy Wadsworth 1.00
Pittsfield — Mrs. Dr. Wilson, for support of Hattie Wilson, Zulu girl in
Mrs. Edwards's school. 30.00

Randolph, East — Aux., by Miss Sarah J. Holbrook, treasurer, in part for support of a pupil in Mrs. Edwards's school $50.10

Swampscott — Congregational Church Sabbath school mission circle, " The Busy Workers, " additional (making a total from this class, Mrs. J. Thompson's, of $61 this year, and, with $18.98 collection, a total of $79.98 from the Sabbath school since January) . . . 4.00

Wellesley — Aux., by Mrs. Charles B. Dana, $175; Miss Adelia Chaffin, for two pupils in Miss Proctor's school, Aintab, $50 . . . . 225.00

RHODE ISLAND.

Providence — Beneficent Church, by Miss Anna T. White, treasurer . 6.00

CONNECTICUT.

Berlin — Aux., Miss Lena Woodruff, treasurer, to constitute Mrs. Martha B. Halleck and Mrs. Mary B. Moore L. M.'s 50.00

Bolton — Ladies, by Rev. W. E. B. Moore, pastor 17.50

NEW YORK.

Buffalo —Westminster Presbyterian Church, Aux., additional (with previous contributions, to constitute Mrs. C. G. Root, Mrs. F. Gridley, and Miss A. E. Elliot L. M.'s) 8.75

Brooklyn — New-England Church Sabbath school, Hattie D. Snook, in part, to educate a pupil in Oroomiah 10.00

Castile — Aux., by K. V. Cochran, secretary, to constitute Miss Cordelia A. Greene, M. D., L. M. 25.00

Penn Yan — Mrs. Charles C. Sheppard 50.00

Smyrna — Sabbath-school Missionary Society, Congregational Church, for support of a pupil at Harpoot Female Seminary 30.00

Warsaw — Aux., by Miss Mary S. Williams 16.00

New York — Anna Mather 75

PENNSYLVANIA.

Philadelphia — Branch, by Mrs. Lynde, treasurer; six ladies, $1 each; " C. A. L.," monthly contribution, $25 . . . . 31.00

TENNESSEE.

Jonesborough — By Mrs. Rhea, from a stranger, half a month's earnings 5.00

OHIO.

Youngstown — Aux., by Mrs. Julia Caldwell, treasurer, quarterly contribution 19.50

INDIANA.

Terre Haute — Second Presbyterian Church Sabbath school, for Sarah Condit, in Mrs. Edwards's school 20.00

FOREIGN LANDS.

Sandwich Islands, Honolulu — Mrs. Jane R. Gelett, to constitute herself L. M. 25.00

Ceylon, Oodoopitty, Jaffna — Rev. J. C. Smith, £5 sterling ($25 of which
. to constitute Mrs. Mary S. Smith L. M.) $27.16

Total of subscriptions and donations for the month $1,070.11
For " Life and Light," quarterlies 55.50
For " Echoes," quarterlies 50

        Total for month $1,126.10

RECEIPTS FOR DECEMBER.

MAINE.

Wells — Mrs. Samuel Lindsay $1.00

NEW HAMPSHIRE.

New Ipswich — Aux., Mrs. M. F. Taylor, treasurer ($25 of which to
constitute Mrs. S. S. Ray L. M.) 37.75
Mount Vernon — Miss M. E. Conant 1.00
Webster — " A Friend " 4.50

VERMONT.

Craftsbury, North — Mrs. D. W. Loomis, to constitute Miss Sarah W.
French L. M. 25.00
Cambridge — Mrs. Mary C. Turner, additional towards L. M. . . . 5.00
Dorset — Aux., by Mrs. Moore, to constitute Mrs. Daniel Kent and Mrs.
Lydia K. Sykes L. M.'s 51.00
Rutland — Aux., by Mrs. Laura P. Flack, treasurer; subscription of Mrs.
Page, $50 (of which $25 to constitute Mrs. Silas Aiken L. M.); other
subscribers, $72.25 (of which $25 to constitute Mrs. James Gibson
Johnson L. M.); and by ladies of Pittsford, $28, a part of which to
constitute their pastor's wife, Mrs. Hall, L. M. 150.75

MASSACHUSETTS.

Amherst — Aux., Mrs. M. A. Allen, treasurer 114.65
Boston — Mrs. M. H. Baldwin, $2; " E. R. L.," $2; Mount Vernon
Church S. S., Mr. Nazro, superintendent, by Mrs. Miron Winslow,
$20; Shawmut Mission School, for support of school under care of
Miss Sarah L. Wood, at Kessab, $50; " A Friend," to constitute
Elizabeth, wife of John C. Webster of Chicago, L. M., $25; Mrs. H.
B. Hooke, sundry small donations from individuals, $1.50; F. D.
Avery, five annual subscribers, $5; Jamie's Bank, $2.25 . . . 107.75
Baldwinsville — Mrs. Stillman Norcross 1.00
Cohasset — Ladies of Second Cong. Church 3.72
Dedham — Ladies of Cong. Church 54.40
Falmouth — Mrs. Samuel P. Bourne 2.00
Foxborough — " A Friend," by Mrs. Lucy H. Dean 5.00
Holliston — Mrs. Fisk 50
Jamaica Plain — Aux., Mrs. M. A. B. Brackett, treasurer . . . 6.75
Milton — Mrs. George P. Field, to constitute herself L. M. . . . 25.00

53

Norton — Aux., C. C. Metcalf, treasurer $16.00
Newton, West — Aux., Mrs. H. N. Judson, treasurer, additional towards
support of Miss Ursula Clarke, at Broosa 6.00
Newburyport — Aux., Mrs. H. A. Ingraham, treasurer (of which to consti-
tute Mrs. L. W. Stanton, Mrs. Hannah B. C. Porter, and Miss Eliz-
abeth Bassett, L. M.'s, $75) 125.00
Plymouth — Mrs. Emily B. Richmond 1.00
Rowley — Ladies of Cong. Society, to constitute their pastor's wife, Mrs.
Lyman H. Blake, L. M. 25.00
Randolph, East — Aux., additional, with previous contribution, to con-
stitute Miss M. Anna Wood L. M. 5.00
Templeton — Mrs. Maria P. Sabin, to constitute herself L. M. . . 25.00
Taunton, East — Ladies of Cong. Church, Rev. F. Reed 7.00
Wellesley — Aux., appropriates funds reported in last Herald, to consti-
tute Mrs. Jane Morse and Miss Julia Jennings L. M.s, and to support
a pupil two years in Miss Fritcher's school, a pupil, each one year, in
Mrs. Edwards's and Miss Smith's schools.
Wrentham — Aux., Miss Emily S. Shepherd, treasurer 26.00
Winchendon — Aux., to constitute Mrs. Mahala D. Butler, Mrs. Mary
H. Brown, and Mrs. Harriet M. Beals, L. M.'s. 75.00

CONNECTICUT.

Ellington — Mrs. Edwin Talcott, to constitute herself L. M. . . . 25.00
Greenwich — Aux., for support of their second Bible-reader . . . 60.00
Hartford — Aux., Mrs. Charles A. Jewell, treasurer, to constitute Mrs.
Austin Dunham L. M., $25; annual memberships, $103.75 . . 128.75
New Fairfield — Ladies of Church, collected by Mrs. C. B. Dyer . 17.25
New Haven — Aux., Mrs. John W. Fitch, treasurer; additional (making
$445 contributed this year), for support of two girls in the Madura
Mission, $50; balance towards Mrs. Edwards's salary, whose support
in South Africa this Auxiliary has assumed 145.00
Wapping — Aux., Mrs. W. S. Hawkes, secretary 5.00
Windsor, South — Ladies of Cong. Church, $20; "A Friend," to consti-
tute Mrs. E. D. Willey L. M., $25 . . . . 45.00

NEW YORK.

Brasher Falls — Mrs. C. T. Hulburd 50
Coeymans — "A Friend" 25.00
Homer — Mrs. J. F. Stewart, to constitute herself L. M. 25.00
Union Falls — Mrs. J. T. Duncan, $8; Misses E. B. and M. B. Duncan,
$1 each 10.00

NEW JERSEY.

Madison — Aux., for support of Sarah White, their Bible-reader in Ceylon 50.00

PENNSYLVANIA.

Philadelphia — Branch, Mrs. J. D. Lynde, treasurer, of which from five
ladies, each one dollar, $5; Mrs. B. Hart, $5; Mrs. J. E. Reynolds,
$5; Mrs. C. Burnham, $5, with previous contribution, to constitute
Mrs. Edward Webb L. M.; "C. A. L.," monthly contribution, to
constitute Mrs. Cyrus Stone L. M., $25; "Woman's Missionary So-
5*

ciety," Vineland, N.J., $15; "Woman's Missionary Society," Jersey City, $43.66; "Woman's Missionary Society," Washington, D.C. (of which $25 to constitute Mrs. Goodrich Smith L. M., by Mrs. Frank Smith; Mrs. S. C. Pomeroy, $50, to constitute herself and Mrs. D. C. Paterson L. M.'s), $110 . . . . $213.66

Belle Valley.— A nice bedquilt, by mission circle.

NORTH CAROLINA.

Raleigh — From a teacher of freedmen 1.00

TENNESSEE.

Jonesborough — Pres. S. S., by Rev. J. G. Mason, towards support of Miriam, a Bible-reader at Bootan 8.50

Lookout Mountain — Educational Institution, for support of little Miriam, at Mardin, $25, and C. C. Carpenter, to constitute Miss Sarah A. Mather, St. Augustine, Fla., L. M., $25 . . . . 50.00

OHIO.

Delaware. — " K. M. H." 2.00

Lafayette — Cong. Church S. S., by Mrs. H. B. Fraser. 5.00

INDIANA.

Fort Wayne — Pres. S. S., for pupil in Mrs. Bissell's school . . . 8.00

CALIFORNIA.

Oakland — Ladies' Missionary Society, Mrs. M. P. Cole., treasurer, payments for last quarter, to constitute Mrs. Jane E. Sanford, Mrs. Kate B. Fisher, and Mrs. Caroline A. Colby, L. M.'s; also from Mrs. S. S. Macondray $25, to constitute herself L. M. 100.00

WEST AFRICA.

Gaboon — Mrs. C. H. Walker, of which $25 to constitute Mrs. Louisa Reutlinger of Gaboon, West Africa, L. M. 27.75

Subscriptions and donations $1,860.18

" Life and Light," quarterlies 225.60

" Echoes " 11.24

$2,097.02

LIFE-MEMBERS

OF THE WOMAN'S BOARD OF MISSIONS.

MAINE.

Bangor. — Duren, Mrs. Emma L.
Low, Mrs. M. G.
Pond, Miss Charlotte M.
Smith, Mrs. Thomas
Brunswick. — Sewall, Mrs. J. B.
Castine. — Ives, Mrs. Mary E.
Cumberland Centre. — Jordan, Mrs. E. S.
Lewiston. — Balkam, Mrs. Annie L.
Danielson, Mrs. Sarah L.
Lockwood, Mrs. A. D.
Lockwood, Miss A. D. F.
Portland. — Foxcroft, Miss A. C. M.
Washington. — Starrett, Mrs. P. W.
Yarmouth. — Shepley, Mrs. M. N.

NEW HAMPSHIRE.

Atkinson. — Page, Abigail Little
Page, Mary Ann
Page, Susan Elizabeth
Bedford. — Damon, Mrs. Stephen C.
Gage, Mrs. Charles
Claremont. — Goddard, Mrs. Ewd. L.
Campton. — Blakely, Mrs. G. S.
Concord. — Blanchard, Miss Sibel
Derry. — Day, Mrs. P. B.
Epping. — Philbrick, Mrs. Nancy
Exeter. — Gordon, Mrs. John
Otis, Mrs. I. T.
Fisherville. — Moore, Mrs. N. P.
Hollis. — Burge, Mrs. Cyrus
Henniker. — Cogswell, Mrs. R. H. B.
Fay, Mrs. S. M. E.
Ray, Mrs. S. S.
Pelham. — Tyler, Mrs. E. W.
Wyman, Mrs. H. C.
Portsmouth. — Adams, Mrs. Geo. M.
Stark. — Cole, Miss Elvira
Stratham. — Sinclair, Mrs. Fannie D.

VERMONT.

Dorset. — Kent, Mrs. Daniel
Moore, Mrs. John
Pratt, Mrs. P. S.
Sykes, Mrs. Lydia K.

East Dorset. — Olmstead, Mrs. F. W.
East Rutland. — Page, Mrs. J. B.
Page, Miss Helen L.
Page, Persis, 2d
Middlebury. — Hough, Miss Martha
Simmonds, Miss Laura
Montpelier. — Eustis, Miss Mary A.
Howe, Mrs. A. J.
Hubbard, Mrs. Mary J.
Newbury. — Keyes, Mrs. Freeman
Keyes, Miss Hattie E.
North Craftsbury. — French, Mrs. Sarah W.
Wild, Mrs. R. S.
Peacham. — Chamberlain, Mrs. D. S.
Pittsford. — Hall, Mrs. Rev.
Rutland. — Aiken, Mrs. Silas
Johnson, Mrs. James Gibson
St. Alban's. — Bittinger, Mrs. J. Q.
Brainerd, Miss Frances M.
Brainerd, Miss Sophia
Brainerd, Mrs. Helen Lynde
Chandler, Mrs. Sabina
Dutcher, Mrs. Luther L.
Farrar, Mrs. Eliza C.
Gorham, Miss Mary
Merrill, Mrs. Eliza W.
Newton, Mrs. John W.
Riggs, Miss Adeline E.
Safford, Mrs. Emily B.
Samson, Miss Henrietta L.
Samson, Mrs. A. J.
Smith, Mrs. John G.
Smith, Mrs. Worthington
Smith, Mrs. M. A.
Smith, Mrs. Maria W.
Stevens, Mrs. Henry M.
Seymour, Mrs. Laura
Whiting, Mrs. Mary F.
Wyman, Mrs. Charles
St. Johnsbury. — Cummings, Mrs. E. C.
Colby, Mrs. J. R.
Fairbanks, Mrs. Henry
Fairbanks, Mrs. Horace

56

St. Johnsbury. — Ladd, Mrs. Daniel
  Thayer, Mrs. W. W.
Wallingford. —Walker, Mrs. Aldace

MASSACHUSETTS.

Abington. — Abbie, Mrs. Mary T.
Andover. — Coburn, Mrs. Geo. W.
  Dole, Miss Sarah A.
  Draper, Mrs. W. F.
  Jones, Mrs. Susan Kimball
  Merrill, Mrs. James H.
  Pearson, Mrs. Emily C.
  Pearson, Miss Helen C.
  Smith, Mrs. John
  Smith, Mrs. Joseph
  Smith, Mrs. Caroline L.
  Smith, Miss Carrie R.
  Taylor, Mrs. H. B.
  Taylor, Miss Adelaide B.
Amherst. — Cooper, Mrs. J. S.
  Ballantine, Mrs. Henry
  Jenkins, Mrs. J. L.
  Lewis, Mrs. Harriet E.
  Stearns, Mrs. William A.
  Thompson, Mrs. Esther E.
Ashby. — Parker, Mrs. Ellen S. .
Athol. — Cutler, Mrs. R. M.
Auburndale. — Alden, Mrs. N. A.
  Cutler, Mrs. Calvin
  Cutler, Mrs. Sarah
  Gordon, Mrs. James W.
  Shedd, Mrs. Susan F.
  Walker, Mrs. Eliza H.
Boxford. — Park, Mrs. H. T.
Brimfield. — Hyde, Mrs. C. M.
  Knight, Miss Eunice B.
  Knight, Mrs. Therza
Beverly. — Choate, Mrs. F. W.
  Lanphear, Mrs. Mary E.
  Odell, Mrs. Charles H.
Bradford. — Kingsbury, Mrs. J. D.
  Ordway, Mrs. Caroline
Brookline. — Conant, Mrs. Rebecca
  Thomas, Mrs. Edward I.
Belchertown. — Root, Mrs. Eliza
Braintree. — Storrs, Mrs. Ann S.
  Storrs, Miss Eunice C.
  Sugden, Miss Mary
Barre. — Adams, Mrs. Arnold
Boston. — Allen, Mrs. Freeman
  Homer, Mrs. S. J. M.
  Lincoln, Mrs. Chastine
  Thompson, Mrs. Louisa
  Turner, Mrs. Celia C.

BOSTON CHURCHES.

Central. — Bates, Mrs. Benj. E.
  Bird, Mrs. James

Central. — Child, Mrs. Linus
  Dennison, Mrs. John
  Freeland, Mrs. Charles
  Grover, Mrs. Wm. S
  Hale, Mrs. Cyrus K.
  Herman, Mrs. L.
  Houghton, Mrs. W. S.
  Kendall, Mrs. Elizabeth
  Russell, Mrs. Thos. S.
  Todd, Mrs. John E.
  White, Mrs. James
Berkeley St. — Snow, Mrs. Barna.
  Snow, Mrs. Franklin
  Wright, Mrs. Wm. B.
Union. — Adams, Miss
  Brown, Mrs. L. H.
  Durant, Mrs. H. F.
  Dunning, Mrs. Wm. H.
  Ellis, Miss Frances
  Fiske, Mrs. J. N.
  Hooker, Mrs. H. B.
  Hooper, Mrs. H.
  Holland, Miss Sarah E.
  Keep, Mrs. Dr.*
  Keep, Miss E.
  Newman, Miss C.
  Newman, Miss A.
  Pierce, Mrs. A.
  Pease, Mrs. Giles *
  Ramsay, Mrs. A.
  Scudder, Mrs. Charles
  Scudder, Mrs. David C.
  Scudder Miss Bessie M.
  Scudder, Miss Vida
  Scudder, Miss J. M.
  Strong, Mrs. Alex.
  Treat, Mrs. Selah B.
  Tappan, Miss E. S.
  Wilkinson, Mrs. Arthur
Maverick. — Bowker, Mrs. Albert
  Bowker, Miss Sarah
  Bowker, Miss Mary F.
  Bingham, Mrs. Joel T.
  Fales, Mrs. Joseph J.
  Folts, Mrs. Harriette E. M.
  Hammett, Miss Elizabeth
  Josselyn, Miss Eliza I.
  Wright, Mrs. Luther A.
Mt. Vernon. — Coit, Mrs. Daniel T.
  Crockett, Mrs. G. W.
  Cutler, Mrs. James
  Kimball, Mrs. J. W.
  Parkhurst, Mrs. S. E.
  Palmer, Mrs. Julius A.
  Safford, Mrs. Dea. Daniel
  Tufts, Mrs. A. W.
  Warren, Mrs. Samuel
  Winslow, Mrs. Miron

* Deceased.

Old South. — Armstrong, Mrs. S. T.
Allen, Mrs. Frederick D.
Blagden, Mrs. Geo. W.
Baldwin, Mrs. James T.*
Bartlett, Mrs. Homer
Bancroft, Mrs. Jacob
Buck, Mrs. David
Cragin, Mrs. ——— *
Cowdoin, Mrs.———
Davis, Miss Elizabeth
Fowler, Miss Mary F.
Fearing, Mrs. M.
Gordon, Mrs. Louise Powers
Gray, Mrs. ———
Howe, Mrs. J. C.
Hardy, Mrs. Alpheus
Johnson, Mrs. S., sen.
Johnson, Mrs. S., jr.
Manning, Mrs. J. M.
Noble, Miss Juliette
Plumer, Mrs. Avery
Plumer, Miss Hattie Mason
Stoddard, Mrs. Charles
Wentworth, Mrs. ———
Park St. — Eustis, Mrs. Wm. T.
Farnsworth, Mrs. Ezra
Field, Mrs. John W.
Garratt, Mrs. Martha V.
Hubbard, Mrs. Samuel*
Hubbard, Miss Florence M.
Hobart, Mrs. Peter
Kittredge, Mrs. Jeremiah
Manning, May
Murray, Mrs. W. H. H.
Pratt, Mrs. G. W.
Quincy, Miss Martha A.
Simpson, Mrs. M. H.
Shattuck, Mrs. Lemuel
Wiggin, Mrs. J. K.
Salem St. — Lovejoy, Mrs. Wm. R.
Lovejoy, Mrs. Wm. Bates
Shawmut. — Blaney, Mrs. Mary A.
Bishop, Mrs. Mary S.
Duff, Mrs. John
Erskine, Mrs. John
Greenwood, Mrs. Ira
Gray, Mrs. Joseph H.
Hyde, Mrs. H. H.
Jones, Mrs. Frederick
Putnam, Mrs. Sarah B.
Rice, Miss Louisa J.
Stone, Mrs. James S.
Webb, Mrs. E. B.
Wilson, Mrs. Chas. B.
Willard, Mrs. Martha A.
Phillips, S. B. — Alden, Mrs. E. K.
Conley, Mrs. C. C.
Drake, Mrs. Jeremy

Phillips, S. B. — King, Mrs. ———
Lincoln, Miss Mary
Meins, Mrs. Jane R.
Shepard, Mrs. C.
Vinton, Miss Eliza
Vinton, Mrs. Laurinda R.
Wheelwright, Miss R. J.
Winchester, Mrs. E. T.
Eliot, Highlands. — Anderson, Mrs. Rufus
Bowles, Mrs. Stephen J.
Bray, Mrs. C. F.
Day, Mrs. Moses
Huntington, Mrs. E. B.
Hodges, Mrs. A. D.
Mills, Mrs. C. L.
Rockwood, Mrs. L. B.
Vine St. — Means, Mrs. J. O.
Parker St. — Stockwell, Mrs. S. N.
Charlestown. — Grant, Mrs. A. W.
Tufts, Miss S. S.
Trowbridge, Mrs. E. A.
Cambridge. — Bates, Mrs. William
Farwell, Mrs. Stephen
Green, Mrs. C. M.
McKenzie, Mrs. A.
Cambridgeport. — King, Miss E. F.
Pratt, Mrs. W. H.
Snow, Mrs. Russell
Cohasset. — Fitts, Mrs. Calvin R.
Concord. — Williams, Mrs. C. H. S.

CHELSEA CHURCHES.

Broadway. — Copp, Mrs. J. A.
Cheever, Mrs. Ira
Gilmore, Mrs. Sarah M.
Herrick, Mrs. S. E.
Sweetser, Mrs. Joseph
Sweetser, Mrs. A.
Tenney, Mrs. Elizabeth C.
Thwing, Mrs. E. Payson
Chestnut St. —Chamberlain, Mrs. M.
Frost, Mrs. Rufus S.
Langworthy, Mrs. I. P.
Lawrie, Mrs. Ellen A.
Mitchell, Mrs. Jacob
Plumb, Mrs. Albert H.
Stone, Mrs. Mary
Dorchester. — Baker, Mrs. Walter
Brooks, Mrs. John H.
Clapp, Mrs. Eliza
Means, Mrs. James H.
Mann, Mrs. Henry E.
Shaw, Miss E. Cornelia
Sharp, Mrs. James C.
Smith, Mrs. Henry
Torrey, Mrs. Elbridge
Wales, Mrs. William

Dorchester. — Wales, Mrs. Elizabeth A.
Withington, Miss Eliza
Dedham. — Edwards, Mrs. J.
Whitney, Mrs. A. B.
Everett. — Bean, Mrs. F. M.
Bryant, Mrs. Albert
East Cambridge. — Munroe, Miss L. S.
Wyman, Mrs. Ruth E.
East Randolph. — Russell, Mrs. Louisa S.
Wood, Miss M. Anna
East Somerville. — Davis, Mrs. E.
East Taunton. — Reed, Mrs. F. A.
East Braintree. — Faxon, Miss R. A.
Falmouth. — Bates, Mrs. William
Bourne, Mrs. S. P.
Kimball, Mrs. Jas. P.
Lewis, Mrs. Thomas
Lewis, Mrs. Thatcher
Lawrence, Miss Lucy
Robinson, Mrs. S. D.
Robinson, Miss Elizabeth D.
Swift, Mrs. Oliver C.
Fitchburg. — Clark, Miss Clara A.
Emerson, Mrs. Alfred
Lowe, Mrs. John
Fall River. — Borden, Mrs. Richard
Borden, Miss Carrie
Durfee, Mrs. Nathan
Remington, Mrs. Hale
Remington, Mrs. Robt. K.
Grantville. — Smith, Mrs. E. M.
Groton. — Aldrich, Mrs. J. K.
Williams, Miss Elizabeth C.
Great Barrington. — Scudder, Mrs. Evarts
Groveland. — Tuttle, Miss Sarah
Granby. — Pease, Mrs. Asa
Hadley. — Ayres, Mrs. Jane E.
Ipswich. — Cowles, Mrs. E. C.
Cowles, Rox. C.
Morong, Mrs. T.
White, Miss Ellen R.
Jamaica Plain. — Capen, Mrs. S. B.
Gould, Mrs. George
Perkins, Mrs. F. R.
Long Meadow. — Harding, Mrs. M. L.
Pynchon, Mrs. Susan M.
Lancaster. — Ames, Mrs. Jane A.
Leominster. — Batt, Mrs. Wm. J.*
Burrage, Mrs. Myra
Burrage, Mrs. Leonard
Haskell, Mrs. Sarah T.
Lexington. — Davis, Mrs. John, sen.

Lawrence. — Cordley, Mrs. C. M.
Fisher, Mrs. Mary H.
Kimball, Mrs. W. A.
Maddock, Miss Phebe A.
Snow, Mrs. Harriet E.
Lincoln. — Farrar, Mrs. A. H.
Richardson, Mrs. H. J.
Lowell. — Carter, Miss Mary T.
Marshfield. — Bourne, Mrs. Sarah T.
Milton. — Field, Mrs. Geo. P.
Wadsworth, Mrs. Lucy
Monson. — Bradford, Miss Sarah E.
Carpenter, Miss Mary L.
Chapman, Mrs. Reuben A.
Deney, Mrs. Hadassah
Field, Mrs. A. M.
Porter, Mrs. A. W.*
Packard, Mrs. John
Sumner, Mrs. Chas. B.
Malden. — Reed, Mrs. Chas. E.
Melrose. — Bale, Mrs. A. G.
Medford. — Haskins, Mrs. Matilda T.
James, Mrs. Amanda J.
James, Miss Hannah
Stinchfield, Miss Louisa
Mt. Holyoke Seminary. — French, Miss Helen M.
Ellis, Miss Mary
Ward, Julia E.
Blanchard, Miss Elizabeth
Bowen, Miss Susan
Bardwell, Elizabeth M.
Ballantine, Miss Elizabeth D.
Burgess, Miss Mary P.
Bowers, Miss Ellen P.
Childs, Miss M. Elizabeth
Clary, Miss Susan M.
Cowles, Miss Louisa F.
Dearborn, Miss Anna
Edwards, Miss Anna C.
Foster, Mrs. Mary A.
Gordon, Miss Alice W.
Hazen, Miss Frances M.
Hood, Miss Anna M.
Holmes, Miss Lucy J.
Noble, Miss Hannah
Nutting, Miss Mary O.
Prentiss, Miss Elizabeth B.
Savage, Miss Helen M.
Sessions, Miss Harriet E.
Shattuck, Miss Lydia W.
Townsend, Miss Mary C.
Newtonville. — Clark, Mrs. J.
Goodale, Mrs. E. A.
Newton. — Cobb, Mrs. Harriet M.
Cobb, Miss Lucy Ely
Ely, Mrs. Alfred B.
Ely, Elizabeth Brewster

Newton. — Hatch, Mrs. I. A.
Hatch, Miss L. E.
Jewett, Mrs. D. B.
Kidder, Mrs. Isaac L.
Reed, Mrs. Charlotte L.
Newton Centre.— Ellis, Mrs. Warren
Furber, Mrs. Daniel L.
Kingsbury, Miss Hattie
Wardwell, Mrs. A. F.
North Somerville. — Hodgkins, Mrs.
W. H.
Virgin, Mrs. Samuel H.
Newburyport. — Bannister, Mrs. W.
B.
Basset, Miss Elizabeth
Brown, Mrs. Newman
Fisk, Mrs. Dr.
Hale, Mrs. Sarah W.
Ingraham, Mrs. Herbert A.
Jones, Mrs. Anthony S.
March, Mrs. Alice L.
Porter, Mrs. Hannah B. C.
Stanton, Mrs. L. W.
Tyler, Mrs. T. C.
Tyler, Mrs. Hannah
North Chelmsford. — Clark, Mrs.
B. F.
North Falmouth.—Nye, Mrs. Francis
North Brookfield. — Ayres, Miss
Harriet M.
Northampton. —Williston, Mrs. C. L.
Oxford. — Bardwell, Mrs. Horatio
Peabody. — Anthony, Mrs. Geo. N.
Gardner, Mrs. Mary A.
Plympton. — Parker, Miss Hannah S.
Plymouth. — Gordon, Mrs. Dr. T.
Gordon, Mrs. Jane P.
Pittsfield. — Harding, Mrs. Wm. G.
Reed, Mrs. Sarah E.
Rowley. — Blake, Mrs. Lyman H.
Southbridge. — Lane, Mrs. S. M.
Salem. — Atwood, Mrs. E. M.
Palmer, Mrs. Charles R.
Stockbridge. — Brown, Mrs. S. B.
Whitney, Mrs. Anna J.
South Amherst. — Dana, Mrs.
Marion A.
Hutchings, Mrs. C. B.
Lyman, Mrs. Maria P.
Miller, Mrs. E. C.
Springfield. — Ames, Mrs. Galen
Gay, Mrs. Mary C.
Swampscott. — Thompson, Mrs. John
South Hadley. — Lawrence, Mrs.
Ithiel
South Marshfield. — Alden, Mrs.
Ebenezer
Seekonk. — Carpenter, Mrs. A. H.

Townsend. — Bertram, Mrs. Mary A.
Farmer, Mrs. Sarah A.
Morss, Mrs. Ellen M.
Proctor, Mrs. Lucy
Templeton. — Sabin, Mrs. Maria P.
Truro. — Noble, Mrs. E. W.
Upton. — Claflin, Mrs. Geo. P.
West Roxbury. — Clark, Mrs. N. G.
Ellis, Mrs. Mary F.
Hubbell, Mrs. Caroline S.
Labaree, Mrs. Susan F.
Smith, Mrs. R. B.
Tolman, Mrs. Julia F.
West Newton. — Graves, Mrs. T. E.
Hitchcock, Miss ——
Newell, Mrs. J. A.
Newell, Miss Elizabeth H.
Whittemore, Mrs. B. F.
Weymouth. — Bailey, Miss Sarah M.
Ellsworth, Mrs. A. A.
Waltham. — Clark, Mrs. Dorus
Strong, Mrs. Elnathan E.
Williamsburg. — Bodman, Mrs. Lu-
ther
Winchester. — Cutter, Mrs. Stephen
Cutter, Mrs. Henry
Chapin, Miss Lizzie
Holt, Mrs. N. W. C.
Holt, Miss Nellie B.
Manney, Mrs. Ellen E.
Patten, Mrs. Hannah
Westhampton.—Clark, Mrs. Newman
Montague, Miss R. Louisa
Williamstown. — Hopkins, Mrs. A.
Lincoln, Mrs. Lucy C.
Pierce, Miss Elizabeth
Stone, Mrs. Cyrus
Safford, Mrs. Jennie T.
Wellesley. — Dana, Mrs. Nathaniel
Dana, Mrs. G. N.
Dana, Mrs. Charles B.
Fuller, Mrs. Augustus
Herrick, Mrs. Charles
Jennings, Miss Julia
Little, Mrs. E. G.
Morse, Mrs. Jane
Phipps, Mrs. G. T.
Rollins, Miss Hannah
Webber, Mrs. A. D.
Webber, Miss Mary S.
Watkins, Mrs. M.
Whitinsville. — Clark, Mrs. L. F.
Whitin, Mrs. Paul
Whitin, Miss Anna L.
Walpole. — Kimball, Mrs. Geo. E.
Thurber, Mrs. E. B.
Worcester. — Ball, Mrs. Richard
Curtis, Mrs. Albert

Worcester. — Moen, Mrs. P. L.
  Peckham, Miss Ruth
  Washburn, Miss E. H.
  Whitcomb, Mrs. M. C.
  Whitcomb, Mrs. G. Henry
  Whitcomb, Miss Ellen M.
Westfield. — Catlin, Miss Ella C.
  Leonard, Miss Mary A.
Webster. — Keith, Mrs. Parmenas
Ware. — Hyde, Mrs. Wm.
  Hyde, Mrs. W. S.
  Hyde, Miss H. S.
  Sage, Mrs. O.
  Sage, Miss S. R.
Winchendon. — Beals, Mrs. Harriet
  M.
  Butler, Mrs. Mahala D.
  Brown, Mrs. Mary H.
  Dole, Miss Clara H.
  Foster, Mrs. Davis
  Mason, Mrs. Calista A. S.
Wilmington. — Buck, Mrs. C. C.

RHODE ISLAND.

Lansdale. — Garvin, Mrs. L. F.
Little Compton. — Richmond, Mrs.
  Abigail B.
Providence. — Cady, Mrs. Isaac
  Carpenter, Mrs. Hattie Z.
  Claflin, Mrs. Geo.
  Cross, Mrs. Wm. J.
  Draper, Mrs. J. L.
  Hazard, Mrs. Roland
  Jackson, Mrs. B. M.
  King, Mrs. Wm. J.
  Knight, Mrs. B. B.
  Lathrop, Mrs. H.
  Mason, Mrs. J. N.
  Merrill, Mrs. M. A.
  Sprague, Mrs. A.
  Sprague, Mrs. S. S.
  Spicer, Mrs. George T.
  Snow, Mrs. J. L.
  Vose, Mrs. James G.
  Wilkinson, Mrs. H. W.
  White, Miss Anna S.

CONNECTICUT.

Berlin. — Gilbert, Mrs. Mary G.
  Halleck, Mrs. Martha B.
  Moore, Mrs. Mary B.
Bozrah. — Abell, Mrs. Wm. C.
  Ghent, Mrs. Nathan S. (Rev.)
  Raymond, Mrs. Fannie
Burnside. — Elmore, Mrs. M. Janette
Colebrook. — Carrington, Mrs. J. P.
Colchester. — Clarke, Miss Martha T.
  Day, Mrs. Maranda M.

Colchester. — Day, Miss Eliza M.
  Fiske, Mrs. H. M.
  Gillet, Mrs. Russell
  Hyde, Mrs. Mary Ann
  McCall, Mrs. C. B.
  Newton, Mrs. Harriet T.
  Wheeler, Mrs. J. B.
  Willard, Mrs. S. G.
Deep River. — Wickes, Mrs. Henry
East Haddam. — Parsons, Mrs. S. B.
Ellington. — Talcott, Mrs. Edwin
Groton. — Copp, Miss Kate B.
Guilford. — Kitchell, Mrs. Alice L.
  Sage, Miss Clara I.
  Talcott, Mrs. Alvan
Glastenbury. — Andrews, Mrs. S. J.
  Hale, Mrs. Susan S.
  Hubbard, Mrs. Almeda
  Hubbard, Mrs. Charlotte H.
  House, Mrs. Vilettie J.
  Kittredge, Mrs. Susan B.
  Lockwood, Miss Priscilla S.
  Williams, Mrs. Mary E.
  Williams, Mrs. Julia E.
Hartford. — Dunham, Mrs. Austin
Harwinton. — Hayes, Mrs. Sarah B.
Middletown. — Coe, Mrs. Linus
  Goodrich, Mrs. E. H.
Naugatuck. — Sherman, Mrs. E. W.
New Haven. — Foote, Mrs. Emily W.
  Foote, Mrs. Amelia Leavitt
  Pitkin, Mrs. Mary A.
New London. — Brown, Mrs. Abby E.
  Field, Mrs. C. C.
  Latimer, Miss Lucretia
  McEwen, Mrs. Harriet W.
  Sisson, Miss Elizabeth
  Smith, Mrs. Abba W. L.
  Wilcox, Mrs. G. B.
New Milford. — Ives, Mrs. Lucy S.
New Britain. — Davis, Mrs. Mary M.
Norwich. — Arms, Mrs. Hiram P.
  Bartlett, Mrs. F.
  Bond, Mrs. S. Ann W.
  Coit, Mrs. Charles
  Coit, Mrs. George
  Dana, Mrs. M. M. G.
  Hubbard, Mrs. Amos H.
  Lee, Mrs. Charles
  Palmer, Mrs. Emeline
  Slater, Mrs. J. F.
  Williams, Mrs. W. W.
Orange. — Bradley, Miss Anna
  Prudder, Mrs. E. C.
Southbury. — Smith, Mrs. Harriet E.
South Windsor. — Bowman, Mrs.
  Ernestine Lord
  Willey, Mrs. E. D.

Thompson. — Hubbard, Miss Elizabeth
West Winsted. — Beardsley, Mrs. M. E.
Lawrence, Mrs. Wm.
West Stonington. — Hubbell, Mrs. S.
Woodstock. — Brown, Mrs. S. H.
Child, Mrs. Peleg C.

NEW YORK.

Albany. — Brayton, Mrs. Elizabeth
Cox, Mrs. J. W.
Wood, Mrs. Margaret
Brooklyn. — Hayes, Mrs. J. W.
Whiton, Mrs. James M.
Buffalo. — Calkins, Mrs. Mary Whiton
Elliot, Miss A. E.
Gridley, Mrs. F.
Heacock, Mrs. Grosvenor W.
Root, Mrs. C. G.
Sawyer, Mrs. Charlotte O.
White, Mrs. Eliza N.
Wilkes, Mrs. Ellen
Castile. — Greene, Miss Cordelia A., M. D.
Coeymans. — Ten Eyck, Miss C.
Fayetteville. — Beard, Mrs. Huntington
Bigelow, Mrs. K. H.
Chipman, Mrs. N.
Pratt, Mrs. Jane
Fredonia. — Stevens, Miss Martha L.
Wright, Miss Lucia E.
Gilbertsville. — Clark, Mrs. H. M.
Homer. — Stewart, Mrs. J. S.
Jamestown. — Anderson, Mrs. Edward
Newburg. — Hall, Mrs. Wm. C.
North Bergen. — Talcott, Miss E. B.
New-York City. — Betts, Mrs. G. F.
Dodge, Mrs. Wm. E.
Lyon, Mrs. Isabella
Leavitt, Mrs. J. T.
Prentice, Mrs. George L.
Safford, Mrs. Helen A.
Smith, Mrs. J. V. C.
Sutton, Miss Caroline
Poughkeepsie. — Lyman, Harriet W.
Stirling, Miss Mary H.
Penn Yan. — Sheppard, Mrs. C. C.
Rochester. — Chapin, Mrs. Lucinda
Hamilton, Mrs. Julia A.
Springfield. — Winson, Mrs. Daniel
Schenectady. — Brooks, Mrs. Isabella
Syracuse. — Leavenworth, Mrs. E. W.
Tenan, Mrs. J. G. K.
Troy. — Warren, Mrs. Samuel

Utica. — Crittenden, Mrs. A. W.
Watertown. — Bates, Mrs. James
Bates, Mrs. James R.
Boalt, Miss Mary L.
Morgan, Mrs. Almena B.
Morgan, Mrs. Susan H.
Porter, Mrs. J. J.
Waverley. — Beaumont, Mrs. H. N.
Williamsburg. — Carter, Mrs. L. Diana

PENNSYLVANIA.

Philadelphia. — Burnham, Mrs. C.
Lynde, Mrs. C. A.
Philadelphia Branch
Edmands, Mrs. John
Fisk, Mrs. Joel
Goodell, Mrs. Wm.
Goodell, Miss Emma L.
Hart, Mrs. Burdett
Hawes, Mrs. Edward
Holmes, Mrs. Samuel
McLeod, Mrs. John
Rhea, Mrs. Sarah J.
Stone, Mrs. Cyrus
York. — Small, Miss Sallie B.

DELAWARE.

Glasgow. — Webb, Mrs. Edward
Webb, Miss Mary E.

MARYLAND.

Frederic City. — Rockwell, Mrs. R.

DISTRICT OF COLUMBIA.

Washington. — Paterson, Mrs.
Pomeroy, Mrs. S. C.
Smith, Mrs. Goodrich

OHIO.

Belpre. — Bates, Mrs. Sarah A. T.
Cincinnati. — Aydelotte, Mrs. B. E.
Brown, Mrs. S. B.
Cleveland. — Taylor, Mrs. Elizabeth E.
Coolville. — Bartlett, Miss Mary
Tidd, Mrs. Fanny
Freestone. — Adams, Mrs. Lucy B.
Granville. — Fuller, Mrs. Deborah
Salem. — Allen, Mrs. David A.
Toledo. — Parmelee, Mrs. W. E.
Williams, Mrs. Anna J.
Troy. — Grosvenor, Mrs. Hannah
Windham. — Angel, Mrs. Cornelia
Shaw, Mrs. James
Wales, Miss A. M.

ILLINOIS.

Chicago. — Brown, Mrs. Wm. H.
Webster, Mrs. Elizabeth
Concord. — Fairbank, Mrs. H. M.
Galena. — Kent, Mrs. Caroline C.
La Harpe. — Gove, Miss Mary C.

MICHIGAN.

Concord. — Shaw, Mrs. A. M.
Detroit. — Noble, Mrs. Charles
Grand Haven. — White, Miss M. A.
Homer. — Foucher, Mrs. Charles
Paint Creek. — Lowe, Mrs. C. M.
St. Clair. — Wastill, Mrs. Wm. P.

IOWA.

Grinnell. — Grinnell, Mrs. Julia A.

TENNESSEE.

Lookout Mt. — Bancroft, Mrs. F. K.
Carpenter, Mrs. C. C.
Wilson, Miss Mary A.

FLORIDA.

St. Augustine. — Mather, Miss S. A.

KANSAS.

Topeka. — McClelland, Mrs. H.

CALIFORNIA.

Oakland. — Bigelow, Mrs. Anna E.
Colby, Mrs. Caroline A.
Fisher, Mrs. Kate B.
Macondray, Mrs. L. S.
Mooar, Mrs Sarah A.
Sanford, Mrs. Jane E.
San Francisco. — Bacon, Mrs. J. A.
Janes, Mrs. E. L.
Stone, Mrs. A. L.

—

IN FOREIGN LANDS.

AFRICA.

Benthinger, Mrs. Louisa
Edwards, Mrs. Mary K.
Lloyd, Mrs. K. C.
Walker, Mrs. William

TURKEY AND SYRIA.

Baker, Miss Isabella C.

Barnum, Mrs. Mary F.
Barnum, Miss Katie
Bliss, Mrs. Daniel
Closson, Miss Sarah A.
Dodd, Mrs. Lydia B.
Leonard, Mrs. Amelia
Morse, Mrs. Eliza Winter
Proctor, Miss Myra A.
Parmelee, Miss Olive F.
Rappleye, Miss Julia A.
Seymour, Miss Hattie
Schauffler, Mrs. C. F.
Wheeler, Mrs. Crosby H.
Washburn, Mrs. George

PERSIA.

Cochrane, Mrs. Joseph G.
Labaree, Mrs. E. W.
Rice, Miss Mary S.
Rhea, Mrs. Sarah J.

INDIA.

Atkinson, Mrs. Culista
Burnell, Mrs. T. S.
Bissell, Mrs. Mary E.
Bruce, Mrs. Hepsibeth P.
Capron, Mrs. Sarah B.
Capron, Miss Annie Hooker
Chandler, Mrs. Charlotte H.
Chester, Mrs. Sophia
Fairbank, Mrs. Mary Ballantine
Herrick, Mrs. Elizabeth H.
Hazen, Mrs. Martha R.
Harding, Mrs. Elizabeth D.
Park, Mrs. Anna M.
Penfield, Mrs. Charlotte E.
Pollock, Miss Sarah
Rendall, Miss Mary F.
Tracy, Mrs. William
Taylor, Mrs. Martha S.
Taylor, Miss Martha S.
Wood, Mrs. Elizabeth P.
Wells, Mrs. Mary L.
Washburn, Mrs. G. T.

CEYLON.

Agnew, Miss Eliza
De Reimer, Mrs. Emily F.
Green, Mrs. Margaret W.
Howland, Mrs. Susan R.
Hastings, Mrs. Anna
Hillis, Miss Hester A.
Smith, Mrs. Mary S.
Spaulding, Mrs. Mary C.
Townshend, Miss Harriet E.

CHINA.

Andrews, Miss Mary E.
Payson, Miss Adelia M.
Williams, Mrs. S. Wells

SANDWICH ISLANDS.

Atherton, Miss Caroline F.
Bingham, Miss Lydia

Bingham, Miss Elizabeth F.
Damon, Mrs. Samuel C.
Flaxman, Miss Margaret
Gelett, Mrs. Jane R.
Gulick, Mrs. L. H.

MICRONESIA.

Bingham, Mrs. Hiram
Snow, Mrs. L. V.